The Wagered Widow

PATRICIA VERYAN

St. Martin's Press
New York

Design by Lee Wade

Library of Congress Cataloging in Publication Data
Veryan, Patricia.
    The wagered widow.
    I. Title.
PS3572.E766W3   1984   813'.54   84-1878
ISBN 0-312-85341-6

First Edition
10 9 8 7 6 5 4 3 2 1

For Audrey and Sheldon

CHAPTER

❧ 1 ❧

London. May, 1746.

" 'Tis not as though she was a foolish girl." Mrs. Albinia Boothe completed another loop of the rosette she was crocheting, held up the embryonic tablecloth, and surveyed it dejectedly. "You know," she went on, apparently addressing her creation, "that dear Rebecca is prodigious resourceful." She sighed and clicked her tongue, and her powdered curls danced a little beneath the constraint of the dainty lace cap she wore. "*Too* resourceful at times, for a gently nurtured Lady of Quality. Indeed, one worries, for if she sets her mind to something one never knows what she may do next." The crochet hook slowed. Mrs. Boothe, a prettily petite lady of middle years and amiable, if somewhat apprehensive, disposition, raised large dark eyes to gaze at the Sèvres clock on the mantelpiece, as though in search of support.

The clock ticked on, far too secure in its own ordered setting to be disturbed by the woes of the little lady and, receiving no encouragement, Mrs. Boothe let her gaze drift aimlessly around the parlour. It was a charming room and properly reflected the polite prosperity of John Street, on which the small house was located. Pale morning sunlight slanted through snowy lace curtains to puddle the rich carpet with lighter patches; the furnishings were discreet but expensive and tastefully arranged so as not to clutter the space available. But although this May morning was decidedly cool, no fire was lit in the hearth of the fine Italian fireplace, and Mrs. Boothe pulled the shawl closer about her shoulders as she took up her work once more. She missed the loop she had been about to complete, however, the crochet hook jumping when a clear, feminine voice called an imperious, "Aunt! Only look at me!"

A simple enough request but, glancing to the top of the

three steps that led to the hall, Mrs. Boothe uttered a squeak and sprang to her feet in dismay.

The girl who posed there was not much taller than her diminutive aunt. Her complexion was clear, and as light as her brows were dark. Her hair, beautifully powdered, was dressed in thick coils upon her proud little head, with one lone ringlet swooping to her shoulder. Eyes of a dusky darkness danced with mischief, and red lips, full and sweetly shaped, fought a smile as they parted to reveal even white teeth. "Is it not marvellous?" she said innocently. "I feel alive again!"

She looked very alive indeed, but Mrs. Boothe did not felicitate her upon that fact, instead pressing one hand to her bosom while remarking in a failing voice, "Rebecca! You have—oh!—you have put off your blacks!"

This was certainly true. The widow of Mr. Forbes Parrish looked a veritable sprite of Spring in the pink silken robe *à la Française* that hugged her slender body to the waist before sweeping out over its hoops. The twinkle in her eyes very pronounced, but her tone repentant, Rebecca asked, "Are you very much shocked, love?" She trod down the steps, holding up her hoops to reveal dainty little feet and shapely ankles. "It *is* a year since Forbes died, you know."

"A year today!" Mrs. Boothe sank back into her chair and wailed, "Rebecca—do you not think you should wait?"

"I *have* waited! A whole year! Oh, Aunt, I thought it would never end! Lucy Farrington put off her blacks only ten months after Harley was killed."

Mrs. Boothe watched, aghast, as her lovely niece crossed to sit on the small loveseat. She remarked in a troubled voice that Rebecca did look quite in bloom again, which was nice, "Only—Harley was killed in *battle*, dearest."

"Does that make a difference? I cannot see why it should. *His* was an honourable dying. More so than poor Forbes—to be slain in that unforgivably wretched duel! Oh, how I despise duellists!"

Refusing to be diverted, Mrs. Boothe argued, "But Harley Farrington fought on the wrong side! He was a Jacobite!"

"He fought for a cause he believed in." Rebecca's dimpled

chin tossed upward. "As did many other fine gentlemen."

Mrs. Boothe uttered a shocked cry and peered nervously around the room. "What a terribly reckless thing to say! *Do* have a care, my love!"

"Fiddlesticks! Even should Falk or one of the maids chance to hear, they likely feel as do I. Besides, they are so loyal, bless them, despite the fact I've not been able to pay them for weeks! They would never betray me. And I did not say that I *approved* of Prince Charles or his Cause—only that I hold it more agreeable to give up one's life for an ideal than because of a foolish quarrel over the turn of a card."

Mrs. Boothe said earnestly, "But you surely will own that poor Forbes died in striving to bring us about? You know, love, how *hard* he tried."

Rebecca was silent. Her late husband, she thought rebelliously, might better have tried to repair their fortunes by some other means than those which had ruined them. Yet, despite his carefree lack of common sense, she had been genuinely fond of the debonair gentleman who had been her husband, and she knew that her aunt's grief at his death had been intense. She tightened her lips over an instinctive response, therefore, and stood, saying gently, "Yes, I know. Come, dear, it is a lovely day, and I must get to the bazaar, for Anthony simply *has* to have a new suit. We can be back in good time for luncheon, do we hasten."

Before the ladies had reached the end of the street, however, Mrs. Boothe was questioning her niece's idea of "a lovely day." The sun was bright, but a stiff breeze sent cloaks fluttering, and it was necessary to hold one's hood when a gust came up—a practice the lady found lowering. "For who can look graceful when one is clutching at one's hood and likely to have one's ankles revealed at any second by so pranksome a wind?"

Amused, Rebecca said promptly, "You can, dearest. And such a sight would gladden the hearts of many gentlemen in old London Town!"

"Rebecca!" Mrs. Boothe's cheeks were as pink as her eyes were bright. "Why, you saucy puss! Oh, dear, here is the corner, and we will be blown to— Ah, that is better, after all!

Where was I? Oh, yes, if any gentlemen were so unmannerly as to be leering at ladies' ankles, your own would claim all the attention, I am sure, and no one so much as notice my elderly limbs."

"Mr. Melton would notice." Rebecca chuckled to see her aunt's blush deepen. "He has noticed you these many months, and with so yearning an eye."

"Re . . . *becca!* Really!"

"And truly! As well you know. And as for being elderly—"

"Never mind! I declare you grow more naughty each day! Besides, if Mr. George Melton *has* noticed I am alive, one might never guess it. He stands. And he stares—when I am not looking. And says nothing! I begin to think 'tis merely that I remind him of someone. But—it is all of a piece." She shrugged. "Pray tell me now, why do we essay this blustery walk when your seamstress is quite beyond our present means? Little Anthony must surely have a suit can be turned, or patched, or something?"

"Not good enough, dear. He is no longer a baby and must have proper apparel. Why, in a year or so he will be off to Eton."

At this, Mrs. Boothe was so astonished as to stop in the middle of the flagway and stare at her niece with eyes as round as saucers. "*Eton* . . . ? We can scarce afford wax candles for the drawing room, and I declare my eyes smart each evening when I go to my bedchamber and endure those dreadful tallow monstrosities! And you speak of *Eton?*"

Rebecca took her arm and they continued once more, encountering few acquaintances upon their way, since the morning was so brisk and most ladies would walk, or drive, after luncheon, rather than at this unfashionable hour.

"Why not Eton?" Rebecca's chin took on the mulish tilt her aunt knew so well. "Something will turn up, I am sure of it."

"You are?" Peering hopefully at her, Mrs. Boothe ventured, "Have—have you a new admirer, dearest? Is that why you are come out of blacks so precipitately?"

"I wish I might find such an article!" And seeing her aunt's mouth opening in indignation, she added hurriedly, "I mean—one who is eligible, comfortably circumstanced, and with matrimony in mind!" Another protest was imminent, so that she rushed on, "The gentlemen who were interested in me when I married poor Forbes are now all wed, love. Most of those who are eligible now are either hanging out for rich wives, or unwilling to take on a lady with a six-year-old son!"

"Hilary Broadbent is—"

"Is no more than a good friend—or ever has been. Oh, he's fond of me, I grant you, but I doubt his heart has been touched by any lady as yet. And besides, I've no wish to follow the drum. Nor will I wed a man old enough to be my grandfather, if it is Lord Stoker whose name trembles on your tongue!"

Lord Stoker was exactly the name that had trembled on Mrs. Boothe's tongue. She sighed and pointed out wistfully, "But you would be a *baroness*, love! And they say he is full of juice, so—"

"Aunt *Alby!*"

"Oh! My goodness! Only see how distraught you make me, wicked one! But you know what I mean. No more worries, Rebecca. The butcher and the servants and the carriage. It was so sad when we had to let the matched team go—and your own Saracen."

Rebecca's eyes fell. The parting with her loved Arabian had been more cruel than even Aunt Albinia could guess. Dear Saracen, so gentle and yet so full of fire, and with a silken gait that— She put such painful recollections away and asked, "How can you be sure his lordship has marriage in mind? The gentlemen are more like to offer me a slip on the shoulder now that I am a widowed lady."

Aghast, her aunt exclaimed, "Never while you are in mourning! Have they?"

"Not quite openly, perhaps. But the insinuations have been there this three months and more."

"Good heavens! How wicked some men are!" But after a brief pause, Mrs. Boothe asked tentatively, "Anyone—suitable, my love?"

"*Wh-what?*" Much shocked, Rebecca gasped, "You cannot be serious?"

"Oh, well, indeed it would be dreadful," gabbled Mrs. Boothe, mending her fences. "And you will certainly be receiving far more proper—er—proposals, now that you are out of mourning."

"Well, I should hope so!"

Mrs. Boothe blinked and murmured, "On the other hand . . . if you really feel yourself to be ineligible because we are penniless, love, and—since you are so hopeful for your son . . . *dear* Anthony! Such a precious little boy, and should have every opportunity in life . . ." Here, she peeped at Rebecca's stormy countenance and, not having been devastated by a furious denunciation, proceeded with care. "Dreams are very well, but—reality is so horribly . . . real! And there are the servants, dear, and the carriage, and—"

"And the candles," Rebecca inserted, tartly. "Never! I shall be no man's mistress only to pay my bills! I place too high a price on myself to sell so cheap!"

Mrs. Boothe uttered a muffled yelp, produced a lacy handkerchief from her reticule, and, pressing it to her lips, wailed, "Oh! How outspoken you are! And now you mean to prose and preach at me, and perhaps send me away when indeed I never meant—"

Rebecca's sunny nature reasserted itself. She squeezed her aunt's arm and assured her that she meant to do no such thing. "For whatever would we do without you? I know your every concern is for me and Anthony, but—I've some plans of my own, and—"

"Aunt Alby! Rebecca!"

The horseman who pulled up his mettlesome grey steed was *point-device*, from the rakishly tilted tricorne to the spurs of his gleaming riding boots. "Good that I came up with you," he said, swinging from the saddle to plant a buss on his sister's cheek and another on his aunt's forehead. "Stand still, you looby! Why in the deuce must you go trotting out on a windy day like this? I was sure you'd be still abed."

Aware that the initial admonishment had been addressed

to his mount rather than his relations, Rebecca smiled fondly into her brother's handsome face and reminded him that she had never been in the habit of snoozing her days away in bed. "How well you look, Snow." She patted the sleeve of his full-skirted riding coat. "Blue always becomes you. I wish *I* had inherited Mama's eyes."

He said sternly, "Never mind trying to turn me up sweet. What are you about, miss? I was never more shocked than to see—damn it, *will* you come down, you blasted whirligig!—than to see you tricked out like any dashed courtesan!" Having pulled down his horse by this time, he turned to his sister, indignation in the blue eyes that, contrasting so vividly with his black brows, played such havoc with the ladies.

"Courtesan?" Rebecca protested, dismayed. "Oh, surely not."

Snowden Boothe was fond of his sister, and his eyes softened before the distress in her face. "Well—perhaps not that, exactly," he admitted. "But it ain't the thing, Becky. You'd best get home before some court card fancies you to be, er . . . You must wait your year out, is what I mean."

It was very apparent, thought Rebecca, that she was the only person to whom this year of mourning had seemed two years long. "But it *has* been a year! How could you forget? The duel was just after Jonathan went to Europe, and he's been away a year last sennight."

"Good God!" Incredulous, he said, "Has he? Oh, well, that's all right, then. Dashitall, I'd best mount this confounded glue pot!" He swung into the saddle again and, grinning down at his ladies, enquired, "Whither away? I'll escort you."

Mrs. Boothe eyed the fiery stallion dubiously. "Do you think he will submit to it, dear?"

"Who? Pax? Oh, he'll be all right. He's a bit—" Snowden broke off, perforce, as his mount essayed a pirouette at the passing of a carter's dray. "He's a shade fresh," he finished breathlessly. "Now, what I came to see you about was—blast and damn!"

The decidedly misnamed Pax reared to protest the approach of a carriage. The fine bay team, no less highly strung and nonsensical than he, reared and screamed, thus all but oversetting the light vehicle, whereupon the coachman pulled it over to the side of the street, and a groom jumped down to quiet the panicked horses.

"Sorry!" shouted Snowden, and went on jerkily, "What I came—to see you about was—I've heard from our Johnny."

Both ladies gave exclamations of delight. Her mittened hands clasped prayerfully, Rebecca cried, "Oh, how splendid! Is my brother well?"

"I collect he is." His mount having subsided a trifle, Snowden said with less erratic enunciation, "He sends his love to all, and says he will be home very soon."

"How soon? Snow, does he speak of finances? Oh, if only he could help us come about! Do you think—"

"No, I don't," he interpolated bluntly and, a frown puckering his brow, added, "See here, Becky, you ain't altogether in the basket, are you? You told me—".

"Yes, I know. Only—" She bit her lip. "There are so many bills. And if—"

He laughed. "Is *that* all? Burn 'em, m'dear. Only sensible thing."

"But—I cannot. The people I owe must be paid, 'tis only honest."

"Oho! Do you mean to be honest, Becky, you'll find yourself at Point Non Plus quicker'n you can skin a winkle."

"But, surely, the servants—"

"Will wait. They're all devoted to you. Won't mind a bit."

Rebecca sighed and her eyes fell.

"Trouble with you," he grumbled, "is you worry too much. Mustn't do that, Becky. It'll make you Friday-faced on Tuesday! Don't do a damned bit of good, neither. Tried it."

She forced a smile. "I expect you are perfectly right, as usual."

Mrs. Boothe, who had remained silent during this interchange, now put in a mild, "Rebecca does not worry for herself, Snowden. But there is little Anthony to consider, you see."

Boothe frowned. He was an improvident, happy-go-lucky

young gentleman, a fine sportsman cast in much the same mold as his late brother-in-law, and following a path that his much harassed father had been wont to prophesy would very soon bring him to ruin. There was no wager too preposterous for him to cover, no dare too foolhardy for him to take, no escapade from which he would back away. His temper was quick to flare and as quick to fade, but his pride was high, so that already he had been involved in two duels, both concluded satisfactorily, since he was a good swordsman. Full of energy, and chafing against the constraints of London's Society, he had toyed with the notion of joining the Jacobite Cause when the Uprising had again exploded the previous September, and only a stern letter from his elder brother, reminding him that he was the temporary head of his house, had dissuaded him. His wildness, however, had seemed to increase of late. Rebecca suspected he had already run through the small inheritance left him when his sire had succumbed to influenza some four years earlier, but he showed no signs of being in desperate straits, his brow as unclouded, his eyes as full of laughter as ever. His friends were legion, for besides being endowed with an unquenchable optimism he was generous to a fault, and his kindness and loyalty were legendary. It was this very kindness that now caused him to say slowly, "Yes. Of course. I should have thought of the boy. I collect you're wishful to send him away to school."

"Yes. But you are not to worry, Snow. You've enough to do not to outrun the constable, I do not doubt, without having to—"

"Pooh! Nonsense!" He waited out two more hops and a dance, then said with the air of one who has solved the unsolvable, "Tell you what, Becky. I'm promised to a party of friends at Brooks' tonight. Three of 'em owe me a—er, good deal. I'll demand they fork over the dibs, and you shall have it. 'Twill be a start, at least. By the time Anthony's old enough to go away to school, there should be sufficient for the first year, at all events."

Touched, Rebecca said, "How very good you are!" But as she reached out to him gratefully, her loving gaze shifted.

A gentleman had sauntered from the carriage and now stood at a safe distance from Pax, idly twirling an amber cane, and certainly able to have heard the last sentence or two. He was a tall, lean man of about thirty, clad in a caped cloak of dark red silk, flung carelessly back to reveal a white velvet jacket with enormous cuffs exquisitely embroidered in shades of pink and red, a waistcoat of red-and-gold brocade, and white knee breeches. His powdered hair was tied back with a riband of deep red velvet. A great ruby gleamed in the Mechlin lace cravat, adding to an over-all effect of dazzling elegance. Rebecca's gaze slanted to his face. The features were strong but gaunt, the nose Roman, the cheekbones high, and the chin a square and determined jut. His complexion was clear, if inclined to sallowness, suggesting that his hair must be very dark, as were his thick, sharply peaked brows. An interesting face, decided Rebecca, if not a handsome one, yet never had she seen such cold grey eyes, nor so mockingly cynical an expression.

Snowden Boothe glanced over his shoulder, and at once his own eyes hardened. "Give you good day," he said with bleak formality.

"No trouble at all, my dear fellow," murmured the newcomer. But he did not look at Boothe, his hard eyes continuing to scan Rebecca from the ruffles of her hood to the little pink slipper that peeped beneath her gown.

Again dismounting, and holding the reins with an unwontedly firm grip, Boothe enquired, "Your pardon?"

The heavy brows lifted, the grey eyes shifted lazily to meet Boothe's level stare. "Did I mistake?" he queried in a deep, insolent drawl. "I had fancied you apologized, Boothe. You came da—er, curst near to oversetting us, y'know."

Rebecca, who had begun to believe herself clad only in her corset, was incalculably relieved by the removal of the rude stare, but at these words anxiety twitched her brows together. Snowden had such a swift temper. Her brother, however, having noted that another gentleman had left the carriage and was inspecting the knees of one of the horses, said a repentant,

"The devil! Have I caused your cattle to be hurt, then? Now curse me if I don't have this clunch put to the plough!"

"I would curse you did you do such a thing to . . ." The cool appraisal slid again to Rebecca, "to—so splendid a creature."

His thin lips eased into a smile, his admiration was obvious, and Rebecca was mortified to feel her cheeks become hot. She turned her head away with lofty dignity and stepped closer to her aunt.

Boothe, meanwhile, led his horse over to the carriage, where he apparently discovered an acquaintance, for there ensued an interlude of shouting and back thumping. Rebecca murmured something trite to her aunt and contrived to ignore Snowden's maddening behaviour, not daring to glance his way for fear of again meeting the smirking grin on the face of this flirtatious Unknown.

Boothe returned at last, bringing his friend with him, and calling cheerfully that they must meet "good old Ward. Peter, I present my aunt, Mrs. Boothe, and my sister, Mrs. Parrish— Sir Peter Ward."

Pinning a smile upon reluctant lips, Rebecca turned about. Her smile died aborning and it was only with an effort that she restored it. A slender gentleman stood before her, and as he removed his tricorne to bow first to her aunt and then to herself, she saw that his thick hair, lightly powdered, revealed here and there a gleam of gold. Straightening, he smiled warmly at her, and she experienced the oddest sensation, as if she had left the ground and was floating off into the clouds. Surely, she thought dreamily, there had never been so perfect a gentleman. His hazel eyes were wide and deepset beneath arched brows of a light brown. The hair framing his high brow struggled to curl despite the severity with which it had been tied back. His nose was classically straight, his chin firm, his mouth well shaped and generous.

A polite cough jolted Rebecca back to earth. A sardonic voice remarked, "Boothe is forgetful, as ever, Peter. Pray present me."

"Your pardon," said Snowden hurriedly. "Ladies—the Honourable Trevelyan de Villars."

"Honourable, is it?" thought Rebecca, dropping a curtsey in response to a graceful bow. "What a farradiddle! The man's a libertine if ever I saw one!"

"How glad I am that you persuaded me to venture forth at so ungodly an hour, Peter," murmured de Villars. "Are you by any chance the widow of poor Forbes Parrish, ma'am?"

"She is," Boothe put in curtly. "And has come out of blacks today."

"Very good of you to point that out." De Villars' smile was bored. "I'd never have noticed it, else."

Uneasily aware of Snowden's tightening jaw, Rebecca asked, "Are you also an early riser, Sir Peter?"

"I am the despair of my friends," he admitted with a wry shrug.

"True." De Villars nodded, his quizzing gaze turned upon Rebecca. "But you do, occasionally, redeem yourself, dear boy."

Boothe took a pace forward. The belligerence of his chin was alarming, and his blue eyes fairly sparked.

"You should invite these charming people to your ball," de Villars went on with a wickedly amused glance at Boothe.

"What a capital suggestion!" Ward turned to the ladies and said in his pleasant voice, "It is to be on Friday next, at my house in Clarges Street. I shall have cards sent round at once, but—do say you will come."

"But, of course they will come," said de Villars.

"Thank you, Ward." Still, Boothe's chin was high. "I shall be glad to attend. My sister is but out of mourning, however, and it would not be seemly for her to do so."

"Have mercy on us, dear Mrs. Boothe," pleaded Ward, who had not missed the bristling resentment in Boothe's voice and was well aware of de Villars' deadly and well-deserved reputation. "Can you not intercede with your nephew?"

"Oh—it would be lovely, of course," said Albinia, flustered. "But—if Snowden feels . . ."

De Villars sighed. "I cannot endure the suspense. What *do* you feel, Boothe?"

Snowden's tightly compressed lips and the glitter in his eyes left little doubt as to what he felt. Alarmed, Rebecca intervened, "Oh, please, Snow. I should like it of all things. It has been such a *very* long time since I went to a party." She crossed to take his arm as she spoke and smiled up at him in the coaxing way he could never resist.

His anger eased. He thought, "Poor little chit, it *has* been hard on her." "We-ell," he said, reluctantly. "There must be no dancing, mind."

"Lord, what a clodpole," muttered de Villars, his voice unfortunately audible.

Boothe's head jerked to him. He said through his teeth, "Your pardon, sir?"

De Villars smiled and with a languid wave of the cane and a lift of his Satanic brows said innocently, "The muffin man yonder—came dashed near to losing his entire tray. . . ."

&

"I have seldom seen Snow so angry." Rebecca paused at the laden table in the busy warehouse to inspect a bolt of green velvet. "But—oh, did *ever* you see such speaking eyes? Or so fine a figure of a man?"

"Very speaking eyes," her aunt agreed, frowning a little. "And I'll allow that I have always been partial to the athletic type. Truly a splendid leg and very good shoulders, but—as to disposition . . ." She pursed her lips doubtfully.

"Oh? I thought him delightful. Do you not think this green would become Anthony with his auburn hair?"

Mrs. Boothe nodded absently. "And a fine grade of velvet. But velvet is so difficult to sew on, love. And if you mean to do it yourself . . . He would be dangerous, and not an easy man to handle. Though he is the type that—were his heart once given it would be for ever, I fancy."

"I *must* do it my—" Rebecca checked and, glancing up at her aunt, echoed, "Dangerous? I thought him all gentleness; all sweet amiability."

"You *did?* With that chin? That devilish smile? Lud! I sensed danger in every line of him!"

"For mercy's sake! I was speaking of Sir Peter! Not that nasty de Villars!"

Her aunt's brows went up. "Ward? You aim high, love."

"Perhaps, but—how could you have thought I meant de Villars? Had I been a man I should have knocked him down, if only for the ways his eyes prowled over me! At one point I feared I had forgot to put on my overdress!"

Mrs. Boothe smiled. "He could not take his eyes from you, I'll admit, and never has cared who he antagonized. Have a care, child. Snowden don't like him above half, and from what I hear of de Villars, a duel with *him* does not end with a polite sword thrust in the arm."

"I knew it!" Startled, Rebecca lowered the blue satin she had taken up. "He has a reputation, then?"

"With swords *and* women. Dreadful!"

"Then thank heaven I want none of him! What about this blue?" But before her aunt could respond, she asked hopefully, "Do you know aught of Sir Peter?"

"Very little, dear. I have not heard of a wife, however."

They exchanged conspiratorial smiles. Striving to be sensible, Rebecca said, "Still, there might be one. In the country, perhaps. Oh, I *do* wish Snow had not gone off to his club! I can scarce wait to ask him a *hundred* questions."

As it transpired it was late the following afternoon before Snowden Boothe put in an appearance in John Street. He wore evening dress, and his aunt and sister exclaimed proudly over the whaleboned coat of blue satin embellished with silver braid on cuffs and pocket flaps, the silver lace of the cravat, and the white satin small clothes. "And blue clocks on your stockings, love," smiled Rebecca. "La, but you put me to shame!"

He grinned, sat in the chair to which they ushered him, took the glass of Madeira that was offered, gazed into it, then set it down on the drum table beside him. "I'd best tell you now," he sighed. "I couldn't raise the wind, Becky."

She was well acquainted with cant, having grown up with two brothers, and although she had not really expected him to rescue her from her financial embarrassments she hid a little pang of disappointment as she patted his hand and told him not to fret. "I've a plan or two of my own," she said, with more confidence than she felt.

He eyed her uneasily. "Now see here, my girl, I'll have nothing smoky! Lord, but Jonathan would never let me hear the end of it did you open a gaming house, or some such—"

He was interrupted by a faint scream from his aunt, who lay back on the sofa, fanning herself.

"The very thought of it," she moaned. "My poor heart! I shall be in my grave before Christmas! I know it!"

"Fustian!" scoffed her unfeeling nephew. "You're strong as any carthorse, Aunt Alby. Do not try to flimflam us! Come now, Rebecca. What is this mysterious plan of yours?"

Rebecca's plan was quite daring and, uneasily aware that Jonathan would not approve and that even the more flamboyant Snowden might forbid it, she wished she had kept silent in the matter. "Oh, nothing definite," she said airily. "I shall tell you when I have all the details clear in my head. But, meanwhile, Snow, tell us of Sir Peter. What do you know of him? Aunt thinks he is quite a Non Pareil."

Half Boothe's mind was still worrying at her obvious evasions. He stared at her blankly. "Sir Peter—who?"

"Odious boy! Ward, of course! The gentleman we met yesterday."

"Oh." He took up his glass and sampled the wine. "Haven't seen him for years. Been rusticating, I understand. He has a beautiful place in—er, Bedfordshire, I think. Spends most of his time up there."

"He must have a very amiable wife," said Mrs. Boothe, all innocence. "Most ladies would wish to spend more time in Town."

"Hmmmnn," said Snowden, maddeningly.

"She must be very beautiful," persisted Rebecca.

Snowden, who had been thinking how delightful it must be to own a country seat, looked up at this and enquired vaguely, "Who must?"

"Lady Ward."

"Oh. As to that, I could not say. Never met the lady. Heard she was a beauty, did you? Surprising, at her age." He added a hasty, "Don't intend no disrespect, mind. I *had* Heard the old lady was a real Toast in her day, but—"

"*Old lady?*" gasped Mrs. Boothe, titillated. "Did he marry for money, then?"

"Oh, I doubt that. No, come to think of it, he couldn't have. Ward Marching has been in the family since the Conquest, I should think." He chuckled. "They likely brought it over with them."

"Then—why—" Rebecca broke off, her bewilderment replaced by amusement. "Snowden—impossible creature! Of whom are you speaking?"

"Ward's grandmama, of course. You said 'Lady Ward,' did you not?" And shaking his head as his relations dissolved into laughter that was more relieved than he could guess, he asked, "Are you sure you two girls ain't been at this decanter before me?"

"No, you wretch. We were referring to Sir Peter's *wife*, not his grandmama!"

"Then you were fair and far off from the start," he said triumphantly. "Ward don't have a wife. Oh, he was betrothed once. Years ago. I believe the lady went to her reward. Shame. She was a great Fair, so they say. Ward never got over it. I heard he hasn't looked at a girl since. Silly gudgeon."

"I think it noble in him to be so loyal," said Rebecca, shocked by such callousness. "There are not many gentlemen would mourn a lady so steadfastly."

He grunted. "I should hope not. Dashed silly thing to do. Now do not fly up into the boughs! I ain't saying a man shouldn't go into blacks for a year or so. But—*six* years? Drivel! If the lady loved him, she'd likely want him to be happy, not wear sackcloth and ashes into his dotage."

"From what I saw of Sir Peter yesterday," Mrs. Boothe murmured, "he was far removed from sackcloth and ashes."

"Nor anywhere near his dotage," added Rebecca.

"Well, whatever he is," said Snowden, preparing to take his leave, "he's lost to the matchmaking mamas. They've all thrown up their hands over him, although he's quite the best catch in Town. Full of juice, y'know. From what de Villars told me, there was a time when poor Ward could scarce set one foot after t'other without foundering, he was so deep in the handkerchiefs dropped for him."

"Indeed?" Rebecca walked with her brother to the hallway and said with a faint frown, "De Villars? I thought you purely disliked the gentleman?"

"Did." Boothe winked at the maid as he accepted the tricorne she offered blushfully. "Misjudged the fella. Had a good chat with him last night at Brooks'. Never dreamed he could be so jolly." He bent to plant a kiss on Rebecca's cheek. "Teach me not to go making hasty judgements, eh?"

"Hasty judgements, indeed!" said Rebecca disparagingly when she relayed this conversation to her aunt. "If that horrid man was 'jolly' to Snow, it was because he has some mischief in mind."

"Yes, and involving you, child! I saw how he looked at you!" Mrs. Boothe shivered. "Like a cat with a mouse. It fairly turned my blood cold."

"Well, I shall be no mouse for Trevelyan de Villars!" Rebecca declared, the mischievous gleam bright in her dark eyes. "I am after bigger game!"

"I knew it!" Gripping her hands apprehensively, Mrs. Boothe moaned, "You mean Sir Peter! Oh, but this is going to be frightful, I can feel it in my bones! What do you mean to do to the poor man?"

Rebecca twinkled at her. "Well, that," she admitted, "is one of the details I've not quite worked out as yet. But I shall catch him, never you fear! Papa once told me that if a person wants something badly enough, no matter how difficult it may seem, it can be done." She held out her skirts and danced around the room. "Lady Peter Ward. . . . Oh, Aunt! Does it not sound delicious?"

Mrs. Boothe uttered a heartfelt wail and reached for her vinaigrette.

CHAPTER
🙟 2 🙟

Rebecca sat at her dressing table, leaning forward, the small round patch balanced on her slender forefinger, her hand wavering as she critically considered her features. With a decisive swoop, she placed the patch slightly below and to the right of her tender mouth. "There!" she said with a pleased air.

"Oh!" gasped her aunt, shocked. "The *Kissing?*" Her niece responding with nothing more than a bright nod, Albinia shook her head and retired to perch on the bed. She already wore her ball gown, a charming creation of dark blue sarsenet embroidered in lighter blue, with the bodice and train also of the lighter colour. Her wig was tall and decorated with clusters of violets, and she looked rather astonishingly youthful. Her eyes, however, were apprehensive, and the mirror informing her of this, Rebecca stood and asked archly, "What is the matter, dear? Do I not look well?"

"You look very well, my love. Save for that naughty patch! And you are causing my poor heart to flutter most distressfully, for I dread to think what you may have plotted against that poor—"

The door swung open to the accompaniment of a hurried scratching, and six-year-old Anthony raced in. "Mama! Mama!" he cried, "I had the most—" And he stopped, his green eyes widening so that they looked enormous in his pale face. "Oooh . . . !" he breathed, and went over to touch the white silken gown with one fine-boned hand. "Are the pink flowers stuck on?"

Rebecca laughed, and bent to kiss his cheek. "No, my darling, they are part of the material." She pirouetted for him. "Do you approve of your mama?"

His awed eyes answered for him, but he whispered, "You are very pretty, ma'am. I never saw you look . . . like that."

"Well, you see, love, I no longer have to wear only black,

or dark colours." Hands on waist, Rebecca surveyed her reflection. The Watteau gown really was elegant. It had been dreadfully dear, but, following Snowden's oft-repeated instructions on How to Proceed When Under the Hatches, she had ordered four new dresses from Madame Olga and ignored the frightening balance of the bills already stuffed into the bottom drawer of her desk. Madame's smile had been a little strained, but she had said nothing, and Aunt Albinia had attributed this to the advertising that so lovely a patron would achieve. Nonetheless, Rebecca's heart had been thundering with nervousness when they had left the modiste's discreet shop, and she wondered now if ever she would be able to pay the half of what she owed. "I suppose I should not have bought it," she sighed.

"Of course you should," said her aunt loyally. "It might have been fashioned for you; how could you resist it after all this time in blacks?"

Rebecca threw her a grateful smile. "I own I love the pleated train and the flattened paniers. But do you know, they say that in France they are starting to turn away from the back pleats?"

"And I suppose the next to go will be the stomacher! The French will stop at nothing! Never have! But, as to those ruffles at the neckline, dearest, *très chic*, but—" She glanced to the child's worshipful face. "A little—ah, *décolleté*, no?"

Rebecca contemplated the expanse of her creamy bosom and had the grace to blush. "The tools of conquest," she murmured provocatively.

Mrs. Boothe gasped quite properly, but her dimples quivered.

Millie, Rebecca's abigail, her voice as blunt as her face was square, asked gruffly, "Which rings, Mrs. Rebecca? With the little roses you'll likely want the pearls and rubies?"

"Yes, thank you, Millie. And my pink tulle scarf, if you please. You really powdered my hair beautifully."

Glancing with fond pride at the richly upswept curls and the pink velvet ribbons she had wound amongst them, Millie said, "Is it very special tonight, ma'am?"

Mrs. Boothe put in, "It well may be!"

Rebecca smiled and turned to her son. "How did you go on in the park, dear? Your cheeks are rosy as any apples."

"I had a jolly good time, Mama." He sank to his knees beside her as she again sat at her table, adjusting the shawl Millie draped across her shoulders. "We met the kindest gentleman. He had a boat. A model galleon. With guns and—and everything! And he let me sail her in the lake. He was a friend of Uncle Snow's. And Uncle Snow took me up with him on Pax, and it was the best afternoon ever!"

She ruffled up his thick auburn curls lovingly, then frowned. "Your hair is wet!"

"Oh. Well—I sort of fell in," he confessed, with a guilty grin. "A little bit."

"A little bit!" She scanned the delicate features in immediate anxiety.

From the open doorway, Mrs. Falk, the housekeeper, tall, starched, angular, and greying, proclaimed in her nasal twang, "The boy was soaked, marm. I told him not to go near the edge, for it is very slippery just there. The gentleman fished him out and thought it most amusing."

"Oh, yes. He was a great gun," declared Anthony, his eyes flashing merrily.

With a grim look at Rebecca, Mrs. Falk said, "Is not the term I had in mind, marm. Nor I do not think you would have—"

There was no time for more, for at this point Snowden entered, a vision in purple and gold. "What's to do?" he asked breezily. "You ladies ready? I fancied you would be waiting downstairs. Jolly decent of old Forty to invite us for dinner, y'know. Shouldn't keep him waiting. His cook's a tiger!"

Typical of the man who is himself invariably late, he was all impatience, and his charges were obliged hurriedly to gather up fans, shawls, and reticules and trip down to the waiting carriage. Once inside, and with the coachman whipping up the horses, Rebecca blew another kiss to Anthony and, settling back against the squabs, said, "How nice it is that one of us still can keep up a carriage. How you manage it, Snow, I cannot guess."

"Couldn't get along without one. There's always some way to arrange these matters. Shouldn't have let yours go. At all events, mine is at your disposal, as I have said. You should use it more often, if only to take my nephew for a drive. Little varmint enjoys sitting up on the box." He added thoughtfully, "He is looking much less down pin these days, Becky. A touch pale, but better."

"Yes. He has recovered nicely, I dare hope. But that dreadful illness has left him much too frail. How I would love to take him into the country for a while."

"It's a frail lad with a lion's heart," he said bracingly. "Never fret, m'dear, he'll be a fine man some day. And his mama is certainly a fine figure tonight. That's a nice gown. But remember—no dancing, lest the *ton* think you disrespectful to poor Forbes."

"As you say, dear," said Rebecca meekly.

"She will be the new Toast," declared Mrs. Boothe, with fond prejudice. "Mark my words, Snowden, no lady can hope to outshine your sister tonight!"

They enjoyed a light dinner at the charming flat of Lord Graham Fortescue, a good-humoured Tulip of the *ton*, who enjoyed the rather dubious distinction of being often referred to as "that young fribble who's a bosom bow of Snow Boothe." His lordship journeyed with them to the ball, and it soon became apparent that Albinia's expressed hopes for her niece had been a trifle premature. They had turned onto Clarges Street and taken their place in the procession of vehicles discharging guests before Sir Peter Ward's large house, when Mrs. Boothe exclaimed excitedly, "Look, Becky! Only look at that *glorious* gown! And the *wig!* I never saw anything so elegant! Who is she, Fortescue?"

Obediently craning his neck, his lordship's brown eyes skimmed the crowd. "The tall girl? That's The Monahan. She's— By Jove! Snow, look at this! D'ye see her escort? You never think . . ."

Snowden looked, and whistled softly. "So *she's* his interest! I'd heard the gossip, but— Gad! They're bringing it into the open, eh?"

"Who? Who?" Trapped by her paniers and trying vainly to glimpse the gentleman with the lady in the magnificent gold brocade robe *volante*, Rebecca said, "I cannot quite— Oh." Her nose wrinkled disdainfully. "'Tis Mr. de Villars."

"Yes. And speaking of dress—look at his!" Snowden chuckled. "Black and silver, to her gold! He'll cause a flurry with the lady on his arm!"

Rebecca asked, "Are you quite sure of their—er, relationship, Snow? The lady is so lovely, surely she could not view *him* with favour?"

"Not much for looks, is he?" Snowden agreed cheerfully. "Yet the women melt at his feet, Lord knows why. I never could believe he'd actually snared The Monahan."

"She seems entranced," murmured Mrs. Boothe, curiously. "Is he very wealthy, Fortescue?"

"Pockets to let from what I've heard, ma'am. Still, he keeps up appearances, don't he?"

"He does indeed," Snowden agreed, with a grin. "The Monahan is expensive, that I *do* know."

Rebecca turned to him, much shocked. "You *do*? How—"

"He—he ain't clutch-fisted, neither," Fortescue interposed, desperate but ever loyal. "No lady leaves his protection with rancour, so they say. And—"

"My—*lord!*" gasped Mrs. Boothe.

"Oh—egad!" groaned his lordship.

"Here we are, at last!" said the vastly diverted Snowden. "Get your pretty selves together, *mesdames*. And remember, Becky: No dancing!"

૱

Had anyone ever told Rebecca that she could have a wonderful time at a ball without once dancing, she would not have believed it. On this warm May evening, however, she thoroughly enjoyed herself. Before they were through the reception line she had become a centre of attention, and she could scarcely have been more pleased than to have two gentlemen vying for her attention when she came up to give her hand to the host.

Sir Peter's greeting was the essence of charm and manners. His hair, heavily powdered, was tied back in the English style. The great cuffs of his green velvet coat were frogged with pale green satin, the pocket flaps and stiffly pleated skirts free of further ornamentation. It was a rather austere habit for so young a man, but Rebecca, entranced, thought that very austerity emphasized his good looks.

Once in the ballroom, she was besieged, as her aunt had foretold, gentlemen pressing in around her, and old friends struggling through the crowd to embrace and congratulate her upon her return to social functions. When she was asked for her dance card, and replied demurely that she would not be dancing, her decision was obviously applauded. Several would-be partners claimed her for the duration of a dance, nonetheless, either walking with her through the cooler halls, or taking her on to the terrace to admire London's myriad lights and the clouds that drifted across the quarter-moon.

Shortly after midnight she was led into the refreshment room by a long-time friend, Major Hilary Broadbent. He was a pleasant young man, with sandy hair (now hidden by powder) and the pale skin and freckles that so often accompany such colouring, and he looked very dashing in his scarlet regimentals. His long, narrow tawny eyes had brightened when they fell upon Rebecca, and, although she might yearn for the escort of a certain baronet, she was very well pleased to accept the major as her supper partner.

The large room was warm, bright with flowers, crowded with guests, and ringing with chatter. Mrs. Boothe was already seated with some of her cronies, and from the corner of her eye, Rebecca saw Trevelyan de Villars, distinguished by his height if not his behaviour, as he flirted with his lady love at the centre of a covey of friends.

Major Broadbent said, "Oh, there's The Monahan. She's the latest Toast. A striking pair, eh?"

She had deliberately avoided a direct look at the group, but now glanced that way. De Villars' twisted grin flashed, and he raised his glass in a brief salute that managed somehow to embarrass her. She nodded frigidly and turned away.

Surprised, Broadbent said, "I'd not realized you was acquainted. Should you like to join them?"

"No. Thank you."

He looked at her sharply, then chuckled. "Taken him in aversion, have you? As well. He's no fit friend for you, m'dear."

She rapped her fan lightly on his wrist. "And you have not the right to so name me, Hilary Broadbent!"

"Those dimples make me want to say a deal more," he said with fond impudence. "But first, I'll get your supper."

He seated her at a small table for two and went off. Rebecca allowed fancy to drift. Moments ago, she had seen Sir Peter lead a pretty girl into the minuet. Soon, the dance would end. He would come in search of the widowed Mrs. Parrish, for he *must* have been struck by the beauty of her gown, and his eyes, when first she arrived, had been full of admiration. He would stay beside her, chatting politely, and she would be her most gracious self. Not a trace would she reveal of the "hoydenish starts" that some-times caused dear Aunt Alby to throw up her hands in despair. Tonight, she would be all demure and pretty propriety, and Sir Peter would be charmed . . . intrigued, even. . . . He would say—

"I give you good even, Mrs. Parrish."

The subtly taunting voice stiffened Rebecca's back, but she looked up and extended her hand politely.

His grey eyes gleaming, de Villars bowed over it. (One had to admit The Creature was graceful.) "A charming picture you make, ma'am. And—all alone? Criminal! By your leave . . ." He did not wait for her leave, however, but in a sort of easy swoop disposed his long self in the chair.

"Oh!" Rebecca blinked. "But—that is Major Broadbent's place, sir."

"We shall guard it for him, you and I. Now tell me, my Fair, of what were you thinking? You looked as enchanted as enchanting."

She did not immediately reply, but surveyed him thought-fully. The thick, crisp hair was expertly powdered and brushed into a style that softened his sardonic features. The magnifi-cently tailored black jacket hugged his broad shoulders without so much as a suggestion of a wrinkle. The silver frogging was dramatic, and the white satin waistcoat, embroidered with black roses, made him look even more suave and sophisticated.

She thought, with an unconscious curl of the lip, "Even more raffish!"

Belatedly, she became aware that he was laughing softly. Aghast, she stammered, "Oh! Your pardon! I was—er—"

"Summing me up. And not flatteringly, alas. Is an unkind return for an innocuous remark."

"To tell a lady you scarce know that she is enchanting, is *not* innocuous, Mr. de Villars!"

He leaned closer, his eyes quizzing her wickedly, his long-fingered hand straying dangerously close to her own upon the tablecloth. "Then we must better our acquaintance, and speedily, so that I *can* tell you how truly enchanting you are."

Rebecca snatched her hand back and began to ply her fan. "I expect your lovely partner must be sighing for you, sir."

"Oh, no. Rosemary is accustomed to my comings and goings. And I left her in good hands."

"Indeed?" Hoping that her down-drooping eyelids would convey her utter boredom with him, his lightskirt, and his comings and goings, Rebecca looked elsewhere. And thus found herself gazing straight at The Monahan and the "good hands" in which she had been "left." Her eyes widened in dismay. She turned away at once, but de Villars had seen and, raising his quizzing glass, directed a keen stare in the same direction. His brows went up. "Aha," he murmured, "my dear friend Ward. So that is the way the wind blows. . . ." He grinned as Rebecca's haughty stare returned to him and, with a revoltingly sympathetic air, remarked, "You waste your hopes, my dear. Peter, alas, is not in the petticoat line."

"Oh!" she gasped, shutting her fan with a snap. "Oh! How *dare* you!"

He stood, leant one hand on the table, and said, soft-voiced, "Here comes your military rattle, so I shall leave you. For the time. But—you have much to learn, ma'am, about what I would—dare."

Rebecca smiled past him and said warmly, "How nice that looks, Hilary. I am very ready to do it justice."

The major, a laden plate in each hand, frowned from the flushed cheeks of the lady to the sneer on the face of the gentleman. "Look here, de Villars," he began.

"As you wish," said de Villars, equably. "Ah, yes. An excellent selection. Thank you, Broadbent." And appropriating a cheese tart, he bowed to the lady, waved his prize in appreciation to the scowling officer, and wandered off.

Rebecca's sense of humour, seldom far from the surface, was tickled by such blatant insolence, and she struggled to subdue a giggle. The major did not share her amusement. "That . . . fellow!" he fumed.

"De Villars?" she said, with arch unconcern. "Is he not droll?"

Broadbent ground his teeth and, looking after that debonair departing figure, snarled, "Droll . . . indeed."

❧

"It is that wretched de Villars," Rebecca hissed. "He means to bring me to a stand, I know it! I've had scarce two words with Sir Peter all evening!"

Mrs. Boothe, sharing the secluded sofa in the wide corridor, had a rather different notion of what Mr. Trevelyan de Villars intended to bring Rebecca to, but, her eyes lighting suddenly, she murmured, "Then he has not yet succeeded, love. Here is Sir Peter coming."

Their host hastened towards them, bowed gallantly to Mrs. Boothe, and implored that she permit him to capture her niece for a stroll in the garden. "For if I have to dance another quadrille," he said with his grave smile, "I vow the soles of my shoes will melt away."

Her heartbeat quickening, Rebecca placed her little hand on his sleeve and allowed herself to be led into the garden.

The night, which before had seemed rather muggy, now became all delight. The moon, hitherto here and gone in a vexing way, was a glory, peeping shyly from behind the lacy fragments of slow-drifting clouds. For the first time, Rebecca noticed the heady fragrance of the flowers, and she seemed more to float than walk beside this splendid young man. He spoke with propriety, his deep voice thrilling her with its gentle cadences. Was there a step to be negotiated, his hand was unfailingly at her elbow, to guide her gently up or down, as though she were a fragility too precious to be allowed to make the attempt unaided. He was overjoyed, he declared, that she and her aunt had been so kind as to accept his invitation on such short notice. "So many of my guests," he said, with a twinkle, "have been demanding an introduction, ma'am."

"Yes," she replied, all bashful innocence, "the ladies have been exceeding kind."

"Ah, but I had not meant the ladies."

Rebecca gave a little gurgle of laughter. "Lud, sir. You will quite turn my head with such flattery."

"That is certainly not my intention. Nor is it flattery, dear Mrs. Parrish. Any host must be delighted to entertain so lovely a guest. I shall hope you will grant us the pleasure of your company again."

She blushed with joy. "Thank you, sir. Do you mean to make a long stay in Town, then?"

"I had, but I am compelled to soon return to Bedfordshire." Guiding her to a stone bench beside which a fountain splashed musically, he dusted a section with his handkerchief and, when Rebecca was seated, sat beside her.

"You must love the country," she said, hiding her disappointment. "I can scarce blame you. London is so exceeding oppressive in the summertime."

He took the fan from her hand and began to ply it for her. "And do you mean to escape it also, ma'am?"

"Alas, I fear it beyond my means. If my brother can arrange something for us, however, I am sure he will. You are acquainted with Snowden, I believe?"

"We were at school together. Is it presumptuous of me to enquire whether there are others in your immediate family? I seem to recollect Snow mentioning another brother, or an older sister, was it?"

"Yes. I have an elder brother, Jonathan, who bear leads an aristocratic young gentleman through Europe at the moment. My sister, Mary, is married to a clergyman and lives in Wales."

"So you number two brothers and a sister, in addition to your son. How I envy you. I, you see, am not merely an only child, but an orphan besides." He said rather wistfully, "I have always thought how fortunate are those with large families."

Rebecca, who had endured all the joys and torments of growing up with sister and brothers, could not imagine life without them and said kindly, "How very lonely you must have been."

He smiled and waited for the inevitable coy remark that he must hope to soon establish a large family of his own.

It was not forthcoming. Rebecca was too sincerely interested to remember to be the designing female. She said, "You have cousins, surely?"

"Oh, I do indeed! And what a bother they are." His rueful grin mitigated the harshness of the words, and he went on, "I am the head of the family, you see, and it is because of my cousin James that I must now return to my country seat."

"Well, I do think it too bad in him to cut up your peace. Is he in a dreadful scrape?"

"Oh, no." He laughed. "Well, perhaps he is, at that. He was still a bachelor when his older brother died suddenly of some intestinal disorder. A year later, the widow remarried and went off to India, leaving her ailing daughter in James's care. He is a good-natured fellow, but now he himself has married. His bride refuses to take the girl into her household, and she and James have removed to Norway, where he is attached to the Ambassador's staff."

"And so they have left the girl with you!" Frowningly indignant, Rebecca said, "Why, I think that perfectly dreadful! The poor creature! Pushed around from pillar to post! She must feel she dwells in a swing, never able to set foot to ground."

"Oh, it is not that bad, I assure you. She will not lack for food and shelter. But I must find a governess, for a young lady should be properly guided before she makes her bow to Society, do you not agree, ma'am?"

"I most certainly do. How good you are, Sir Peter. Do you mean to keep her with you, then?"

"For the time, at least. And only listen to me boring on about my troubles." Rising, he asked in his courteous way if Rebecca wished to go back inside. "There is a new summer house I had hoped to show you, but perhaps . . ."

She lost no time in asserting that she would love to see the new summer house, and they walked slowly along the path that wound through flower beds and little clumps of trees and shrubs towards the centre of the garden. Sir Peter did not again refer to his family, and the conversation turned gradually to politics and the recent tragic conflict. "How sad it is," he observed, "that so many fine fellows should have flocked to the banner of that pretty princeling, with never a thought for the consequences to themselves or their loved ones. Such gullibility is very well for callow youth, but for mature men to have taken up the Jacobite Cause shows a sad want of steadiness, do not you agree? For myself, I can but deplore the irresponsibility of those who plunged into so sadly lost a Cause, and must now pay so frightful a price for their folly."

This view was not one that Rebecca shared, but despite her admiration of the gentleman beside her, her own thoughts were much taken up with other issues. As he expounded on the subject she made few comments other than to murmur an occasional acquiescence, so that he judged her a very comfortable girl, this strengthening his good impression of her.

It was not until they were leaving a rose arbour to come out onto the hedge-lined path leading to the little summer house that either of them realized the structure was occupied. A sudden burst of feminine giggles was followed by a squeak, the sound of a slap, and the abrupt emergence of The Monahan. Laughing softly but hilariously and concentrating upon lifting her paniers so as to negotiate the three shallow steps down to the pathway, the statuesque beauty did not at once see the approaching pair, but fled towards them, still looking back and calling, "No, *really*, Treve! You would not dare—"

A shout from her amused pursuer alerted her too late. Rebecca had made a belated effort to step aside, but was trapped by the hedge. Glancing around at the last instant, The Monahan swung in the same direction. For two ladies wearing the wide-hooped paniers and voluminous skirts of full evening dress, a collision could only be disastrous. Caught off balance, Rebecca staggered backwards. The Monahan stumbled over Rebecca's foot; Rebecca was undone by the hedge, and down they both went.

Paniers had been designed for dramatic effect. They had never been intended for reclining. Scarlet with mortification, Rebecca saw her skirts shoot into the air. Her efforts to contain them were as fruitless as her attempt to get back on her feet. Not only was she revealing a shocking expanse of her chemise, but her romantic interlude with Sir Peter was quite ruined, for how could he do anything but laugh at so clumsy a finish to their walk? Her humiliation was magnified as she heard a smothered male chuckle. That *wretched* de Villars! Of all the men she would least prefer to be rescued by!

His strong hands gripped her upstretched ones. His mocking countenance bent above her. "Oh, dear! Oh, dear!" he chortled. "What a contretemps! *Poor* Little Parrish!" He slipped an arm about her waist, steadying her as she stood, and breathed into her ear, "We *did* spoil things for you. But it would not have worked, you know. Did you hurt yourself?"

Pulling away and glaring at him ferociously, she hissed, "You are *horrid!* Did you know it?" And, remembering her manners, "No, thank you. I am not hurt."

"I think I am in love with you," he countered, grinning broadly.

"Oh!" she exclaimed, yearning to scratch him.

"Who could blame me? You look extreme edible. Especially with your hair so deliciously at right angles."

She reached up. It was truth; her elaborate coiffure had paid a dreadful penalty. She gave a little whimper of despair.

De Villars gripped her wrists as she attempted to rectify the matter. "Let be, girl!" He proceeded to busy himself with her hair. "There! Good as new!" He stepped back, eyes dancing with laughter. "I apologize. No, really. I will prove it. I shall be so unselfish as to contrive in your behalf. It might be amusing, at that."

"How I dread to deny you amusement, sir," she said coldly. "But—pray do not contrive!"

He stepped closer again and, with a very different gleam warming his eyes, breathed, "You mean I am free to be—*selfish* with you, m'dear?"

Seething with indignation, she turned her back on his impertinence and managed to smile as her host came anxiously to console her.

❧

Sir Peter Ward stretched his long legs, sank deeper into the comfortable chair in his parlour, and sighed his satisfaction. "It went off quite well, eh, Treve?"

Chin on fist, de Villars surveyed him thoughtfully. It was almost dawn, and both men had shed their finery and wore dressing gowns over their night rail. Even *en deshabille* the difference between them was marked, for de Villars' dressing gown was an Oriental design of black with heavy red frogging down the front closure, and although the sardonic gleam was still apparent in his grey eyes, he looked rumpled and far more human than the elegant exquisite who had graced the ball. Sir Peter's hair had been brushed free of powder and neatly tied back, and he was if anything better looking than he had appeared earlier, the lamplight waking a rich golden sheen on his head, and his fair colouring enhanced by the blue quilted satin of his dressing gown.

"It went very well," de Villars acknowledged. "Did you suppose it would not?"

Ward shrugged. "It has been a long time since I hosted a London ball. I am very glad you agreed to come, my dear fellow. Did you enjoy yourself?"

"Enormously." De Villars took a pull at the liqueur in his glass, then said with a slow smile, "I've not laughed so much in years."

A tiny frown touched Ward's eyes. "The collision?"

"Mmmnn. Lovely ankles has the widow."

"Which one?"

De Villars glanced at him and thus glimpsed the frown. "By Jove, you're right! Two widows! *L'embarras des richesses!*" He chuckled. "Now, why do you scowl? Never tell me you have a *tendre* for the chit?"

"You came with The Monahan. I'd have supposed her woman enough for any man."

"Oh, she's a delicious creature, I grant you, but . . ." De Villars paused and asked curiously, "*Are* you warning me off, Peter?"

"Why should I? I am not in the petticoat line."

"No. As I told her."

"The deuce you did!" With uncharacteristic heat, Ward snapped, "You had not the right!"

"Aha! So the gentleman *is* interested!"

"No, but she is a Lady of Quality. I'd not wish to see her ruined, de Villars."

"De Villars, is it? Woe is me! I am in deepest disgrace!" He laughed at Ward's tight-lipped exasperation. "She is a *widow*, my dear Peter. A lonely little lady, ripe for the taking, I'll warrant. And besides, why should you assume I mean to ruin her?"

The injured air brought Ward to a reluctant smile. "Spare me a seizure. Do not say you mean marriage."

"I could not bear to see you suffer a seizure." De Villars held his glass to the light and scanned it drowsily. "She amuses me, merely. One might be spared boredom for a year, per-haps, with her in keeping."

Ward was silent for a moment, then asked, "What of your present lady?"

De Villars yawned. "Rosemary is delightful. And desir-able. She excites, but—" He interrupted himself with a gesture of impatience. "Our relationship was entered into with the awareness on both sides that it could not become permanent, for temperamentally we do not suit. From the start we agreed that if either of us found our situation becoming—*ennui*, we would part while still friends."

Sir Peter threw him an awed look. "And you have found *The Monahan* to be *ennui* . . . ?"

"Now, what a fellow you must think me, that I should make so gauche a remark about so enchanting a lady. Let us instead own that she has become bored with me."

"Gallant," thought Ward, "but not true." He warned in his grave fashion, "Have a care, Treve. I suspect The Monahan would make a loyal friend, but a bad enemy, and does she

suppose you to slight her because you find another lady more
alluring—"

"Alluring! Did I imply that? By God, but I must be extreme inarticulate tonight! Rosemary has sufficient and to spare
of *that* commodity." He went on slowly, "'Tis just that . . ."

"That—what?"

"Lord! What an inquisition! If I must be blunt then, I find
Rebecca Parrish to be a rare article. An honest woman who
balances practicality with a—a sort of elfin gaiety; who copes
with many problems that are, I fancy, somewhat crushing, yet
who has retained a naïve and rather heart-warming romantical
outlook . . ." His eyes even more thoughtful, he said, half to
himself, "And who, withal, manages to be a very lovely little
creature."

"I'll allow she is different," mused Sir Peter. "When I expected a platitude, she showed me sincerity."

"And when I rescued her, she asked me did I know I was
horrid!" De Villars chuckled. "Outspoken to a fault, The Little
Parrish. Now you frown again. My poor Peter. For how many
years have you endured me?"

"Six."

"I wonder you put up with me. I have always been a burden to my friends."

He sounded sincere. Glancing at him, Ward wondered if
he was. Ever. How little one knew the man and what was behind his sneering mouth and cold eyes. He could be so insen-
sitive, so merciless, yet at times a boy almost, full of teasing
and laughter. "I shall never forget how kind you were, when—
when Helen was killed," he said simply. "Yet—sometimes I do
not . . . *can*not like what you do. Sometimes, I think I know
you not at all."

"But I know you. Is sufficient."

"Is it?" Ward said with a faint smile, "You probably find
me a bore at times. Own it."

"I find everyone a bore. And there dawns the frown, very
predictably." Definitely bored, de Villars stood and put down
his glass. "I shall bid you goodnight, mine host."

Ward said nothing.

At the door de Villars paused and, his hand on the latch, turned back. "Peter," he said softly, "I have never taken a woman who was unwilling. And no lady has suffered—because of me. I am a rascal, I own it. But—I trust I am not a rogue."

Ward looked at him levelly. "I suppose we none of us really know ourselves."

"Oh, very good!" But with a suddenly wistful smile, de Villars said, "Do you know, I have few real friends. I should purely detest to lose one."

"A most unlikely eventuality," Ward acknowledged, returning the smile.

De Villars swept him a bow. "In the matter of The Little Parrish?"

"I—er, scarce know the lady."

"Nor I. We start even. Shall we make it a wager? Do I obtain a 'yes' from the lady, you owe me a thousand. A 'no,' and you win. What say you?"

"'Tis something steep, considering I've not said I seek a wife. What have I to gain?"

"A very great service. Only think, if the chit is willing to me, then she's no proper wife for you. And *your* wife must be proper—no?"

Ward looked steadily into the jeering grey eyes. "Oh, yes. Assuredly."

"A double incentive, then. Do I fail, you get one thousand guineas and the knowledge she is *sans reproche*. For I tell you this, Peter, if she is persuadable, I'll persuade her."

"I believe you might." Ward's lips curled a trifle. "And—the limits?"

"One month from today. *Still* the man cavils! What now?"

Ward said hesitantly, "It does not seem quite—honourable. Almost as though we tested the lady."

"If she is chaste and pure, she has nothing to fear from me, I swear it."

"Very well, Treve." Sir Peter reached out. "You've my hand on't."

CHAPTER

✿ 3 ✿

Rebecca tilted her white parasol so that the pink silk fringe cast a dappled shade across the pink damask of her gown. "No," she said reluctantly, her mournful gaze on Anthony and his boat. "'Twas not an upset but a full-fledged disaster, dear Aunt. I failed us all."

"What fustian you do talk, my love." Mrs. Boothe shifted her position on the wooden park bench they occupied, having paid a groat for the privilege, and patted her niece's hand comfortingly. "Was you to ask me, many gentlemen were captivated, for I seldom have seen you in better looks. Besides, only Sir Peter and Mr. de Villars saw your tumble, and de Villars is very obviously interested."

"Oh, *very* obviously! And has already stated he fancies himself 'in love' with me!"

With a squeak of shock, Mrs. Boothe cried, "He never did! Oh, but dearest, it will not do! 'Any port in a storm' may be well enough, but not *that* port! The gentleman has a reputation from Land's End to John o' Groats! He has fought four duels that I know of, and had to leave the country for six months only last year when poor Lord Kadenworthy nigh died after their meeting. His birth is impeccable, I grant you." She shook her head and hove a wistful sigh. "And his person. Such a leg! And those magnificent shoulders—what a waste! But the best you would get from him would be a slip on the shoulder, certainly not a gold wedding band. He is not the marrying kind. And as to fortune, I have learnt now that he was cut off with no more than a competence after he ran off with a poor child barely out of the schoolroom, so if you—"

"For mercy's sake!" cried Rebecca, breaking into this lengthy indictment with considerable indignation. "How could you think I would even *consider* such a—a reprobate? I—Anthony! Have a care, dearest! I would sooner lie in my grave in Potter's Field!"

Mrs. Boothe blanched and flapped her dainty hand-kerchief in the general area of her cheek. "Do not say such dreadful things! Now I shall dream of it, I know I shall! And me in the next box to you! Oh!" Her wail was brief, however, and she sat straighter, exclaiming, "Yet it is all flimflam, for after the stir you created last night, I will be amazed are you not inundated with callers and cards of invitation. You may have to cross Ward from your list, as you say, but—"

"Oh, but I did not say that," contradicted Rebecca with a tiny smile.

Mrs. Boothe blinked. "But—I understood you to imply . . ."

"That I failed. Which I did. But"—Rebecca bestowed a dimpling glance upon her—"'twas just the opening hand, as Snowden would say. The game is scarce begun yet, and already I've an ace up my sleeve."

"You have? God bless my soul! What—"

The ladies had been too engrossed in their discussion to notice the gathering of bandsmen, but now a sudden roar of music shattered the quiet of the warm early afternoon, sending pigeons rocketing into the air and causing a dozing elderly gen-tleman to topple from his chair.

Anthony, his pale face alight with excitement, added to the embarrassment of the casualty by clamorously aiding him back into his chair. This done, he galloped up to deposit his dripping yacht in his mother's lap. His aunt foiled this dastardly scheme by snatching the yacht and setting it on the grass. He threw a beaming grin at her, and panted, "May I please go and listen to the band, Mama?"

Being conversant with the mental processes of small boys, Rebecca refrained from pointing out that the efforts of the mu-sicians could probably be heard in Hampstead. "Yes, dear. But please stay where I can see you."

He darted off. Mrs. Boothe watched the vigorous pumping of those bony knees, but she had not lost track of the conversa-tion and probed, "Now, as to this ace of yours . . . ?"

"Well," said Rebecca gleefully, "it seems that Sir Peter has become temporary guardian to the daughter of a cousin. He means to launch the girl properly, and wishes her to be groomed for her come-out by an exceptional, er—companion or governess."

"Very good of him, I'm sure. But I do not see how this happenstance can be viewed as an ace card for you, love."

"But only think! Sir Peter is an only child. What can he know of the type of lady who would be suitable for such a post?" Seeing that her aunt was preparing to enter a caveat, she rushed on, "It seems to me that were I to offer to help him in selecting a suitable candidate, 'twould be logical enough that I must also meet his charge, no?"

"It is scarce a certainty, and—"

"And from what he told me of her upbringing, the poor girl has known little of love and less of guidance." Her eyes dreaming, Rebecca went on, "She has been sickly, and is likely a dowd, poor creature. 'Twill be a positive joy to instruct her. I shall take her to Madame Olga, perhaps, and by the time I am finished, will have transformed the girl into a poised debutante of whom Sir Peter can be proud."

Mrs. Boothe mulled this over in silence. Life, she knew, had not been easy for her niece since, at seventeen, she married Forbes Parrish. Rebecca had accepted her father's choice of a husband with no outward evidence of dismay. They had made a handsome couple, she thought, with a nostalgic smile. Forbes, the most generous and well meaning of men, had gone through his quite respectable fortune within three years of the marriage, however. The jewels he had showered upon his bride had been the first casualties to result from his gaming, and had kept them solvent for another two years, but the luck he was sure would come to his rescue had (after the fashion of such capricious commodities) deserted him, and only his aunt and his widow knew how perilously close they now were to bankruptcy.

Rebecca's tendency to fantasize was well known to Mrs. Boothe, who had judged the trait a blessing that enabled the dear girl briefly to escape harsh reality. Besides the romantical, however, Rebecca harboured a wilful streak, and an occasional disregard for the bounds of convention that could be alarming.

What other lady would have paid heed to that old man who had fallen in the middle of Bond Street last winter? Why, he had given every appearance of being inebriated and, if the gentlemen passing by chose to ignore him, a *lady* should certainly not rush into the traffic to aid him. Much less a lady wearing *blacks!* It made one palpitate just to remember the uproar it had caused. Especially when Becky had demanded that those two unwilling chairmen convey the man to a doctor, and then paid for the chair (which she could ill afford!). She had insisted the victim was not intoxicated, and admittedly one could not smell wine upon his breath, but the entire unhappy fiasco was so typical of her headstrong nature. And then there had been the instance of those wicked boys and the little brown cat, and Becky running from the house to lay about her with Snowden's amber cane, and getting properly clawed for her trouble when she had untied the creature's tail from the back of the carriage! Mrs. Boothe sighed. The cat had remained with them. He not only ate like a horse, but was grown so fat and lazy he could likely never chase a rat, much less catch one! Whisky's affectionate nature was undeniable, but— Mrs. Boothe sighed again and cast an oblique glance to her niece. The big dark eyes were faintly smiling. She was undoubtedly indulging a dream in which she accompanied Sir Peter's radiantly transformed cousin to her triumphant come-out ball. . . .

At this point, Mrs. Boothe became aware that the air rang with laughter and that the rhythm of the music had become erratic. She turned to the bandstand, and cried, "Becky! Look!"

Rebecca was jerked from a rosy dream that had progressed much further than her aunt guessed. She looked, and said laughingly, "Oh, that scamp!"

Anthony had beguiled his way onto the bandstand, and a grinning bandmaster watched as the boy wielded his baton to the amusement of the musicians and the delight of the crowd. The selection lurched to a stop, the crowd applauded, and the maestro pro tem bowed low.

"What a way he has, dear child," said Mrs. Boothe, clapping heartily. "He will go far, mark my words."

Whatever his future prospects, Anthony was not going far at the moment. Rebecca watched curiously as a man wearing green livery spoke with her son at some length. She was about to go and join them when Anthony nodded, seized the man's hand, and led him towards her.

"This is Hale, Mama," he announced cheerfully. "Hale, this is my aunt, Mrs. Boothe, and my mama, Mrs. Forbes Parrish. My papa is dead, you know, but I remember him very well."

Hale expressed polite regrets and ventured an understanding smile to the ladies. He handed an engraved card to Rebecca, remarking that he had been charged to deliver it into her hands at once, then bowed and left them.

Rebecca read the brief message and gave a squeal of triumph. "Aunt Alby!" she cried joyously. "It is from Sir Peter. He begs that we join his party for the weekend at his country seat in Bedfordshire."

"How splendid!" exclaimed Mrs. Boothe. "Becky, you clever minx!"

"Uncle Snow!" shrieked Anthony, hurling himself at the gentleman who strolled towards them on the arm of a friend. "Oh, you *do* look funny!"

Snowden, awesome in a high French wig and puce satin, snatched up his nephew and rounded on his companion in high dudgeon. "There! Now blast you, Forty! Did I not say it?"

Choking on a laugh, Rebecca said, "Oh, dearest! You never cut off all your pretty curls?"

"'Tis the fashion, Mrs. Rebecca," pointed out Fortescue, striking in yellow brocade. "You must own that Snowden looks much more the thing in his wig."

"May I try it on, Uncle Snow?" begged Anthony, tugging at one glossy ringlet.

Snowden all but cringed. "Do not touch the curst contraption! Already, I scarce dare turn my head for fear it will fall off and reveal my nakedness!"

Mrs. Boothe gasped and blushed fierily.

"Really, Snow!" Rebecca scolded. "Anthony, leave your

uncle's wig alone." She smiled at Graham Fortescue, causing that shy young Buck to blush almost as deeply as Mrs. Boothe. "Sir Peter Ward," she told her brother, "has been so good as to invite us to join a weekend party at Ward Marching."

Snowden set his nephew down and took the card Rebecca handed him. "Hmmnn," he said dubiously. "Don't know about this." He gave the card to Fortescue. "What d'you think, Forty?"

His lordship scrutinized the invitation critically. "Not too bad. A touch plain, perhaps. Ward never was much of a one for frills, and—"

"Not the *card!*" Snowden exploded. "The message, you slowtop! Is it proper for my sister Parrish to jaunter off to Bedfordshire with Ward?"

"Oh," said his lordship, grinning. "Well—why not? You will be going as well, so—"

Boothe threw him an irked scowl. "No, I shall not! No more shall you!"

"What? But I am invited, and—" His lordship encountered the full force of Boothe's meaningful grimace, and his indignant protest faltered to a halt. He said lamely, "Forgot. Sorry. No, we cannot go, of course."

"Do you say I cannot either?" wailed Rebecca, who had waited out this odd discussion with much anxiety.

Snowden looked from her dismayed countenance to his friend. "Well, you're the expert in all things having to do with dress and manners. What d'you say?"

His lordship reread the invitation painfully. Watching him, Anthony's face was one big grin. He opened his mouth to comment, caught his mother's eye, assumed the mien of a martyred saint, and was silent.

"Don't see why she should not go," Fortescue opined at length. "Not a green girl, after all. Y'r pardon, ma'am, but 'tis truth. Says here a small party go. Ward's a perfect gentleman. Besides, aunt will be with her. What?"

Snowden pursed his lips. "Trouble is, Ward cries friends with de Villars, and if *he's* to go . . ."

Rebecca said innocently, "But I thought you said you had misjudged Mr. de Villars, Snow?"

"Might have," he admitted with a brooding look. "But it's one thing for *me* to enjoy his company, and quite another for *you* to be seen with him!"

"Shouldn't worry about de Villars," offered his lordship. "Gone into the hinterlands to see his great-uncle Boudreaux." Evidently fearing this information would be suspect, he tapped the end of his snub nose and added owlishly, "Told me so. Personally. Didn't ask him, mind. Not polite. We was talking of something else at the time. I collect he thought I might like to know it."

Staring at him, Boothe asked, "Why?"

His lordship, misunderstanding the question, considered it, and shrugged. "Probably he's going to try and turn the old fella up sweet. Always going down there. Except," he appended with shrewd perspicacity, "when Boudreaux is here in Town. Then he goes to Grosvenor Square, instead."

"Good gracious," Mrs. Boothe fluttered. "I'd no idea Lord Boudreaux was related to de Villars."

"Head of his house." Fortescue took out his snuff box and tapped it meditatively. "Old boy's a bit of a martinet. Disappointed in de Villars. Cut him off without a penny when he run off with poor little Miss Rogers in '30—or was it '32? Lord, what a bumble broth that was!"

"Yes, indeed," agreed Mrs. Boothe. "A very dreadful scandal. Poor girl. But she married Dutton the following summer, as I recall. I remember wondering at the time whatever could have induced a clever boy like Trevelyan de Villars to ruin himself by compromising a widgeon like Constance Rogers."

"She was a *lovely* widgeon, probably," said Rebecca dryly. "She must have been, if she achieved an eligible connection within a year of her disgrace."

"I still do not see, Forty," Snowden persisted single-mindedly, "why de Villars should think you interested in the fact he visits his great-uncle."

"Stands to reason, dear old boy. Anyone would be.

Dashed great fortune like that, whistled down the wind for a schoolgirl. His papa suffered a seizure, I believe. They came near to burying him. Had to, finally. He died."

Aghast, Rebecca cried, "How awful! The poor man died of shame?"

"Pneumonia," his lordship corrected. "Contracted it when he—"

Rebecca was unable to repress a giggle, and Anthony jumped up and down a few times to contain himself. Snowden laughed and cuffed his friend lightly. "Don't pay no heed to Forty," he advised his amused family. "Fell out of his cradle when he was an infant!"

"What he means is that I'm not awake on every suit," said Fortescue with a rather endearing grin. "It's truth. I ain't a clever one." He pondered a minute, then asserted with simple pride, "But I never brought disgrace on a green girl. Nor got cut out of a fortune. So I ain't altogether past praying for, am I, Snow?"

"You most certainly are not, sir," said Rebecca. "And you are a supreme authority on fashion and etiquette besides!"

His lordship beamed at her and promptly volunteered to escort the ladies home, were they intending to leave. They started off very shortly, Rebecca and Lord Fortescue leading the way and the other three following.

Tugging at his uncle's dress sword, Anthony chortled, "Lord Forty moves his lips when he reads, sir!"

"Silence, scapegrace!" hissed Snowden, much amused. He turned to Mrs. Boothe. "Now, Aunt Alby, I rely upon you in this business. Becky's been shut away from the world so long, she might not—ah, that is to say, sometimes she don't quite understand—"

His aunt tucked her hand into his arm and murmured comfortingly, "Never worry, Snowden, dear. I'm more than seven, and am all too aware of dear Rebecca's impulsive nature. You may be perfectly easy. I shall not take my eyes from her."

Snowden thanked her and promptly forgot all about it.

&

Because of the length of the journey, the carriages conveying Sir Peter's guests were to leave London at an early hour on Thursday morning. Rebecca and her aunt, determined not to be late, were delayed when Whisky was discovered to have disposed himself upon Mrs. Boothe's travelling gown, which Millie had laid on the bed while the family breakfasted. The cat, a part-Persian, had long tawny fur, and in addition to the fact that his weight had set a mass of creases, the gown was covered with hairs that stubbornly resisted anything but individual removal. By the time Rebecca had donned her own travelling dress of peach linen, the underskirt embroidered in orange and white, and Millie had positioned a dainty matching cap, frilled with white lace, upon her powdered coiffure, the carriage was waiting at the door, and a man's voice could be heard downstairs.

Anthony had been carried off by his uncle to see a military review in the park so that they found Sir Peter Ward alone in the small drawing room, gazing up at the portrait of the late Forbes Parrish that hung above the mantel. He turned and bowed when the ladies entered, and upon Mrs. Falk hurrying in with her mistress's shawl, he begged the honour and himself bestowed the white lace about Rebecca's shoulders. She slanted an oblique and triumphant glance at her beaming aunt and murmured, "You knew my late husband, Sir Peter?"

"Very slightly." He looked pensively at the portrait, apparently having forgotten the guests waiting outside in the carriages.

Watching him, Rebecca thought how fine he was in his riding clothes, the high top boots and spurred heels combining with his sword to lend him an air of strength and masculinity. She sighed dreamily.

He murmured, "Do you miss him very terribly, ma'am?"

She started and, knowing that of late she thought far less often of her dear Forbes, knew also a pang of guilt, and evaded, "He was a fine gentleman."

"Yes. I am very fond of sparrows."

Rebecca's eyes widened, and her aunt stared her bafflement.

"S-sparrows . . . ?" echoed Rebecca.

Sir Peter pointed with his gold chased riding whip to the sky beyond the low wall against which the artist had chosen to portray Mr. Parrish. "There are three of the little rascals," he said. "Do you not see, ma'am? Here—and two over here."

"Why—yes. So there are. What very keen eyes you have."

Not one to let an opportunity slip past, Mrs. Boothe imparted the news that her niece was extremely interested in birds. "I declare as a child she used to gaze at them by the hour," she lied staunchly.

Rebecca blinked.

"Are you, indeed?" Sir Peter turned from his absorption with the sparrows, his usually grave eyes bright with enthusiasm. "Jove, if that's the case you are in for a treat, ma'am. My estate in Bedfordshire is something of a bird sanctuary. I permit no shooting there, and you may see many different—" A shout from outside startled him. "Gad!" he exclaimed remorsefully. "Whatever must you think of me, keeping you standing here and my guests waiting! Are you ready, ladies?"

Two luxurious carriages were drawn up on the flagway, and several mounted gentlemen were gathered about the open windows, conversing with the ladies seated inside. Rebecca, her fears eased by the absence of Mr. de Villars' sardonic features, heard her aunt utter a small cry, and glanced to her curiously.

"I believe I see at least one old friend," said Mrs. Boothe, blushing.

Rebecca searched the faces of the guests, and said a surprised, "Why, is that not Mr. George Melton, Sir Peter?"

Their host nodded affably. "He is a good fellow, do not you think?"

With a sudden flash of intuition, she asked, "Is he also a close friend of yours?"

"I think I could not claim his friendship, Mrs. Parrish. But de Villars is rather attached to him, and asked that I invite him. I was more than glad to do so. Especially when I learnt you have his acquaintance."

Rebecca looked thoughtfully at her aunt. Decidedly

flustered, that lady enquired as to whether Mr. de Villars himself would join them, and it appeared that Lord Fortescue was infallible, as ever, and de Villars was at the country seat of his great-uncle. "He is," vouchsafed Sir Peter in his gentle fashion, "extreme fond of the old fellow."

"To say naught of the old fellow's fortune," thought Rebecca, cynically.

She and her aunt were guided down the steps and across the flagway as though highwaymen lurked in each areaway. To be accorded such reverence after her lonely year of seclusion was bliss for Rebecca, and she smiled gratefully as she was handed into the luxurious vehicle. Complacency left her abruptly. A purring voice said, "Why, it is the fallen lady!" Rebecca stiffened and looked up quickly. A beauteous face smiled upon her, but there was a glint behind the languor in the green eyes. "Oh, dear," murmured Mrs. Monahan. "How clumsy of me. I was speaking of our collision, of course, dear ma'am."

Managing to squeeze onto the seat beside her aunt, Rebecca said in puzzled fashion, "Collision? Oh! You must be the lady de Villars chased from the summer house! Faith, but I'd not have recognized you in the daylight."

The glint in the green eyes became a spark. A flush brightened the dewy cheeks, and the chin of The Monahan lifted dangerously. Beside her, a very pretty girl with clear grey eyes and fair skin exclaimed in amusement, "That gave you back your own, Rosemary!" She leant forward, extending her hand. "How do you do, Mrs. Boothe? It has been a long time since we met. Can you place me, I wonder?"

Albinia's brow wrinkled. Dismayed, she said, "Oh, mercy! Your face, I know, but . . . for the life of me, I've no name to put to it."

The girl laughed merrily. "We were never introduced, dear ma'am, and met under prodigious adverse circumstances. In fact—"

"The flood!" exclaimed Mrs. Boothe. "Now I remember! Your party was marooned with ours when a bridge was washed away. We were coming home from Stratford, as I recall, and we all sought shelter in some remote hedge-tavern. Goodness me! That must be six years ago, at least. What a memory you have, Miss . . . ?"

"Allow me," said The Monahan, in her drawling, lazy voice. "Miss Letitia Boudreaux, Mrs. Boothe, and Mrs.—Perish."

Miss Boudreaux hesitated. Mrs. Boothe went into an involuntary peal of laughter. Rebecca smiled with an unusual expanse of pearly teeth. "Lud, ma'am. I vow I'd not believed all the gentlemen say of you, but I see they were right on one count. You are quite comical."

They smiled sweetly upon one another.

A very few seconds had passed since Rebecca and her aunt had entered the carriage. It was only just, in fact, beginning to move off, the gentlemen clattering along behind. But each of the four ladies knew that battle had been joined.

During the balance of the journey, Rebecca and The Monahan contrived to deal together politely, if not sincerely. The truce was temporary, as both of them knew, but manners must be served, and each lady was far too well bred to continue sniping at the other in a way that would cause embarrassment to their fellow guests. Thanks largely to Mrs. Boothe's volubility and Miss Boudreaux's sunny nature, the conversation went along easily, as did the miles. At each stage of the journey the gentlemen came to the windows of the carriage to chatter to their fair companions. Sir Peter divided his attention nicely between the two vehicles, and nothing could have been sweeter than the demeanour of Rosemary Monahan when his handsome face appeared beside the window. Mrs. Boothe fairly sparkled, for George Melton, a stocky gentleman of middle years, wearing a conservative tie wig that seemed to add to his solemnity, did not once divert his attentions to the second carriage, but came shyly up to her window each time they halted. If he said little, his brown eyes were admiring, a smile hovered about his firm mouth, and his very bashfulness added to the lady's regard for him. Rebecca, who had privately agreed with Snowden's opinion that Mr. Melton was a very dull dog, found herself warming to him, if only for her aunt's sake, and when his square, guileless face turned to her, she granted him a smile that brought a momentary surprise into his eyes. He returned the smile with a rather touching eagerness, and she wondered for a selfish instant whatever she would do if he popped the question and Aunt Albinia departed from the little house on John Street.

At the second stage they all left the carriages to be ushered into the Duke and Duck by a beaming proprietor and shown to bedchambers where their various servants already awaited to minister to their needs. Downstairs again, the coffee room had been commandeered by Sir Peter, and hot chocolate and little cakes for the ladies, ale and pies for the gentlemen, were waiting. Rebecca was again impressed by Miss Boudreaux's friendliness. Such a warm, kindly girl, it was a pity she was so tall, that feature probably explaining why she was not betrothed, despite her looks and her eligibility. There was little time for private thought, however, for the guests from the other carriage had to be introduced, the gentlemen who had ridden escort also pressed around, and soon they all were enjoying the light repast and merry company.

Rebecca was part of a chattering group when her glance aside discovered The Monahan flirting outrageously with their host. Sir Peter displayed no more than his usual courtesy, but Rebecca was dismayed. She turned away and found that Miss Boudreaux was watching her smilingly. Rebecca was briefly flustered; her cheeks blazed. Miss Boudreaux stepped closer and asked softly, "Have you known Sir Peter for very long, ma'am?"

"I only just met him, to say truth. Do—you know him well?"

"Oh, yes. I have known Peter ever since Miss Edwards was killed. It was an accident and happened only a week after I first met your aunt. My cousin de Villars was escorting me back to my Seminary. We saw a tree struck by lightning, and it fell just as Sir Peter's coach came around the corner. There was no slightest chance for him to stop." Her eyes became blank for a moment. She murmured in a hushed tone, "It was—frightful. Treve ran to help, of course. Peter's arm was broken. He was quite helpless, and utterly distraught. Miss Edwards was thrown from the vehicle, and her head struck a boulder. She was killed instantly."

"How ghastly!" Her warm heart touched, Rebecca put a hand on Miss Boudreaux's arm and said with sympathy, "Do not think about so dreadful a thing."

"I seldom do. But, do you know, I saw Helen Edwards lying there in the rain, and I have never forgotten it. She was so lovely and looked quite untouched—like someone asleep. It is small wonder poor Peter has never been able to look at another lady."

"She must have been very beautiful. How fortunate that you were close by."

"Yes, for there was no one else about. It was a terrible storm, and Treve—my cousin—would not have ventured abroad, save that I was to be in a play at the Seminary that evening, and bedevilled him to get me there. He took care of everything. Peter was past caring, but later he was rather pathetically grateful. They have been bosom bows ever since."

"I see. What a tragedy to lose her before they were even wed."

"Ward is rather a dear, do not you think? I have always hoped he might find someone else."

"It would appear," murmured Rebecca, glancing to the side, "that he has done so."

"Who? Mrs. Monahan? Oh, no. Rosemary actually has—ah, interests elsewhere."

Striving to appear surprised, Rebecca said, "Indeed? Is a most indulgent gentleman."

"Is an absent gentleman," Miss Boudreaux corrected, her eyes twinkling.

The two girls exchanged understanding smiles. It would appear, thought Rebecca, that although she had undeniably made an enemy of one lady, she had found a friend in another.

Soon they were back in the carriages and resuming their journey. The weather was fair, if not bright, and the countryside lush and green and ablaze with the flowers of early summer. They took luncheon at a charming old hostelry in St. Albans, and when they set forth again it was agreed to split up the guests so that they might better get to know one another. Much as she had liked the tall girl, Rebecca hove a sigh of relief to see Miss Boudreaux and The Monahan go to the second coach. Their places were taken by a sister and brother. An amiable pair, they appeared to be in their early thirties, and were distinguished only by their odd habit of finishing one another's sentences. When it developed that the gentleman was as interested in birds as was their host, Rebecca lost no time in requesting that he identify some species for her as they went along. He gladly agreed, and she was instructed that there were many different species and that the British Isles was blessed with a great number of these, although the wholesale slaughter for "sport" bade fair to soon render many species extinct. She was shocked, and her interest spurred Mr. Street's enthusiasm. The resultant flood of instruction became so confusing that she sighfully admitted at length that she must be a feather-wit, and was able to remember very little of what she had been told.

"Never fret," beamed Mr. Street encouragingly. "Sir Peter will—"

"—tell you of them all," Miss Street finished, her round face as full of good-natured cheer as was her brother's.

Fascinated, Mrs. Boothe asked, "Do you and your brother always—"

"Talk like this?" Miss Street smiled, pulling her shawl closer about her plump shoulders. "Oh, yes. You see, we are—"

"—twins," chuckled her brother. "I am nine and twenty, and—"

"—I am also," Miss Street declared.

"Oh," said Mrs. Boothe, understandingly. "Then that—"

"—explains it." Miss Street nodded.

Rebecca thought, "My goodness! I wonder if Snow has met this strange pair!" Still, she liked them, for they were as friendly and unassuming as two puppies, and besides, she had learnt something from them that might very well assist her in The Plan; at least she would not be totally without knowledge of sparrows, rooks, and cuckoos!

It was late afternoon when Sir Peter rode up to the windows to announce that they were now on his preserves. Mr. Street and his sister continued their mutual instruction, and many different varieties of birds were pointed out for Rebecca's edification. She tried to pay attention, but her interest had waned, and she found more to admire in the estate they traversed. Save for an occasional low rise, the terrain was largely flat. The park was a very good size and well wooded. It had been left in as natural a state as possible, so that she thought what a happy time Anthony could have here. The house came into view when they rounded a curve in the drivepath. Rebecca experienced a feeling of disappointment, for although it was impressive and in excellent repair, it was a grey brick structure, sitting with uncompromising squareness in a broad treeless hollow. She could not but think how much more attractive it would appear were it surrounded by trees and shrubs, and found herself wondering why the original builder had not set it on some of the higher ground rather than in the hollow. The welcome they received, however, left nothing to be desired. Sir Peter had an excellent staff, and the butler and several footmen and lackeys were on the terrace to receive them as the carriages rolled up to the wide-spreading front steps.

Inside, the mansion was much bigger than Rebecca had anticipated. Maids and powdered footmen and lackeys were everywhere, low-voiced, efficient, and obviously eager to welcome and assist the master's guests. Somehow, in the confusion of ushering his friends about, conferring with his butler, and doing all he might to be the perfect host, Sir Peter found time for a few words with Rebecca and Mrs. Boothe. He seemed almost overly concerned as to their comfort and summoned his housekeeper to enquire which suite had been assigned to them. Their disposition apparently satisfying him, he told the immaculate, white-haired woman that every possible effort must be made to ensure that Mrs. Parrish and her aunt receive anything that might make their stay more pleasant. He left them then, to attend to his other guests, but his smiling gaze lingered on Rebecca's face, and she felt dizzied with happiness.

The housekeeper, Mrs. Kellstrand, placed them in the

charge of a magnificent lackey and urged that they rest and refresh themselves after their long journey. "If you wish it, your dinner will be brought up to you," she said courteously. "But if you are not wearied, Sir Peter will await you in the green saloon at half-past six o'clock. Dinner will be served at half-past seven."

Following their assigned lackey across the hall and up the wide staircase, Rebecca looked about with interest. Despite its now crowded state, everything was orderly, the Great Hall seeming, like its owner, to reflect an air of calm refinement. The marble floors gleamed; Florentine gold benches were spaced about the walls which were painted a pale blue-green; two marble pillars soared to the ceiling at each end of an oval dome of blue and green glass that filtered an arboreal light into the room; and the draperies at the tall windows were of green velvet. The stairs climbed against a wall hung with many portraits: the largest of these depicted a flock of starlings, and there were smaller individual paintings of robins, sparrows, blackbirds, and an especially fine likeness of a snowy owl. Somewhat taken aback, Rebecca glanced at her aunt and encountered such a stunned look that she had to battle a sudden urge to giggle.

In keeping with the luxurious quality of the mansion, their suite was sumptuous. It consisted of two large bedchambers, each with an adjoining dressing room, and having between them a cosy little parlour. The carpets were so thick that Rebecca's slippers seemed to sink into them. The furnishings were rich, but not ornate, the drawer and wardrobe space more than ample. Several fine old bird prints graced the walls, and the view from the windows was delightful.

There was no sign of Millie, but they had no sooner removed their bonnets and mittens than a knock at the door heralded the appearance of a maid bearing a tray with a pot of tea, cups and saucers, and, in addition to the milk and sugar, a plate of scones and sliced cake. Curtseying to Mrs. Boothe, the girl advised that Madame's abigail would be up so soon as what she'd got the luggage straightened out, as there was "some sort of bumbling in the stables just now."

Rebecca began to pour the tea and her aunt watched, holding her sides and bemoaning the fact that she would not have time to put off her corsets did Millie not hasten. She sat down to accept the cup Rebecca offered and, stirring in her customary three teaspoons of sugar, took a sip, sighed blissfully, and said, "Was you as surprised as I, love, to discover The Monahan amongst us? Lud, but you could have knocked me down with a feather."

"And me, Aunt. And did you notice how she scratched at me? Wretched woman! It is de Villars' doing, I make no doubt. He has sent her, in his stead, to thwart me at every turn!"

"Thwart you? But—whyever would she do such a thing, dearest? She cannot wish to aid you, if to do so means *she* will lose de Villars."

"If she adores him so, why is she here *sans* her love? He would be just cunning enough to convince her she is helping to protect his friend against a designing woman, never allowing her to suspect what his *own* evil designs are! I tell you, Aunt Alby, de Villars means to prevent me attracting Sir Peter, for he plots that I am to become another of his collection of light-skirts!"

One hand pressed to her bosom, Mrs. Boothe squawked, "Re—*becca!* What a naughty expression! Besides, if de Villars does not mean you to become—er, better acquainted with Sir Peter, why would he have urged the man to invite you to his ball last week? And why did he not bring his influence to bear so that we were not invited here? Ward obviously rates him high, and would listen."

Stirring her tea thoughtfully, Rebecca admitted the logic of this. "If Ward followed de Villars' suggestion that Mr. Melton be invited, he would—"

"Do you know, I had quite forgot that," Mrs. Boothe interpolated. "Lud! How ungrateful in me, when I should instead feel a kindness for the scheming rascal!"

"Should you, dearest?" Rebecca chuckled at her aunt's blushes. "I vow each time I looked your way, there were Melton's eyes, fairly glued to you. Has he not so much as thrown out a hint yet?"

"He looks, and smiles, and sometimes seems *about* to say something significant, but when he does speak"—Mrs. Boothe hove a mournful sigh—"'tis only to mumble about the weather, or what fine cattle Sir Peter keeps in his stables, or some such commonplace. Alas, I fear is a *most* bashful gentleman!"

"Poor dear." Rebecca smiled sympathetically. "We both are hampered, it seems. You by a shy swain, and me by a predatory rake! Well, never mind. We shall come about. Now, tell me what you think of this estate."

"I think it charming. A shade formal, perhaps. And did ever you see so many servants? Ward must indeed be plump in the pockets." An arrested expression came into her eyes. "Can that be why Rosemary Monahan is so prodigious syrupy to the man?"

Dismay seized Rebecca, but then her chin set doggedly. If The Monahan fancied to amuse herself by captivating another victim this weekend, she was going to encounter some stiff opposition!

CHAPTER
❧ 4 ❧

*R*ebecca blinked sleepily as the brocade bedcurtains were drawn and Millie's phlegmatic countenance looked down at her. The abigail vouchsafed the information that it was a cloudy morning, but the boat party had not as yet been cancelled, and Mrs. Rebecca had best take her breakfast now did she not wish to be tardy. Millie was tolerant of modern ideas; she knew her mistress would never eat in the morning before she had washed and cleaned her teeth, and hot water was already steaming in the washstand bowl. Yawning, Rebecca stretched and threw back the bedclothes.

Ten minutes later, feeling alert and refreshed, she was seated at the round table in front of the windows, partaking of toasted crumpets and strawberry jam. The crumpets had been created by the sure hands of a master, the jam was rich and full of luscious berries, the coffee hot and of a fine brew. Yet Rebecca's expression was glum.

For a while last evening everything had gone beautifully. She had been seated at table between Hilary Broadbent, who had arrived at the mansion with several other dinner guests, and the shy Mr. Melton, who had surprised her with pleasant if not scintillating conversation. The gentleman spoke like a sensible man, wherefore one must assume shyness attacked him only when in the company of the lady he meant to court. Rebecca smiled sympathetically at the fragment of crumpet she held. Her own efforts had been no more successful than those of Mr. Melton. Sir Peter had looked her way often during the meal, and she had managed to appear unaware. Save for the one instance in which he had glanced at her just as a scallop had slipped from her fork and managed in some perverse fashion to plop into her glass, splashing wine over her neighbour. Hilary had teased her for her embarrassment, demanded that none but her own "fair hands" should wipe his cuff, and then created a good deal of amusement by "fishing" for the immersed scallop. Rebecca's blushes had faded. Vastly diverted, she had entered into the merriment, glancing up at length to find Sir Peter's grave eyes still upon her, and Aunt Albinia directing an unmistakably warning glance down the table.

She popped the crumpet into her mouth and wondered pensively why it was that she invariably forgot to be poised and sophisticated just when it was most important that she be so. Nonetheless, her jollity must not have been too hoydenish or given Sir Peter a deep disgust of her, for later, in the drawing room, he had three times wandered to her side, and when musicians began to play soon after ten o'clock, he had solicited her as his partner in a country dance. The Monahan, ravishing in a very *décolleté* gown of fawn damask embroidered with pink flowers, with hoops rounded in the old style, had been won by Major Broadbent, his narrow tawny eyes triumphant as he led her through the measures. Completely happy, Rebecca had known she herself looked well in her Watteau dress of cream satin trimmed with blue and having blue knots clustering about the flounce of her petticoats and the elbow-length lace of her sleeves. She had danced well, until someone had accidentally trodden on her train. She had been staggered and purely horrified when she heard the sound of ripping fabric.

Her shining little teeth savagely attacked the remaining half of the crumpet. It *had* been an accident—no? When she'd glanced around, The Monahan had been some distance off, but in the movement of the dance, perhaps . . . She growled to herself. If it had been deliberate, it had succeeded, for by the time Millie had repaired the ravaged train and she had returned to the party, the musicians were packing up their instruments, The Monahan had Sir Peter fairly trapped, and Hilary was chatting with Letitia Boudreaux. She herself had at once been pounced upon by the Streets and borne off for a tour of the bird paintings, accompanied by a joint lecture she would have found a crushing bore had not her sense of the ridiculous arisen to rescue her.

Well, she thought, her chin setting determinedly, the boat party today would not be spoiled! She would watch that designing lightskirt like a hawk! She stood and went over to the wardrobe. What to wear. . . . Running her eyes along the rainbow of colours that hung there, she fairly pounced on the green taffeta she had so recklessly purchased from Madame Olga. It was daringly plain, the stomacher of striped green and white satin being edged on both sides with a band of white fur that swept from waist to shoulder in a gracefully expanding "V," this the only ornamentation, save for the ruffled edges of the chemise sleeves. It was a little frightening to be so far ahead of fashion, and she eyed the gown uncertainly. The skirt *was* rather stark, for it was neither tiered, flounced, nor scalloped. Still, when she had tried it on, it really had looked delicious, and Madame had been so enraptured that, despite the unpaid bills of this undistinguished client, she had called in her assistants to see "eggsackly 'ow the *robe à l'anglaise* it *should* be wore!"

Calling to mind the colours of the Great Hall and Sir Peter's interest in things pastoral, Rebecca took down the dress and, holding it against her, postured rather nervously before the oval standing mirror. Oh, but it *was* delicious! Surely, she would captivate Sir Peter this time! She smiled, her eyes taking on their far-away look. . . .

She was stepping aboard the barge . . . how the gentlemen stared! And the envy in the faces of the ladies, especially That Cat who clung tenaciously to Sir Peter's arm. He was trying to free himself. The Monahan clung tighter. Looking down at her sternly, he put her aside and, ignoring her sobs as she collapsed into Mr. Melton's arms, came to take Rebecca's hand and guide her to a seat. He refused to sit down, but proclaiming himself unworthy, knelt at her feet. With his own strong hands he gathered her luncheon (having stood up again, of course!) and watched adoringly as she ate. All through the hours that followed, he scarcely strayed from her side, and when the boat docked in a glory of sunset, he swept her into his arms, carried her ashore, and with a regal gesture sent the barge off, oblivious of The Monahan's heart-broken wails. His voice husky with emotion, he said, "Shall we fight your corsets now?"

Jolted, Rebecca comprehended that the voice had been real and not imaginary. "Oh, Millie! It's *you*," she gasped.

Millie smiled indulgently. Dreaming again, poor little lass. Lord knows, she deserved that at least one of her dreams come true. . . .

The sky was clearing by the time they were ready to leave, but a brisk breeze was tossing the treetops about. The guests had been told that it was only a short drive from Ward Marching to the dock where the barge awaited. Nonetheless, Millie draped a light but warm shawl about Rebecca's shoulders, and tied a fruit-bedecked straw hat with a wide brim atop her curls. Knowing that the long day on the water might well play havoc with her hair, Rebecca had told Millie to use no powder and had chosen a style that she herself could restore did it become disarranged. When she walked down the stairs beside her aunt, a chorus of admiration arose from the gentlemen gathered in the Great Hall. The full, red lips of The Monahan tightened as The Beauty took in Rebecca's sophisticated gown. The green eyes flickered to the shining jet locks. She murmured, "But how charming. Quite a gypsy look. Were your parents foreign, perhaps, ma'am?"

Seething, Rebecca (whose grandmama had been a Spanish lady) retaliated sweetly, "Why, yes, I suppose they were in a sense. My ancestors were—Norman, as I understand." And she swept past and out on to the front steps.

A hand was under her elbow. A deep chuckle caused her heart to leap. "I see that you are in form—as ever, Mrs. Parrish."

Rebecca's heart reversed direction and thudded into her shoes. She all but wailed, "De Villars! Oh, but I thought you were not coming."

He also had abandoned powder today, and his thick brown hair was less severely dressed, betraying a tendency to curl that made him seem more youthful and somewhat less menacing, despite the wicked glint in the shrewd eyes. Leaning to her as he ushered her to the waiting carriage, he murmured a provocative, "I could not bear that you should miss me, sweeting."

"Do not *dare* call me that!" she hissed. "If my brother knew it, he would—"

"Call me out?" The thin lips sneered. "I try not to judge silly fribbles, having been one myself. Still, I think even Boothe would not be so unwise."

The cruel voice pierced Rebecca's heart with an arrow of ice. He was *more*, not less, menacing! If only half of what she had heard of him was truth, Snow would be an easy prey for him. Her dear brother was a fine swordsman, but this man was sure death! She wrenched her arm away and then was climbing into the carriage, no easy task with her voluminous skirts and that confounded hat. Settling herself at last, she was breathless and still frightened and had to force a smile when Letitia Boudreaux took the seat opposite. The tall girl scanned her suspiciously. "Mrs. Parrish, I saw my cousin—" Miss Street was being handed up the steps, talking as she came, and leaning forward, Letitia said swiftly, "Ma'am, do not allow de Villars to frighten you. He can be a wretched tease, but—believe me, he is not near so wicked as he is painted."

Rebecca's smile warmed, but she wondered what this gentle girl would think had she heard her evil cousin's remarks. She did not join in the ensuing flow of happy talk and responded only briefly when her aunt climbed in to sit beside her. Looking blindly into the blustery morning, she decided that one thing was perfectly clear: de Villars must be repulsed, but she must do the business herself. Whatever happened,

Snowden must not know how The Lecher hounded her!

Sir Peter rode up to the window, his eyes brightening to a smile when he saw her. Rebecca's heart lifted. Why should she fear de Villars? Ward was interested in her, beyond doubting, and de Villars was his friend. No gentleman would poach on the territory of a friend and, however base he might be, de Villars was assuredly a gentleman. She put her fears away. Today, The Plan would prevail!

In only a few minutes they were driving along the banks of the river as it wound through meadow and copse and hamlet, sparkling in the brightening sunlight, and carrying upon its broad back ducks and mudhens, an occasional swan, and a few small pleasure boats. Soon, the carriages slowed and stopped beside a sturdy dock whereat a long, brightly painted barge was tied up, the breeze flapping the red and white canvas awnings, and a flag flying merrily at the stern. The air was fresh and invigorating and full of the scents of summer, but as the ladies were handed out of the carriages and the gentlemen gathered around them, Mrs. Boothe murmured uneasily that the water looked rather choppy. "Do you think," she appealed to Mr. Melton, "that we might have a storm?"

"No, ma'am. Looks to be clearing up, in fact. It will likely be warm this afternoon."

"How lovely the river is," said Rebecca, gazing at it appreciatively.

"The Ouse," Ward imparted, and quoted, "'slow winding through a level plain.'"

"When it ain't overflowing its banks and flooding said level plain," put in de Villars cynically.

Rebecca flashed him a look of indignation, and thought, "How typical!"

Major Broadbent laughed. "Don't be such a curst unromantical clod, Treve."

Taking de Villars' arm, The Monahan said throatily, "Whatever else he may be, sir, Trevelyan is far from unromantical, I do assure you."

De Villars chuckled and patted her hand, but Ward's eyes held a frown. In full accord with his disapprobation and outraged by such vulgar flirting, Rebecca stuck her little nose into the air and tripped up the companionway. The effect was spoiled by the breeze that whipped her broad-brimmed hat to the back of her neck. She halted, clutching at the straw instinctively, whereupon the perverse breeze sent her skirts flying.

Steadying her, de Villars clicked his tongue. "Good gracious! What an abandoned display!" His eyes held amusement rather than shock, and he went on, "Never float away from us, lovely one."

How he could have come up with her so quickly, when only seconds past The Wanton Woman had been hanging on his sleeve, Rebecca could not imagine. To say truth, his strong grip was welcome, for the swing of her gown had all but overset her balance. "One can but hope," she said primly, "that any further abandonment this day will be as innocent as was mine, Mr. de Villars."

"To each his own hope, ma'am," he said with his leering grin.

There was no shame in him, decided Rebecca and, making her way to the bow, resolved to stay as far away as possible from the miserable pair.

Happily, Mr. Melton's prediction proved to be correct. The barge, drifting lazily along the river, was soon bathed in warm sunlight, and it became apparent that the revellers were to be treated to a perfect day. Sir Peter had hired three minstrels who wandered about performing charming old airs for the delectation of the guests. Several flirtations were being vigorously conducted, the dashing Major Broadbent apparently finding Miss Boudreaux a pleasant companion despite her inches; Mr. Street rather pathetically bewitched by The Monahan, and behaving so like a moonling that de Villars could scarce contain his amusement; and Mr. Melton's tongue-tied pursuit of Mrs. Boothe continuing until Miss Street attached herself to that lady. Hardly able to credit her good fortune, for a time Rebecca had Sir Peter all to herself, since the remaining female ladies, of rather advanced years, settled happily into a little group and thoroughly enjoyed themselves by blackening the characters of everyone else on board, while the four other gentlemen appropriated one end of the luncheon table and started to throw dice.

Comfortably disposed on one of the chaises that had been set along the decks, Rebecca gazed blissfully at the sylvan scene and murmured, "What a perfect day."

"Yes. I am a fortunate man," Sir Peter agreed, leaning against the rail and looking at her with deliberate double entendre. Rebecca blushed prettily, and he went on, "Had I known you've a little son, ma'am, I would have asked that you bring him. Children always enjoy the river. And it is educational for them."

"How kind you are. I fancy your cousin would have enjoyed this, also. When does she arrive, sir?"

He sighed and, having begged permission and received it, seated himself at the foot of her chaise while deploring the fact that he had been unable to find a suitable governess for the girl. "Patience arrives next week, but I am determined that the lady to take her in hand *must* be a gentlewoman well acquainted with our level of society. I had hoped to persuade one of my own indigent relations, but . . . well, whatever else, I do not mean Patience to be pushed off on some inferior creature incapable of ensuring that she be well instructed in all the proficiencies so essential to a young lady. Sketching, I can help her with, for I am accounted adequate in that art, but music, alas, is not my forte, and as for deportment—" He grinned and shrugged whimsically. "You see my problem, Mrs. Parrish."

Pensively recalling Forbes's decidedly haphazard efforts in his son's behalf, Rebecca murmured, "I fancy few fathers are willing to show such an interest in their own children. Your conscientiousness, your generosity, do you much honour, Sir Peter."

"Oh, come now, Mrs. Parrish," an unwelcome voice intruded, "you surely can do better than that."

Rebecca caught her breath. Surely, The Horrid Creature did not mean to humiliate her in front of their host? Her gaze flew to de Villars and found a not unkind smile on the lean features. "I cannot guess what you mean, sir," she said.

"Can you not? Look you, ma'am. Here is poor Ward, a

dreadfully afflicted man, and here are you, a lady who has vast experience in the matter of tutors, governesses, feminine apparel, and what-have-you. You *must* know of some well-bred lady—perhaps not, er, indigent, exactly . . ." Out of Ward's range of vision, his left eye winked meaningfully. "But who would be glad of a summer passed in so idyllic a setting."

For one of the few times in her life, Rebecca was rendered speechless. The colossal impudence of the man! Did he really fancy her so lost to propriety that she would accept such an offer? And then de Villars' glance angled to where Aunt Albinia smiled in response to some sally from Miss Street, and Rebecca's outrage was drowned in a flood of excited comprehension.

Sir Peter cried eagerly, "Can that be so, ma'am? Faith, 'twould be a blessing to me, I own. My grandmother has agreed to come up for a while, but she is of—er, rather eccentric temperament, and accustomed to Cornwall's milder clime, so that I cannot say how long she would remain."

"Nor whether she would be willing to interview an endless string of applicants for the position," de Villars put in mildly.

Sir Peter shuddered, and de Villars fastened a smile of saintly benevolence upon Rebecca.

The wretched man was smugness personified, she thought. How confidently he waited for her to pounce on the opportunity he had created! And yet, what else could she do? It would be folly to reject so magnificent a chance. How dear Anthony would love Ward Marching, and how it must benefit his health. With a fine nonchalance, she said, "Alas, the only lady I know who would answer that description is my aunt, Mrs. Boothe. She is wonderful with young people, and there is no one has a kinder heart, so that she must appreciate your predicament, Sir Peter. As to how to go on—why she would be perfection itself. . . . But"—she sighed regretfully—"dear Aunt Alby is devoted to us and would never come so far away, however she might enjoy a sojourn here."

Ward's eyes were glowing. "By Jove!" he exclaimed. "Could you not persuade her, Mrs. Parrish? I cannot express to you how grateful I would be, for such a lady would be the ideal answer to my dilemma. And—and as for leaving you, that is easily got over. Or, at least, it would be if— Oh, I should not press you, I know, but—is it possible you could see your way clear to accompany the lady?"

Resolutely ignoring the grin on de Villars' face, Rebecca gave a gasp and took refuge behind her fan. "Sir! You cannot have considered! Your—yours is a—a *bachelor* establishment!"

"Oh, but I have, dear ma'am!" Ward said earnestly. "There are several cottages on the estate, and one, the closest to the house in fact, now stands empty. I can have it readied in jig time, and you and your aunt can have it all to yourselves. Only think, ma'am, you were but telling me last evening of your concern for your son's health. Might not this pure country air be good for him, also? I would not ask you to remain for very long, I promise you. Only until we could find someone suitable to take charge on a permanent basis. Mrs. Parrish, I beg of you—say you will!"

"Mercy!" said Rebecca, with an anxious frown. "How difficult it is! I should be most pleased to help you, sir. But it does not seem quite . . ."

"After all," de Villars put in, his expression grave but his eyes dancing with laughter, "you *are* a widow, ma'am, not a naïve young ingenue. Your reputation would not suffer."

"Well, dash it all, Treve, *that* has nothing to say to the matter," Ward protested, in a rare display of anger. "Were Mrs. Parrish a debutante straight from the schoolroom she would be perfectly safe on my property!"

"Have I not said it?" murmured de Villars, with an injured look. "Only think, ma'am, a trout stream runs through the Home Wood, and there is a fine pool where Anthony could sail his boat. Any boy must love it here."

Rebecca needed no urging, as he knew perfectly well, the sly fiend. Her hopes were soaring to dizzy heights and, however insincere, his words added to her joyous anticipation. She hesitated through a proper space that seemed endless. "We-ell," she said hesitantly, "I suppose I *could* put it to my aunt."

❧

Very soon, large hampers were being unpacked below

decks, and so many tureens, bowls, and platters were conveyed to the tables that there seemed scarcely room for the plates of the diners. Sir Peter's butler rang a silver gong, and the guests crowded to the board. They found cold roast duck and turkey, ham and beef, shrimp, lobster, and fish in aspic, these accompanied by artichoke hearts, pickled beetroots, glazed carrots, olives, and tiny pearl onions. There were six different types of cheese, breads and rolls and crispy croissants, and mellow, fresh butter. When justice had been done to these offerings came the next remove, with raised veal, mutton, and pork pies, tongue and sweetbreads, herrings in a cream sauce, green peas and string beans, cheese tarts, a chocolate gâteau, lemon puffs, grapes, cherries, rhubarb pie, and bowls of walnuts. Four varieties of wine were served with the meal, and by the time the ladies left the gentlemen to their cigars, two hours had slipped away and most of the guests were not only replete, but decidedly sleepy.

Major Broadbent made his way to the starboard side where sat Rebecca with her aunt, watching the gurgle and flow of the waters. He offered his arm and a "jaunt about the decks." Rebecca accepted, and several other couples followed suit. A charming picture they made, the great barge with its bright awnings fluttering as it floated along, the shimmering river, the gentlemen in their colourful silks and brocades, the ladies with their highly dressed curls or elaborate wigs, their white shoulders and sweetly curved bosoms, the delicate pastels of their gowns with the tiny waists and the provocatively feminine sway of the great skirts. It was a picture to be treasured through all the years to come and one that seemed, to Rebecca at least, in keeping with the joy of knowing that not only was The Plan working, but it had progressed much faster and further than she had dared to hope.

The golden moments drifted past; the air grew warmer. By half-past three the afternoon was very still, the countryside seemed to be dozing, and all that could be heard were the gurgling chuckle of the river, the snores of several guests who had dropped off to sleep, and the occasional drowsy song of a bird. The musicians, having been given trays and tankards, were happily occupied in the stern; the servants were enjoying their own meal; and even Mr. de Villars seemed content to perch quietly on the rail close to The Monahan. Having returned Rebecca to her chaise, Major Broadbent went off to throw dice with Ward. Mrs. Boothe and Mr. Melton were standing in the bows together, and Rebecca watched them thoughtfully. The gentleman appeared to be saying very little. It was debatable whether her aunt would be able to bring him up to scratch, yet surely this delightful excursion must be a perfect opportunity—

"May I join you, ma'am?"

The gentle voice was that of Letitia Boudreaux, lovely in her blue muslin trimmed with white lace.

"Pray do," said Rebecca warmly. "I have been hoping for a cose with you."

A blush of pleasure warmed Miss Boudreaux's cheeks. She occupied the chair Mrs. Boothe had vacated, murmuring shyly, "Do you know, I feel as though we were old friends."

"And I expect we would be, had I not been in mourning, for we would certainly have met at some function or another. Perhaps you are acquainted with my brother?"

"Do you mean Mr. Snowden Boothe?" Miss Boudreaux pleated a fold of her gown with nervous fingers. "I have danced with him a time or two. It was brave of him to stand up with me, under the circumstances."

Rebecca's gaze sharpened. The blue eyes were lowered, but the blush in the cheeks had deepened. She thought, "Oh, no!" but said kindly, "Why, I am sure Snowden was honoured."

"He said so, of course, for his manners are beyond reproach. But—" Miss Boudreaux gave a wry smile. "I am so *wretchedly* tall, you see. He could only have been embarrassed."

Despite the deprecating words, she was very obviously in hopes of an encouraging reply, and Rebecca positively ached with sympathy. The poor girl harboured a *tendre* for Snow! And there was no hope at all, for not only was he enjoying a mild flirtation with a petite damsel, but Rebecca suspected that he had a pronounced interest in a certain Green-Eyed Cat who was at present exerting every wile at her command to keep The Lewd Rake at her side. What a pity it was, to be sure, for there was not another girl in all London Rebecca would sooner have had for a sister-in-law, or who might have made her rackety brother a more suitable wife.

"I am sure he was not at all embarrassed," she lied staunchly. "If you did but know how I envy you your height, for tall ladies always look so superb in their garments. Have you never noticed that all the styles in the fashion magazines are worn by extreme tall creatures—so very elegant."

"Yes. And one wonders if any woman living could have such incredibly long"—Letitia glanced around cautiously and lowered her voice—"long *legs!* I vow even so tall a gentleman as my cousin de Villars would not dare stand up with one of them!"

They laughed merrily together, and by the time Miss Boudreaux went over to chat with Martha Street, their friendship was firmly cemented.

Rebecca was not accustomed to taking a large luncheon and, although it seemed wasteful to nap, she was beginning to feel drowsy. She yawned, put back her head and prepared to close her eyes, just for a few minutes. She had reckoned without the wide brim of her straw, and found it necessary to remove the obstructing article.

"Would you wish that I place your bonnet on the table for you, fair conspirator?" asked de Villars, suddenly materializing at her side.

She jerked her hat away, even as he reached for it. "I most decidedly would not! And furthermore, Mr. de Villars, I never have, nor ever shall, conspire with you in aught, and would be grateful did you not address me in such fashion."

The gleam left his grey eyes. He looked levelly at her for a moment, then, as though invisible guards had been lowered, said wistfully, "That is unkind in you, pretty one. Did I not pave the way for your—er, summer amusement?"

However she might begrudge the admission, it was truth.

She had been rude, behaviour as foreign to her as was this new side of Trevelyan de Villars. Confused because she felt so at sea, she stammered, "If you consider it amusing to guide a young lady to her come-out—yes. And I *do* thank you for your, er, help."

His gaze held on her, but in some subtle way his expression had changed. He said, "Patience? I take it that Ward has described her to you?"

"Not in so many words." He had sounded faintly incredulous. The poor girl must be *extreme* ill-favoured! Uneasy, Rebecca pointed out that it was her aunt who might perhaps guide Miss Ashton. "I," she reminded, "shall be here purely—"

"Oh, very purely, I do not doubt."

Rebecca blushed scarlet and lowered her lashes, scored by guilt and yearning to scratch the odious creature.

De Villars grinned. "I assume that Boothe is capable of arranging his own summer holiday and will not require my assistance."

Stiffening, Rebecca rested a frowning gaze upon him.

"However," he went on musingly, "unless I mistake the fellow, he will wish to express his—ah, appreciation for my efforts in your behalf. If you've writ him . . ." Rebecca not rising to the bait, he nodded and said in a thoughtful way, "It would be better, of course, had you not mentioned my part in your . . . scheme."

Feeling like a conniving Jezebel, Rebecca unclamped her locked jaws and uttered a saintly, "I do not lie to my brother, sir."

"No." His head bowed. "Of course you do not. One can tell at a glance that you are all that is pure and good. And . . . there's the snag, d'you see? Any brother worth his salt, and Boothe is worth that at least, would seek to shield so innocent a girl from such an—ignoble rascal as . . . I." Lifting his head, he revealed again that oddly boyish humility, so that Rebecca, who had bristled because of his sly jibe at Snowden, was inexplicably touched.

"I had not heard you described in just that way, Mr. de

Villars. Your reputation, so far as I am aware, has largely to do with the ladies." She glanced at the dozing Monahan, and could not forbear to add, "Of a certain class."

He turned swiftly away and when next he spoke his voice was somewhat muffled, as though choked by emotion. "You are too kind. Ah, had I only been so fortunate as to meet a girl of your character long ago. Alas, it was otherwise. And I, a stupid young fool, betrayed by my love, and—" He broke off with an impatient gesture. "Forgive me. You cannot wish to hear all that ancient history."

"From what little I *had* heard, sir," she said, watching his averted profile intently, "the shoe was rather on the other foot."

He turned back to her, a whimsical half-smile on his lips. "You do speak your mind, Little Parrish!"

Again flustered, she gasped, "Oh, good gracious! I have no right—I mean—"

"No, no. Never guard your tongue with me, I implore. So few people say what is truly in their hearts. Is what makes you so refreshing. As for your remark, 'twas well justified, perhaps—" He shrugged. "But, enough. I will not bore on about my lamentable past—it was all very long ago."

Intrigued despite herself, she said, "You cannot be *that* old, surely!"

Down went his head once more. He said meekly, "I was but nineteen at the time."

"Oh, my! And—and the lady?"

"Older."

This was a most improper conversation that must not be pursued. Rebecca lowered her voice and probed, "*Much* older?"

"Fifteen years."

"But—but . . . she must have been nigh twice your age!"

"But very lovely, ma'am. One of your ethereal beauties. I worshipped her."

"And—she betrayed you?"

A reluctant nod of that abased head. Waiting, fascinated

by the story her romantic heart could relate to so well, Rebecca asked, "But—you did run away with her?"

He nodded again, but said nothing for a moment. Then in a remote, sad voice, he murmured, "She left me. After three glorious days. And nights."

"How dreadful," she breathed, overlooking the innuendo. "But—could you not have prevented her?"

"You must be thinking me a very great fool. And rightly so. But—I was in no condition to prevent anything, ma'am."

"No con— A *duel*?" she gasped. "The lady's father or brother, perhaps?"

"Nothing so proper, I grieve to confess. We were overtaken by her—lover."

Rebecca's eyes were very round indeed. "She had—more than—than you?"

"Alas, had I but known that ghastly truth, I could have spared myself a mortifying and painful defeat."

"Good . . . God!" Breathless, she could all but see that misty field in the dawning, and the valiant youth fighting vainly, staggering back at last to lie with his blood soaking and soaking into the dewy grass. . . . Clasping her hands, she cried, "Never say they just went off and left you lying there? Whatever happened to you?"

"I recovered, of course. Eventually." He said heavily, "But—the word had got out, you see. My reputation was forever fouled. Dishonour . . . disgrace . . . inevitable and unrelenting."

A lump came into her throat. Almost she could have wept for that cruelly betrayed youth. "And—the lady?" she asked in a much more kindly tone. "What became of her?"

"She chose to stay with her lover." He looked at her, his eyes grave. "The last time I visited her, she had twelve children."

Rebecca's jaw sagged. "Tw—twelve . . . ? And—and you *visited* her?"

"It's dashed difficult to avoid them, Fair One. You see, as it turned out, the lady's secret lover was—my grandpapa."

The gleam was in the grey eyes with a vengeance. The quirk beside the thin lips could no longer be contained and spread into a wide grin.

"Oh!" exclaimed Rebecca furiously. "Odious! Horrid—deceiving—*creature!*"

With a shout of laughter, de Villars stood. "That will teach you, m'dear, to be a little more gracious when someone does you a very large favour!" He started back to The Monahan, who had awoken and was watching them with mild curiosity.

"Wretch!" Rebecca hissed, jabbing her hatpin furiously in amongst the fruit around the crown of her hat. "Monstrous—*rake!*"

De Villars retraced his steps and placed one hand on the side of her chair to lean above her. "You are extreme lovely when you are kind, Little Parrish. But even more delicious, I think, when you are angered."

Not deigning him an answer, Rebecca turned towards the river, put back her head, and closed her eyes.

Chuckling, de Villars went away.

Rebecca lay there, fuming. Gradually, however, the warmth, the delicious meal, the soft song of the river, combined to dull her indignation. She thought, "Twelve children, indeed!" His mirthful voice echoed in her ears, "The lady's secret lover was my grandpapa!" The nuances of such a situation began to titillate her. She smiled in spite of herself, and in a little while, drifted into slumber. . . .

She was walking down the main staircase at Ward Marching, and she walked slowly, for she wore a magnificent gown of white and could not see clearly for the lacy veil before her eyes. At the foot of the stairs, Sir Peter, heart-stoppingly handsome in his bridal raiment, waited with one hand on the baluster rail, smiling worshipfully up at her. Glowing with happiness, she moved towards him. Birds began to flutter about her; one at first, then three, and suddenly a veritable flock of doves, swooping and calling all about her, coming so close, in fact, that their feathers tickled her nose. . . .

Rebecca opened her eyes with a start. A gentleman's

waistcoat hovered just abo 'e her, and recognizing the superb cut of it, she demanded indignantly, "Whatever are you about, Mr. de Villars?"

He glanced down. "Not following my natural instincts when so close to a beautiful and recumbent female," he said, stepping back a pace. "I was, in fact, engaged in so plebeian an endeavour as to try to rescue your bonnet."

She glanced quickly to the right. Her outflung arm trailed below the bottom rail, and her hat, loosely held by one ribbon, was about to float away.

It had been *such* an expensive hat! With a wail of dismay, she tightened her grip on the long ribbons and sat up. Impossibly, the hat pulled back.

"What—on earth?" She frowned, tugging at it in turn.

Peering over the side, de Villars gave a whoop. "You've got a bite!"

The hat was quite definitely resisting Rebecca's efforts. "A—a bite?" she echoed in disbelief. "Do you mean—oh! Is some nasty wet little fish trying to eat my hat?"

"Not so little, by God! Hang on, ma'am! And—pull!"

She gave an incensed exclamation and entered the battle. De Villars, hilarious, shouted to the other guests, and everyone hurried to watch. Excitement knew no bounds. Bets were placed, and Rebecca was inundated with instructions, cautions, and compliments. At one point her reluctant captive tugged so hard that she feared she would be pulled through the rails, but a strong arm slipped about her waist. She could well imagine whose strong arm it was, and, glaring over her shoulder, was pleasantly surprised to find Ward smiling into her eyes. "Allow me, dear ma'am," he said in his gentle way, reaching for the impromptu line.

Captivated she might be, but this was Rebecca's fish. "No!" she cried determinedly. "I want to try and catch him, if you please, Sir Peter."

He looked dubious, but allowed her the struggle while he guarded against her being pulled overboard.

"Why on earth does not the silly fish let go?" trilled The Monahan mirthfully.

"He has probably become hooked on Mrs. Parrish's hatpin," said de Villars. "I noticed it looked rather lethal when she stuck it in amongst her fruit assortment."

Hanging over the rail, Major Broadbent exclaimed, "Jove, but he's a fine specimen! Reel him—I mean, haul him in, if you can, Rebecca."

"Yes, do haul him in, but gently does it," cautioned de Villars.

Someone advised, "If you're slow, ma'am, your ribbon will come loose and he'll get away."

"If you pull too hard," warned another, "he's like to pull off the fruit!"

"What kind of fish is it?"

"Why on earth does she fish with her *bonnet?*"

Such remarks, interspersed with whoops of laughter, assailed Rebecca's ears as the tussle went on, but she followed de Villars' advice. The delighted crowd pressed in around her as the strange contest went on. Rebecca was dishevelled and hot when at last she gave the "jolly strong heave" de Villars recommended. The fish apparently running out of fight at the same instant, Rebecca's heave was much stronger than required. The bedraggled bonnet, a large trout attached, shot through the rail. Still firmly grasped by Ward, Rebecca tumbled backward. Sir Peter staggered, bearing Rebecca with him, willy-nilly, and bonnet and fish slapped into the trim middle of the fascinated Mrs. Monahan.

"Oh! I am drenched!" wailed The Beauty.

Convulsed, de Villars hooted, "Jupiter! What a magnificent victory!"

"Let me see him! Oh, do let me see him!" cried Rebecca eagerly, emerging from Sir Peter's embrace.

Broadbent had retrieved the bonnet and trout. Holding them high, he shouted, "Three cheers for The Little Parrish and the finest catch of the day!"

Rebecca clapped her hands and danced with jubilation as the cheers rang out. To her surprise, The Monahan joined the applause. Whatever else, the lady was a good sport.

Mrs. Boothe had reached a quite different conclusion.

Slipping through the throng, she shuddered at the sight of the fish, took Rebecca's arm, and whispered, "My love, whatever are you *thinking* of? You look a wreck! Do come and let me try and tidy you."

Aghast, Rebecca slanted a glance at their host. He stood some distance apart, watching Miss Street attempt to dry The Monahan's gown. Disregarding her aunt's pleas that she first restore herself, Rebecca hurried to them. "I am indeed sorry, ma'am," she said repentantly, surveying the sodden peach satin.

"Well, do not be," said Mrs. Monahan. "A fine marplot I should be to chastise you when you provided us with such a fine entertainment. I vow 'tis a tale I shall be able to tell forever."

Rebecca blushed scarlet and her heart sank. What the Beauty meant was that The Little Parrish had behaved like a clown and made a complete spectacle of herself. From the corner of her eye she saw Sir Peter watching her with a grave expression. She again conveyed her apologies, then went with her aunt to the small cabin that had been converted to a cloakroom for the ladies. Fortunately, it was unoccupied. Fighting tears of mortification, Rebecca was swept into a consoling embrace. "Oh, Aunt!" she whimpered. "I was doing so *well!* Why did I have to spoil it? Whatever must Sir Peter have thought? To see me heave that enormous mackerel, or whatever it was, right into The Monahan's stomacher! And then to stagger and—and jump about like any hobbledehoy! He looked . . . absolutely *appalled!*"

"No, no, my love. A little surprised, perhaps. But you were ever a spirited child. I'll own it might have been just a touch wiser had you allowed one of the gentlemen to—ah, catch the fish."

Dabbing at tearful eyes, Rebecca turned to the mirror. "Yes, for only *look* at me! Red-faced, and my hair all anyhow! And—oh, Aunt! See here, my new gown is *ripped* and such a nasty stain!" She wailed miserably, "Small chance of catching the fish I really want, now!"

"Do not give up hope, dear girl. We shall arrange your

hair as prettily as ever. The gown will dry in no time, and the tear is very tiny. Perhaps you can embroider a flower here and there, to hide it." Working busily at the tangled locks, Mrs. Boothe murmured, "Mr. de Villars was most amused, at least."

"Oh, to be sure! And egged me on, the wretch! Much he cares if I make a spectacle of myself, for he seeks only to—" She broke off, and sighed. "No, that is not really so. I stopped him when he was trying to retrieve my hat. But we did not know the fish was trying to eat it, then. And he laughed so, and—so did I. And it *was* funny, you'll admit, but—oh, dear, oh, dear! What a birdwit I am!"

"Well, Sir Peter will love it if you are," said her aunt with a twinkle. She won a rather watery laugh for her efforts and went on staunchly, "Cheer up, love. Your Plan may yet work."

Her Plan! Rebecca's heart gave a hopeful little lurch. Sir Peter could not go back on his word at this juncture, and when they were peacefully alone at Ward Marching, she could really concentrate on her campaign. It was very apparent that he was the conservative type and admired gentle, mannerly behaviour—as indeed he should. Well, she would be the quietest, most timid, and clinging lady he could desire. Of course, she had not yet broken the news of her impending duties to dear Aunt Albinia. . . . She slanted a glance at that lady. Meeting her eyes in the mirror, Mrs. Boothe stiffened. "Rebecca . . . ?" she said nervously. "I *know* that look! What is in your head?"

"Nothing dreadful, ma'am," Rebecca asserted with a meekness that further alarmed her aunt. "Merely an invitation. But I shall tell you all about it later on. Hush! Here is Mrs. Monahan!"

❧

When Mrs. Boothe and Rebecca returned to the deck, the tables and benches had been folded and stacked along the sides, the musicians were tuning their instruments, and a minuet was about to begin. Sir Peter came over to the two ladies at once, all anxious solicitude for the "Fair Fisherwoman" who was, he averred, "the belle of the boat." Rebecca's heart lightened, and optimism increased when he solicited her hand for the dance. Moving through the measures, she was the recipient of many smiles, and if she met also with teasing, there was little evidence of censure. Hilary Broadbent said merrily that she had given the guests a good laugh, which could but endear her to them; de Villars' eyes glinted at her, and he murmured that there was no telling what she might catch did she but use the right bait; and when she rose from her fourth curtsey to her partner, Sir Peter said with his charming smile that thanks to her this was the very jolliest party he had ever hosted. During their next pause in the stately dance, he asked eagerly, "Have you by chance spoken to your aunt as yet?" She shook her head and, as they paced along together, imparted the word that she meant to do so this very night, but would be unable to give him a definite answer until her brother had been approached in the matter. His grip on her hand tightened. Facing her, his bow was the essence of grace, his smile approving. "Very properly," he said. "I shall await with the greatest anxiety."

Elated, Rebecca knew that *somehow* she would persuade her aunt to acquiesce. And tomorrow—oh, how quickly the time was passing!—tomorrow, she would be very good, and do nothing even remotely hoydenish.

CHAPTER
❧ 5 ❧

"*I* . . . will . . . *what?*" Mrs. Boothe fell back against the pillows of her bed, her eyes all but starting from her head. "What have you done? Oh, my poor heart! Only moments ago I awoke and thought 'twas a glorious morning! And now— Had ever a dutiful aunt so mischievous a niece? Oh, but I shall faint! I shall suffer a spasm! I shall—"

"You shall make a perfectly splendid chaperon, dearest," cajoled Rebecca, perched on the side of the bed, and chafing one of her aunt's limp hands. "Only think—to spend the rest of the summer on this beautiful estate! It would give me a perfect opportunity to—"

"To weep as you watch them lower me into the ground," moaned Mrs. Boothe, clutching her brow. "Oh, that it should come to this! To be sold into bondage! At my time of life, too! I thank God I was too sleepy last night for you to tell me of this wretched new Plan of yours, else I'd not have slept a wink!"

"But, dearest of aunts, you are so splendid in matters of dress and deportment. Miss Ashton will be—"

"A lump!" prophesied her aunt mournfully. "A stodgy, ill-featured girl. With pimples, belike, a neighing voice, and a sour disposition!"

"Were she fat as a flawn, turned in her toes, had a squint in each eye, and teeth like tombstones, *you* could make her into a beauty, love! And only think what a challenge it would be." Mrs. Boothe regarded her glumly but with a little less of tragedy and, pursuing this small improvement, Rebecca bribed, "Sir Peter has taken a prodigious liking to Mr. Melton and told me he means to invite him to the Midsummer Festival. It might be quite . . . enjoyable, were we all together."

Mrs. Boothe brightened, but protested that she had never *been* a chaperon, that she knew nothing of being *employed*, and—whatever would dear Mr. Melton make of it all? She rather spoiled the effect by next asking, "What Midsummer Festival?"

"I am not perfectly sure why, but it seems there has been a costume ball on Midsummer's Eve at Ward Marching since time immemorial. It is said to be a very festive occasion. We could have such fun, dearest. Oh, 'twould be heavenly, but— of course, if you feel I ask too much of you . . ." Rebecca bowed her head, though continuing to watch her aunt from beneath the ribbon frill of her pretty cap.

Indulging a little dreaming of her own, Mrs. Boothe envisioned a summer night with a great full moon, and Mr. Melton . . . "Well, never look so heart-broke," she sniffed. "I must make the sacrifice, I expect. For you, and dear little Anthony."

She squeaked then, vowing her ribs were being crushed by the power of her niece's gratitude.

❧

De Villars left early that afternoon, so as to escort the coach of The Monahan back to Town. He wore a coat of dark blue; a sapphire glowed amidst the snow of his neckcloth. With one gauntletted hand carelessly resting on his thigh, the jewelled scabbard of his sword glittering, and his top boots mirror bright, he was an impressive gentleman, and watching his magnificent black Arabian dance down the drivepath, Rebecca was forced to own that the man had a splendid seat. She waved her handkerchief as the other ladies were doing. He turned at that instant. His eyes, she would swear, looked only at her. He removed his tricorne and bowed low and gracefully. He did not wear powder today, and the sun awoke bright gleams of auburn amongst the thick brown hair.

Miss Street sighed, "Oh, were I but ten years younger."

"Is a something notorious gentleman, ma'am," said Rebecca, rather startled.

"The attractive ones always are," Miss Street replied. "And—what an air! What a leg! What a merry humour 'neath all that assumed cynicism."

They walked back into the house together, and Rebecca echoed curiously, "Assumed? Do you indeed judge it so? From what I'd heard there is nothing gentle about the man. Rather, he is all steel, and his heart as merciless."

"But then, a man who is struck by such a tragedy when he is little more than a boy can scarce be expected not to carry scars. Such a wicked tale. You are familiar with it . . . ?"

"He told me a tale. I fancied there was little of truth in it. Indeed," she chuckled, "I do trust there was not, else theirs must be a most odd family."

Mr. Street approached at that moment, to announce that they also must leave. "Those clouds," he said, glancing eastward, "look rather—"

"Ominous," his sister finished. "Perhaps we could—"

"Travel with Mrs. Parrish and her aunt," he said. "Sir Peter is not to return to Town, and it would be our very great pleasure—"

"To escort you," beamed Miss Street.

Rebecca smiled and thanked them, but she felt saddened. So soon, this lovely idyll was over. Now she must return to London's noise and heat, and to bills and worries. And to Anthony, of course, and dear Snow. Her heavy heart lifted. How silly she was! And how glad she would be, to see their loved faces again!

And besides—she would be coming back. . . .

&

"Is enough, ma'am," panted the wiry abigail, her knee in the middle of The Monahan's back, and the corset laces gripped firmly in each hand.

"Non . . . sense . . ." Clinging to the bedpost, Mrs. Monahan whispered, "I almost can . . . sigh. Tighter . . . Annie."

And so Annie gritted her teeth, hauled and strove and, at last triumphant, summoned the parlourmaid, who watched with hands fast gripped and eyes big as saucers, to put her finger on the knot whilst the bow was secured. For a moment, The Monahan could not move, then, one hand clasped to her tiny middle, she tottered around the bed and was assisted into her long-legged camisole. A soft scratching was followed precipitately by the opening of the door, and an elegantly powdered head appeared. The parlourmaid uttered a small squeal and fled. The abigail frowned. Glancing to the door, The Monahan managed, "Come in, if you must, Treve. My wrapper, Annie."

Annie presenting a cloud of cerulean taffeta and net, Mrs. Monahan slipped into it and seated herself at her dressing table.

Trevelyan de Villars held the door wider, bowed, and ushered the abigail through. Annie bestowed a curtsey and a frigid stare upon him, and he closed the door after her and moved to the dressing table, chuckling to himself. Coming up behind The Monahan, he viewed her vivid beauty in the mirror, bent and pressed a firm kiss upon the curve of her lovely neck, followed by another . . . and another. She shivered and closed her eyes, but the kisses ceased and, looking up, she watched him for a moment, then shrugged and took up her patch box. "Well," she murmured, "we had a lovely time."

"Ward's party, do you mean?" He took a long, flat leather case from his pocket and laid it on the vanity, bending once more to slide his lips down into the hollow of her throat. When he straightened, she had not touched the case but was still watching him in the mirror, a speculative look in her green eyes.

She said, "No. I did not mean Ward's party. But I've not seen you since."

"Until—last night," he reminded, kissing the top of her ear.

She jerked away with a petulant movement and picked up the box. The necklace was of small diamonds, graduating to a larger stone at the centre, and each suspended from a baguette. It was a dainty thing, and sparkled with all the colours of the rainbow as he took it from her and fastened it about her throat. He did not kiss the clasp once it was secured, and, very aware of that small omission, she asked, "A farewell gift, Treve?"

One of his high-peaked brows lifted. "I have been clumsy about it, have I?"

She smiled rather sadly. "No—not clumsy." She touched the necklace, watching it gleam as she turned her head from side to side. "You always had good taste, I'll give you that."

"I chose you," he agreed, knowing the remark was expected of him.

"And choose now to discard me."

A troubled look came into the grey eyes. He argued gently, "Let us say rather—it is a mutual decision. It is, you know."

"Thank you. Though mine was not as final. Nor as honest, perhaps." She met his steady gaze in the mirror and said with brutal candour, "She'll not suit you. She has neither poise nor dignity."

Something in his eyes stilled. She knew that look and knew that he had withdrawn, and her heart sank.

"There is not an ounce of affectation to her," he corrected, making no attempt to pretend puzzlement.

"Save where Ward is concerned," she snapped, irritated. "In that direction she is all coquette." De Villars was silent. She set a patch under her right eye, surveyed it critically, received his approving nod, and advised, "She wants Ward. You have no chance with her. Unless you mean to force her."

He wandered to the window, half sat against the sill, and scanned the busy London morning. "I have never forced a woman, Rosemary. As well you know."

Her eyes travelled his profile. His nose was too hawkish for beauty, his chin too pronounced. The mouth was delicately sculptured but down-trending, and, although it could curve into a smile of great sweetness on occasion, that particular smile was seldom seen. Still, the high forehead, the deepset grey eyes, the lean planes of the face had, for her, a rare charm, an appeal that sent a sudden pang through her and caused her to leave the dressing table and run to him. He stood at once and held out his arms, and she came into them. For a moment he hugged her tight, then he put her from him, but still holding her, smiled down at her sad face, and this was the rare and very special smile that she and some other ladies before her had found so captivating.

"Only think, my dear," he said kindly, "we have had a wonderful relationship this year and more. We part best of friends. How many husbands and wives can say the same?"

Her eyes widened in astonishment. She leaned back in his arms, searching his face. "Lud, Trevelyan! You never mean to *wed* the chit?"

He laughed softly. "Heaven forfend!"

"I think," she said with a thoughtful frown, "you'll not have her, else."

"And I know she'd not have me to husband, Rosie, even were I of a mind to it—which I ain't. Gad, what woman wants a spendthrift with small expectations?" The laughter faded from the grey eyes. He asked lightly, "Would you, for instance?"

Even more shocked, she gasped, "Do I hear aright? Are you offering?"

He chuckled. "Now, lovely creature, you very well know we would not suit." She scowled and pulled away from his embrace. He went on, "But—suppose I had been—more to your heart's delight. *Would* you have accepted me?"

She bit her lip, hesitating, for she was deeply fond of him. Then, "No," she said, and went back to her dressing table and took up the hare's foot. "I am too expensive. I could not endure poverty."

"I do not envision poverty, exactly," he demurred, one slim finger straightening the Mechlin ruffles at his waist. He looked again into the street. "You have another caller, I see, so I'll be off."

He came towards her with his lithe, lazy stride. She suffered another pang and so said in anger, "Your Little Perish is no better than am I!"

"Perish—is it?" He grinned. "'Tis not like you to unsheathe your claws."

Paling, she spun around. "Is not an idle name, I think. Oh, Treve!"

His eyes narrowed. Placing quieting hands on her shoulders, he asked, "What is it? Another of your 'funny feelings'?"

"Yes! She spells danger for you! Death, belike! I know it! Oh, Treve—have a care. She's not worth it. She wants Ward, I tell you!"

"And loves him, think you?"

"Loves him! If she loves anything 'tis that boy of hers, and money. She makes it very plain she means to catch herself a rich husband!"

"Yes, but then, she does it so charmingly, my dear. . . ."

Her head tossed up. "Whereas I—"

"Mr. Snowden Boothe," announced the lackey, fortuitously swinging wide the door.

Mrs. Monahan flirted an irked shoulder and turned her back on de Villars. "Snow," she cried, holding out both hands to the newcomer. "How kind in you to come and cheer my loneliness."

Striding briskly into that feminine chamber, Boothe checked and regarded de Villars with dismay. "Oh—er, de Villars," he said lamely.

"You are very acute," drawled de Villars. "Which is more than could be said for our blockheaded lackey. Well, Boothe, do you mean to finish it?"

"Finish what?"

"Your entrance, my dear fellow. I believe you should next say, 'What a surprise to find you here,' or something as inane."

Boothe reddened, frowned, then laughed. "What a hand you are!" He bestowed a kiss on the fingers of The Beauty, and enquired, "Am I *de trop*, m'dear? Shall I come back later? Since you both are here, I should like to— But if it ain't convenient . . ."

"Good God," murmured de Villars. "One might suppose you to have caught us *sans* apparel."

Snowden gave a gasp, and his blue eyes became very wide indeed.

As white as he was flushed, The Monahan said with acid finality, "Mr. de Villars was leaving."

De Villars bowed and turned to the door. "Give you good day, dear lady. You also, Boothe."

Snowden, however, requested Mrs. Monahan's permission to leave her for a moment while he walked with de Villars to the front door. She gave an indifferent shrug and returned to her dressing table.

In the hall, de Villars warned, "That was unwise, Boothe. Rosemary is very angry with me. You would have done well to stay and comfort her."

"And that would not—ah, vex you?" asked Snowden carefully.

"*Mais non*. The lady has told me she has—new fields to conquer, as it were."

"Jupiter!"

One hand on the stair rail, de Villars flashed his cynical grin. "Oh, I think not. I doubt even Rosemary aims at such Olympian heights."

Boothe frowned, baffled, then uttered a shout of laughter. "I—I meant only that I was surprised to hear she had turned you off," he imparted gleefully.

Watching him, his face expressionless, de Villars thought that there was little wonder several ladies of his acquaintance sighed for this handsome young man. And he thought also that one could see much of his sister in him. But he said only,

"Surprised? Why? We enjoyed a delightful—friendship. But sixteen months is, frankly, longer than I had expected her to endure me."

"Sixteen months? Egad, but—her husband was alive then, I'd have— Oh, damme! Y'r pardon! What I *mean* is—"

With a soft laugh, de Villars said, "You know, you really put me very much in mind of your sister."

Boothe gripped his arm. "Have a care, sir! I'll not have Rebecca spoken ill of by any man!"

De Villars put up the glass that hung from a carven ivory chain about his neck. Surveying the younger man, he asked, "Do you tell me it is an insult to compare your sister to yourself? The devil! I'd no idea you was such a reprobate. Tell me why you are seeing me off the premises."

The glitter in Boothe's eyes faded to a gleam of mirth. "What a flat you must think me!" Slipping his hand through de Villars's arm as they continued down the stairs, he explained, "I really came to see Mrs. Monahan, for I knew she was at that accursed party of Ward's, and I hoped to discover— But you was there also and can tell me. De Villars, what the deuce is this ridiculous rumour that is sweeping Town?"

"I have heard no new rumour. But then gossip bores me, for it has been my experience that nine-tenths of it is fabricated by the lurid fancies of those who circulate it."

Boothe slanted an uncertain glance at the aloof countenance beside him. "Oh, quite. Couldn't agree more. As a rule. Trouble is—well, I am the head of my house, d'you see, while my brother is on the Continent. And Rebecca's such a trusting chit. . . ." He faltered into silence as de Villars turned eyes of grey ice upon him. Boothe felt transfixed by that chill gaze, and stammered, "I—er, had told her 'twas convenable for her to go, but Jonathan—my brother—will have my ears have I encouraged her to—er . . . She's so *dashed* naïve! If she's made a cake of herself, he is sure to hold me responsible, and—"

"Do you doubt your sister's morals," de Villars interpolated coldly, "one might suppose you would speak to her yourself."

"No, well, I don't! It—it ain't *that* exactly, but—" Boothe

bit his lip and blurted, "Fiend seize it, man! Everyone is talking such infernal balderdash! All I can make of 't is that my
sister Parrish has landed some poor fish, and be damned if I
can find out who 'tis!"

The sound of de Villars' laughter could even be heard in
the quiet bedchamber where The Monahan frowned thoughtfully at her diamonds.

ꝛ

Although Snowden Boothe dealt his repentant sister a severe scold in the matter of her fishing prowess, he was secretly
amused and not a little proud of her because of the incident.
Sensing this, Rebecca was encouraged to broach the subject of
Ward's request that their aunt guide Miss Patience Ashton to
her come-out. She proceeded with caution, neglecting to mention the extremely generous amount Ward had offered by way
of payment. It was as well, for Boothe's pride was affronted and
his temper flared. How had Ward *dared* suggest so infamous a
thing? Did he fancy them to be in dire straits that he must offer
Mrs. Boothe employment? Did he suppose Snowden so incapable of providing for his relations that his aunt must hire herself
out as a *menial?* Mrs. Boothe wept and wailed that she had
known this was how it would be! and even Rebecca, quite sure
that she could talk her fiery brother around her thumb, decided to let a few days pass before she attempted to do so.

Both ladies were astounded, therefore, when, while walking beside their chair next afternoon, en route to a musicale,
Snowden informed them he had decided they could accept
Ward's offer. "Talked to Forty about it," he said. "Seems Ward
told him we grant him a great favour. True, of course, though
I'd not thought of it in just that light. Forty says that under the
circumstances, and in view of our family name being what 'tis,
the arrangement is quite unexceptionable." He grinned and
added a teasing, "Wouldn't do for *you* to trot down there and
serve as ape leader, Becky. But, being as it's my aunt, it will
serve."

Overjoyed, Rebecca avoided Mrs. Boothe's anguished
eyes and said she thought it quite the outside of enough for Sir
Peter's cousin to have dealt him such a turn, and that dear

Aunt Albinia would likely prove so indispensable to Miss Ashton that Ward must be eternally grateful. "Who knows," she said brightly, "the lady may prove to be as beautiful as she is rich, and after one glance at her, Snow, your heart be won." She sighed dreamily. "How wonderful that would be, for Sir Peter would, by then, be so in our debt he could not refuse the match. All London would envy you. . . . It would be the wedding of the year, and you and Patience live happily—"

"Thunder and turf, but she's off again!" Snowden exclaimed indignantly. "I'll tell you what it is, Becky, my girl. This romancing of yours will land you in the suds one of these days! Marry Patience Ashton, indeed! A girl I never so much as heard of, much less saw! Ten to one she'll have a face like a frog, and if you think I'd wed such a one only to help you captivate your sainted Ward—think again, sister mine! Think again!"

Snowden was not known for his perception, and this was Rebecca's first intimation that he'd been aware of her *tendre* for his handsome friend. Thrown into confusion, she blushed scarlet and was relieved when they reached Tanterdale House and she was able to mingle with the other guests climbing the steps of the mansion. Miss Boudreaux was amongst the throng in the foyer, escorted by a clerical young man almost as tall as herself, whose raw-boned awkwardness was offset by a winning smile. She introduced him as her brother, FitzWilliam. His pleasant grey eyes had widened when they rested on Rebecca, and he proceeded to hover about her with such inarticulate but earnest admiration that Mrs. Boothe, desperately anxious for a private word with her niece, was denied the opportunity, and it was not until the interval following an excruciating recital by a vast soprano that she was able to take Rebecca into the garden for a breath of air.

Leading the way to an isolated marble bench, Mrs. Boothe seated herself and, when Rebecca had occupied the space beside her, wailed, "Whatever are we to do *now?* Snowden will straitly *forbid* you to accompany me! You know he will! And I shall *not* go to Bedfordshire alone. No—do not attempt to sway me, for nothing could tempt me to be isolated from my near and dear. I had come to think it might be a jolly summer, but—oh, Becky! You must tell Sir Peter we cannot accept."

Rebecca patted her trembling hand and said a consoling, "Good gracious, ma'am. What a piece of work to make over so simple a matter. Snowden has not forbade me to go. Not in so many words. Exactly. No, listen, dearest. All I have to do is avoid any direct statement of the nature of—of our plans, and we shall be—"

"*Our* plans! Naughty minx! You know very well—"

"My plans, then." Rebecca's conscience was somewhat strained by the prospect of deceiving the brother she adored, but Anthony's future (she told herself) was of even more import, and despite some sleepless nights, she had refused to abandon her scheme. Mrs. Boothe was tearing her handkerchief to shreds. Removing the tattered lace from her fingers, Rebecca soothed, "Never worry so. We shall come about, wait and see."

As it developed, their worries were needless. The following morning Snowden rode up on a dapple-grey thoroughbred he had lately purchased from Lord Fortescue. After the somewhat hazardous business of dismounting without being trampled by this animal, he called a passing link-boy to hold the horse, ran up the front steps, and came into the house with rather less than his usual cheeriness. He responded with an abstracted air to Rebecca's bright greeting, settled himself into his favourite chair in the sunny parlour, stared blankly at his sister, stood up, then sat down again.

Alarmed, Rebecca asked, "Snow? Are you quite under the hatches, love?"

"Eh? Oh, no. Had a turn of luck, in fact." Instead of elaborating on this phenomenon in his customary manner, he rose once more, took a turn about the room, and stood with one hand on the mantelpiece, gazing down into the empty grate. "It is no use your getting up in the boughs," he remarked, frowning. "Cannot take you to the Dawes' rout party tonight. Nuisance, I know, but—there 'tis."

Snowden had agreed to escort them tonight, only because Major Broadbent, whose plea to partner The Little Parrish to the party had been accepted, was now suddenly recalled to duty, and a hastily scribbled note declaring that he was shattered, desolate, and utterly distraught had arrived too late for Rebecca to accept any of the other offers she had received. There had been many of those, for her popularity had bloomed after the weekend at Ward Marching. News of her merry good humour, her unstilted nature, her charm and beauty had swept the *ton*. She had, Snowden acknowledged with a grin, won the heart of every ramshackle rattle in Town, to say nothing of several very well to pass older gentleman who were excellent matrimonial prospects was a girl prepared to wed a man thirty years her senior.

Rebecca had looked forward to the party on two counts. Firstly, because she knew Sir Peter Ward was expected to arrive in Town today and there was a chance he might be in attendance, and secondly, because she had hoped her brother would have such a jolly evening he would be in an expansive mood and she might be able to tell him she meant to accompany her aunt to Bedfordshire, if only for a few days. One look at Snowden's unusually grim expression drove such plans from her mind. She crossed to place her hand on his arm and, her eyes anxious, she asked, "Whatever is wrong, dear? I care nothing for the party, but—if you are in difficulties, please tell me."

"Nothing to tell," he said, adding a severe, "And don't you go making up no ridiculous Cheltenham tragedy, Becky! If truth be told, Forty's—ah, well he's got himself into the most caper-witted bumble broth, and—he ain't fit to go, y'know, at the best of times. Nothing for it, but I must go up there and see can I bring him about."

The suggestion that as irresponsible a young Buck as Snowden Boothe could bring *himself* about, much less rescue a friend, would have sent several gentlemen in London's Corinthian set into whoops. Even his doting sister might have registered stupefaction at this expansive statement had not her own brain been busily spinning webs in other areas. The truth was that she was overjoyed by the news that her brother meant to leave Town, and, instead of delving deeper into the matter of Lord Fortescue's embarrassment, she enquired, "Go up where?"

"Newcastle."

Rebecca stared. "Newcastle? Upon-Tyne?"

"What? Lord, I don't know what it's on! Is there another one, then?"

"Well, I expect there is. We seem to have so many towns with the same name. But if you mean the one in the north, Snow, it must be hundreds of miles distant! What on earth would take Forty up there?"

"Nothing that makes any sense, I can tell you!" Snowden stared broodingly at the grate, then exclaimed, "Jove, but you're right! Do I ever inherit the title—which it stands to reason I won't with all the dirty dishes on the other side of the family cluttering up the succession—but if ever I do, I dashed well think I shall stand up in the Upper House and register a protest about the whole dirty mess! Blest if ever I come to think about it before, but it is an absolute disgrace and should be stamped out before it goes on into perfidy or whatever that jawbreaker is."

"Perpetuity, love," supplied Rebecca, fond but baffled.

"All right. Before that."

"Do you really suppose Forty's troubles will—"

"Thunderation, Rebecca! I ain't speaking of Forty! It's the towns I mean. Look at Dorchester, for instance. We've a Dorchester in Dorset and another in Oxfordshire. And there's Farnham in Dorset and another in Surrey and Lord knows how many more lurking about! Too dashed confusing is what it is! And no call for it. Lots of good names. Something should be done!"

Accompanying him to the door, Rebecca said, "Yes, but—Snow, how long shall you and Lord Fortescue be gone, then?"

"Forty ain't going with me."

Surprised, she exclaimed, "But I thought you said he was in some kind of difficulty?"

"Well, he is. But it would pay no toll to take him. He's such a block, he'd just muddy the waters." He turned at the door to put both hands on her shoulders. "Now you be a good chit. No more hare-brained starts, mind! Forty will keep an eye on you. Did I tell you he will take you to the party tonight? Said he'd bring the carriage round at nine, so don't be late." He kissed her, told her not to worry and that he'd be back in a week or two, and ran lightly down the steps to where the link-boy had resorted to wrapping the reins around a tree trunk and hanging on for dear life. At the foot of the steps, Snowden bethought himself of something and came running back up again.

"About that fellow de Villars . . ." He hesitated. "Has he been causing you any—ah, embarrassment?"

Rebecca answered cautiously, "I've not seen him since the boat party. Why? I understood you to say—"

"Never mind what I said. Someone mentioned— Well, at all events, you stay clear of him! And if he makes any—I mean, if he says— Hell and the devil confound it, *must* you stand there looking so blasted angelic? You know dashed well what I mean!"

She laughed. "Yes, dear. But why you should think de Villars has eyes for me, when I understood you to say it was The Monahan who—"

Suddenly very red in the face, her brother coughed, and intervened with a stern stricture that she put up with "no humbug from ramshackle rakes!" He next advised her with a fond grin that she wasn't up to the rig, that widows was fair game but with Forty and Aunt Alby to chaperone her she'd be all right and tight, and took himself off to rescue the wailing link-boy.

Rebecca waved her goodbyes wondering if he'd completely forgotten that Aunt Albinia was going to Bedfordshire. Dear Snow, she would miss him. But, "Two weeks!" she breathed, her eyes bright with anticipation. It must *surely* be ample time in which to captivate one very lonely gentleman!

❧

Rebecca had visited several country seats, but she had never lived in one and although she enjoyed their peace and beauty, it occurred to her that to spend a few days at an isolated estate as one of a merry throng of guests was one thing, but to live in such a setting for any length of time might be a touch lonely. It was perhaps for this reason that she had so looked forward to attending the Dawes' rout party before journeying into Bedfordshire.

She had chosen a gown of dusty rose pink silk that she and her aunt had worked feverishly to bring up to style. It had always been a charming dress, but with the addition of many tiny satin bows, gathering the soft material into a ruched effect, and a billowing underdress of lace, also embellished with the little bows, it looked very pretty indeed, and she felt quite pleased with herself when she descended the stairs with her aunt.

Lord Graham Fortescue awaited them in the drawing room, a vision of sartorial splendour in a powdered bag wig, a coat of scarlet cloth with quantities of gold lace, and white satin knee breeches. Gold ladders adorned his stockings, and on his high-heeled shoes ruby buckles glittered. He jumped up as the ladies entered, and presented each with a corsage of white roses.

"Thank you, dear sir!" said Rebecca gratefully. "It is very good of you to step into the breach like this. I trust you were not discommoded."

He was, he assured her, not only pleased, but proud to be escorting a lady who had become quite the rage. He was a cheerful and attentive escort, and Mrs. Boothe remarked that it was delightful to receive such courtesies. "I vow"—she smiled—"you will pamper us just as much as would Snowden."

"Oh, no! A good deal more," said Rebecca, well acquainted with her brother's affable but careless attentions.

His lordship disclaimed, a rather troubled light in his honest brown eyes. Rebecca saw that look and apprehension touched her. She fancied she was being very clever as she manipulated the conversation around to Snowden's reason for having gone into the north. Her tact was wasted. Fortescue acquired a hunted expression and embarked upon an explanation that became so muddled and involved that he was still in the midst of it when the footman swung open the crested door and the ladies were handed tenderly from the carriage. The

usual vociferous crowd was watching the guests arrive, but as
she made her way up the carpeted steps to the front doors of
the mansion, Rebecca scarcely heard their admiring comments.
Snowden had said he was going to Newcastle in an attempt to
extricate his friend from some sort of sticky dilemma. According to Fortescue, the journey had been necessitated by a business transaction having to do with a boat and a scaly scrub of a
dealer in Irish hunters. Since Newcastle was on the east coast,
and an Irish transaction would more logically have been conducted in the west at Liverpool or Blackpool, Rebecca could
make no sense of it all.

Once inside the mansion, however, she forgot the matter.
The large foyer was a press of great skirts, perfumed ladies, and
their glittering beaux. Wigs towered, feather plumes swayed,
silks and satins and taffetas shushed across the marble floors,
and fans fluttered busily. The strains of music drifted from the
rear ballroom, and the air was not, as yet, oppressively warm.
Rebecca was greeted with enthusiasm by old and new friends.
Mr. Dunsmuir, a balding but vivacious gentleman with a turn
for wit and poetry, composed an ode for her which he titled,
"Fairest Fisher of the River," creating much merriment; two
eager young beaux instantly solicited her hand for a minuet and
a quadrille; rotund Lord George Francks wished to tell her the
tale of a fish *he* had almost caught; and Miss Letitia Boudreaux
embraced her and exclaimed that she was the talk of the Town.
"I declare," she murmured, "you shall achieve a brilliant match
before the Season ends!" Rebecca thanked her, but her own
eyes sought ever for the handsome head of one distinguished
gentleman, and found it not.

She was returning from having been led down to supper
by Lord Fortescue when a page brought word that she was
wanted in the gold ante-room. Her question eliciting the further information that her presence was desired in connection
with the arrival in Town of a Miss Patience Ashton caused her
politely to decline his lordship's offer to accompany her.
Heaven forbid that Forty should become involved in a conversation that might very well apprise him (and thus Snowden) of
her intentions to journey into Bedfordshire the very next day!

Her kindly cavalier went wandering off and, with a sigh of relief, Rebecca hurried into the hall. The page led her to a side corridor and indicated the third door on the left.

Rebecca opened the white-and-gilt door with caution. The room was luxurious, quiet, and deserted. She walked in and crossed to a small adjoining chamber. Finding it also empty, she decided this must be the wrong apartment, although the décor was decidedly golden. She turned back to the outer room and halted abruptly.

An elegant gentleman appeared as if from thin air to bow before her. A gentleman with a cynical mouth and a physique that did full justice to a superb blue velvet jacket embroidered with silver thread. His small clothes were blue satin; a sapphire glowed in the lace at his throat, and another and larger sapphire was worn on one finger of his right hand. An impressive gentleman, but instead of curtseying, Rebecca tensed and drew back.

De Villars said with his twisted grin, "I bring you word from Miss Ashton. Perhaps I should instead have sought out your brother."

Her powdered head tossed upward. She said triumphantly, "Snowden is not here, so you cannot."

"How very obliging in him. . . ." He wandered closer, his eyes alight with deviltry.

Lifting one small but determined hand, she cautioned, "Stay back!"

"Wrong, lovely one. You should say 'Stay back, dastardly villain!' because, I assure you, that is in the best tradition of—"

Large her hoops might be, and tiny her shapely form, but Rebecca was nothing if not fast on her feet, and in a trice the gilt-and-cream-brocade sofa was between them.

De Villars laughed softly, with a flash of white teeth that she perversely found exceedingly attractive. "Egad, but you're a lovely article, Little Parrish," he declared, standing before the sofa, hands on hips. "Come now—such a fine sportsman as you are! A kiss in exchange for my message, yes?"

"No! And—do you lay *one hand* on me . . ." she said between her teeth.

"I would not," he vowed piously, but spoiled the effect by adding with a twinkle, "Two hands, or nothing!"

"Oh! You are without shame! Tell me the message, sir! Stay! Another step and I shall scream for help!"

"Do not, oh, pray do not! I swear I'll not step," he said earnestly and, with a lithe bound and one hand briefly placed atop the sofa, stood beside her.

Rebecca uttered a squeal and darted away, barely eluding his grasp. "Lecher!" she gasped, breathless, but anxious to obtain the message he brought. "Horrid libertine! You *lured* me here!"

"But of course." He said with an apologetic gesture, "There was no other lady half as lovely, you see, else I'd merely have sent the message to you." He swung one long leg over the sofa and perched on top of the back, his grey eyes glinting with laughter. "Come, sweeting, you want your message and I ask only a small forfeit, surely."

"Sooner," she panted, "would I be dead!"

"You would?" He eyed her curiously. "I wonder why. I think I am not an inept lover. At least I've not as yet been told my kisses are repulsive. Now, Ward, on the other hand, is pitifully lacking in experience, and—"

"Oh, base! And he your *friend!*"

"There—you see? You *do* prefer experience. Now, as for myself—" Even as he spoke, he sprang with a fluid leap that came with astounding swiftness.

With a gasp of fright, Rebecca tried, too late, to escape. She was seized in a grip of steel and crushed close against him, her little scream muffled against his cravat. His head bowed over her. In his eyes was a new light of tenderness that reduced her knees to the consistency of custard. "Jupiter," he breathed, "but you're an exquisite little creature."

"I," she whispered without much resolution, "shall . . . scream . . ."

"In that event"—his lips caressed her temple—"I must be deafened. . . ." He was planting little kisses down to her chin, up her other cheek, and upon her half-closed eyelids. "Ah, sweeting," he breathed, "how delicious you smell."

A floating sensation had taken possession of Rebecca's mind. She had a heady impression of drifting among clouds, and at the same time experienced another emotion as shocking as it was unfamiliar: the yearning to return those kisses; the need to feel his lips not upon her cheek, or her brow, or her eyelids, but claiming her mouth. . . .

Distantly, someone laughed, and the simple sound restored sanity. With a shocked gasp she tore free and uttered an incensed, "How *dare* you! Oh, how dare you take such advantage of a helpless lady!"

De Villars said ruefully, "But consider, Little Parrish. I did not kiss you on the lips, as I had every right. And—"

"Every—*right?* Oh! When my brother hears of this, he will—" But she bit back the words, knowing she dared not tell Snowden.

"I had thought you had bought and paid for your message. However," he shrugged, "do you mean to terrify me with blackmail . . ."

Much he was terrified, she thought, yearning to scratch him. It was poor Snow who— Her fears for her brother ceased abruptly. Despite his light and teasing manner, The Lecher had shifted his position and now stood between her and the door! Her heart began to hammer wildly. She turned her back on him, her head bowed, but her eyes searching for something to use as a weapon. "You have no right," she murmured coyly, "to—to force me, sir."

"And will never do so, loveliest. Come now—" He was moving up close behind her. "Admit," he said huskily, "that you enjoyed—"

With a pantherish leap, Rebecca snatched up the only article that offered, a large cut-glass bowl of roses. She whirled about. De Villars was in the act of reaching out for her. Without an instant's hesitation, she dashed the contents of the vase into his face.

He gave a yell and reeled back.

"How right you are," Rebecca snarled. "I have enjoyed *this* moment immensely, at the least!"

He dragged a sleeve across his eyes and gasped, blinking

at her through the streams of water that ran down his face to soak his blue-and-silver brocaded waistcoat. A rose had become entangled in the sagging wreck of his powdered hair, and a spray of fern hung incongruously over his right eye.

"Lud, but you're a sight!" giggled Rebecca. "Here—let me help you." She sprang closer before he could recover himself, and balanced the upended bowl on his head. "I crown you King of the May-have-been!"

He muttered an oath and lunged for her. With a squeak of fright, she ran for the door. De Villars' attempt to pursue her was foiled as the bowl fell and landed with a thud on his toe. He yelped, grabbed his foot, and hopped, groaning, to the sofa.

Laughing in triumph, Rebecca watched him from the open door.

"Next time . . . enchanting . . . vixen!" he warned, nursing his battered toe. "Next time—I shall even the score!"

Rebecca glanced around. The corridor was empty. Distantly, music lilted in the final strains of a gavotte, and happy laughter and talk could be heard. "I foiled your despicable wickedness," she said proudly. "Own it!"

Sagging and bedraggled, he glared ferociously at her. But gradually, a reluctant grin dawned. "Aye," he admitted. "You did that."

Her own anger faded. "If I come back and help restore your appearance, will you swear to behave like a proper gentleman?"

For a moment, he gazed at her, then, a whimsical smile in his eyes, he stood and limped towards her, shaking his head. But as she tossed her own and started away, he called, "Peter cannot be here, for his cousin is to arrive at Ward Marching this night. His carriage will call for you and Mrs. Boothe tomorrow morning at ten o'clock."

Rebecca turned back; but even as she started to him, a man and a girl came hand in hand around the corner. De Villars swung shut the door, and Rebecca hurried away.

The balance of her evening was triumphant in a different

sense, for no sooner did she reappear in the ballroom than she was surrounded. Eager gentlemen vied for her dance card and quarrelled over the right to put down their names. It was wrenching to have to leave at one o'clock while the festivities were in full swing, but she and Albinia had to be up early. In the carriage, her aunt, echoing Miss Boudreaux's sentiments, told her that even was she unable to snare Sir Peter, there was no doubting now but that she could achieve a highly respectable marriage. Rebecca said sleepily that she hoped that was so—and thought it did not matter, for she *would* snare Sir Peter!

Lying in bed an hour later, drowsily content, her cheeks reddened suddenly even in the darkness, as her thoughts turned to that horrid ante-room. How strong the wretched man was! His arms had all but crushed the breath from her. She forced away the recollection of how contrastingly gentle had been his kisses, but then frowned at the canopy. He *was* strong, so strong he might easily, as he had said, have claimed her lips. Grudgingly, she acknowledged that The Lascivious Libertine had played fair and, irked by that admission, banished him from her mind. In only a few hours they would be en route to Bedfordshire and Sir Peter. Dear Sir Peter, with his haunted, wistful eyes, courtly manners, and gentle charm.

Lady . . . Peter . . . Ward. . . .

Rebecca yawned, smiling.

And fell asleep in the midst of an uneasy awareness that this happiness was to be hers only because The Wretched Rake had so manoeuvred it.

CHAPTER
❧ 6 ❧

"*O*h, but how lovely!" Rebecca looked eagerly from the armful of long-stemmed pink roses Millie held, to the plain card she offered. Taking it, Rebecca unfolded it and read, "One for every kiss, my adored Little Fishwife." There was no signature—nor any need for one. Her cheeks flaming, she tore the card to shreds and tossed the remnants onto the hall table. "Throw them away," she said loftily. "We certainly cannot carry them with us."

"Throw them away? But—Mrs. Rebecca, they're so pretty. Falk will like to have 'em, if you don't mind. She loves flowers."

They *were* pretty. A soft, blushing pink. Her own complexion matching the blooms, Rebecca relented and, trying not to notice that her aunt watched apprehensively, agreed that Millie should present the roses to Mrs. Falk. She took up her reticule and gave a twitch to her shawl. "Are we ready at last, Aunt Alby? Wher*ever* is that child?"

"Anthony is outside, admiring Ward's carriage." Adjusting her bonnet with the aid of the Chippendale wall mirror, Mrs. Boothe asked with trepidation, "Why did you tear up the card and tell Millie to throw away those lovely roses?"

Rebecca was spared the necessity of a reply, for the front door burst open and Anthony erupted into the hall. Jubilant, he imparted the information that Sir Peter's coachman was called Todd. "And the right wheeler is a young 'un and full of spirit, so it would be very nice if we might leave afore he kicks over the traces! Can we not go now, Mama? Can we not?"

Rebecca smiled, her heart warmed by his radiance. "Of course we can, dearest. Come, Aunt." She rang the bell, and Millie and Mrs. Falk bustled along from the kitchen stairs, the former now swathed in a woollen cloak and a black bonnet with a severely curtailed poke; and the latter worrying over them all and muttering subdued remarks anent what she was supposed to tell Mr. Snowden did he come home all of a sudden.

Rebecca hugged her and for perhaps the twentieth time said that she was accompanying Mrs. Boothe only until the lady was comfortably settled in and would doubtless be home long before her brother returned from the north. Seized by a belated thought, she added, "If Lord Fortescue should call, be so good as to tell him that my aunt and I are gone to visit friends. Nothing more, if you please."

The housekeeper wrung her hands and looked frightened. Millie pursed her lips and uttered a snort. Mrs. Boothe moaned and went feebly outside, prophesying dire consequences. Anthony leapt, whooping, down the steps.

Rebecca followed with hope in her heart. They were off!

❧

The day was fine, if not warm, the sun playing hide-and-seek with scurrying clouds that were fluffily white, betraying no hint of rain. By the time the first stage was reached, there was no containing Anthony. His prayerful requests granted, he scrambled up to the box and sat between Todd coachman and the guard, his green eyes all but shooting out sparks of excitement.

Rebecca devoted herself to allaying her aunt's feelings of guilt—no easy task, and one that succeeded only when she was inspired to turn the conversation towards Mr. Melton. Mrs. Boothe blushed like a girl and was soon joining with her niece in dreams of a rosy future.

The miles and the hours flew past. Once, Rebecca's heart jolted into her mouth as Anthony uttered a piercing shriek. He had not, however, tumbled from the box as she feared, but had seen a deer "with antlers and everything!" grazing in the preserves of an estate.

They came to a stretch of rather desolate open country, and Mrs. Boothe began to fret about the possibility of encountering highwaymen, but they reached Harpenden without mishap and lunched at a bustling posting house where a private parlour and a meal had been arranged for them by the ever-thoughtful Sir Peter. Mrs. Boothe urged that Anthony eat lightly, in view of the long journey still ahead of them, but Rebecca was inwardly elated by the glow in her son's pale cheeks and the enthusiasm with which he attacked his food, a marked departure from his usual finicking appetite.

The journey was resumed shortly after three o'clock. The carriage rattled merrily through Bedfordshire's flatter terrain, past neatly hedged fields with crops ripening to the golden caress of summer; past quaint old villages where the women sat in open doorways, weaving their famous lace, and children ran, shouting, after the luxurious coach. The afternoon ticked away, and the view from the carriage windows became routine:

sunshine and shadows across the white ribbon of the road; meadows and woods; low gentle hills and dimpling hollows; hamlets, becoming fewer; and, occasionally, the loom of some great castle or manor house. And then, at last, another shriek from the boy, and they were rumbling between great stone gates and passing a gatehouse, neither of which Rebecca had noticed on the first journey.

They had travelled far more swiftly on this occasion, probably because the two outriders were Sir Peter's grooms, not pleasure-seeking, unhurried guests, and most stops to change teams had been brief, the fresh horses ready, the changes accomplished with swift efficiency under the watchful eye of Todd coachman. At all events, they rolled up the drivepath and halted before the great square grey house at a quarter to seven, with the sun still far from setting.

As before, the butler was on the terrace to see the carriage door opened, two lackeys flanking him, impressive in their green satin and powder. The ladies were bowed into the mansion, and the coachman drove on with Anthony, Millie, and the lackeys, to unpack the luggage in the cottage Mrs. Boothe would eventually occupy. Sir Peter, the butler explained, had not expected quite so early an arrival and was from home, having taken Miss Ashton for a drive, but he would be back directly. Meanwhile, the visitors were conducted to a bedchamber where a petite French maid waited, eager to be of assistance to *mesdames*. As soon as they were tidied and refreshed they were taken down to a small saloon wherein the butler himself served them with hot tea and shortbread. They were finishing this pleasant snack when the sounds of wheels and hooves could be heard outside.

Mrs. Boothe grasped Rebecca's hand nervously. "Whatever shall I do if she is an unkind girl and treats me with contempt? After all, she likely thinks I am but a servant!"

That possibility had not occurred to Rebecca, but it was a valid one, and for the first time she comprehended the difficulties that her aunt might have to surmount. "Oh!" she thought, "what a wicked girl I am!" But footsteps were in the hall; it was too late now! Her heart gave a bound as Sir Peter's deep voice said, " . . . and with me not here to receive them!" She hissed, "Then we shall leave at once, love! Never fear!"

Mrs. Boothe did fear. She whimpered, "She—she may be a regular harpy! Do not leave me alone with her! I *beg* of you!"

There was no time for more. A lackey flung open the door, and Sir Peter entered. Eyes bright with pleased welcoming, he bowed and then hastened to stretch forth eager hands to both ladies while conveying his profound apologies for such unforgivable tardiness in greeting them. "Whatever must you think? I am quite disgraced, and would never have left the house save that my cousin is not capable of rational thought and had worked herself into such a condition that I feared lest she fall down in a fit."

This dismal statement caused Mrs. Boothe to blench and throw a horrified "I told you so" glance at her niece. Even Rebecca was stunned. A spoiled beauty, or a hoydenish tomboy, she had been prepared for. Madness was a possibility that had never crossed her mind. "Wh-where, sir," she managed, "*is* Miss Ashton?"

"Why, she is here—" He turned about, startled. "She was beside me. I—Miss Ashton? Where are you gone to? Come here, if you please."

A portion of Miss Patience Ashton entered the room—the frill of a dainty dress. A strangled snuffling presaged the gradual appearance of more of her. Staring at the red eyes, red nose, and twitching mouth that reluctantly inched around the door edge, Rebecca comprehended at last that there was no possible way for her aunt to groom this person into a ravishing debutante.

Miss Patience Ashton was not quite three feet tall.

"Good . . . God!" Rebecca gasped. "She is—only a *child!*"

"Oh, the poor mite!" Her kind heart touched, Mrs. Boothe stretched forth her arms and invited, "Come—sweet baby."

The tearful eyes overflowed. From the rosebud lips came a wail unutterably forlorn. Little Miss Ashton turned on her heel and fled.

Sir Peter spread his hands helplessly. "That is how it has been all day! She whines, and weeps, and wails. There is no dealing with her!"

Recovering from her momentary stupefaction, Rebecca muttered, "What a shock!"

"I cannot agree more," sighed Ward. "I'd no comprehension that one small girl could be so very vexing."

"Well, that is only because she is frightened, poor little creature," Rebecca pointed out with a touch of indignation. "Sir Peter, you did not tell us that Miss Ashton was a *child!*"

He blinked at her. "But of course she is. She is only four years old, you know. Had I not mentioned to you that she is my elder cousin's child?"

"Yes, but when you said 'elder'—and you indicated she must be groomed for her come-out—I thought . . ."

"By Jove! You never fancied her to be a *grown* girl? But that is not the case at all." He turned to Albinia and said earnestly, "I do pray you will not change your mind, dear ma'am. I have always held that a young woman's training begins in the cradle, and with Patience, alas, much time has already been lost."

"The *child* will be lost, do we stand here and chat all evening," said Mrs. Boothe with uncharacteristic acerbity. "By your leave, sir, I will try and find her."

All contrition, he said, "No, no—do not distress yourself, ma'am. Ecod, but I'd no thought to wish such a difficult situation upon you. I'll confess Patience appears to have a penchant for hiding under things. She is likely at this moment curled up under the hall table, convinced she is completely invisible. I have found her there twice. Twice! And it is the very—er, deuce, to lure her out again!"

"How very sad," Rebecca murmured with a sigh. "The dear little soul must feel utterly lost. Have no fear, sir. My aunt is the kindest creature and will prevail upon her, I am very sure."

Patience was not under the table, however, or under any other item of furniture in that long and elegant hall. They proceeded to search the Great Hall and then the dining room, breakfast parlour, and book room, and the ladies were becoming alarmed when Anthony joined them at his customary headlong pace.

"Mama!" he cried eagerly. "You should only see the stables! And the hunters! Jolly fine bits o' blood! How do you do, sir? And there is a bay mare has dropped her foal this morning—it is the very *prettiest* thing! Oh." He turned to detach a chubby hand from the tail of his coat. "This is Patience. She was running away, but did not know which way to run. I didn't know either, so perhaps she had better not."

Rumpled curls the colour of winter sunshine appeared from behind young Mr. Parrish. Great blue eyes peeped at the relieved adults.

Anthony gave her an impatient push. "Make your curtsey, do," he adjured sternly.

A finger was removed from the dimpling mouth. The child bobbed something vaguely resembling the first stage of leapfrog. "My name ith PaythenAth—" she lisped, her last name fading into a deep breath. She smiled shyly, thus revealing that one front tooth was noticeable by its absence.

"Awful!" Anthony held out his hand. Hers was at once tucked trustingly in it, and he led her over to Rebecca. "This is my mama, Mrs. Forbes Parrish. Say 'How do you do?' No! Not like *that!* Hold out your skirt. *Out*—not *up*, silly shrimp!"

Rebecca battled a smile and said gravely, "I am most glad to meet you, Patience."

"How do do?" The child nodded. "You pretty."

"And this," said Anthony, continuing the tour, "is my great aunt, Mrs. Boothe."

Patience's awkward salutation was followed by the offer to "Have a hug now. If you want to," an offer that was at once accepted, though it reduced Mrs. Boothe to tears.

Sir Peter said gratefully, "Anthony, you have saved the day! Now, I am assured you ladies would like to see the cottage. May I drive you, or would you prefer to walk? It is just a short distance."

❧

Rebecca gazed around the spacious bedchamber, noticing

rugs that were not in the least bit worn, a large, comfortable-looking bed, an ample chest of drawers, and a large press. The curtains were pretty, the pictures charming, and even the fireplace gave no hint that this was the home of a servant, for it had none of the tell-tale stains above the mantelpiece that bore mute witness to a smoking chimney. The other two bedrooms in this "cottage" were as impressive; the parlour was a delight, and it was as well that the faithful Falk, who combined the duties of cook and housekeeper in London, did not see the splendidly equipped kitchen.

Anxiously watching Rebecca's expressive countenance, Ward asked, "Will it serve, ma'am? There are other cottages about the estate, of course, but this is at a—er, proper, but not taxing, distance from the main house. Or so I think. Should you wish to inspect the others? I assure you they are all very livable, and—"

"No, no," she interposed with her lilting laugh. "If I seem speechless, it is because I am! My goodness, sir! If this is your notion of a cottage, whatever must you think of my London house? It would fit into one corner of this establishment!"

He said in a more hopeful tone, "Then you think you could endure it for a week or two, at least? If your aunt does not desire to take on the girl, it will give me a chance to search about for someone else."

Mrs. Boothe, Patience's tiny hand fast clamped on her skirt, intervened to say that she thought the cottage a veritable delight, and as for Mistress Ashton—she rested a fond hand on the pale curls—"Who could not love such a darling child?"

Overwhelmed by such kindness, Patience nursed Albinia's hand to her cheek and smiled mistily up at her.

Rebecca said, "May she stay here tonight, Sir Peter? It would be as well for us to get started on the right footing, do you not think?"

He beamed. "Capital! But may I propose an exchange?"

For one shocked moment, Rebecca could scarce breathe, and Mrs. Boothe stared at him in outright astonishment.

"I regret the lateness of the hour," he said, sublimely unaware of the consternation he had aroused. "But my chef promises dinner at eight o'clock. I trust you are not too wearied to honour me with your company?"

Rebecca pulled herself together, and assured him they were not too wearied. Evans, the buxom housemaid who was to serve them, had already taken Anthony off to the kitchen, and Patience was now conducted thither while the ladies went to change their gowns.

The air was cool and sweet as they walked through the park to the main house. They arrived in the glow of sunset to find lamps already lit, and candles waking a thousand sparkles from the prisms of the chandelier that hung above the table in the dining room. Sir Peter, his gaze lingering appreciatively on Rebecca's demure white gown, explained that this was the small, family dining room. "I trust you will forgive us, but the large dining room is so"—he waved one graceful hand—"so—large."

There were no other guests, but he seemed not in the least discomposed by the lack of another gentleman and, with a lady on each side of him, was the perfect host. Rebecca tried not to make any remarks which so conservative a gentleman might judge unfeminine, and even when the recent tragic Rebellion somehow found its way into the otherwise innocuous conversation (a topic on which she held deep and rather treasonable opinions), she contrived to remain meekly tactful.

Mrs. Boothe, who had several times trembled lest her niece's hasty tongue lead her into indiscretion, was gratified by this restraint. Rebecca was a picture tonight. The white taffeta gown with dainty red scroll embroidery about the hem looked pure and virginal and was complemented only by a simple ruby pendant that glowed against her white bosom. Sir Peter, impressive in brown velvet, his fair hair unpowdered and gleaming in the candlelight, could scarce tear his eyes from her. He was the very epitome of good breeding, however, and never once slighted the elder lady whilst catering to the younger. Watching him with the critical eyes of a prospective aunt-in-law, Albinia could find nothing to displease. He was gracious without being condescending and amusing without having that regrettable tendency to flirt exhibited by so many gentlemen.

Although he certainly led the conversation, he never monopolized it and would listen with interest did a lady venture an opinion, even if later he felt obliged gently to point out aspects of the subject of which she might be unaware. His smile was warm, his laugh well modulated, his manners exquisite. And he was very rich. Her prior conviction that he would make a kind and devoted husband was strengthened, and she could not wonder that her niece had lost her heart to the handsome fellow.

At eleven o'clock Sir Peter escorted his guests back to the cottage. As they strolled through the fragrant gardens under a bright half-moon, Albinia contrived gradually to fall behind, leaving the young couple to chatter together. Sir Peter did not take advantage of the situation by indulging in a little light flirtation. Instead, he chose to speak of the history of Ward Marching, which had been awarded to his ancestors soon after the Battle of Hastings, in 1066. "The original pile," he said, "is gone, of course, but you may see the ruins still, about a mile to the west of here. My great-great-grandfather, Sir Montague Ward Marching, had the present house begun in 1635."

Rebecca thought it a pity that no one had instructed Sir Montague as to the benefits of building on high ground, rather than in a hollow. "Did he choose the site so as to be away from the wind?" she asked.

He chuckled. "No, ma'am. So as to be away from his wife. If history speaks truth, she was a fearsome lady of violent moods, and with a tongue like an asp."

"Poor man! And did he dwell here all alone, then? He must have been very solitary."

"Yes. But—er, he was something of a rascal, I fear, and—ah, he—"

"Brought his *chère amie* here?" She gave a ripple of laughter. "And right under his wife's nose! Lud, but there must have been some royal battles!" The nervous cough from behind them caused her heart to thud. Slanting an uneasy glance at her companion, she saw a surprised expression. Why, oh why, must she say such things!

Sir Peter murmured without looking at her, "Yes. I believe their life was not tranquil."

She had shocked him, of course. Something must be done at once. . . . She stumbled and reached out for support. With a startled exclamation, he swung out an arm. His movement was very fast. Unhappily, Rebecca had moved just as fast, turning her head to him. His knuckles collided violently with her jaw, just below the ear, and every star in the heavens seemed to explode.

&

"There, my love." Mrs. Boothe laid a cold wet cloth across Rebecca's brow and straightened. "Are you better now?"

Rebecca blinked up at her, stupidly. "Whatever . . . ?" she gasped, and clapped a hand to her chin.

"It was purely an accident, dearest. But—alas, I fear 'twill bruise."

Struggling to sit up, Rebecca peered about. She was laid down upon the sofa in the cottage parlour, and of her selected mate there was no sign. "Is he gone, then?" she cried. "Lud! What a fiasco! I vow, Aunt, I can do nothing right!"

Mrs. Boothe put a hand over her lips and glanced to the open doorway. "He is outside," she whispered, her eyes dancing with mirth. "So far he has vowed three times to blow out his brains! Play your cards right, my sweet, and you may have him yet." She checked her niece's position, adjusted her skirts carefully, then hastened to the door. "She is awake now, sir, and asking for you."

A pale, distraught face appeared around the door. Eyes haunted by terror scrutinized Rebecca. Ward tiptoed into the room, wringing his hands and asking an anguished, "Are you . . . are you better now, Mrs. Parrish?"

Mrs. Boothe winked mischievously, and slipped away. Quite unaware of either her wink or departure, Sir Peter stumbled to kneel beside the sofa and take the hand Rebecca held out. "My God! My God!" he moaned, bowing his face upon it. "I have never struck a woman in all my life!"

Infuriatingly, Rebecca had to battle an urge to giggle. "But you never did such a thing," she said comfortingly. "'Twas purely accidental."

Grasping at this straw, he looked up. "Yes! That is truth, but— Oh, your poor sweet cheek is so red and already swelling! What a brute I am! What a clumsy fool! And you so gentle as to forgive so heinous an offence!"

"Nay, how could I judge it so when you have been all that is kind."

"Do you know," he said, looking at her wonderingly, "almost, at times, Mrs. Parrish, you put me in mind of—of my dear, lost lady." His eyes fell. Stroking her hand, he went on, "I need not tell you how frightful it is to lose your love, for you know too well, poor gentle creature. All these lonely years, Helen has been seldom from my thoughts."

"How unhappy you must have been," said Rebecca, squeezing his hand sympathetically.

"Oh, no. For I have my birds, you see. But—" he sighed. "Always I have felt there could never be—another, to replace her. And yet, of late . . ." His eyes lifted again, gazing into her own. "Of late, it has been in my mind to . . . to ask you . . ."

Rebecca's breath began to flutter. "Yes, dear sir?" she prompted gently.

"If you might . . . consider . . ." He wrenched his eyes away and gabbled with frantic haste, "Consider coming up to the main house tomorrow morning. There is a portrait of Lady Ward Marching in the gallery. I know you will like to see it, and then, if you are feeling up to it, we could—we could picnic on the Home Farm."

Disappointed, Rebecca thought that the gentleman was nothing if not adept at extricating himself from a dangerous moment. She forced a smile and said she would like very much to see the portrait and would be quite recovered after a night's sleep. Very daring, Sir Peter pressed a salute upon her hand and left, bowing to Mrs. Boothe as she returned to her patient.

Waiting until he was safely out of earshot, Albinia demanded to know what had transpired. "What did he say? Did you suffer heart-rendingly?"

"Probably not. I should have, shouldn't I? But the poor man was so repentant I *could* not punish him further."

"And so wasted a golden opportunity!" Mrs. Boothe shook her head and offered a fresh cloth. "Well, what did he say?"

Rebecca sat up, holding the cloth to her aching head. "He told me that he has never got over his dead love, but he is very brave about it, and says he has not been lonely because he has his birds."

Mrs. Boothe gasped and sank into the wing chair opposite.

"Did you see him drop to his knees, dearest? Well, he did. And he said—"

"What? What?"

"That I reminded him of his Helen."

"Huh!" said Mrs. Boothe.

"And that he had never thought another could take her place, but of late he'd had it in his mind to ask me—"

"Yes? Yes?" cried Mrs. Boothe, leaning forward, her eyes bright with anticipation.

"If I would care to see the portrait of his great-great-grandmother."

Albinia's jaw dropped. "The man is alone with you, on his knees, and you lying ravishingly lovely before him, and he talks of his *birds* and his *grandmama?* Dear heaven, Rebecca! Is he short of a sheet?"

"Why? Because he did not take advantage of my helplessness?" Rebecca defended, indignant. "I make no doubt de Villars would have been tearing the gown from me in such a situation! Ward's gentleness, his dignity, his nobility, are the very qualities I so admire. He has been much courted, do not forget. And I suspect he is—a trifle wary. Unless . . ." She hesitated and, her brows a little knit, went on, "Poor fellow, he has been so very lonely all these years, that I think he may perhaps have forgot how to court a lady."

"Faith, it sounds to me as though he's forgot a sight more than that!"

"Aunt!" gasped Rebecca, much shocked. "Whatever do you mean?"

Mrs. Boothe blushed and disclaimed, "I—we—oh, my!"
She rallied, saying with a remarkably girlish dimple, "Well,
you have the right of it, I do not doubt. He is wary."

"Yes." Rebecca nodded. "And is going to be more difficult
to snare than I had fancied." She felt her jaw tenderly. "I *must*
look my best, dearest. Shall this be dreadfully unsightly tomorrow?"

Mrs. Boothe assured her there was little cause for worry.
"We can always arrange your curls so as to hide it, never fear."

By the following morning, the bruise was quite lurid, but
the swelling had gone down, and between her aunt's skill at
arranging her hair, plus a careful application of cosmetics, the
desired result was achieved. The bruise was evident, but not to
the extent of being unsightly. One did not wish that the gentleman forget his brutality entirely!

Anthony burst into the room while Millie was busied with
pounce pot and pomatum, powdering his mother's curls. He
announced with several leaps and bounds that it was "a lovely
day! Oh, what fun this is, is it not? But how noisy it was last
night. I never heard such a clamouring of creatures! I wonder
country folk ever get any sleep. Do we take the shrimp with us
today? Her legs are very short, you know."

Inwardly amused, Rebecca said that he should not criticize
Patience. "She has had a very sorry time of it, and besides, we
all were little once, Anthony."

He thought this over and asked in some awe if that in-
cluded Sir Peter. "I cannot make *him* into a little boy."

She laughed. "I fancy he was a very handsome little boy."
Reaching out to ruffle his hair, she smiled fondly. "Though not
as dashing as another young gentleman of my acquaintance."

His guileless eyes met hers earnestly. "Do you think that,
too, Mama? Mr. de Villars *is* a great gun even if he is not
handsome."

Startled, Rebecca said, "You like him?"

"Oh, yes. I did not at first, but then I found out that his
eyes say different to his words."

Millie chuckled. "From the mouths of babes . . ."

"Hmmnnn," said Rebecca. She sent her son away then,

while Millie dressed her. She had chosen a frock without hoops purchased two years earlier for a picnic that had been postponed due to inclement weather. It was a simple style, of powder-blue India muslin with a tiny fitted waist and many petticoats. The neckline, very low cut, was edged with white lace, and the same lace, threaded with blue ribands, fell in rich gathers about her elbows. Standing to scan herself critically, she had to admit that Millie had been right in suggesting they bring the gown although it was not of the latest style. It looked fresh, and, with her hair powdered and arranged in ringlets that fell over her bruised jaw, added to an impression of youthful purity.

She smiled faintly at her reflection. Today, Sir Peter was going to see a different Little Parrish. Today, she would be all rustic simplicity, enjoying the country delights, with the children romping happily about her. He would discover she could remove from London's sophistication and be just as at ease amid gentle rural pleasures. . . .

Nature seemed to lend its good will to her hopes. The sun shone brightly, the skies were azure, and a very few clouds drifted slowly across the heavens. Mrs. Boothe and the children were to be taken up later for the picnic, but Rebecca had promised to be at the main house by eleven o'clock and, taking her parasol, walked through the dewy gardens, looking glad-eyed on the beauty all about her.

Sir Peter met her on the steps of the main house. He looked very well, as always, his unpowdered hair shining in the sunlight. To his anxious enquiries Rebecca turned a smiling face, and he touched her cheek with one gentle finger and groaned over his misdeeds. She comforted him and said teasingly that he might make amends by giving them a memorable day.

"How could it be otherwise, Mrs. Parrish? For me, at least. Jove, but were I an artist we'd not stir from the house till I had put you on canvas, you look so charmingly in that dainty gown."

She blushed and was happily elated as he led her into the Great Hall. All here was bustle; maids and flunkeys scurrying about, dusting and polishing, the air redolent with the fragrance of several large bowls of cut flowers.

"My grandmama arrives tomorrow," said Ward, by way of explanation for the flurry of industry. "The dear soul abhors travel and comes only so as to help with Priscilla."

"Patience," Rebecca corrected softly.

He sighed. "I know. But the very young and the elderly are both sore trials at times, do not you agree?"

She could not forbear to giggle at this. "I meant, Sir Peter, that your cousin's *name* is Patience."

"You're right, by Jupiter! What a chawbacon you must think me. Even so, whatever her name is, I do apologize for her. Your poor aunt's nerves are likely shredded. Was she very vexing? Lud, but I'd not a moment's peace with her!"

All gentlemen, of course, found children trying. And how many scarcely ever saw their own offspring, consigning them to the care of nurses and governesses, with an occasionally administered evening kiss to remind them of who their fathers were. One must not, thought Rebecca firmly, expect Sir Peter to be as carelessly (lovably) ramshackle as her own dear sire had been. In fact—she stifled a sigh—perhaps it was Papa's very indifference to the conventions that had caused Snowden to be so cheerfully uninhibited, and herself so—hoydenish, at times. . . . She realized with a start that her companion was talking once more and, accompanying him up the broad stairs, said, "Your pardon, sir. I did not quite hear your remark. You spoke of a scarlet coat, I believe? Are there military hereabouts?"

"Oh, yes. They are everywhere just now, hunting down these hapless Jacobite fugitives. But I referred to the cardinal—the bird in the painting to your right, ma'am. A splendid fellow, eh? Whilst we picnic today, I hope to be able to point out many of my feathered friends, for Ward Marching abounds with the little rascals. I'll not have 'em harmed, you know. In fact"—he shot an uneasy glance at her—"I allow no cats on the premises. You—ah, have a cat, I believe?"

With a strong feeling of guilt, she admitted this. "Our Whisky is a lazy old ruffian, I do assure you. I doubt he could catch a bird, if he wished. Not that he *would* wish it, since he is much too fat to contemplate violent exercise." Sir Peter smiled and, anxious to change the subject, she went on, "You feel strongly about the Jacobites, I collect. How tragic it all is. And how dreadful for families of divided loyalties. Whatever must people do in such a situation, I wonder?"

"Another evil of their alleged Cause! So you think on such weighty matters, do you, dear lady? One never knows what goes on in those pretty feminine heads, I vow. For myself, I have sometimes puzzled over what to do if some dear relation or friend who had harboured sympathies for Prince Charles should come here imploring sanctuary." He shook his head and ushered her to the second pair of stairs. "What a frightfully difficult decision to contemplate."

She agreed, but asked, "And what *would* you do, sir?"

"One's first loyalty must be to King and country," he said frowningly. "But yet I fear . . . however great the risk, I should feel bound to give the poor wretch aid and sustenance and speed him quietly on his way. The conflict, after all, is over now. And so long as the miscreant left our dear island, I cannot think any great harm would be done." He gave her a whimsical smile. "Have I shocked you beyond reason?"

"Indeed no," she said, warming to him. "I agree. Though such gallantry could well cost you your head, sir."

He replied without bravado, "One has to accept whatever the cards may hold in life. Ah—here we are, and as well to turn us from so grim a discourse. This, ma'am, is my gallery. Very many ancestors, I fear, but I'll not take too much of your time."

A flunkey hurried to open one of the large double doors, and a long, low room was revealed, the walls lined with portraits. Rebecca thought it would be easy to spend an entire day in here, but as it turned out they did not linger above half an hour. Sir Peter had a few interesting anecdotes to relate concerning his more illustrious antecedents, and introduced Rebecca to his great-great-grandmother, whose portrait hung in a small bay on the east wall. The lady was depicted in early middle age. She was plump and not unattractive, being blessed with a splendid bosom that she thrust out, while smiling fixedly from the canvas as though defying any other lady to compete with her charms. Amused, Rebecca remarked that there was no denying Lady Ward Marching had possessed a pronounced and determined chin. Moving along, she looked with mild curiosity at a clerical gentleman next to my lady, the frame of his portrait obviously too small for the faded outline of some former occupant of the wall.

"You are looking at my late Uncle Nathaniel," said Ward. "He is quite out of place here. I really should put him back where he belongs, and likely will one of these days." He smiled when she gave him a questioning look, and explained, "It was de Villars's doing. My great-great-grandfather's portrait belongs in this space, of course. Trevelyan took it into his head that the old gentleman was miserable residing next to the lady he had avoided during his lifetime. He kept at me about it until, much against my better judgement, I gave in, and Sir Montague is now at the far end of the gallery."

Rebecca laughed and clapped her hands. "Oh, excellent! I quite agree. The poor man must be much happier there."

Ward said whimsically, "Do you know, ma'am, I rather suspect you and Trevelyan are kindred spirits."

She sobered at once and said a rather stiff, "You are very wrong, sir."

He begged her pardon most humbly and assured her he had intended no offence. She had the impression, in fact, that he was excessively pleased by her reaction.

CHAPTER
❧ 7 ❧

The Home Farm proved to be a model of neatly laid out fields, well-kept gardens of herbs and flowers, and a charming old whitewashed house with thatched roof and mullioned windows. Anthony and Patience explored every inch of the barn and stables, exclaiming delightedly over the various farm animals, as intrigued by a hen's new brood as by the fine Hereford bull-calf that was the farmer's pride and joy. The day continued fine, and it was pleasantly warm by the time the inspection tour was finished and the picnic lunch was served. The food was plain, yet having that extra deliciousness that is always to be noted in al fresco meals, and they washed it down with chilled home brewed ale and cowslip wine, lemonade being provided for the children.

The combination of warmth, food, and wine soon set Mrs. Boothe's head nodding. Rebecca and Sir Peter left her dozing comfortably under the tree, and went off for a walk with Anthony and Patience.

Sir Peter needed no urging to expound upon the various birds they saw fluttering about, and Rebecca listened attentively. His knowledge of the subject soon palled on his younger listeners, however. Anthony had brought along a ball and begged that Rebecca play with them. She agreed willingly. Ward joined in for a while, but became diverted by what he thought to be a kestrel and was soon absorbed in the possibilities of an old jackdaw nest high in the branches of an elm tree that he thought the kestrel may have appropriated.

Not for nothing had Rebecca grown up with two older brothers. She enjoyed sports, and the sight of Anthony's bright cheeks, the sound of his happy laughter, warmed her heart. It was a joy also to watch Patience's clumsy toddling after the ball and complete, worshipful acceptance of the boy's good-natured teasing. Rebecca quite forgot that she had determined to be serene and gracious and even forgot Sir Peter until she chanced to look up some time later and discovered him sitting on the root of a tree, watching them. In the act of blowing a wayward lock of hair from her eyes, she was horrified by the awareness that she was hot and dishevelled and, turning quickly away, made a frantic attempt to tidy her hair.

"Mama!" Anthony ran to look up at her appealingly. "You're never going to stop so soon?"

"I am rather warm, love. Do you teach Patience how to catch now, like a dear."

"Like a deer! She cannot even catch like a boy!" But he went off without further protest.

Catching her breath, praying that she looked not blowsily

flushed, Rebecca turned about and began to wander gracefully up the slight rise to where Sir Peter stood to greet her. As always, her heart quickened when she looked at him. So tall and fair, and with that eager smile in his fine eyes. Her concentration on the man of her heart proved disastrous, alas, for her attention wandered from the placement of her feet. The sense that she had stepped into something other than the meadow grasses was followed by the unhappy realization that the little bull-calf's kindred had lately occupied this meadow. Even as that unpleasant fact was brought home to her, she heard a hail from the farmhouse and all but groaned her chagrin.

Trevelyan de Villars, carelessly elegant in buckskins and boots, a broadcloth coat of brown, and with his powdered hair neatly tied in at the neck, sauntered across the meadow to them. It was, Rebecca thought bitterly, typical of him to arrive at the very instant of her unhappy predicament. Her attempts to cleanse her little sandal on a tuft of grass without being too obvious in the matter did not appear to be altogether successful. She summoned her most dazzling smile and bestowed it on Sir Peter. "I had not known you expected other guests, sir."

He glanced rather ruefully at de Villars. "No more had I, to say truth, ma'am." And then, in a louder tone, "Welcome, Treve. Are you en route, or remaining?"

De Villars came up, shook his outstretched hand, and bowed to Rebecca. "Could I do anything but remain, when you've such fascinating company?" His nose wrinkled. "Gad, Peter! How do you endure this pastoral scene? It smells so dashed—countrified!"

Her cheeks hot, Rebecca said, "Yet how lovely it is after London's heat and noise, and the endless pursuit of pleasure."

The Intruder raised a topaz-encrusted quizzing glass to view her and drawled, "One might suppose you to have been engaging in that very same pursuit, Mrs. Pe—er, Parrish. I saw you catch that last ball. How—lustily you play." His lips quirked, and the narrowed grey eyes glinted at her wickedly.

Her cheeks hotter than ever, she indulged a scorching disposition of his future, but said with a wry smile, "No, was I being juvenile? I expect you could entertain the children far better than I, Mr. de Villars, for I believe you already know Sir Peter's cousin."

All innocence, he answered, "Patience? A lovely mite, is she not? Will your aunt guide her to her come-out, do you suppose, ma'am?"

"Of course not," she said haughtily. "You knew perfectly well that she was a child! Why did you not tell me?"

"What—and ruin so many well-laid plans?" That revoltingly mocking eyebrow twitched upward, and he went on, "You would not have come, and only think of our poor Peter."

"Indeed, yes," said Ward. "I own myself grateful you did *not* warn Mrs. Parrish and her aunt away. I shall have to—"

"Mr. de Villars! Mr. de Villars!" Anthony came puffing up, Patience wobbling some distance behind.

De Villars had recourse to his quizzing glass. "Who," he said with abhorrence, "is this revolting urchin?"

Rebecca gave a gasp of rage. To her surprise, Anthony showed no resentment of such a greeting, but sprang to grip de Villars' hand and tug at it urgently. "Come and play ball with us," he beamed.

"I shall do no such thing. Begone, brat, lest I toss you in the nearest pond."

Stunned, Rebecca gawked at him. Anthony, however, uttered a squeal of delight and only tugged harder. Patience, toddling up, breathless and flushed, promptly seized de Villars by one muscular and immaculate leg, and tugged also.

"Good Gad!" he moaned. "Will no one rescue me from these fiendish creatures?" He flung out one hand and gripped Rebecca's wrist, declaring, "I am a shockingly poor sport, but I'll play any game *you* choose . . . lovely one."

"Let go!" she said indignantly, struggling to free herself.

"Gladly, if you will desire your son to release his clutch! Tony! Desist, you little varmint!"

"No," chortled Anthony, dragging his prize toward level ground. "You're captured, sir!"

"Cat-erred," echoed Patience, happily.

Rebecca made a bid for some vestige of independence and

remarked, as she was borne helplessly along, that she did not like the nickname "Tony."

"Then you should never use it," said de Villars pontifically.

She scowled at him, and only then did it occur to her that although Anthony had spoken of de Villars several times, to the best of her knowledge they had never met. "Good gracious!" she exclaimed. "How are you acquainted with my son, sir?"

"I refuse to reply on grounds of self-defence," he declared solemnly.

"He is my friend from the park, Mama." Anthony tossed a sparkling glance over his shoulder. "The man who helped me to sail my boat and 'lowed me to sail his."

"And allowed you to be nigh drowned." She nodded. "I should have guessed!"

"Never mind," de Villars said kindly. "Not everyone can be quick-witted. Prepare for a throw, halflings! Here—" He shrugged out of his jacket and thrust it at the seething Rebecca. "Hang this up somewhere, will you? Hey! Peter! Never stand there counting leaves! You'll get a crick in your neck. Go and get the bat. I left it on your picnic table. Hurry up, there's a good fellow!" He caught the ball Anthony sent whizzing at him, and threw it far off, proclaiming, "First one to find it wins a shilling!"

The children squealed across the meadow in hot pursuit of the bouncing ball.

De Villars turned and said breezily, "What? Haven't you got that thing hung up yet?" He retrieved the jacket and tossed it onto a convenient bush. "Must I do *everything* myself?"

Rebecca's comprehension was much too slow, and even as she started to retreat, his arms whipped around her, the grey eyes twinkling down at her in a most disconcerting way as he bent closer.

"Devil!" she gasped, struggling wildly. "Oh, how evilly you contrive!"

He kissed her brow. "I appreciate your appreciation."

"No! Horrid, *horrid* man! You will ruin everything!"

He chuckled, but straightened, still holding her. "With

our Peter, do you mean? You've not a chance there, my delicious dear. Were you a bird's nest, now . . ."

"You planned this entire thing," she hissed, vainly trying
to force his arm away. Faith, but the man was made of iron!
"You influenced Sir Peter to bring my aunt and me down here,
purely so that you could force your attentions on me!"

"Not 'purely,'" he admitted with an unrepentant grin.
"There is much less competition in this pastoral solitude. And
besides"—he succeeded in planting a quick kiss on the tip of
her nose—"your perfume is so—earthy. What is it, love?
Musk? Or musk ox, perhaps?"

"Odious!" wailed the mortified Rebecca. "Sir Peter will see
us! Oh, please! Please! If you spoil this for me, I shall *never*
forgive you!"

"Foolish child." But with a glance to the picnic area, he let
her go and stepped away. "He *would* come back at once. I was
hoping a vulture might captivate him. You really have set your
heart on becoming Lady Ward, have you?"

Busied with straightening her gown, she ignored that
question and said tartly, "I think it typical in you to poke fun at
him, even while you enjoy his hospitality. For shame!"

"Oh, no. I am shameless. And I do not poke fun at our
Peter, my adored rustic. I merely point out that he is a slowtop. A lovable fellow. And extreme handsome, I grant you. But
decidedly a slowtop. Never fear, I do not say it with malice or
on the sly, for Peter knows what I think of him. And he, in
turn, thinks me a cynical, graceless, immoral womanizer. You
see, we harbour no illusions about one another. Perhaps that is
why we are such good friends. Your Peter is all nobility. I"—he
bowed with a flourish—"I am all depravity. And shall remain
so until I am converted by the love of a good woman, whereupon I shall settle down, breed fourteen fat children, and
never look at another lady so long as I do live!"

"Hah!" she snorted, watching rather impatiently as Sir Peter meandered towards them. "You left out one word, my Lord
Smirk—'marriage'! Is the lady to bear you such a brood, you
might at least wed her!"

"Well, of course I shall wed her! Good God, woman! Do you fancy me to take after my grandpapa? I would not keep a mistress who presented me with fourteen children! She must be wits to let to land herself in such a bumble broth!"

Despite herself, a gurgle of laughter rose in Rebecca's throat.

Watching her, de Villars said, "So I am quite safe, d'ye see, Little Parrish, for I learned early in life that you ladies may sigh and pine for romance, but there's not one amongst you would wed a gentleman who has neither fortune nor expectations. Thus shall I die a lonely bachelor."

A different note had come into his voice. Glancing at him sharply, Rebecca was surprised to see that his eyes were bleak.

Anthony pounded up, sank to his knees, and panted, "Here . . . 'tis, sir. I—I win . . . the prize!"

"Jolly well done!" De Villars made a great show of presenting a shilling to the boy. "But now you must go and help the wee Patience, and give her this groat for a consolation prize. Her little legs did their very best, I think."

Anthony groaned. "*Must* I, sir? Is a pest!"

De Villars bent to him and imparted in a stage whisper, "All ladies are pests, my lad. Only—we gentlemen could not get along without them, alas. Hurry now, and then we shall have our game. *Come* along, Peter! *Do!*"

&

It was almost five o'clock before they turned their steps homeward, and they were, as Mrs. Boothe observed, "a sorry looking crew." Rebecca's gown had a grass stain, acquired when she slipped while catching an elusive ball; Anthony had managed to split his breeches; Patience seemed mud from head to heels and was ensconced upon de Villars' shoulder, one hand fast gripped in his once elegant locks. Sir Peter was the least disreputable amongst them, but even he sported a streak of mud down one cheek, and a lock of golden hair had fallen across his brow. His courtesy was undiminished, his hand ever ready to aid her or Albinia, and Rebecca thought him more handsome than ever, a becoming colour in his cheeks, and a warm glow in his eyes when he smiled down at her.

"What a jolly good time we have had," he remarked. "I vow I cannot recall when last I played bat and ball."

Rebecca lied that she would never have guessed it for he had hit the ball so hard she had supposed him to be an excellent cricketer.

De Villars moaned and murmured under his breath, "*What* a rasper!"

Rebecca cast him a look that must have raised blisters on his skin had it not been, she thought to herself, so thick as that on a rhinoceros! Her scorn was wasted, for he was glancing off to the side and following his gaze she saw an officer riding towards them, followed by a small troop.

"Soldiers!" howled Anthony, and raced to meet them.

"Goodness," Rebecca exclaimed. "You have surely not been practising your treasonable kindnesses already, Sir Peter?"

De Villars said curtly, "Treasonable—what?"

Ward laughed. "Mrs. Parrish and I were deciding what we might do if some wretched Jacobite appeared at the door, begging sanctuary, and I said my conscience would not allow that I render him up for execution, but that I most probably would have to give the poor fellow what aid I might."

De Villars' mouth twisted. "How very noble," he said sardonically. "And likely accompany the thimble-wit to the block!"

Albinia said nervously that they should not even speak of such matters, but Rebecca persisted. "I suppose there is no doubt what *you* would do in such a situation, Mr. de Villars?"

"None. Any man so stupid as to embrace a cause that was obviously doomed from the start has no business whining when inevitable retribution catches up with him."

"Such strong views," she said with a scornful laugh. "I declare I am impressed—if only by your vehemence. Is it that you are for the House of Hanover, sir? Or do you dislike Rome?"

"I do not relish having a German prince on the throne of England, but even less do I admire impractical dreamers, ma'am! And as for offering up my head to be stuck on a pike on London Bridge, or allowing my limbs to be hacked off before a jeering mob whilst yet I live— Gad! One would have to be an utter gudgeon to invite such a death and thus compound pure folly!"

The soldiers were very close now, with Anthony, tireless, leaping along before them.

"For heaven's sake, do not say anything rash, Becky," Mrs. Boothe implored.

"Excellent advice, ma'am," said de Villars. "Let us have no mention of treasonable sentiments in front of these men." And he called, "Good afternoon, Captain. Lost, are you?"

The young officer reined up and eased his position in the saddle, the men behind him looking with envious eyes at the apparently carefree group. "No, we are not lost. My name is Holt. Have I the honour to address Sir Peter Ward?"

Sir Peter stepped forward. "I am he. Is anything amiss, Captain Holt?"

"I shall let you be the judge, sir. We were obliged to search your house and properties this afternoon. You will find your staff upset. My apologies. Duty is duty."

"Well!" Rebecca exclaimed, indignantly. "I should think—"

"Just so," de Villars interposed. "The man is but following orders, m'dear."

Her angry gaze flashed to him, but his eyes were like shining steel. She felt as though she had been slapped and knew then how dangerous he judged the situation. Her gaze lowered, and she said no more.

De Villars met the captain's hard stare, and he rolled his eyes heavenwards in a long-suffering manner. Holt relaxed slightly and deigned to give him a tight but sympathetic smile.

"We have rebels in the neighbourhood, I take it?" Ward enquired.

"We have been advised several are headed this way, sir. I am sure I need not remind you that they are the King's enemies, thus anyone aiding them becomes as guilty and will be hanged, quartered, and beheaded."

Mrs. Boothe paled and shrank, trembling against Rebecca.

Ward assured the captain that if any Jacobite fugitives were seen, a message would at once be relayed to the authorities.

De Villars watched the troop ride off and said dryly, "There goes a man fairly slathering for promotion."

Patience lisped, "Wha doth quarted mean?"

"It—it means," Mrs. Boothe faltered, "er, put to death, dear. Very cruelly. Oh! Those wretched soldiers have thrown a shadow over our happy day!"

"Never!" argued de Villars. "Nothing could mar this day! Except this great lump that breaks my back! You may become the beast of burden for a while, Ward. She's your kin, after all."

Rather gingerly Sir Peter took the tired child on his shoulders, and Mrs. Boothe walked ahead with him, asking anxious questions about the possibility of desperate fugitives lurking in the vicinity.

De Villars fell into step with Rebecca. "Well, lovely one," he murmured, "now you have seen me at my bucolic best, what say you to a tour through Europe? I've a cosy little villa in—"

"Good God!" she exclaimed with repugnance. "Do you never give up, Mr. de Villars?"

"Never!" He ran a hand through his dishevelled locks, succeeding in restoring very little of neatness. "I will win you yet. When you face the fact that poor Peter can elude the keenest hunter—"

"Oh!" she cried. "*Must* you be so—so crude?"

"Crude? Come now, Mrs. Becky. Why dissemble? You want a rich husband—no?"

"A pretty fool I would be to want a poor one!" She reddened, knowing that had sounded hard and grasping, and amended hurriedly, "I've my son's welfare to think of, after all."

"No, no! Do not soften your candour, beloved. Is what I most admire in you. No gloves, and straight from the shoulder." He chuckled as her lips tightened, and asked idly, "Have you never loved a man for himself?"

She spun on him, infuriated. "Do you fancy me without a heart? You seem to forget I was wed for nigh six years to a gentleman who was not at all rich."

"Not when he died, at least," he amended, cynically.

Rebecca's small jaw sagged. "What . . ." she gasped. "What do you now imply? That *I* frittered away my husband's fortune?"

"No, I'd not thought of that." He asked curiously, "Did you?"

"Oh! Of all the— You are the most— You— *Oh!*" And she ran ahead to walk beside her aunt, despising herself for having, just for a little while this afternoon, begun to entertain kinder feelings towards The Lascivious Libertine.

❧

The afternoon sunlight threw a mellowing glow over the rather stark lines of Ward Marching, for it was almost six o'clock before the picnic party climbed with a trace of weariness up the steps. Sir Peter set Patience down and ushered Mrs. Boothe and her niece into the dim coolness of the interior. "You will do us the honour of remaining for dinner, I hope," he said. "I should have arranged company for you, but—"

"Never mind," put in de Villars. "I did."

Ward stared at him. "Did—what?"

"Arranged company for your guests. Forgot to tell you, old fellow. I was commanded to escort your grandmama up here."

Sir Peter gave a shocked gasp. "You—brought Lady Ward here and *forgot* to tell me?"

"Oh, ecod!" Throwing a hand to his heart, de Villars groaned, "Am I utterly beyond the pale? Never fear, Peter. The old lady was quite fatigued and likely will have enjoyed a peaceful nap." He added with questionable gravity, "But I really do think you had best seek her out now, and—er, mend your fences."

Visibly irked, Ward excused himself and beat a hasty retreat, all but running up the stairs. Mrs. Kellstrand, who had been watching this by-play with an air of amused fondness, shook her head chidingly at de Villars. He called the housekeeper to him, slipped an arm about her slender waist, and engaged her in a brief, low-voiced colloquy. She nodded and led Mrs. Boothe and the muddied children towards the kitchen. De Villars bowed Rebecca to the stairs. She hesitated, but he would not dare attempt anything wicked while Lady Ward was in the house, so she went up with him, resolutely keeping her eyes turned away. When they reached the landing, she forgot, and her eyes met his. He looked far less elegant than she had ever seen him, but her satisfaction over that circumstance was tempered by the awareness that she also must be in sorry disarray.

De Villars smiled in a chastened way, but said a provocative, "Back to the bird sanctuary, eh, lovely one?"

Her lips twitched. She turned sharply away and declared with more vehemence than complete honesty that she was and always had been a bird fancier.

"Lud! I'd not have thought it of you," he said reproachfully. "You and Peter are better matched than I had supposed." He accompanied her along the hall towards an open door and an apparently petrified lackey. "Only one thing for it, m'dear," he went on. "You'll have no choice but to take a hatchet to that cat of yours."

Automatically proceeding as he ushered her across the threshold, Rebecca looked up at him in total indignation. "I shall do no such thing!" she declared angrily. "I'll have you know, sir, I am prodigious fond of Whisky!"

"Oh! My heavens!" exclaimed a horrified female voice. "How very dreadful!"

Stunned, Rebecca jerked her head around. She had supposed she was being taken to a bedchamber so as to refresh herself. Instead, she was entering a lavish saloon all red, white, and gold, occupied by Sir Peter, who looked aghast, and an angular but well-preserved lady of about sixty-five; a modishly gowned lady who was very stiff of manner and patently much shocked.

No less appalled, her cheeks flaming, Rebecca heard a muffled snort from The Monster beside her.

"Never a dull moment," he chortled, *sotto voce.*

Sir Peter had sprung up at their arrival and, faint but ever gallant, said, "M-Mrs. Parrish, I must make you known to my grandmother. Lady Agatha Ward; Mrs. Forbes Parrish."

Rebecca stumbled forward to make her curtsey, and stammer, "I th-think you may have misunderstood, ma'am, but—"

"Not at all, Mrs. Parrish." A lorgnette was raised to an eye of brown agate. "Ward, is this the—er, lady who has so kindly volunteered to guide Prudence?"

"Priscilla, dear ma'am," her grandson corrected gently.

"As you please, but— *Whatever* is that dreadful odour?"

"Patience," Rebecca put in desperately. "And you see, ma'am, it is my cat who is called—"

"*Cat?*" The lorgnette darted about the large room. Unnerved, her ladyship shrilled, "If 'tis not housebroke I shall have no patience whatsoever!"

"Not the cat, ma'am," de Villars put in, grinning from ear to ear. "The little girl."

"Good God! Prudence is not properly trained? Why, she must be four or five years—"

"No, no, Grandmama," Ward began, then turned suddenly frantic eyes to Rebecca. "You did not truly bring your cat here?"

"Of course I—"

"She said distinctly that her cat is responsible for that noxious odour!" Her ladyship's observation was rather muffled as she clapped a tiny, lace-edged square of cambric to her thin nostrils.

His voice almost suspended with laughter, de Villars pleaded, "Peace, my children." He took Rebecca and Sir Peter by the elbows and ushered them to the door, murmuring, "I cannot think when I have been more diverted. Now begone, and I will attempt to clarify matters."

Sir Peter said a grateful, "Good of you, Treve. You always know how to handle her."

"I know how to handle all the ladies." With a quirk of the lip and an audacious wink at Rebecca, de Villars returned to the dowager.

As Ward closed the door, Rebecca heard his grandmother say tartly, "You did not see fit to tell me, Trevelyan, that the widow was such a pretty piece. What a pity she is a tippler. . . ."

Lady Ward proved to be as tyrannical as she was diminutive. That her tall young grandson was under her sway was obvious. He all but trembled when she scolded him, hastened to do her bidding, and strove always to win her approval. The servants were terrified of her, as was Mrs. Boothe, who paled whenever my lady addressed her.

It soon became apparent that the grande dame had no intention of contributing towards the care and nurture of Miss Patience Ashton. She demanded to see the child on the morning after her arrival, and when Patience was conducted into her presence, surveyed her through her lorgnette, pronounced her "a foolish little gel" when Patience began to cry, and summarily dismissed her, not to mention her name again for the duration of her stay in Bedfordshire.

Mrs. Boothe was seldom singled out for attention, a fact that did not in the slightest offend that timid individual. Rebecca, however, was judged to stand in need of instruction on almost everything, and my lady, always willing to share of her vast store of knowledge, gladly undertook the task. On the few occasions when Rebecca was allowed the opportunity to venture an opinion, she managed to be meekly diplomatic, but the effort required to keep her tongue between her teeth, as the saying went, was considerable, partly because she could not like so autocratic a personality, and partly by reason of the faint sneer with which her subdued responses were observed by a certain Wicked Lecher.

De Villars' attitude to Lady Ward was one of amused tolerance. Her tantrums he viewed with indifference and, although he was never less than respectful, it was clear to everyone, including my lady, that he had no intention of allowing her to bully him. Neither did he make any more attempts to continue his unorthodox pursuit of The Little Parrish. He was pleasant to all the ladies, but no more to one than another. He never called at the cottage without Sir Peter's company, and the occasional remarks he addressed to his avowed quarry were models of propriety. Mrs. Boothe was convinced that he had abandoned his evil schemes. Rebecca indulged a guarded optimism.

He might very well, she reasoned, be unwilling to harass her for fear that she call upon the formidable Lady Ward for protection. Almost certainly such a step would result in her immediate return to London, a development that would further the plans of neither of the plotters.

Her own Plan progressed satisfactorily. She was most pleased when Sir Peter took to accompanying her while she led Patience and Anthony on their morning walks. Much of the time was spent in listening to learned ornithological discourses, but often she contrived to change the subject and with a very little effort she was able to set him to laughing merrily, either because of her recounting of some humorous episode involving her brothers or Anthony, or by reason of her rather unconventional views of politics. There was no doubt but that he was becoming much more relaxed and at ease in her company, and Rebecca's hopes rose accordingly.

Despite her acceptance of the current situation, she had seldom been more relieved than when Sir Peter called at the cottage on the fourth morning after his grandmother's arrival and announced that Lady Ward was removing to London.

"She cannot abide Town, you know," he said earnestly. "But in her eyes Bedfordshire is infinitely worse. Her maids are packing now, and she will be leaving within the hour."

"Oh, dear," said Rebecca, jubilant. "Shall you miss her dreadfully, dear sir?"

"No," he answered with a wry smile, "for I am to escort her."

In the act of pouring her guest a cup of tea, Rebecca almost dropped the cup, and had to struggle to keep her voice calm as she asked if he would be long away.

"I cannot say with any degree of assurance. I—there are matters requiring my attention in London, but I shall return at once if you and Mrs. Boothe find it expedient to go back to Town yourselves. I had hoped, however, that you might be able to remain until our Midsummer Ball, at least, by which time I must certainly have found a suitable governess for my cousin."

Rebecca replied that she would have to be guided by her brother's wishes. She waved goodbye with her usual bright smile. Alone, however, she sank onto the sofa in utter dejection. Her Plan had collapsed again, like a house of cards. Not only had she failed to win an offer from Sir Peter, but now he was blithely riding off to the metropolis and all the ladies lying in wait to entrap him, leaving her marooned miles from anywhere, with not a single beau in sight, and nothing more exciting to anticipate than a dashing game of croquet!

"It was Lady Ward's doing," she told her aunt as they sat in the parlour after dinner that evening. "She likely warned Sir Peter it was not at all the thing for two single gentlemen to be here, despite the fact that I am a widow and well chaperoned. So off he has gone leaving us high and dry in this wilderness!"

"But—my love," said Mrs. Boothe, blinking her bewilderment. "If that is how you feel, we can return to Town at once."

Rebecca abandoned the fringe she had been making and walked over to the secretary desk and the letter she had earlier started to write to Snowden. "How can we? Ward advanced us a perfectly ridiculous amount for you to spend a month here, and—"

"A . . . *month?*" gasped Mrs. Boothe, beginning to fan herself feebly. "You said nothing about a month!"

"Well, I—I did not think it would really be that long, and if he had found himself a governess for Patience before the time was up, I knew he would not ask for a refund, so I sent the cheque to Mrs. Falk and instructed her to pay the servants at least a little something." Rebecca put a quivering hand over her eyes and said unsteadily, "You know, dearest, I . . . have felt so dreadful about not paying them in all these weeks."

"Of course you have, my love, and much credit it does you. But—why so gloomy? Perhaps Sir Peter will find a governess tomorrow! I should think there must be hundreds of ladies would jump at the chance to come to so beautiful a home, with a generous employer, and a . . ."—her voice became slightly uneven—"a . . . precious child. . . ."

Rebecca glanced around to catch her aunt in the act of

wiping tearful eyes. "Oh, dear! Another complication! I am scarce surprised. I fancied you were becoming attached to her."

Mrs. Boothe blew her nose delicately. "Is a little darling of a girl, and so exceeding tragic that no one wants her, for she has the sweetest, most giving nature imaginable."

"Yes." Rebecca sighed. "She adores de Villars. One might think he would at least have come down to bid her farewell. . . . But what fustian I talk! Who could expect a charitable impulse from such a one?"

"Good God! Is *he* gone, too?"

"Oh, yes. And not so much as a word. To Patience, I mean. Well"—her nose tilted defiantly—"much we shall miss them. And as for that dreadful old lady, Lud! We will be far happier here alone."

For the next three days she strove to convince herself that the lazy peace of the country was all she could wish for. But on the following morning the sound of hooves on the drivepath sent her running eagerly to the parlour window. Expecting to see Sir Peter's graceful figure, she was surprised when Mr. Melton came into view and dismounted in his deliberate fashion, handing the reins to the stableboy who had run out to him. Even Mr. Melton was welcome in this desert, she decided, as she opened the door without waiting for Evans to perform that service.

He bowed to her, his colour a little heightened, and, entering the parlour, said that he had "chanced to be visiting friends in the neighbourhood" and had dropped by to see how she and her aunt went on. Stifling a smile, Rebecca made him welcome, offered refreshments, which he declined, and in a moment or two reprieved him by suggesting he might like to walk towards the north because her aunt had taken the children to the pond so that Anthony might sail his boat. "I had a letter to finish that has been several days delayed," she explained, indicating the epistle to Snowden, "so I did not accompany them."

Mr. Melton proving not unwilling to go for a walk, Rebecca closed the door behind him and wandered back to the desk.

She had scarcely sat down again than there came another knock on the door. Millie was busied upstairs, and Evans was apparently snoozing somewhere, so once again, Rebecca got up, thinking this the busiest day since the gentlemen had left.

When she opened the door, however, it was to reveal only the broad expanse of the park, with not a human being in sight. Puzzled, she stepped onto the porch and glanced about. To her right, a short distance from the cottage, a basket containing a colourful bouquet of flowers had been left on one of the wooden garden chairs. Her heart lifting, Rebecca ran to take up the card, but there was none. She searched about vainly, then carried the basket into the cottage.

She closed the door, and her heart gave a terrified leap, for two hands came from behind to cover her eyes. "De Villars!" she thought. "And I am all alone!" With a squeak of fear, she dropped the flowers, tore free, and spun around.

CHAPTER
❧ 8 ❧

With one hand upflung to strike, Rebecca checked and cried in surprised relief, "Snow!"

Boothe had drawn back and, his blue eyes alight with laughter, said, "Oho! What a termagant! A fine welcome for your weary traveller!"

She threw herself into his arms and kissed him heartily. "Wretched boy! How you frightened me! I had not expected you for another week and more."

"So I gather!"

Her heart thudded, but the smile was still in his eyes; at least he did not appear enraged. He picked up the basket of flowers and set it on a table and Rebecca went to the sideboard to pour him a glass of the wine that was kept on the silver tray for Sir Peter and de Villars, did they chance to call.

"Are you angered, love?" she asked meekly, and lied, "I'd

not thought you would mind. My aunt and I stay here, quite apart from the main house. She was loath to come alone, so I thought—just for a few days it would be all right."

Boothe settled himself on the sofa, stretched out his long legs and, taking the wine she handed him, sampled it, then gave a beatific sigh. He looked tired, she thought; still, she was inwardly amazed when he shrugged and said he saw nothing improper in her having accompanied her aunt to Ward Marching. "Ward's thoroughly decent, after all, and you are no schoolroom miss."

"True," she agreed quickly. "Besides which, Lady Ward has been here."

"Never say so! That harridan?" He toasted her with a grin that had an element of strain about it. "You've my sympathy, Becky. Is she gone? You must be enjoying the peace, no?"

"Yes. But I cannot like you to be alone in Town."

He laughed. "Falk mothers me. I am occupying your house for a week or two. Hope you've no objection?"

"Of course not." She went over to sit beside him. "Rascal! What are you about? Does some angry papa seek you with blunderbuss in one hand and whip in the other?"

"Never that!" He tugged a ringlet in retaliation. "Give me credit for more finesse, I implore you. 'Tis simply that my flat is being painted, and I'd planned a dinner party, so I made the move."

She pointed out with a dimple that "a dinner party" did not last "a week or two." Snowden laughed loudly, and said she was a rogue and would not be told everything. "Not just yet, at all events," he finished.

He was concealing something. She wondered if he had met his fate at last, and attributed her sinking heart to the fact that she was fairly well aware of his lady friends, and only Letitia Boudreaux, who was not among them, had impressed her as being a suitable wife for the volatile young man.

The important thing, of course, was that he had not only countenanced her stay here, but was actually encouraging her to prolong it. For a fleeting instant she wondered if anything was wrong, but a brisk rapping at the door dispelled that odd little qualm.

She went to answer that peremptory summons, and her earlier fear became justified.

Trevelyan de Villars, a picture of elegance in pale blue velvet, bowed low. "Hail, fairest of the— Oh, dear!" His gaze had slipped past her to encounter Boothe's uptilted chin and stern glare. He stepped over the threshold, nonetheless, and closed the door.

"He will ruin it!" thought Rebecca, but her frantic search for something politic to remark was useless. Her tongue seemed to cleave to the roof of her mouth, and she followed helplessly, glancing with trepidation at her brother's scowl as he came to his feet.

"You came, I presume, sir," drawled Boothe at his coldest, "in search of Ward?"

"Do you really?" With his usual cool effrontery, de Villars sauntered across the parlour. "I suppose I should claim something as asinine, but the fact of the matter is that I came"—he turned to Rebecca with a smile that banished the boredom from his eyes—"to leave this for young Anthony."

He proffered an instrument resembling a small flute.

Taking it, her hand slightly trembling, Rebecca said in a faraway voice, "How kind in you, sir. He will be pleased."

"One can but hope you also will be pleased." He grinned faintly in response to her startled look. "It makes bird calls. I thought 'twould be a pity if he failed to benefit from all the— ah, instruction he has received."

"I most appreciate your kindness to my family," Snowden imparted with frigid formality. "Although my sister is far from home, she is far from being unprotected, though I am sure I need not point that out, de Villars."

Rebecca's heart skipped a beat. Snowden's partiality for this man had obviously undergone an abrupt change when he caught him on the doorstep. De Villars' eyes were gleaming with mockery, and Snow's temper was so quick. . . . She could have wept with relief when Anthony erupted into the room, closely followed by a rosy-cheeked Patience. The little girl went at once to fasten her chubby fingers on de Villars' spotless coat, and with a joyous whoop, Anthony flung himself at his uncle. For a moment all was happy confusion, then Mrs. Boothe came in with George Melton behind her, and more greetings were exchanged.

Almost, Rebecca forgot the menace constituted by Trevelyan de Villars. Glancing to him, she was surprised. His expression was sombre as he watched them; for a moment she almost fancied to see sadness there. Then, he winked, blew her a kiss, and having removed Patience's clasp from the skirts of his coat, slipped quietly outside.

Rebecca drew a breath of relief. The danger was averted. At least, for this time.

₪

"Not kept my eye on her?" His face flushed with indignation, Lord Graham Fortescue faced Boothe across the dining table in his cosy flat and flung his fork ringingly onto the plate of roast beef recently set before him. "If that ain't the outside of enough!" he protested. "You come bursting in here in the middle of m'dinner, snorting, and smoking at the ears, with not a thought for what your mischievous sister has put me through these past two weeks!"

"Dashitall, Forty," Boothe intervened, his face dark with anger. "You know blasted well I'd no choice in having to leave in such a flurry! I asked you, as a friend, to guard her during my absence, and I come back, purely to see if Johnny— Well, never mind that. I come back and find Becky cavorting on Ward's preserves, with—"

"Cavorting on his—what?" Fortescue interrupted, leaning forward curiously.

"His *preserves*, damn you!"

"Oh. No need to be so starchy. I thought you meant she was—"

"Well, I didn't. No thanks to you!"

The butler came in, and conversation languished as Boothe was provided with a plate and various comestibles. His guest satisfied, my lord motioned the butler from the room.

"I'll tell you what it is, Snow," he said soberly. "That girl is a veritable will-o'-the-wisp! There ain't no keeping a check-rein on her, for she's gone before you know she's even thinking on it! And if you cared to ask, you would learn I've spent the past week galloping the length and breadth of the south country, trying to find her! She told her housekeeper she was gone to visit a friend. When she didn't come back after a day or so, I tried to get more out of the woman, and she threw her apron over her head and went into a blubbering that was enough to make any man of sensitivity run for his life!" Fortescue raised a forkful of beef, eyed his friend aggrievedly over it, reiterated his belief that Snowden should have taken Mrs. Rebecca with him, and conveyed meat to mouth.

"Taken her *with* me?" echoed Boothe, his own fork suspended. "Forty, you're wits to let! How the deuce could I have taken her with me? She don't have the wisp of a suspicion why I went trotting up there." A grim look came into his tired eyes. "And what's more, she ain't going to have, can I help it!"

The indignation faded from his friend's mild features. Boothe, his lordship recollected, was in the devil of a dilemma. Not envying him it, he said a soothing, "Well, now she's safe back in Town again. No damage done."

"Oh, no. None. Only—she ain't."

Lord Fortescue goggled at him. "You never *left* her there?"

"Why not?" Boothe evaded his eyes. "Anthony is in alt in the wilderness, and Becky and my aunt reside in a jolly nice little house some distance from the main pile." He sank his teeth into a roast potato and said rather indistinctly, "'Sides, old Ward's a good fellow, as you said. No problem there."

Fortescue mulled over the several warnings that came to mind and, with rare shrewdness, decided there was nothing to be gained by providing fuel for a potentially disastrous fire. Therefore, he replied with only a trace of uncertainty, "No. Well, I'm for Brooks' and some cards. You're more than welcome to stay here tonight, dear old boy."

Snowden thanked him, but declined, saying with a somewhat heightened colour that he had an assignation for the evening and that he was staying in John Street while Rebecca was away. "Never can tell who might break in whilst the knocker's off the door."

They exchanged sober glances. His lordship broke the short silence, exclaiming, "The devil's in it if you're after that titian-haired witchery again! Jove, but I understood she'd set her cap for—"

"Why, that's just it," Boothe interposed with a knowing wink. "So long as her cap ain't set for *me*, there's no danger, eh? And she's a toothsome morsel, Forty. A very toothsome morsel indeed."

His lordship waved his fork and intoned broodingly, "Is a morsel I'd not dare crave. Have a care, Snow!"

Boothe laughed merrily, finished a most excellent supper, and, feeling much restored, parted from his friend in high good humour.

An hour later, seated on a secluded bench in Vauxhall Gardens, the "toothsome morsel" fast clasped in his arms, he claimed a kiss, and chuckled when his lady reached up to straighten the glittering mask she wore, and glanced uneasily along the moonlit path. "Snow," said Mrs. Monahan, pushing him away, "*anyone* might come down here! But no! Behave, you naughty boy!"

"I *am* behaving," he said, pulling her closer. "I'll wager you do not treat de Villars so!"

She stiffened. "Do not mention that creature and his silly wagers! I vow—" She broke off. Behind the mask, her lovely green eyes widened. In some confusion, she urged that they return to the masquerade before they were missed. Boothe, however, was predictably intrigued by both words and attitude. "What wagers?" he asked. "Come on, Rosemary! You cannot dangle the carrot and then back away! What mischief is de Villars about? Something smoky, I warrant. Concerns a lady, eh?"

Affecting agitation, Mrs. Monahan pulled free of his embrace and got to her feet. "I am a total ninny," she confessed, busily straightening her pink domino. "But that I should have let anything slip to you, of all—" And, again, with an irked little exclamation, she broke off and started along the path.

Coming up with her, Boothe caught her arm and drew her to a halt. The laughter was gone from his fine eyes, and a blue glare transfixed her. He said in a harsh voice, "I'm not the quickest brain, ma'am, but I'm more than seven! This concerns my sister Parrish—no?"

The lady uttered a moan of dismay and strove (not very hard) to break free.

Tightening his grip, Boothe grated, "I'll know the whole of it, if you please. Rebecca's far from being up to every move on the board, but she's a good chit, and I'll not have her name bruited about by such a one as Trevelyan de Villars. He engaged in a wager, I take it? With you, ma'am?"

"Of course not! It was with Ward, and— Oh, *now* see what you have made me say! I think you are very clever to take me off stride in that cunning way, but I shall not say another word. However you may seek to trick me." Despite this brave speech, her voice was unsure and a convincing alarm lurked in the green eyes.

Snowden Boothe smiled a grim smile. And blundered deeper into the silken web.

❧

At midnight Brooks' Club was crowded. The card tables were well patronized; a large bet had just been recorded as to whether or not it would rain on Midsummer's Eve, and a noisy discussion was under way in front of the lounge fireplace anent the possibilities of Bonnie Prince Charlie's rallying his followers and essaying another strike against the Crown. In the south corner of the large room, Lord Graham Fortescue smoothed a wrinkle from his silk-clad arm, even as the wrinkles in his brow deepened. Beside him, his usually placid features reflecting anxiety, George Melton muttered, "I fear it is but a matter of time before Boothe hears of it. And when he does—Gad!"

"Of all the caper-witted starts! Who the deuce put it about? De Villars?"

Mr. Melton pursed his lips. "I cannot allow that to be the

case. Whatever one may say of him, he is a gentleman and of unquestionable honour. To put about a rumour such as this is in very poor taste, and—"

"And I'd best come at the root of it before Snow does, or we shall have a— Ah! Here is our man now!" Fortescue waved his handkerchief to a new arrival.

De Villars, elegant as always in a splendid bottle-green coat embroidered in shades of lime and olive, his small clothes impeccable, a great emerald winking amongst the Dresden lace at his throat, turned his quizzing glass upon them, then wandered over. "Hello, Forty," he said with his bored smile. "If you mean to persuade me in the matter of my Arabian, I warn you I'll not sell."

"No, it's a deal more serious than—" His lordship's glance shifted and became dismayed. "No! Now, Snow—" he began, anxiously.

De Villars was seized by the arm and wrenched around. His face distorted with rage, Snowden Boothe snarled, "I mislike your wagers, sir!" And with one well-placed fist, he knocked de Villars down.

❧

The morning air was warm and fragrant, the birds sang blithely, the bees buzzed about their eternal collecting, and Rebecca hummed as she wandered among the rose bushes, basket on arm and a fair-sized bouquet already cut. Two days had passed since Snowden had come and gone. Two quiet, balmy days. A little dull, but Anthony, bless him, was having the time of his life and already looked less frail, and Patience, whom he privately stigmatized as being a millstone around his neck, trotted after him with total adoration, as sweetly enduring his superior attitude as her name might imply, and perhaps sensing that the boy secretly enjoyed her companionship. Her devotion was not without peril. She had twice fallen into the pond and only yesterday had become petrified with fear, having clambered up a tree after him, so that a groom had been summoned to climb up and retrieve her. Neither of the ladies was greatly alarmed by such escapades. Any small girl growing

up with older children was subjected to such risks, and seldom
the worse for them. Rebecca could not but wonder, however,
what Sir Peter might have said had he seen the little girl
stranded in the tree. He was such a decorous person. De Villars,
now . . . She smiled. That Wretched Rake would shrug a
disinterested shoulder and drawl that it would do the brat
good; and then keep an eagle eye on her to ensure she did not
fall! And—good heavens—why should she ascribe such kindly
impulses to the man? Her smile faded, and the hand outstretched to the red rose paused. Her feelings for de Villars
were changing. Why that should be so was more than—

"Rebecca! Oh, thank heaven I have found you!"

Letitia ran to her across the lawns. Rebecca had never
seen her other than calm, poised, and fully in command of herself. Now, the breath was hurried, the gentle voice agitated,
and tears glinted on the long lashes. "I came . . . just as
quickly as I could." Miss Boudreaux's lips trembled pitifully.
"Your—your brother—" But she could not continue and
gripped Rebecca's outstretched hand, while her tears overflowed.

Rebecca felt chilled. "Snow?" she said in a breathless
voice. "Has there been an accident?"

"No. But . . . I am so frightened! I tried and tried to stop
them, but it is useless. And—and if they meet . . ." Again, her
words were suspended by a choked sobbing.

Trying to control her own terrors, Rebecca put an arm
about this unexpected visitor and led her to a stone bench. "Sit
down for a minute, and then I shall take you to the cottage for a
nice cup of tea. My poor dear, you are white as a sheet.
There—that is better. I fear I can guess what has happened.
Snowden has—has got himself involved in a duel
with . . . someone?" Letitia nodded, teardrops scattering.
Dreading the answer, Rebecca asked, "Is it—with your cousin,
de Villars?" Again, that convulsive nod. Rebecca closed her
eyes, fear gripping her heart with fingers of ice.

"I am so sorry," gulped Letitia. "I never thought I
would . . . would give way like this." She dried her eyes with a

hand that shook. "I was all right, driving up here. But—oh! If I should . . . lose . . . both of them!" She began to tear at the fine cambric and lace of her handkerchief.

Rebecca thought in a numb, detached fashion, "So she does love Snow. Poor girl. She has no least chance with him!" Impatient with such digressions, she said, "I'll admit I had feared that. Do you know how it happened? But I suppose you could not—gentlemen are so ridiculously secretive about their savageries."

Letitia gripped her hands tightly, as though striving to overcome her emotions. "I was not meant to know," she quavered. "Indeed, I discovered it quite by accident. I chanced to encounter my brother when I was leaving a dinner party last night. He was coming out of Brooks' Club, and detached me from my friends, saying he had something to discuss with me. He walked home beside my chair, but said nothing other than the merest commonplaces. I was never more astonished than when he took me to the front door and said his goodnights. When I asked him what it was he had wished to speak about, he gave me some nonsensical answer about having a lot of work to do." The troubled grey eyes lifted; Miss Boudreaux said earnestly, "Fitz is Chaplain to the Duchess of Waterbury. She is the dearest old thing and has never made the least demand of him that would cause him to work late at night."

"Did you tax him with it?"

"No, for he seemed to brighten, and went off quite cheerfully. I went to bed and tried to read, but I could not overcome the fear that something was very wrong. At last, I put on my dressing gown and went downstairs, meaning to send a note round to Trevelyan and ask him to call on me. You can imagine my surprise when I went into the drawing room and found Fitz in there with my cousin. I was so astonished that I stood quite still without speaking for a moment. They had not heard me come in, and by the time I collected my wits, I had heard enough to know what was about." Her hands wrung. Biting her lip, she scanned Rebecca's intent face, then faltered, "You— you will not like what I must tell you. It seems de Villars had made a—a very vulgar wager with—with someone regarding . . . yourself."

"Good . . . God! And Snow learned of it?"

"Yes. He was incensed. I'll own he had every right. He rushed to Brooks' and—and—"

"Knocked de Villars down, unless I mistake it!"

Letitia nodded.

Struggling to sound calm, Rebecca asked, "When do they meet? De Villars must have choice of weapons. Heaven grant he did not choose pistols?"

"Swords," Letitia said dully. "They meet early tomorrow morning. That much I heard before they saw me, else I would not have learned of it, but—" She gave a cry of alarm and threw her arms around Rebecca. "Oh, my poor soul! You are faint. Rest here, and I will run for assistance."

"No." Rebecca managed a wan smile. "I am better now. It is only—my husband was . . . was killed in a duel."

Appalled, Miss Boudreaux stared at her, then bowed her head into her hands. "My God! Oh, my God!"

There was a heavy silence. Letitia sat down again and each was lost in her own apprehensions. With devastating clarity a face came into Rebecca's mind's-eye. Not her brother's handsome features, but the cynical mockery of Trevelyan de Villars. As unwanted, and as clearly, she saw him laughing as they had played bat and ball that happy day—just last week. And his so different expression when they had been walking home across the fields; he had looked younger, happier . . . with little Patience held on his shoulder and his thick hair all rumpled and askew because of the clutch she'd had on it.

Turning on her companion she said fiercely, "How *dare* they do this to us! Had your horrid cousin a vestige of decency he might have made an attempt to apologize!"

"He did! I swear. When I had learnt as much as I was able, I was frantic and flung every accusation imaginable at him. He said nothing until I was done. But I had shaken him, for then he snarled at me that he *had* apologized, in front of all the gentlemen in Brooks'! And my brother said that Treve had told your brother not only that he was fully to blame, but that he would not meet him. I gather Mr. Boothe remarked to the effect that Treve *had* to meet him because he had knocked him down, and—oh, you know my cousin's way! Treve laughed, and said he fancied *his* reputation would survive. Mr. Boothe likely thought he was being insulted, and flew into a passion and—and struck Treve again. Treve had been lifting his glass, and the wine splashed all over him. There was—*nothing* he could do after that . . . don't you see?"

Rebecca knew this to be truth. No gentleman could refuse a meeting once he had been struck. But, struggling against that admission, she exclaimed, "Stuff! He is an experienced duellist, and not only a finer swordsman, but *years* older than Snow! He—"

"Four," sniffed Letitia, dolefully.

"He could have—" Her attention arrested, Rebecca said, "What? Only *four?* But I had thought . . ."

"I know. Trevelyan looks older than five and thirty. I fancy it is because . . . oh, never mind that. Mrs. Parrish, whatever are we going to do? If Mr. Boothe dies . . ." She pushed back her hair in distracted fashion. "Or—if my cousin . . . Dear God! What are we to *do?*"

"It must not happen," thought Rebecca. "Neither of them must die." She said slowly, "I think I may know how to stop them." She stood, and Letitia sprang up, searching her set, pale face with new hope.

Rebecca smiled at her; a calm smile, having behind it a budding and highly dramatic scenario for the resolving of this deadly predicament. She took the other girl's arm. "It is time for that cup of tea."

ଈ

Opening the door of the impressive house on Berkeley Street, the equally impressive butler said in mild surprise, "Miss Letitia! Dear me. The master dines from home this evening, and Cook has not—"

Rebecca was startled by such presumption, but Letitia recognized it for one of her cousin's diversionary tactics and, suspecting Treve had left instructions that she was to be denied admittance if possible, said breezily, "That is perfectly all right, Linscott, we will wait." The butler blinked but necessarily retreated as she ushered Rebecca into the foyer, while asking, "Is my cousin from home?"

"He is upstairs, miss. Changing into his evening dress."

The girls exchanged a quick, relieved glance.

Letitia said with assumed lightness, "I've a small surprise for Mr. de Villars. Would you please ask that he come down for a moment? Oh—pray do not mention I have a friend with me."

The butler, a gentleman with a balding head, a kind heart, and four young daughters, slanted an oblique glance at the friend in question and thought her one of the loveliest confections he'd ever laid eyes on. Whatever the surprise, it could not be too outlandish. Therefore, allowing his professionally disdainful features to relax into something reminiscent of a smile, he said, "As you say, miss." And having sent a footman scurrying to light candles in the book room, he made his own sedate way up the stairs.

Going with Letitia towards the rear of the house, Rebecca glanced about in no little surprise. She had expected a comfortable flat. The size, location, and magnificence of this abode did not at all equate with the polite penury in which she had imagined de Villars to exist. The matter was of little importance, however, besides which, many gentlemen hovering on the brink of financial disaster still contrived to appear very well to pass. She turned her thoughts to the crushing urgencies of the moment. Her plan to avert the threatened duel had seemed so cut and dried when she had conceived it in the gardens of Ward Marching. She had known this morning exactly how she would handle the situation. But now, it did not seem cut and dried at all. Now it loomed as a frightful ordeal, and her knees shook so at the thought of what she must say to The Murderous Wretch that she was inclined to think she would swoon long before she said anything at all.

The sun was going down, but, obedient to Rebecca's request, Letitia blew out all but one branch of candles in the large, comfortable book room.

"Am I tidy?" Rebecca asked urgently. "If your cousin finds one least thing to sneer at, I shall be quite undone!"

There was nothing at all to sneer at, Letitia judged, scanning her critically. On returning to Town, they had gone first to John Street, where she had begrudged the time it had taken for Rebecca to change her clothes. Now, she could appreciate the strategy of it. The little widow looked very lovely in the wide paniered gown of blue silk, with Brussels lace foaming beneath the deep scallops of the overskirt and at the elbows; a simple rope of pearls about her throat, and her curls powdered and piled high on her head. What gentleman could fail to be enchanted by so fragile and appealing a lady in distress? Especially a gentleman already captivated. Whether it was Rebecca's intent to dazzle or denounce her cousin, she had no least notion, for beyond saying that she would try to bring them all off safely, Rebecca had refused to divulge her plan.

Admiring her courage, Letitia also knew her cousin, and thus said, "You look adorable, dear ma'am. I know not what you mean to do, but—but Treve has something of a temper, and if he is still in the humour that he was last evening, I fear—oh, I *dare* not leave you alone with him!"

"You must. I thank you for your concern, but if you stayed I would be too nervous to say a word." Rebecca darted a glance to the door. "He *will* come? If he does not wish to talk with you, might he not just go out and—"

De Villars's voice, upraised in exasperation, put an end to her worries.

"Linscott? Where in the *deuce* have you hidden Miss Boudreaux?"

Rebecca grabbed weakly at the chair beside her, and her knees fairly knocked together.

"Oh!" Letitia paled, and ran to a door at the rear of the room. Glancing back, she cried distractedly, "You are quite sure . . . ?"

"Yes! Yes! Hurry!"

The door closed, and Rebecca was alone. She bit her knuckles, subdued a panicked impulse to run away, and made herself stand very still, praying de Villars would not notice in this dim light that she was much too small of stature to be his cousin.

She heard a quick, firm tread in the hall and closed her eyes, drawing a deep breath.

The door was flung open.

"Where in the devil have you been, Letitia? Uncle Geoff has—"

Trevelyan de Villars, striking in blue and silver, stalked to face her, broke off, and recoiled. The very sight of his shocked disbelief lent Rebecca courage. Her chin tossing higher, she said scornfully, "Does the sight of me cause you to know guilt, sir? Lud, one scarce could wonder at it!"

He seemed momentarily too stunned to reply. Then he went over to swing the door closed, and returned to bow low before her. "You honour my home with your presence, ma'am," he said, pulling up a chair for her.

Rebecca ignored the gesture, continuing to stand with head high, and eyes blazing with contempt. "I am not come for a sociable cose, Mr. de Villars."

"What a pity. I should like that of all things. But—since it is not proper for you to be here at all, I cannot but wonder why you *are* come."

"You know very well! Oh, never look so innocent, sir! It ill becomes you!"

De Villars leaned back against the desk, folded his arms, and regarded her with the vestige of a frown. It was almost dark outside, but the candlelight fell upon his face, and Rebecca saw that one side of his mouth was cut and swollen. She thought, "Snowden struck hard!" and strove unsuccessfully to feel triumphant.

"I admit that I can think of only one thing that would bring you to my house in such headlong fashion," he said thoughtfully. "But it is beyond belief that even so careless a fribble as Boothe would have told you of—"

"Of your contemptible wager?" she put in, her voice sharp with disgust. A flush darkened his cheeks, and she went on, "Well, he did not! I learnt of your reprehensible conduct from—another source."

"Did you now? And—er, dare one enquire as to the nature of that knowledge?"

"I know that you have fouled my name abominably!"

"Yes." He stood straighter. "I have apologized to your brother, and I now apologize to you, most sincerely. Although, you know, lovely one," he added musingly, "I never made any secret of my hopes, or of how desirable I find you."

"Your hopes were disgraceful, sir! And I did not dream you meant to bandy my name about! To make me the—the laughing-stock of all London!"

"No more I did," he denied with a touch of anger. "Only two gentlemen were involved in the conversation, and—"

"A conversation in which I was discussed as though I were a piece of Haymarket ware!" The sudden dance of laughter in his eyes told her that she had rushed into another impropriety, and she hastened to add with assumed regret, "I had not thought you so base, Mr. de Villars."

He bowed. "You are very good, ma'am. And I am more than grateful that you endow me with godlike qualities. But— you must not. I am, alas, full of faults, and not above entering into a stupid and tasteless wager concerning a very lovely lady. Nonetheless, I would have you believe that same wager was a private matter. Knowledge of it should have gone no further than the two of us. That it did was—"

"That it did," she intervened stormily, "indicates your crass friend to have been incapable of even so small a vestige of chivalry as to have kept his tongue between his teeth! Be so good as to give me his name, sir, in order that I may thank him."

De Villars became absorbed with straightening the lace at his cuff. "I think you know him not at all," he said slowly. "But I assure you that he *is* a gentleman, and was aghast when he learnt of this."

"When he *learnt?* Did he not *know* what he had done?"

His eyes lifted to hers, a faint, quirkish grin curving his mouth. "Again, my thanks, dear lady. I take it you had not considered that *I* might have been the one so indiscreet as to have gossiped it abroad."

She was confused, because that notion had *not* occurred to her. "True. But you will forgive me if I fail to be grateful for that, when my dear brother lies dead at your feet!"

De Villars' head jerked up, and sudden wrath lit his eyes. He said impatiently, "My God! Did the young fool tell you of our meeting also? I wonder he does not publish the entire affair in *The Spectator!*"

"Do not seek to lay the responsibility for this ugliness in Snowden's dish! Had you not made your revolting and ill-judged wager in the first place, my brother's life might not now be at stake!"

"Jupiter! What a Cheltenham tragedy you enact me! I own the fault, but for Lord's sake, child, do you fancy I mean to kill your brother over so trite a thing?"

"*T-trite?*" she exploded, her eyes wide with rage.

He gestured his irritation and, with one hand lightly resting on the hilt of his dress sword, paced across the room, saying, "Stupid, then. Vulgar, crude, vainglorious, if you will. But not vindictive, ma'am! Oh, do not mistake—I've no thought to mitigate my guilt, but if vindictiveness was brought to bear, it was in the heart of the lady who wheedled out the tale, deliberately embellished it, and carried it to where it was sure to cause the most harm!"

"A charming lady, indeed," she said acidly.

"Most charming," he reiterated, pausing to fix her with a level gaze. "But she chances to have a score to settle. With me."

"Which offers me a wide assortment from which to choose, I fancy."

His frown eased into a grin. "*Touché*. And you have my pledge that the lady in question will breathe not another word in the matter."

"Oh, my! You—you never mean to—"

"What else?" Her obvious trepidation restored the sardonic gleam to his eyes. "I shall visit her tonight, take her lovely neck and choke the life from her, and then bury her 'neath the floorboards."

Her chin went up. She said, "How can you jest at such a

moment? Have you no understanding of what this means to me?"

"I understand that you are saddled with a hot-headed young fool for a brother, who, having come upon an admittedly vexing rumour, chose not to handle it with tact, but to bungle it into a full-fledged scandal. But I do not hold that against you, I assure you."

Rebecca gasped, "You—you do not hold it . . . against . . . *Oh!* You are—"

"Dastardly, dishonourable, and depraved," he supplied helpfully.

She stamped to him, her small jaw set. And with her nose under his chin, she ground out, "I fail to find it laughable that my beloved brother might be slain in just such another ridiculously 'honourable' confrontation as that which killed my husband!"

His hands went out at once to clasp her arms. A tender sympathy banished the mirth from his face. "Now may God forgive me! I'd not considered this." He gathered her to him very gently and, stroking her hair, murmured, "Poor, sweet girl. How you must have worried."

Hate and rage melted away. Rebecca clung to him, her eyes blurring with tears, and whispered, "I knew it! I knew that—if you cared for me as you claimed, you could not serve me so."

De Villars was quiet for a moment. Then he put her from him and gazed into her dewy eyes and pale cheeks; at the tremulous, sweetly curved mouth, and resolute little chin. Truly, an adorable creature, The Little Parrish. A small pucker tugging at his brows, he asked, "What would you have me do?"

"Draw back! Oh, I know it would be difficult, but—"

"*Au contraire.* It would rather be quite impossible, m'dear." He removed Rebecca's gripping hands from his ruined cravat. "I am sorrier than I can say for having triggered this deplorable fiasco, but I cannot in honour draw back."

Despite the quietness of the words, his eyes were bleak, his face set and cold. Rebecca swallowed an instinctive denunciation. If she was to win, she must use all her feminine wiles;

rage would serve her not at all. And so she stepped even closer, until her skirts brushed his legs. Clasping her hands prayerfully before her, she pleaded, "Treve . . . I beg you. I *beg* you. You said you did not mean to kill him, and I believe that. But Snow is a fine swordsman. What if he pushes you so hard you have no choice? My papa used to say that in any duel, however little death may be considered, there is a high element of risk, and tragedy can strike too swiftly to be averted."

He shook his head, and said with a calm smile, "Extreme unlikely, I promise you. Try to accept that I've been out before, ma'am. I know what I'm about."

"I do know that, but . . . were I bereft for a second time . . . I think I would die. . . ."

He watched her with a speculative expression. "I would do all in my power for you, my little lovely thing. But—"

Swaying towards him, she interposed tremulously, "You— you once said . . . you desire me. . . ."

The grey eyes narrowed. He pulled her to him. "You—are *serious?* You really offer yourself to save that young idiot?"

"I love him," she said simply.

His arms whipped around her. She was crushed so tight she could scarce breathe. His eyes glowing, he bent to her. With surprisingly little effort, she forced her arms to go around his neck, and wondered with an odd remoteness if it would hurt his bruised mouth when he kissed her.

But a new and very different emotion was in his eyes.

Rebecca stiffened, bristling.

De Villars uttered a muffled snort, tottered to the desk, leaned there, and burst into laughter.

Outraged, crouching, yearning to feel the handle of a sturdy axe between her hands, she panted, "Rake! Deplorable—wicked—evil—*lecher!*"

"My—my apologies . . . dearest girl," he gulped, between whoops. "But—but it was . . . so deliciously melodramatic! *What* a . . . villain you judge me! Oh, how good old Will Shakespeare would have . . . loved it!"

All but incoherent with frustrated fury, she managed, "Oh! If I but—had a—a pistol! You are . . . vile! *Vile!*"

"Beyond all doubting. And—there is a pistol in the drawer, yonder."

Running around the desk, Rebecca tore at the top drawer so violently that it flew out, sending the contents over the floor and de Villars into new howls of mirth. Her second attempt was more successful. She snatched up the large horse pistol she found, and aimed it with both hands.

Wiping tears from his eyes, de Villars groaned, "Shoot straight, sweeting, and my troubles are over. But—your brother will not love you for't."

The thought of what Snowden would say made her blood run cold. "Beast! If you but *knew* how I hate you, de Villars!"

"Hatred," he wheezed, sagging weakly against the desk, "is akin to love, so they say. Only think, Little Parrish, how you will grieve if tomorrow morning I am doomed to lie stretched on the greensward." He placed one hand on his chest and intoned theatrically, "'Come away, death, and in sad cypress let me be laid;/Fly away, fly away, breath: I am slain by a fair, cruel maid.'"

"Grieve? *Grieve*, is it? You are fair and far out there! I should rejoice!"

He mopped at his eyes. "And yet, I live. 'The lady doth protest too much, methinks.'"

"*Loathsome!*" she shrieked and, flinging the pistol at him, ran to the door and along the hall. Not staying for her cloak, she sped through the front door that an astonished lackey flung open, and was down the steps and in the street in a trice. Vaguely, she was aware that de Villars was shouting, and in a moment the lackey sprinted ahead and called up a passing chair. Panting her thanks as he assisted her inside, she snatched the cloak and reticule he offered, and was borne off to John Street.

She wept all the way, but regrettably not one tear was shed for her brother's predicament. Rebecca's tears rather were of rage and humiliation.

CHAPTER
❧ 9 ❧

*I*n view of the activities planned for the following dawn, Rebecca was sure that Snowden would not be late home. He had said he was occupying her house, and Mrs. Falk confirmed this. The good housekeeper was horrified by Rebecca's woebegone appearance and when, as the due of an old family retainer, she was told the reason behind her mistress's headlong journey back to Town, she shed a few tears of her own. Rebecca was fussed over, coddled, and every effort bent towards making her comfortable and lightening her spirits. Having changed gratefully into a nightdress and a pink wrapper that was a cloud of gauze and lace, she went down to the snug parlour, ate a light supper from a tray, and determined to await her brother's return. When she heard voices in the hall an hour later, she was sure Snowden had arrived, and was surprised when Letitia Boudreaux burst into the room and tripped down the steps, hands outstretched and an expression of stark tragedy on her lovely face.

"Oh, Lud!" moaned Rebecca, standing to greet her. "What now?"

"Treve told me what happened," Letitia answered, allowing Mrs. Falk to take her cloak and bonnet. And when the door closed behind the housekeeper, she went on, "I wonder you did not strangle the unfeeling brute."

Rebecca showed her guest to a chair by the fire and sat down again. "I nigh shot him! You will never know how close I came to pulling the trigger! I panted—I positively *yearned* to pull it!"

"I am only astounded you did not," said Letitia, betraying no least concern at these murderous inclinations towards a cousin of whom she was deeply fond. "To laugh in your face—I heard him!—when you must have been nigh distracted with anxiety!"

"He said," Rebecca uttered broodingly, "that it was deliciously melodramatic! And that Will Shakespeare would have loved it!"

"The beast! Whatever did you say?"

"I told him he was vile, and—and heaven knows what else."

"Very right! Did he cower?"

"Cower! He roared! He laughed so much he could scarce stand."

"Monster!"

Rebecca nodded, but a dimple peeped beside her red mouth, and she said with what Snowden called her pixie look, "It *was* rather delicious, now that I come to think on it. Especially when I offered myself to him if he would only spare my brother."

Her eyes as big as saucers, Letitia gasped, "You—oh! You *never* did!"

"Yes. That is when he seized me and crushed me to his breast. And—" She frowned suddenly. "And I thought he was going to smother me with burning kisses."

"D-didn't he?" breathed Letitia, awed.

"No. That's when he sort of—snorted, and began to laugh, the wretch!"

"There is but one answer—he must be demented. But, what shall you do now?"

"I mean to try and reason with my brother, and if—"

The door burst open, and Snowden came into the room, still clad in his ball dress, and with a look of anxious anticipation on his handsome features. He checked when he saw Miss Boudreaux and his sister, and his expression changed to one of rather comical dismay. "Hello, hello," he said hollowly. "What's all this? Thought you was entrenched in your pastoral paradise, love?" He crossed to drop a kiss on his sister's cheek and say a polite, "Good evening, Miss Boudreaux."

"I—I trust, sir," Letitia stammered, blushing furiously as she shook hands with him, "that you do not find my presence here repugnant."

He stared at her. "Repugnant?" The candlelight was playing softly on her face. It was a very pretty face, he thought, mildly surprised that he had not noticed that fact before now, and the dusty blue gown she wore became her admirably. Pity she was so tall. . . . "Why on earth would I think so shatter-brained a thing?"

She gave a helpless gesture. "My—my cousin."

"Who? Oh—de Villars! Well, even were he an ogre, I'd scarce allow that to turn me against a very charming lady."

Miss Boudreaux was spared betraying her total confusion by the return of Mrs. Falk with a tea tray. The housekeeper's emotions were so overset when she saw Boothe that the plate of biscuits went into Miss Boudreaux's lap, and by the time they had recovered from that small contretemps, they were on easier terms.

Boothe declined the offer of refreshments and, when he had comforted the housekeeper and watched her sniff her way from the parlour, he went to the sideboard to pour himself a glass of wine. "Poor Falk," he murmured in amusement. "Her wits are wandering tonight."

"No, how can you say that, Snow?" said Rebecca reproachfully. "'Tis only that she dotes on you, and worries—as do we all."

Boothe's hand checked briefly in the act of setting down the decanter. "Worries?" he said, a shade too innocently, as he wandered to the fireplace. "Now what have I been about to disturb you gentle creatures?"

"There is no need to dissemble," said Rebecca with severity. "When first you came in, I could tell you was disturbed. And I've no doubt Miss Boudreaux could, as well."

He directed an apprehensive glance at the quiet visitor. "I fancy you are at your make-believe again, miss! If I was worrying about anything, which I ain't, I'd certainly not wish to bore a guest with it."

"Oh, Letitia knows all about it," said Rebecca.

Boothe paled. "She—does? Good God! Is *that* why you come romping home, then? Of all the caper-witted things to do, you must be—" He broke off, a wary light coming into his eyes. "Knows about—what?"

Rebecca sprang up, and stamped her little foot at him. "Oh, *Snowden!* How can you be so provoking? Your *duel*, of course! I came just as soon as I heard of it."

Boothe's taut features relaxed. "Oh, the duel! Why would you come home for that? I've been out before."

"Am I not to be concerned when my dear brother's life is thrown into such fearful jeopardy?" she cried, indignantly. "A fine stone-heart you fancy me! And poor Miss Boudreaux is as distraught as am I!"

Boothe's quick glance to Letitia was met by eyes that shyly lowered, while a flush again crept becomingly up her white throat and into her pale cheeks. He crossed to her chair and said kindly, "You must not worry so, ma'am." He bestowed his charming smile on her. "De Villars is far more likely to pink me than I am to run him through, I do assure you."

Miss Boudreaux did not appear consoled by this reassurance. Her eyes flew up again, so filled with anguish that an odd little flutter disturbed Boothe's hitherto untouched heart, and he was seized by a foolish wish that some of this pretty girl's anxiety might have been for himself.

Letitia said in a low, husky voice, "I should be . . . most grieved if—if *either* of you was to be hurt, Mr. Boothe."

He smiled down at her, making a mental note that he must call on her tomorrow.

Rebecca, meanwhile, had been seized by a notion of her own. "Snow," she said with marked suspicion, "if you was not worrying about the duel when you came in—what caused you to look so put about?"

For a moment, absorbed by the lovely face turned so anxiously up to him, he made no answer, then, recollecting himself, he said hurriedly, "What? Oh—well, I was, of course. But I—er, didn't think you knew of it, and— How the deuce *did* you learn of it?"

"Miss Boudreaux overheard her cousin speaking of the duel, and came at once to me."

"Oh, well, that's all right, then." He resumed his contemplation of Miss Boudreaux. "I regret if my calling out your cousin has caused you pain, ma'am. But—ladies must be protected from dishonour, y'know."

Entranced, Letitia breathed, "Indeed, I quite understand your gallantry, sir. Though I cannot suppose my cousin to have intended . . ." Her words trailed off and for a long moment they regarded one another, while Rebecca looked hopefully at the silent interchange.

"I must tell you," Miss Boudreaux went on dreamily, "that Trevelyan was most disturbed to learn that word of his wicked wager had leaked out. He did not dream the other gentleman would be so—unwise."

Boothe slanted a glance at his sister. "Did de Villars tell you with whom he made the wager?"

Mistakenly thinking the question intended for herself, Rebecca shook her head. "He said I do not know the man, but—"

"He—*what?*" thundered Boothe, his brows jerking into a black bar above his nose. "You—*went to* de Villars?"

"Oh . . ." stammered Rebecca. "I—er, I—that is—"

"You went to *beg* for my life!" Boothe raged, his tones vibrating the prisms on the candelabra. "By God, girl! Are you gone *daft* to interfere in an affair of honour? I can well imagine the Cheltenham tragedy you enacted him!" He began to pace up and down the room, quite forgetting Letitia's presence, and driving one fist angrily into his palm, groaned, "I shall never be able to hold up my head again! Never! Lord! How de Villars must have laughed!"

All too aware of how The Villain had laughed, Rebecca bit her lip and sought desperately for something to say that would mitigate her heinous offense.

Watching the man of her heart, Letitia's calm good sense returned. She dropped gracefully to her knees, clasped her hands, and gazed up at Boothe. "Then you shall be able to laugh together, sir. For it is in just such a cause I am come here tonight."

"Dear . . . heaven!" yelped Boothe, cringing away. "No—no, ma'am! This will not do! Please allow me to help you up."

Instead, she reached out, saying piteously, "Sir, I beg of

you. Abandon this madness! I love my cousin deeply. If you feel he has offended—as indeed I fear he has—then settle it with your fists. In a boxing ring, dear sir! Not with cold steel! I *implore* you!"

The unhappy Boothe tore out his handkerchief and began to mop at his brow. "Oh, Gad! This is awful! Oh, burn it all . . . Rebecca, for mercy's sake, make her get up!" Meeting his sister's adamantine look, he wailed, "Ma'am—Miss Boudreaux . . . I cannot bear it! Please—*please* get up!"

"I will gladly do so," sighed Letitia, "if you will only give me your word not to persist with this murderous folly."

He ran a hand through his already wildly disordered locks. "I *cannot!* Surely you must understand that—"

Lord Graham Fortescue, also in full ball dress, rushed in. "He is here then," he cried eagerly, then recoiled with a gasp as he took in the dramatic scene.

"Forty!" exclaimed Boothe with unmitigated relief.

"Wrong house!" squeaked his lordship, deserting.

"Wait!" cried Boothe, anguished.

"Sorry!" The word was flung over the shoulder of the vanishing craven.

In hot pursuit, Boothe tore after him.

"Snow!" called Rebecca, but her angry attempt to stay him was doomed. Pale and perspiring, Boothe dodged around her, took the steps in one wild leap, and was gone. "I shall wait up!" she shrilled after him.

"Oh, dear," sighed Letitia, climbing to her feet. "I suspect he is in full flight, Rebecca. He'll likely not come home at all, for fear we might follow him to the duelling ground."

Stamping her foot, Rebecca said, "How wretched they are! He is just as bad as de Villars! I wash my hands of them! Let them have their silly duel!"

"Well—we tried, at least."

"And failed miserably. Here, let me pour you some fresh tea."

Letitia accepted the cup and sat down again. Stirring her tea, she said, "Oh, I don't know. I have heard that Mr. Boothe is a splendid swordsman, but—forgive me—I hold my cousin to be the greater menace."

"In every sense," Rebecca agreed gloomily. "But I do thank you, for you were superb in your little drama."

"Was I?" asked Letitia eagerly. "I own I had hoped I might be doing quite passably."

"Passably!" Rebecca giggled suddenly. "Did you not see Snowden's face? And—and poor Graham Fortescue! Were ever two men so totally petrified?"

They burst into laughter, but in a moment the merry peals faded and they eyed one another askance.

Rebecca said contritely, "How dreadful of us to laugh so when—when in the morning . . . We must be very wicked, I think."

"Perhaps, but the gentlemen do not seem in the slightest concerned."

"No. But gentlemen have so little sense when it comes to duelling and wars and such."

"No less than I! Do you know, dear Mrs. Parrish, that I have been here all this time, and never told you the real reason I came? I dare to think Trevelyan's guns are rather soundly spiked, ma'am. I made him promise me faithfully that he would neither kill nor gravely wound your brother."

Rebecca leaned out to clasp her hand. "How good you are. Do you think he will keep his word?"

Letitia's brows arched. "I have never known him to break it."

"My apologies. I meant no offence." Rebecca sighed. "It is something, for which we must be grateful."

Letitia was silent, staring rather blankly at the tea cosy. "I only hope," she murmured uneasily, "that in attempting to spare your brother, Treve may not himself fall."

Three hours later, Rebecca leapt up in bed, her heart thundering, and with those ominous words echoing in her ears. Panting for breath, she lay back down again, staring wide-eyed at the canopy high above her. It was ridiculous, of course. A bad dream merely. Snowden would not do anything really dreadful, even if given the chance. Yet she could hear again de Villars' odious voice, so full of laughter, "'Come away, death . . . I am slain by a fair, cruel maid.'"

The picture of him, stretched bloody and dying at her brother's feet, would not be banished. She did not sleep again.

≥ঌ

The skies began to lighten shortly after four o'clock, and by five the heavens glowed faintly pink; a luminous pink, as delicate as clear jade, with not a cloud to mar it. The air was cool, full of the fragrance of hedge roses, and wet grass, and trees from which the dew dripped softly. The birds were beginning to twitter, their pure voices the only sounds to disturb the sylvan silence save for the hushed conversation between two young men who stood at the edge of the clearing, cloaks close drawn against the chill. One of these, very tall, wore a tricorne over his powdered hair. He sneezed, and raised his handkerchief, and his cloak fell open to reveal the simple stock and dark garb of a clergyman. The other man, not above middle height, wore a moderate wig whose loose curls framed a lean face, marked by laugh lines at the corners of the green eyes. Well-shaped lips that could curve swiftly to an impudent grin were set now, his intent regard fixed on a third man some distance off.

"Look at him," muttered Viscount Horatio Glendenning. "All business, as usual. Treve fights so well because he never makes the mistake of setting his opponent's worth too cheap, or failing to inspect the ground. This is how he was when he met Kadenworthy. Lord, what a battle that was! I made sure Treve would fall! Matter of fact, I lost two hundred guineas on it!"

Shocked, the Reverend FitzWilliam Boudreaux exclaimed, "But you was his second, I thought!"

"Was." His lordship's grin flashed. "I did not *wish* that he should fall, you understand, Fitz. Purely a matter of odds. Didn't think Treve had a chance—not against Kadenworthy. Of course, I hadn't seen him fence, then. Have now." A thought seizing him, he asked, "Don't suppose you would be interested in putting a few guineas on—"

The reverend gentleman's grey eyes regarded him steadily.

Unabashed, Glendenning chuckled. "You wouldn't. Sorry.
I forget sometimes that you're now a man of the cloth. Damned
if I can see why you agreed to be old Treve's second. A trifle
removed from your—er, persuasions, ain't it?"

Boudreaux sighed and nodded. "I chanced to be there
when Boothe struck him. And—well, I'm very fond of Treve.
He's my cousin, after all. My sister's fond of him, too. Trouble
is, I like Boothe's sister. Delightful. Beastly situation. I agreed
to serve mostly in the hope my presence might deter Treve
from putting a period to Boothe."

"Good Lord! Oh, sorry, Fitz. What I mean is, this ain't
going to be a killing matter, surely? Swords, dear old boy. Not
pistols."

"True. But Boothe struck him *twice*."

They looked at one another with foreboding, but their discussion terminated as a pounding of hooves announced the
headlong arrival of a light travelling coach that tore up to halt
beside a cluster of tall elms. The door was flung open and the
steps let down before the groom could perform those services.
Snowden Boothe jumped out and hurried over, followed by
Mr. Melton and Lord Fortescue.

"Dashed sorry I'm late," Boothe apologized, as de Villars
wandered to join them. "Couldn't wake Forty. Sleeps like a
veritable Mephisto, dashed if he don't."

De Villars regarded his lordship with ironic amusement.

"Methuselah," Boudreaux corrected gently.

Boothe began to put off his cloak and said with a hard look
at de Villars that he didn't see what difference it made. "We're
all the same in the water closet, ain't we?"

The reverend looked shocked.

De Villars mused, "Somehow I have never pictured
Mephisto in a water closet."

"Why not?" Boothe demanded, defiantly. "Who the devil
is the fellow?"

"Just so," de Villars said with a grin.

Glendenning noted Boothe's irked frown and said
placatingly, "Mephisto is a devil, Snow. Or *the* devil, perhaps,
according to Greek mythology."

Boothe broke into a shout of laughter. De Villars chuckled. Taken aback by such levity, Fortescue put in, "Are we ready, gentlemen?"

"By all means," said de Villars, shrugging out of his jacket.

"Hold hard." Glendenning pointed out, "Surgeon's not here yet."

"Well, where the deuce is he?" Boothe demanded. "Dashitall, I'm famished. Hadn't time to stop for breakfast."

"Perhaps," drawled de Villars, as he folded back the lace at his cuffs, "you would prefer we adjourn to the tavern first?"

Boothe's face lit up. "Jove, but I would!" He saw de Villars' incredulity and flushed. "You was quizzing me, eh? Very funny, I'm sure. But if you was as hungry as I am . . ."

"Had you arisen at a proper hour . . ."

"Arisen! I did not arise because I did not go to bed, damn you!"

De Villars' lip curled unpleasantly. "Nervous, Boothe?"

"Another witticism like that," Snowden grated, looking up from attending to his own shirt sleeves, "and I'll call you out, sir, devil take me if I don't!"

Lord Fortescue, who was nervously anxious to fulfil his duties as a proper second should do, protested, "You can't call him out now, Snow! Ain't allowed! Must finish *this* one first, dear boy."

"What? Oh. Well, blast it all, de Villars, I vow I cannot understand why some public-spirited citizen ain't put a period to you long before this."

De Villars, whose cynicism had given way to amusement during this interchange, said, "Are you public spirited, Boothe? I'd not have thought it."

Boothe was mulling over the matter when a third carriage approached, was drawn to a decorous halt, and the surgeon alighted, to be met by Melton and Glendenning.

Lord Fortescue, meanwhile, apprised his principal in an undertone that the rules must be adhered to. "You two gentlemen," he pointed out solemnly, "ain't supposed to be brawling like this."

"We ain't brawling," said Snowden with an indignant air. "We are enjoying a civilized discussion. Eh, de Villars?"

"Oh, decidedly."

"And if truth be told, Forty," said Boothe, turning on his friend, "you and the rest of 'em ain't doing what you should, neither. Has anyone checked the swords? Have you looked over the ground?"

My lord flushed guiltily, and hurried to the coach to collect the long, flat case that held the duelling swords.

De Villars said, "I've checked the ground, Boothe. There's a slight rise at the western side. Over here."

They wandered off together to inspect this irregularity. Returning with the sword box, Fortescue paused and stood staring after the departing principals with such a bewildered expression on his face that Glendenning came over to ask, "Are you thinking there still may be a chance of effecting a truce, Forty?"

Fortescue sighed. "I wish we might. Like 'em, y'know. Like 'em both."

Boudreaux came up, and having heard the last few words, said, "Does anyone know why they fight?"

"Not a word out of either of them," Glendenning replied. "I heard there was a woman at the root of it. Here they come— Gad, you'd think them bosom bows!"

Hope for a reconciliation faded, however, when it was seen that the principals were engaging in a sharp discussion as to whether to remove their shoes. Boothe was shocked by de Villars' refusal to do this, and de Villars said unequivocally that he did not propose to prance about the wet grass in his stockinged feet.

"Then I shall have an advantage over you," Snowden said with a frown. "I always fight better without shoes. Anyone does."

Glendenning put in, "You give him an advantage, well enough, Treve."

"I rather doubt it will prove of any moment," drawled de Villars.

Bristling, Boothe snapped, "Did each of you hear that piece of braggadocio? I want no whining afterwards that I set him under a handicap."

"Nor I." De Villars yawned. "I cannot abide whining. I find foolishness much to be preferred, so do by all means remove your shoes, Boothe."

Boothe ground his teeth, and tore the shoes from his feet.

Glendenning met FitzWilliam's glum look, and shrugged. "Best get started, Forty."

Fortescue offered the box first to de Villars, who took the weapon closest him, flexed the blade between his hands, and nodded approval. Boothe took the remaining sword and made a pass or two, testing the heft of it.

"If you are satisfied, gentlemen," said Melton quietly.

They were satisfied, and walked to the selected ground, side by side. The seconds, also with swords drawn, took up their positions.

The salute was brief. With typical impetuosity, Boothe wasted no time in feeling out his adversary, but at once opened in *carte*. His thrust, lightning fast, was parried at the last instant. De Villars' blade glittered as it then whipped into a *flanconade*, the flat slapping hard against Boothe's hip. His eyes flaring, Boothe got out of distance and threw up a hand.

Mr. Melton stepped forward. "What is it, Boothe?"

Ignoring him, Boothe fixed his antagonist with a piercing stare. "What do you think you are playing at, de Villars?"

De Villars answered with a patient smile, "I believe we are playing at a duel, my dear Boothe."

"Then let us do so in a dignified fashion. We are not oafs, sir."

"Boothe," sighed Mr. Melton, "have you a foul to claim? I saw nothing unethical."

"He slapped me!" Boothe asserted with considerable indignation. "You blind, George?"

"I saw a *flanconade*, merely."

"He struck me with the *flat* of his blade. I did not come here to have my arse spanked, and so I tell you, de Villars!"

De Villars, his eyes dancing wickedly, bowed. "Thank you for clarifying your wishes, Boothe, for I was certainly labouring under a wrong impression."

Boothe flushed scarlet. His lips gripped tightly. Then he snarled, "*En garde!*" And the duel resumed.

Boothe was all too aware of the furtive grins that had been exchanged by the seconds. De Villars' sarcasm was added to the dastardly affront to Rebecca, and, seething with the fires of vengeful fury, Boothe fairly leapt to the attack, his need to wipe out the insults suffered at this man's hands driving him to set a punishing pace. The seconds became sober and intent; the treacherous minutes slipped past, the steel flashed and rang, the antagonists displaying excellent footwork and balance as they moved dexterously in and out. Boothe continued to carry the offensive, de Villars contenting himself with a defence that seemed haphazard, yet brought a glow of admiration to Glendenning's eyes, and caused Boudreaux twice to whisper an awed "By Jove!" But then Boothe ventured a parade. De Villars' wrist turned in a blur of speed. A *glissade* sent his sword singing down Boothe's blade, and Boothe's sword spun from his hand. For a split second, de Villars' weapon still quivered to the attack. Fortescue's heart seemed to stop. He jumped forward to strike up the sword, but there was not the need: De Villars had already moved back, eyes glinting, and his blade held down and to the side.

Boothe rubbed his wrist, looked thoughtfully at the impassive features of his opponent, and took the sword George Melton handed him. "Damn," he muttered.

"It is difficult to fight well when . . . one is tired," observed de Villars, parrying a rather weak lunge. "You would have done better to get to your bed."

His foot stamping, Boothe thrust in *tierce*, was blocked, and in turn parried a flashing riposte. "Aye," he grunted. "And . . . I might have done so had not your cousin . . . driven me from it."

De Villars tensed. Boothe's attack in *carte* was countered by a sizzling return and the resultant *volte* again all but tore the sword from his hand.

"I'll have an explanation of that remark, when we are done," de Villars said curtly.

Talk ceased. The fast pace of the duel became even more accelerated. The clearing was hushed and still, save for the murderous flash and flurry of steel in seeking thrust and defensive parry; the stamp of feet; the sway of lithe bodies, each in perfect condition; the quick, tense breathing of the duellists. The seconds shifted about, their narrowed, alert eyes missing no facet of the furious battle. Glendenning cursed under his breath as, for the third time, de Villars held back a logical attack, and a moment later Boudreaux exclaimed, "Jupiter! That was close! Boothe nigh had him!" Not a little astounded, Fortescue said, "I'd not have dreamed Snow could last this long! He's giving a good account of himself, eh?" Melton said nothing, but his eyes were worried.

Time ticked away, and still Boothe strove passionately but vainly to penetrate that deceptively lazy guard, his thrusts parried by a defence often so tantalizingly tardy as to lure him on to the next, useless effort. The excitement of those watching was intensified. Glendenning swore. "They cannot keep up this pace! It is madness!" But the pace did not slow, although both men were now breathing hard. Boothe's lungs were agonizing, his hand wet with sweat. He was bedevilled by the awareness that he was slipping very gradually from attack to defence, and it was borne in upon him that he might have been run through several times. The suspicion that he was being played with, that the jeering de Villars was laughing at him, sent his ready temper flaring and brought a surge of renewed strength. He swept into the offensive once more, with the fast and hard thrust under the wrist known as *seconde*. Not expecting this sudden revival, de Villars retaliated instinctively with a prime parade, that dangerous manoeuvre bringing gasps of excitement from the watchers. In the nick of time, he checked the following riposte that would have finished the duel, but might very well have also finished Boothe. His hesitation was minuscule, but almost fatal. Boothe's sword flashed at him in a full thrust in *tierce*. De Villars disengaged but he was a split second slow, and the point of Boothe's sword raked across his chest. Angered, de Villars' reaction was quicksilver. The disengage completed, he drew in his arm a little and his blade whirled, the steel becoming a dazzling blaze in the light of the rising sun. Boothe was conscious of a blinding flash. Something smashed violently against his sword. A flame shot up his arm, and he clutched his wrist as his weapon for the second time fell from his numbed hand. The point of de Villars' sword was at his throat. Melton leapt to strike it up, even as it was once more withdrawn.

"Fool!" said de Villars, glaring at him.

Not in the least dismayed, and ever the fine sportsman, Boothe cried breathlessly, "Jove, what a . . . beat! Jolly well done, sir! Jolly well done!"

Panting, de Villars stepped back and paid Boothe the honour of a salute before handing his sword to Boudreaux. The other seconds and the surgeon, who had stood in a state of petrified stillness through these last breathtaking moments, now rushed forward with shouts of acclaim.

The surgeon hastened to Boothe and grasped his arm, drawing a yell from his patient. A swift examination, then he turned to de Villars, who attempted to deal with the enthusiasm of the men gathered about him. "He caught you in the chest, I think, sir," said the surgeon, unbuttoning the slashed shirt.

"Nothing of consequence," said de Villars, cheerfully. "Are you badly hurt, Boothe?"

"No, save that you damn near broke my arm." Boothe grinned. "A fine lot of seconds I have, to allow my sword to be struck with a sledgehammer."

They all laughed. Boothe came over to watch as the surgeon set de Villars' fine linen aside, revealing a shallow gash across the muscular chest, directly above the heart. His eyes darting to de Villars' impassive face, Boothe said an aghast, "By Gad! I might have killed you, man!"

"You were curst slow to parry, Treve," said Boudreaux solemnly. "My poor fellow, that must burn like the very deuce!"

Glendenning proffered a brandy flask. "You were far off your form, dear boy. What ailed you? I swear I never saw your defence so careless."

"Took too dashed many chances," Boudreaux agreed.

Watching de Villars, Boothe's expression became thunderous. "I know what ailed him. Though I'd not suspected it until that brilliant riposte at the finish. You could have had me—how many times, and did not, sir?"

"I counted seven," murmured George Melton, as de Villars took a swallow from the flask. "A dangerous game you played, Trevelyan."

"Nonsense." De Villars slanted a covert glance at his erstwhile opponent. "Boothe's a dashed fine swordsman, is all. Gave me a run for my money."

Boothe cursed savagely. "Never! It was those confounded girls! I collect they wrung a promise from you to spare me?"

De Villars' brows arched into the familiar look of boredom. "Your imagination is, I see, as fertile as your sister's."

"Oh, no, it ain't! Don't try to gammon me! I know, all too well! What Miss Boudreaux put me through last evening! I was so demoralized I wonder I could even *hold* a sword this morning!"

The doctor said despairingly, "Mr. de Villars, it appears to have escaped your notice, but your wound bleeds, sir. If you would just sit down for a moment, I might more easily come at your hurt."

Glendenning waved for the surgeon's carriage, and the coachman touched up the horses and drove to the little group.

De Villars sat on the step and, suffering the doctor to remove his ruined garment, said, "Now, if you please, Boothe—what's all this about your bed and my cousin?"

"Not what you are thinking," said Boothe, but without resentment. "I've been racking up at my sister Parrish's house while she's away—just to keep an eye on the place, d'ye see? At all events, there I trotted last night. Perfectly natural thing to do. And Miss Boudreaux was ensconced with m'sister. The pair of 'em turned on me like a pair of archwives because of our meeting! Most awful thing! Had to make a run for it!"

De Villars said with a grin, "I appreciate your predicament. I endured much the same scene, unless I mistake it."

"You do mistake it! Unless you've far more backbone than I."

Leaning back in response to the surgeon's request, de Villars glanced up at Boothe curiously. "Never say you were treated to tears—and all for my sake?"

"Worse. Your cousin fell to her knees before me!"

"My sister? *Letitia?*" put in the reverend, astonished.

The surgeon, attempting to bathe the cut across de Villars' chest, abandoned the effort as his patient threw back his head and uttered a shout of laughter.

"Fitz . . ." gasped de Villars. "Did—did you know naught of this Machiavellian ploy?"

Still unconvinced, the man of the cloth said, "Faith—I did not. Are you quite sure, Boothe? My sister ain't the type. Deuced calm and collected usually. I cannot conceive why she'd succumb to such megrims."

"She didn't seem megrimish to me," said Boothe meditatively. "Matter of fact, she struck me as being a dashed nice girl. Pretty, too."

"Very pretty," de Villars agreed. "And a perfect lady, Boothe."

His eyes held a warning. Meeting them, Boothe stiffened and retaliated, "Just as *my* sister is a perfect lady, I'd remind you!"

"Never doubted it," said de Villars, his cynical grin dawning. "Of course, your sister is a widow, my dear Boothe."

"Be damned if that makes her fair game! Apologies, Fitz. My sister did not become Haymarket ware on the day her husband was killed! And furthermore, de Villars, if you imply I ain't fit to call on your cousin, you'll answer to me for't!"

Glendenning groaned and bowed his forehead against Fortescue's shoulder.

Mr. Melton smiled slightly and shook his head in disbelief.

The surgeon, looking from sardonic boredom to flaming wrath, said with dry disgust, "I take leave to tell you, Mr. Boothe, that you will engage in no more duels for some time to come. Unless I mistake it, your wrist is badly sprained."

Boothe, who had suspected something of the sort, peered at the swelling wrist in dismay. "Is it, begad?" he muttered. "Well, if that don't beat the Dutch!"

CHAPTER
🦢 10 🦢

How Nature could have been so perverse to make this a beautiful morning was beyond understanding. The clear skies, the birds that sang with determined enthusiasm, the sun that shone with such beneficent warmth, all seemed to mock Rebecca's crushing anxieties. Wringing her hands, she turned from the parlour window to pace for the hundredth time across the snug room, then jumped, her heart leaping into her throat as the clock began to chime. Ten. It seemed an age since she had glanced at it, but only five minutes had passed. The duel was long over, of course. It would take some time for Snow to get back into Town, despite the fact that he always drove at so headlong a pace. Still, it was fully five hours since the sun had risen. Five endless hours. So—why were they not back? Snow knew how worried she had been, and, despite his carefree and rather selfish nature, he was not unkind and would have come at once. Unless . . .

She halted, closing her eyes. Dear God—do not let him be hurt. Do not let him be killed. Do not let Treve— Her eyes opened wide. *Treve?* Mr. de Villars, she corrected primly. That either of them should be slain was—

In her absorption she had not heard the carriage stop outside and was startled when the door was flung open. Whirling about, she uttered a sob of joy and relief. Snowden stood on the threshold, as handsome and devil-may-care as ever, and apparently unhurt. He staggered as Rebecca fairly hurled herself upon his chest and said an indignant, "No, really, Becky! I'd the very devil of a time to tie this cravat! Gad, what a pother you women make about these things!" But for all his grumbling, the signs of strain in his sister's face were so evident that he gave her a hug and dropped a kiss on her brow.

"You are all right?" She ran her hands over his chest and arms as though to reassure herself there was no concealed wound.

"Lord, yes." He readjusted the velvet sleeve anxiously, and added with a twinkle, "Cannot say as much for de Villars, however." Glancing up, he gave a shocked gasp, grabbed Rebecca's swaying figure, and guided her to the sofa. Rushing to pull the bellrope, he then returned and flapped his coat skirt at his sister's white face.

She put up a staying hand and said faintly, "Only tell me—is Mr. de Villars . . . killed?"

"For mercy's sake! Never fear, love. Had I a killing on my hands I'd be galloping for Dover and the first departing packet!"

Mrs. Falk came in. She gave a cry of thanks to see Boothe, peered into Rebecca's wan face, and hurried away to bring the brandy Boothe requested.

"If ever I saw such a birdwitted start," he grumbled, sitting beside Rebecca and chafing her hand. "Why must you fret yourself into such a state?"

Despite the fear that was causing her to feel drained of strength, she managed to say, "Tell me what happened. How badly is de Villars wounded?"

"Not near bad enough! I tell you, Becky, I'll have at him again as soon as my arm—" He bit his lip. "Well, er—that is to say—"

"Your arm?" she cried in new anxiety. "Snow! Were you—"

"Come down from the boughs! A sprain, merely." With a reminiscent grin curving his shapely mouth, he said, "De Villars, blast his miserable existence, is a curst fine swordsman, I give him that."

"Yet you mean to meet him again! Why?"

Mrs. Falk returning at this moment, Boothe followed her to the sideboard and poured his sister a glass of brandy. "Come along now—sip away! That's a good girl. She'll be all right now, thank you, Falk." He patted the housekeeper's bony shoulder, assured her he was unhurt, and ushered her to the door. "Now," he said, turning back into the room, "where was I? Oh, yes. De

Villars. Well, I'll tell you, Becky, that damnable rogue is—"

What the damnable rogue was, Rebecca was not destined to discover. Again there was a scratching at the door, followed by the entrance of Lord Fortescue, who trod into the room, bowed shyly to Rebecca, and gestured to Boothe. "A word, Snow," he entreated, with a hideous grimace intended to warn his friend subtly of the need for secrecy. "Pardon, Mrs. Becky, but—must speak with y'r brother, by y'r leave."

"Of course," said Rebecca, variously irked by the interruption and sorry that poor Forty appeared to have such a bad stiff neck.

The two young men adjourned to the top of the steps. Snowden inclined his head and listened to his lordship's rapidly conveyed message. He started, scowled, and spun about. "Well, I must be off!" he declared breezily. "Now, you pay heed, Becky. No more farradiddles! You should get back to our poor aunt at once. A fine state she will be in." He grinned. "Likely renovating her blacks this very minute!" And he strode to the door.

Indignation restoring her spirits, Rebecca sprang to her feet. "Snowden! Wait! You cannot just rush off like this! I must know—"

"Later, dear chit." He blew her a kiss, bundling his lordship unceremoniously from the room even as that worthy strove to make his bow to Rebecca. "I shall come up to see you so soon as I can. Promise you. Be good, now!" And he was gone.

"Well!" gasped Rebecca. "If that is not the outside of—" Running to the hall, she called to them in vain. The door of Fortescue's smart town carriage was swung shut; the groom snatched at the side rail and swung up behind, and the vehicle rolled swiftly away.

❧

Rebecca followed the lackey along the wide hall of the quiet house on Berkeley Street, her heart beating very fast. Convinced that Snowden's abrupt departure was in some way connected with his duel, she had swiftly bridged the gap between that fact and the likelihood that de Villars was either dead or dying. Distraught, she had ordered Snowden's carriage and required that the coachman drive to the Boudreaux residence, but when they arrived, the porter had said that Miss Boudreaux was gone to her cousin's house. It sounded very ominous, and Rebecca had trembled all the way here. It was not, of course, that she cared for The Wretched Rake, but, if he had fallen while trying to keep his word to her . . . if *she* was responsible . . . "Oh, dear, oh, dear!" she thought miserably, "I should not have placed him under such a crippling restraint!" Yet, had she not done so, dear Snow might even now be dead! She shuddered and was glad she'd insisted the coachman return to the stable at once. Poor Snow might need the carriage was he fleeing the country.

The lackey bowed her into a room and stepped aside. Entering, Rebecca did not hear the door close behind her, for she stood frozen with horror. She was in a large, richly appointed chamber, the window curtains drawn so that the light was dim. She was able, however, to distinguish Trevelyan de Villars, and her apprehensions had been well founded, for he lay on a sofa, one hand pressed to his chest. His head, propped with cushions, was turned towards her, a faint, sad smile on his pale face. "How very . . . good of you . . . to come," he murmured, the words barely distinguishable. His right hand, trailing onto the carpet, rose weakly, but fell back.

A great surge of remorse seared Rebecca. With a muffled sob, she sped to kneel beside him and, her eyes blurred with tears, faltered, "Oh! I am . . . so *sorry!* Is it—is it very b-bad?"

"I expect . . . I may fool 'em all, and—and live," he said in that same thread of a voice, but on the last word his face twisted; he coughed and jerked his head away.

"Oh . . . my!" wailed Rebecca. And seeing how that one limp, long-fingered hand stirred feebly on the carpet, she took it up and clasped it to her bosom. "But—how dr-dreadful that they have left you alone . . . like this! You should have been carried at once to your bed. I will summon—"

"No!" He clung desperately to her hand. "Don't leave me! I do not want to . . . to die . . . all alone."

Shattered, she held his hand higher, under her chin. She

had a vague sense that there was some resistance to this movement, but perhaps it was only that his arm was so helpless and
thus, heavy. And all that really mattered was that he lay here—
expiring. "It is my fault!" she gulped. "All my fault!"

"No, no." The pale lips again quivered to the gallant smile
that was tearing her heart to shreds. "I could ask no more of
life than . . . than to have been of service to you, my
lovely . . . lovely one."

"Do not!" She wept. "Oh, how *can* they treat you so? I
must go and get—"

"My cousin is gone . . . for new bandages and—a draught.
The—the surgeon is on his way. 'Tis just—" The fine grey eyes
flickered and closed. "They dared not carry me—upstairs," he
whispered.

How splendidly he was behaving. How chivalrous to have
risked his life only to keep his promise to her. The long, curl-
ing lashes fluttered, the clear eyes peered up at her. Why had
she never noticed how tender they could be? Why had she
never remarked how sweet was his smile?

He sighed weakly. "I cannot seem to—to see you . . ."

Was this the dimming touch of approaching death? Appalled, she leaned nearer. "I am here, Treve. You're going to
be well again, never . . ." But the unsteady words faded to a
whimper of fear as his eyes closed wearily, and his hand became a dead weight in hers. "Oh, pray do not die! Treve,
Treve! Pray do not," she sobbed.

He looked up, as though reclaimed by her sorrow. "Would
you," he breathed, "kiss me—just once, before . . ."

She bent above him, taking care to avoid the hand pressed
over his heart. His kiss was so weak; no more than a faint stirring of the lips, but that her embrace had much restored him
was immediately obvious. The hand she still held, tightened,
his other arm slipped about her, and he raised himself a little,
to kiss her again. Harder. His hold on her became crushing. A
thrilling tide swept her up, and she was floating far from dull
reality. She could scarcely breathe, yet the touch of his mouth
was an ecstasy that must not cease. . . . In all her life she had
known no kiss like this one; never had she been so ruthlessly

held. Never had a man's mouth sent such a flame burning through—

"Treve . . . ? Wherever have you got to?"

Letitia's voice.

Spinning through a golden glow, Rebecca heard the call as from very far away. But it snapped her back to reality.

De Villars was sitting up, his arms tight-locked about her as he kissed her throat, murmuring endearments. She lay limply in his arms, breathless, her ribs feeling as though one or two might still be intact. And his caressing hand had slipped under the lace at her bosom . . .

Fury boiled through her. "*Villain!*" she shrilled, springing back and beating at him with clenched fists. "Oh—you *wicked*, odious, shameless—"

"Ow!" De Villars laughed, raising a protecting hand. "Now, sweeting"—he caught a flying fist—"admit you liked it. Only—"

"Monstrous trickster!" she shrieked, fighting him wildly. "I did not—"

"Kiss me back? But you *did*, love. No, do not struggle so."

"I thought you were—were *dying!* And I wish you *were!* Oh, *how* I wish it! Of all the loathsome—"

"Treve!" Letitia came in and cried a shocked, "Are you run mad?"

De Villars relinquished his grip on Rebecca's wrists, ducked the flying swipe she aimed at him, and sprang agilely to his feet. "Now do not rail at me, Letty. Only see how I am restored. I was lying in here, trying to rest when Mrs. Parrish invaded my privacy and—"

"*Lecher!*" Rebecca hissed through clenched teeth. "The lackey *showed* me in here—at your command, I do not doubt!"

"Besides which," said Letitia, coming to slip a supportive arm around Rebecca's waist, "you was laid down in the *red* saloon, Treve!"

"Of course he was! He learned I had come and acted out this whole horrid death scene purely to lure me into his wicked embraces!"

Letitia shook her head at her cousin reproachfully. "Oh, Treve. How could you?"

Perching on the end of the sofa, he replied with a shocking lack of contrition, "With the greatest pleasure, m'dear."

⁊⁊

Miss Boudreaux insisted that Rebecca be carried home in her own carriage. It was a luxurious vehicle and accomplished the short journey in smooth, well-sprung comfort, but Rebecca had no wish to be delivered to her house in a coach with the Boudreaux crest on the door, and so required to be set down at the top of John Street. She walked along slowly through the bright afternoon, pondering the situation. She had gone into a small ante-room with Letitia, and while the carriage was being readied, had talked at some length with her new friend. Letitia had done all she might to apologize for her cousin's outrageous behavior and, in also expressing her anxieties for Boothe, had blushingly confessed her regard for him. The two girls had embraced, Rebecca assuring Letitia that she could only be delighted were there to be a happy resolution to her affections. She had tried to conceal how little hope she felt there was of this, but the tender episode had done much to calm her own fury.

Now she thought of Snowden and his sudden exit. Whatever his reason, it could have nothing to do with picking another quarrel with de Villars. A second duel between the two men must be averted at all costs, but the immediacy of such a meeting was obviated by the fact that Snow would be unable to hold a sword for some time to come. Rebecca scowled at a blithely hopping sparrow. How selfish men were! One might suppose that having been spared today, Snow would be sufficiently grateful to refrain from subjecting her to such misery again. Or Letitia. He did not know the depth of Letitia's *tendre* for him, of course. But he had seemed most decidedly interested in her last evening. . . . Even so, being a typical, contrary male, he would very likely wind up in the toils of some flamboyant creature like The Monahan. . . .

Despite herself, her thoughts slipped back to de Villars. From what Letitia had told her, it was apparent that he had taken some desperate chances during the duel. And had received precious little thanks for it. Her features, which had softened to a faintly remorseful look, became indignant again. She must be all about in her head! The Brute had been exceeding well paid! Only think how he had acted out his revolting drama! A gleam came into her eyes at the memory of the touching way he had allowed his hand to lie so limply on the carpet during the moments of his "expiring nobility." Faith, but it was a winsome villain; and a strong one! Her ribs still ached! And the kisses he had so basely tricked . . . a sudden confusion warmed her cheeks, and she looked down, her heartbeat becoming oddly erratic. Mr. Trevelyan de Villars was a cynic, an unprincipled rogue, a dangerous fighting man, and perhaps even a libertine. But it began to be apparent that the lady taken under his protection would be wooed by an accomplished lover. . . .

She took a deep breath and pulled her scattered wits back into order. She simply *must* not allow these vacillations! Sir Peter Ward was neither cynic nor rogue; she had never heard of him engaging in such savage behaviour as duelling, and he was as far from being a rake or a libertine as one could imagine. And he was rich. She shut out a vague disquiet. It was very well that Snowden had told her to return to Bedfordshire. It would not do to let the grass grow under one's feet!

≈

In the garden of the house on Berkeley Street, Letitia Boudreaux was also engaged in meditation. She wandered slowly across the lawn, reflecting that her prayers had been answered: Snowden Boothe was practically unhurt after an encounter that might very easily have left him crippled or slain. And yet, the future looked grim. He had gone gaily off somewhere, apparently without having given her another thought. Only—last night the look in his blue eyes had been unmistakable. She was sure that he had become a *little* interested in her. She had even dared to hope that he might eventually grow fond of her, despite her infuriating height. She sighed. But—of what use? His sister loathed Treve. And Boothe had sworn to fight again. Even was the duel averted the next time, animosity between the two families must mar any chance for a happy marriage, for who could be happily wed if cut off from all the relations who were so dearly beloved? No, it was hopeless, unless . . . She checked and stood motionless, gazing blankly at the kitchen cat who lolled against a tree while cleaning one upflung back leg. The cat abandoned its pursuits if not its position. Two yellow eyes contemplated the girl watchfully and, no caresses being offered, the elevated limb was stretched a shade higher and the ablutions resumed.

"Hmmn . . ." said Letitia, and went thoughtfully into the house.

She found de Villars standing at the window of the drawing room, looking into the street. Considering his tall, athletic figure dispassionately, she thought that although he was not handsome there was a magnetism about him that was undeniable. Had it not been for that wretched Constance Rogers, he would be wed these many years, and likely as sunny-natured as before he met the chit. She had done more than ruin him, for she had blighted that once delightful personality. And yet—perhaps it was purely wishful thinking, but of late it had seemed that his cynicism was a little less marked.

As though he sensed her presence, he turned and smiled wryly. "Am I in for a proper raking down, Letty?"

"I own you deserve one. However, I must admit to feeling more puzzled than censorious."

His head a little bowed, he watched her steadily, waiting.

"One cannot but wonder," she went on, "how you came by your reputation."

"Unjustly," he declared promptly.

"I agree. Surely, a genuine rake must handle these matters with far greater finesse."

De Villars tensed, and a dark flush rose to his lean cheeks.

"That was clumsily done, coz," Letitia murmured. "And no way to win the lady."

A frown came into his eyes, but instead of the acid comment she half expected, he said nothing, resuming his surveillance of the street, so that only his profile was visible.

"One might almost think," she went on softly, "that you do

not really wish to—er, conquer The Little Parrish, as you call her."

He glanced at this shy, quiet girl, wondering at her venture into so improper a conversation. She seemed to be anxiously awaiting his reply. He hesitated, then said musingly, "She is a worthy opponent. And—if a general changes his plans, love, defeat is not inevitable, I think."

"Perhaps," said Letitia idly, "Ward will intervene. I suspect he is most fond of the lady."

"Perhaps. But the game is not over yet. Though it has taken a turn I'd not expected."

The surgeon was announced, and came bustling in, demanding to inspect the cut across de Villars' chest. His patient protested hotly, but was borne off to his bedchamber nonetheless.

Left alone, Letitia knit her brows. It was so difficult to know what he was thinking. His last words may have been a verification of the hopes she had begun to entertain. On the other hand, was it her imagination, or had a sudden grimness come into his eyes as he spoke them?

ᔰ

Ward Marching's usual serenity was decidedly ruptured by Rebecca's return. After she emerged from Anthony's boisterous greeting, and the many hugs, kisses, and unintelligible chatter of Miss Patience Ashton, she was able to embrace her aunt and ease that lady's anxieties as to Snowden's safety. It was necessary that Rebecca feign cheer, for she was plagued by an apathy as puzzling as it was unfamiliar, but she had no need to feign interest in what had transpired during her brief absence. Anthony, it seemed, had driven Millie and the normally phlegmatic Evans to distraction with the flute Mr. de Villars had given him, so that it had been confiscated for a day or two. He and Patience had gone to explore the ruins of the original house, telling no one whither they were bound, and the little girl had tumbled through a rotten floor into the cellar. Fortunately, Mr. Melton had chanced to ride by and had been able to rescue her. Shocked, Rebecca gathered Patience into a hug and asked if she had hurt herself.

"Paythen not hurted," the little girl lisped with a sweet if sticky smile. "But Anth'y a bad boy!"

His face scarlet, Anthony said defensively, "Well, for heaven's sake, I *had* to go and find help!" He turned to his mother in desperation. "The silly shrimp don't understand, mama! She thinks I run off and left her, but I didn't!"

"Of course you didn't, dear. But perhaps you should not have taken her to so dangerous a spot. When she is with you, Patience needs your judgement and protection, you know."

The boy nodded shamefacedly. His sense of guilt was obvious. Rebecca judged it far more punishing than anything she might do, so turned to remark with a lurking smile that it was "exceeding fortunate that Mr. Melton chanced to be riding this way. . . ."

Mrs. Boothe lapsed into a blushful sea of confusion, from which Rebecca was able to extract the information that the bashful suitor had taken lodgings in the village and had been coming to call at least once each day. Later, when they were alone together, Mrs. Boothe admitted that despite this evidence of particularity, her swain had not as yet popped the question.

"There can no longer be any doubt that he means to do so," said Rebecca supportively. "It must indicate a great interest to others, also."

"Well, it might," said her aunt dubiously. "Unless people think he just is staying for the ball."

Rebecca said blankly, "Ball? But that is not until. . . My heavens! It is—oh! It is next *Friday!*"

"Yes, my love. And Sir Peter returns tomorrow, so Mrs. Kellstrand says. Have you brought your costume with you?"

"Costume!" wailed Rebecca, throwing both hands to her face. "With all the fuss and feathers of that horrid duel, I had quite forgot it!"

"Good gracious me! Well, you shall have to turn about and go to Town again. Madame Olga will—"

"I dare not face that woman again! Not with all her bills hiding in my drawer at home! And there is no time for Falk to make something; besides which there is never any telling whether her garments will fit properly! What on *earth* am I to do?"

"Oh, Lud! Oh, Lud!" cried the warm-hearted Mrs. Boothe, equally as dismayed. She gave a sudden squeak of excitement. "I have it! Graham Fortescue! He is such a Pink of the *ton*, he's sure to know where you could purchase—"

"He is gone away!" Rebecca wailed tragically. "And I know not when he will come back."

At this point, Evans waddled into the parlour bearing tea and biscuits on a small tray which she proceeded to set with a thump on the sofa table. The country woman's lethargic ways and unpolished manners had been a source of considerable irritation to Millie during their sojourn in Bedfordshire. She was, asserted the energetic Millie, as clumsy as a cow and of the same order of intelligence. It had early become apparent, however, that Evans was as amiable as she was bovine, took criticism with never a sign of offence, and although she might accomplish an assigned task at a snail's pace, was ever willing to undertake it. Gradually, she had won her way into their affections, and perhaps because of her stolid manner her presence often went unremarked so that conversation was less guarded in front of her.

In desperation, therefore, Mrs. Boothe did not hesitate to suggest that there might be something that could be constructed from their present wardrobes so as to serve the purpose.

"There is nothing I could alter so as to wear to a fancy dress ball!" wailed Rebecca. "They *do* all wear costumes, do they not, Evans?"

"Aye, ma'am. And some *that* laughable! Belike you could sew one your own self, Mrs. Parrish."

Rebecca uttered a moan. "There is not the time, and besides, I am not clever with a needle, nor ever was. Aunt Albinia, what do *you* mean to wear?"

"Why, I have begged a uniform of Evans. I mean to go as an abigail. I thought 'twould be jolly."

"And a jolly time we've had a'taking of it in, for Mrs. Boothe lacks half my inches," said Evans with a chuckle. She closed the window against the evening's cooler air. "Be ye wishful to borrow some clothes, Mrs. Parrish, 'tis a pity ye cannot use some of they pretty things o' Sir Peter's."

"Dress like a *male?*" Much shocked, Mrs. Boothe exclaimed, "Are you quite witless, woman? Mrs. Forbes Parrish would never do such a thing!"

Evans went into such whoops at this, that the sight of her bulk shivering and shaking moved the two ladies to answering giggles. Drying tearful eyes, she said that she had meant nothing of the kind. "Dear me, no, ma'am. I were meaning the clothes in the Fiji Room. Hasn't Sir Peter taked you there yet?" She shook her head. "Likely so busy with showing ye all the birdies, he forgot the best part. Belike ye'll be going for a walk in the morning, ye could ask Mrs. Kellstrand to show you."

The ladies lost no time in following this suggestion and, shortly after eleven o'clock next day, Rebecca was asking the housekeeper if they might see the Fiji Room. Mrs. Kellstrand tilted her shining white head in such obvious perplexity that Rebecca prompted, "Evans said Sir Peter has some beautiful garments in there."

The housekeeper laughed. "Oh—she must mean the Hall of Effigies! But of course you may see it." She led the way to the top floor of the great house, motioning to two of the lackeys to follow. "How quiet it is up here," she said when they had surmounted the last flight of stairs. "I sometimes think Sir Peter quite forgets this floor, for he has lived so quietly of recent years that we seldom put out covers for guests, and these suites go quite unused." Checking through the keys that hung at her waist, she added, "I expect you have heard, Mrs. Parrish, that his fiancée died in an accident six years ago, which quite broke the poor man's heart. But before that tragedy we had many jolly parties, and this floor fairly hummed with company. Here we are!"

She unlocked wide Gothic doors, opened one side, and stood back for the ladies to enter. The lackeys who had brought up the rear of the little procession hastened to draw curtains and open windows, and Rebecca and her aunt gazed in astonishment at the extraordinary sight laid out before them.

At first glance the room seemed full of people, but a closer look revealed that the occupants stood extremely still, no faintest breath stirring the luxurious garments they wore. The room was long, with high arched ceilings, and in the middle of one wall a vaulting stone fireplace. The figures were grouped about; some ten or twelve little knots disposed here and there in conversational attitudes. With a cry of wonder, Rebecca hastened to inspect a gentleman clad in cape and doublet, white hose upon his somewhat knobby legs, and a black cloth hat with a white plume set realistically upon the dark wig.

"Why," she gasped. "How alive they look!"

"Extreme alive," agreed Mrs. Boothe, drawing back uneasily from a regal dowager in a farthingale of green silk, all set about with pearls, and wearing a jewelled tiara on her powdered hair. "I wonder they do not get dusty up here!"

"They are usually kept under Holland covers," Mrs. Kellstrand explained, in her soft, cultured voice. "We unveiled them today, in preparation for the ball, for some of the guests are sure to want to come up here. And they look so lifelike, ladies, because the hands and faces are of wax, you see. Is it not clever? I believe several great artisans worked on the collection. Sir Peter's grandpapa started it so as to keep a memory of his favourite uncle—the naval officer in the corner—and very soon, other figures were added. On Public Days this is the most popular room in the house, and we have to rope off a path so that the clothes and figures may not be damaged by curiosity."

"The workmanship is exquisite," said Rebecca, admiring the half-smile on the face of a pretty damsel in a ruff and jewelled stomacher. "Do they actually resemble real people, or was that not possible?"

"Only the original gentleman was fashioned to a likeness, ma'am. My Lord Samuel Ward found the resemblance unnerving, which is why his uncle speaks to the lady in blue brocade in the secluded corner. Subsequent effigies were designed at the whim of the artist, but the garments are true to the various periods, so that the collection has become a re-creation of times and fashions past, rather than a remembrance of friends or relatives."

Fascinated by a bold young man attired in short tunic and extremely tight hose, Mrs. Boothe murmured, "It is astonishing that *everything* looks so real!" Rebecca smothered a giggle. Mrs. Boothe blushed scarlet and added hurriedly, "It must have cost a prodigious amount, but—is a shade eerie."

"I assure you, ma'am, that to come up here in the dusk, or at night, can be *very* eerie!"

Rebecca was inspecting an Elizabethan lady whose gown boasted a very high-standing collar of jewelled brocade, behind which were butterfly wings supporting a flowing veil. "My heavens," she breathed. "What a large farthingale. However could they have moved about, or sat, I wonder, in hoops of such a size."

"That would be a fine costume for you," said Mrs. Boothe, eyeing the wide skirts thoughtfully. "I've no doubt you could manage it, Becky, and the size looks close enough."

Mrs. Kellstrand asked uneasily, "Had you wished to borrow a gown, Mrs. Parrish?"

Rebecca turned to her eagerly. "Not if it is forbidden, of course. It is that—well, I am so recently come out of blacks that I've had little time to replenish my wardrobe. And there was not the time to order a gown for the ball."

How prettily appealing, thought Mrs. Kellstrand, were the great dark eyes fixed so hopefully upon her. She had a fair idea of why Sir Peter had found it "impossible" to hire a suitable governess for the small cousin who had been foisted upon him. If Mrs. Parrish was to be the new mistress of Ward Marching, what folly to antagonize her. Summoning her most gracious smile, therefore, she said, "I think you would look charmingly in this gown, especially with your dark hair and eyes."

She led the way to a Spanish lady wearing figured red velvet, the long free-hanging outer sleeves edged with white fur. The gown was superb, but Rebecca cried, "Why, it is the biggest farthingale of all! Oh, I could never wear it! How are the hoops called?"

"It is a wheel farthingale, ma'am, and I'll own it enormous.
You would certainly attract attention."

"I should look a quiz," said Rebecca, but her eyes glowed,
and touching the sleeve, she murmured, "My grandmother was
a Spanish lady, you know. . . ."

Mrs. Kellstrand smiled, and began to remove the stomacher. "You might at least like to try it on," she said.

CHAPTER
❧ 11 ❧

*T*hree days later, Sir Peter and his grandmother returned. My lady had apparently endured a brief sojourn in
London only to decide she would attend the Midsummer's Eve
Ball at Ward Marching before going back to her beloved Cornwall. Sir Peter lost no time in repairing to the cottage to invite
the ladies to join them for luncheon. The invitation was accepted with alacrity, but no sooner were they upstairs than Rebecca began to inveigle her aunt into a small conspiracy.
Albinia moaned that she would certainly have a spasm before
they were done with all this, but she agreed, of course. As a
result, Sir Peter had ushered his ladies only a short distance
across the park when the much-tried Mrs. Boothe discovered
that she had "forgotten" her reticule. She rejected Rebecca's
innocent and very insincere offer to go and retrieve it and
begged instead that the two young people walk on slowly, for it
would, she said with a rather warning look at her niece, take
her only a minute or two to go back to the cottage.

Left alone with the gentleman, Rebecca found herself hor-
rifyingly tongue-tied. She did not relish what she had to say to
him, but it must be said and, as she held down the skirts a
mischievous breeze tugged at, she sought desperately for the
proper words.

Gallantly keeping his eyes from a pair of occasionally revealed and nicely turned ankles, Sir Peter observed in his well-
modulated voice, "There is a most becoming colour in your
cheeks today, dear ma'am. Indeed, if I dare remark it, you
seem lovelier each time we meet."

Rebecca brightened. This was a good beginning, surely? She summoned up her courage, but before she could utter anything more than a properly modest assertion that it must be the wind that made her cheeks rosy, he remarked admiringly, "Always so unassuming, so charmingly devoid of the slightest conceit. Speaking of which, Mrs. Parrish, I have found you out!"

Her heart leaping into her throat, Rebecca stammered, "Oh—d—dear me! I did not mean— I would never have—"

He smiled down at her. "How clumsy I am. Have I alarmed you, gentle little lady? I meant only that I have learned—I shall not tell you by what devious means—that you sing very prettily."

She drew a breath of relief. For a minute she had been sure he'd been told of the borrowed gown and that he was angered. "Oh," she said. "I assure you, sir, my voice is small, and nothing to brag of."

"Allow me to be the judge of that, dear ma'am. And I hope I may judge it very soon, although I am already so indebted to you that I scarce dare ask another favour."

"You want me to sing for you, Sir Peter?"

"Yes. At the ball. Would you? I promise you will not be the only volunteer, for I have been so ruthless as to press several of my guests into entertaining us."

She smiled up into his hopeful eyes. "It would be my very great pleasure, sir. But as to your being indebted, I must tell you that is far from the truth. In point of fact, I have something to confess to you." He looked so apprehensive at this that she went on quickly, "It is about my costume for the ball. I hope you will forgive me, but I—"

Aghast, Sir Peter halted and threw up one hand in a graceful gesture of restraint. "Stop, I beg of you! I must know nothing of your fancy dress. I am sure that it can only be delightful, for you would not purchase any that was otherwise. Even so, you cannot discuss it with me. The costumes are kept an absolute secret. That is what makes the ball so excessively jolly."

"But, you do not understand," she persisted earnestly. "Mine was *not* purchased. I have, you see, been so bold as to—"

"I shall not listen!" he said, laughing, but backing away from her. "Do not spoil the surprise for me, fair one. Ah, here is Mrs. Boothe coming."

"For goodness' sake!" muttered Rebecca, frowning a little as she watched him turn with a gleaming smile to greet Albinia. She shrugged. There was no point in worrying about it, and perhaps it was just as well. At least, she had tried.

Lady Ward received them with charm laced with condescension. To see them once more was very nice. They were so kind to bear this wilderness for the sake of little Pamela. It could only be hoped that the ball would provide ample recompense, as it should, since it was always The Event of the summer season and all the County *prayed* to be invited. As for herself, whilst in Town she had conferred with her modiste, and the most original and striking costume imaginable was even now being completed and would be rushed to Bedfordshire at the first possible instant. She coyly refused to divulge the nature of this masterpiece, pointing out that it would not be fair if the judges knew her identity prior to the unmasking lest this bring undue influence to bear. Nonetheless, she admitted she would certainly win the prize for the best costume.

Mrs. Boothe threw an indignant glance at her niece. Rebecca, however, was looking elsewhere. She had chosen a blue muslin gown this afternoon, a charming concoction with an underskirt consisting of row upon row of white eyelet ruffles. She knew she looked well, but was rather surprised by the depth of admiration in Sir Peter's eyes. Returning his smile with becoming shyness, she reminded herself that it would not do to become overconfident. He was certainly interested, but he was also interested in The Monahan, and his close friendship with The Wicked Rake might have resulted in notions that did not include matrimony. The presence of his grandmama was a hindrance also, for Rebecca was quite sure the lady would not approve of her becoming the future mistress of Ward Marching. All things considered, time was of the essence. When the ball was over, their month was also almost over. Sir Peter may have already interviewed a suitable candidate for the post of governess to Patience. There was another item Rebecca refused to consider at all: an item that lurked at the back of her mind, agitating for acknowledgement, its very presence rendering an early conquest even more imperative. She feared this persistent whisper and knew it was becoming stronger so that almost it was as though she fled before an impending disaster that crept nearer with each passing day until the threat would loom so large it must be faced and dealt with.

She cudgelled her brain for the schemes that had once come so readily to mind but that now seemed to elude her. At length, she decided that her entire reliance must lie in the glory of her ball dress. When she had tried on the great farthingale it had been found that only minimal alterations would be required. It was wretchedly uncomfortable, and in order to squeeze even so small a waist as her own into it had necessitated a much tighter lacing of her corsets than she usually affected. Once the rich crimson velvet was draped over those enormous hoops, however, and the pearl-edged stomacher was in place, they had all been able to comprehend why the ladies of that earlier period had been willing to endure such misery. Even with her hair informally dressed and minus the jewels she would wear at the ball, the effect had been bewitching. Mrs. Kellstrand, Aunt Albinia, Millie, and Evans alike had been rendered speechless at the sight, and, although it was odious even to think so conceited a thing, Rebecca had to admit that the rich colour did complement her jet hair and eyes, and she could not but be grateful that she had inherited the clear, pale skin of her British antecedents. If Sir Peter did not succumb when she was arrayed in that magnificent gown, it would be useless to make any further schemes to wring an offer from him.

This decision was arrived at, of course, before she had been introduced to the mouse.

❧

The day before the ball dawned fair and windy, with curtains blowing and windows rattling so that at length they had to be closed against the pranksome gusts. Several guests were to arrive this afternoon, and already the great house had begun to hum with preparations. Carts and wagons of tradespeople rumbled up the drivepath continually, the gardeners worked frenziedly at flower beds and shrubs, while house servants rushed about with mops and brooms and polish, as though the mansion had not been cleaned for years, rather than being maintained always in the first style of immaculate elegance.

Seated in her bedchamber while her aunt and Millie laboured over the shortening of her borrowed ball gown, Rebecca stitched busily at the torn frill of her best chemise. She was kept abreast of developments at the main house by an excited Anthony, who periodically would gallop up the stairs with Patience puffing behind him, to report to his mama. The ball gown was ready to be tried on; Rebecca laid her work aside and unfastened her wrapper. The wheel hoop was fastened about her, and the luxurious velvet draped over it. The length, Mrs. Boothe announced, after much fussing and adjusting, was perfect! Bearing the gown reverently, Mrs. Boothe and Millie went downstairs to undertake the final pressing, and Rebecca, replacing her wrapper, was left alone. Thirty minutes had passed since the children's last departure, and she was worrying over whether they were getting underfoot at Ward Marching, when shrieks arose from the direction of the kitchen. Another instant, and the door was flung open, and Anthony trod gingerly across the floor, his face rapturous and both hands carefully encompassing Something.

"Here, Mama," he whispered. "Only see what I found in the music room."

Eyeing his almost closed hands with the caution born of long acquaintance with large and small little boys, Rebecca said carefully, "Show me, love. I trust you are not making yourself a nuisance up there?"

"Oh, no. I was helping one of the flunkeys and he asked if I could move the bench, so I did and then I found it, but I said nothing for they would have been silly, you know, as Aunt Alby and Millie were just now. Is is not the prettiest thing?"

Lulled to a sense of security by that last sentence, Rebecca smiled and bent forward. She drew back hurriedly. The mouse was quite small, but the tail compensated, and the bright eyes and busy pink nose combined to send the foolish shiver down her spine that all rodents caused in her. "Good—ah, gracious," she said faintly.

"Ith a mouthie," Patience beamed from the doorway. "Lottha mouthieth."

Rebecca glanced to her. "All in the music room?"

Anthony nodded. "I only brought this one. I was thinking, though, that I had best take them away, or there might be a rumpus, do not you think? For lots of ladies are come now."

"Are they so? I had thought no one was to arrive until this afternoon."

"Ith art'noon," lisped Patience, and, coming forward, squeaked, "Art'noon, mouthie!"

"Do not scare him," Anthony rebuked angrily, swinging the little creature away.

Her eyes following his hands, Patience's vision encompassed the window. "More peopleth!" she chirped.

Anthony gave a whoop. "Three carriages, by Jupiter! And two with crests on the panels!" And he was gone, Patience trundling faithfully in his wake.

He relinquished his captive as soon as he left the cottage and, comforting himself with the recollection that cats were anathema at Ward Marching, charged in the direction of the main house. He completely forgot about the unauthorized inhabitants of the music room.

At six o'clock, Rebecca and Mrs. Boothe, who always dined at the main house, entered the drawing room. It was quite crowded. Rebecca knew most of those present by sight, if not intimately. Letitia Boudreaux had arrived and ran to greet her. She was followed by the gentleman with whom she had been chatting, a singularly handsome young man who begged an introduction and was presented as Horatio, Viscount Glendenning. Rebecca liked his friendly smile and the lack of any height to his manner and thought it remarkable he was not wed. Walter and Martha Street came over and said in their cooperative fashion that they had so hoped to find Mrs. Parrish present.

"You are certainly—" began Miss Street.

"—in looks," said her brother heartily. "Dare we ask—"

"—what you mean to wear to the ball?"

Giving a hand to each, Rebecca apologized for being a marplot, but, "Is a secret," she finished with a dimple.

"So everyone says," Mr. Street observed. "Including Lady Ward. But we know—"

"—how *she* means to dress!"

"*Do* you?" said Rebecca, highly intrigued. "Oh, *do* pray tell me! Is it Joan of Arc? My lady let fall a little hint about a warrior maid."

Mr. Street said confidingly, "Wrong warrior, ma'am. She will come as—"

"—Queen Boadicea!" Miss Street finished in triumph.

"A warrior, indeed. Though I had thought she was wed— no?" Rebecca could not imagine that sharp-featured face hidden beneath a great helm, and, dubious, murmured, "Are you quite sure? I doubt it will become her."

"Several of the gentlemen have a tidy wager riding on it," Miss Street said confirmingly. "The Reverend Boudreaux, Colonel Shephard, my brother—"

"—and de Villars and Glendenning," said Mr. Street.

Rebecca's heart gave a jolt. "De Villars?" she echoed, hollowly.

"At your service, dear lady," purred a deep and familiar voice at her elbow.

It was ridiculous to tremble so as she gave him her hand. Many in the room must be watching her reaction to this man who had fought her brother. She should appear cool, and was infuriated to feel her cheeks burn because of a treacherous memory of being crushed to his breast and smothered with kisses.

"Not *too* ardent, love," he teased softly, as he kissed her hand. "Else they may guess 'twas your bewitching self we fought over."

She bit her lip. What an uncanny knack he had for putting her at a disadvantage! Suppressing a powerful desire to rap her fan over his horrid head, she said in an undertone, "What a pity you are so well recovered of your deathbed!"

Walter Street, who had been engaged in converse with a military man, now turned to ask, "May I make you known to Captain Holt, Mrs. Parrish?"

Rebecca gave the captain her hand, and he bowed over it stiffly. "And did you track down all your poor Jacobite wretches, sir?"

"Had I done so, ma'am," he said, his eyes chips of ice, "I might already wear a major's epaulettes."

De Villars gave him a surprisingly friendly smile. "Better luck next time. Ah, there you are, my Peter. Have you seen The Little Parrish?"

"A vision well worth the waiting for." Sir Peter bowed over Rebecca's hand, then turned to greet Holt.

The Duchess of Chilton came up to say she had met Anthony earlier in the afternoon and found him a delightful child. She was a large lady of late middle age, with a jolly face and an amiable but lethargic disposition balanced by a tireless tongue. De Villars' attempt to monopolize Rebecca was foiled, and he turned with faint boredom to the discussion of the rebellion that now occupied Ward and Captain Holt. The Duchess was well under way with an enumeration of the sterling qualities of each of her numerous grandchildren. Rebecca managed to appear politely attentive, but her attention drifted to Ward and de Villars as they stood side by side.

They presented a marked contrast, for although both had the easy assurance that comes with birth, breeding, and a fine education, there all resemblance ceased. Ward, his powdered hair enhancing the perfection of his features, was clad in a coat of maroon velvet, open to reveal a superb brocaded waistcoat. His knee breeches were of deep pink satin; diamonds glittered in the buckles of his shoes and in a great ring he wore. He presented a handsome, gallant figure, the very essence of masculine grace and charm. De Villars, on the other hand, looked positively Satanic. He also wore a velvet coat, but it was black, the only trim being heavy silver embroidery worked on the cuffs of the great sleeves. His waistcoat was of silver lamé, his breeches a light grey. His hair, which, when allowed to curl, tended to soften his gaunt features, was well powdered, but far more austerely dressed than were Ward's softly waving locks, and the only jewellery he affected was a great ruby ring. He was not Satanic, of course, Rebecca thought judicially. But he lacked Sir Peter's gentleness and kindness. His manners were haughty and often offensive, his every thought and action directed towards the furtherance of his own schemes. Her verdict, arrived at with regret, was that he was, at best, a care-for-nobody; a violent gentleman of lascivious appetite. And of minuscule fortune.

Sir Peter proffered his arm. She cut off her deliberations and went with him to be presented to those guests whose acquaintance she lacked. The ladies were gracious, the gentlemen gallant, and Rebecca chattered and laughed and won them all with her gaiety and unaffected good manners. But her heart was heavy, and her mood did not improve when a flurry of activity at the door marked the entrance of a tall lady whose hair shone red-gold in a ray of sunlight. Rebecca was fairly sure that The Monahan was the "charming lady" who had informed Snowden of the wager which had precipitated the duel. If she had "a score to settle" with de Villars, however, there was no visible sign of ill-feeling between them now. He lost no time in joining the small crowd surrounding The Beauty and kissed her hand with obvious affection, while she laughed and appeared to flirt with him merrily.

The room became warmer and noisier as more and more guests arrived. Many were bachelors, and soon Rebecca stood at the centre of a group of admirers. She was teased about her fishing prowess, scolded for having deprived London Town of her divine presence these past few weeks, flattered, and flirted with to a highly satisfactory degree. From the corner of her eye she noted when Sir Peter gravitated to The Monahan and a little later was amused when Mr. George Melton came in, looked about, and wandered nonchalantly to the side of Mrs. Boothe. His sober visage seemed to be even more grave than usual, marking which, Rebecca wondered if he was jealous because her aunt had been chatting with Colonel Shephard, a chubby, red-faced, and genial retired heavy dragoon with a splendid pair of whiskers.

Mr. Street was Rebecca's dinner partner, and she was seated between that gentleman and Captain Holt. A tall, extremely ornate silver epergne blocked her view of the person sitting opposite, until that individual summoned a footman to remove the offending article. A laugh went up. From across the table Rebecca encountered two deeply lashed eyes of grey that twinkled at her irrepressibly. Scarlet, she saw Mrs. Monahan lean forward slightly, so as to see who had requested the adjustment, then settle back, an enigmatic smile on her lovely face. Rebecca could only be grateful when Mr. Street engaged her in a lengthy discussion of the merits of Mr. Walpole, despite his scandalous relationship with Molly Skerrett. Captain Holt was not a bright companion, but after a few glasses of wine, he become fairly human and dinner went along merrily enough.

Someone asked Ward what he planned for them in the way of entertainment at the ball. "A few surprises," he said smilingly, "and—I hope—several delights. Among which will be our lovely Mrs. Parrish, who will sing for us."

De Villars asked through the applause, "Before midnight, Peter?"

"No. It will have to be after the unmasking." Ward explained to Rebecca, "Did you sing before midnight, ma'am, everyone would recognize that pretty little voice of yours."

The Reverend Boudreaux said that Ward was too good to them, but over his mild tones could be heard Lady Ward's comments that Mrs. Parrish *did* have a pretty enough speaking voice, although it was rather husky. As the reverend stopped speaking, her following remark was murmured with disastrous clarity, "I wonder if that could be because she tipples."

Mr. de Villars, who had just taken a mouthful of wine, choked, and had to be pounded on the back. His chivalry aroused, Lord Glendenning launched into the tale of a jaunt he had made to Wales in search of a splendid stallion who had proved to be a perfect slug.

Rebecca knew that several diners were looking at her sympathetically, but her dislike of Lady Ward's arrogant manner was fanned to a flame. She stared fixedly at the blancmange on her plate, and hoped with all her heart that tomorrow at least twenty other ladies would have decided to be Queen Boadicea. Warming to the notion, she decided that each of their costumes would be far more attractive than that of Lady Ward. From here, it was but a step to envision the great house fairly crawling with Boadiceas. Ward Marching would be positively overrun with versions of the fierce first-century Queen. There would be some famous mix-ups, thought Rebecca gleefully, and the ball might turn out to be a much livelier affair than one might have— She stiffened with shock as her ankle received a brisk kick.

De Villars was regarding her with a look of warning. She was appalled then, both by her lapse of manners in having allowed her thoughts to drift while at table, and also by the knowledge that she must have presented a picture of dejection. De Villars' eyes turned to the right. Glancing that way, Rebecca discovered another gaze pinned to her. She responded brightly to a remark of Mr. Street's, but her heart sank. My Lady Ward had very obviously noticed her behaviour and was probably thinking her an ill-bred girl, sadly wanting in manners.

She looked gratefully at The Wicked Rake. He was conversing politely with Mrs. Shephard, a flirtatious woman considerably younger than her husband, but as though he sensed her regard, he glanced at Rebecca. She smiled a silent "thank you." A grin flickered, then he returned his attention to his dinner partner.

From the head of the table, Sir Peter Ward marked this small exchange. His own polite smile faded into something approaching a frown.

Mrs. Monahan, who had also missed none of it, was affected differently; her reaction was, in fact, exactly the reverse of Sir Peter's.

❧

When the ladies adjourned to the withdrawing room, Lady Ward entertained them with a kindly lecture anent the ills of absent-mindedness, which was, she declared, the product of an inferior intelligence. Her austere gaze rested often upon Rebecca during this monologue, and there was little doubt but that the widow was being reprimanded. Happily, Rebecca was rescued. A footman approached to tell her that Sir Peter sent his compliments and the suggestion that she might wish to look through the music and make her selections. She agreed at once, and he led her to the music room, adding, "The master says he will join madam so soon as the gentlemen are done with their port and cigars, and that if it is convenient, you could practise your songs with him in the morning."

A fire burned in the large pleasant chamber, although the evening was not very chill, and the room was a blaze of light from the many branches of candles. The footman, having ascertained that Mrs. Parrish was comfortable, bowed and departed. Rebecca found quite a lot of music in the armoire chest he had opened for her, but upon leafing through it, discovered that it consisted mainly of pieces for violin or harpsichord, and there were very few songs. She could accompany herself, if necessary, but she always sang more smoothly if she could concentrate on the words without having to attend to the music as well. It occurred to her then that the lighter pieces might be more often played, and thus be stored in the harpsichord bench.

When Anthony had told her of his encounter with the mice, she had supposed the creatures to have been lurking somewhere underneath the bench. She discovered her error when she opened the lid. There were four of them: a mother and her offspring, and they had been busy, for the music was in shreds. They began to scurry wildly about and, with a yelp of fright, Rebecca dropped the lid and retreated. She was almost to the door when she heard Sir Peter's pleasant laugh ring out. The gentlemen must be leaving the dining room. She paused, her eyes thoughtful.

"No, really," called Ward. "I shall return directly."

He was coming to fetch her. She ran swiftly back to the bench. Quick light steps were approaching as she opened it. The resultant confusion was chaotic. "I am sorry," she whispered. "But there are no cats, you know."

The steps were very close. She let out a discreetly quiet scream, and swayed convincingly.

A startled exclamation. Swift movements, and a strong arm was supporting her. She could smell the fragrance of him. A faint essence of shaving soap; a hint of a clean, manly scent. She sagged limply, not daring to peep. Her pulses leapt with triumph when she heard a quick intake of breath, then felt a kiss pressed tenderly on her brow. He would do better than that, surely? She had not long to wait. His lips were soon caressing her cheek, her throat. Her heart began to thunder when the kisses moved lower. Ward was more daring than she had thought. *Much* more daring! She shivered to an electrifying thrill.

And she knew. Her eyes flew open.

With a mocking smile, de Villars bent above her.

"You!" she exclaimed, leaping back.

He bowed. "Am I not the most fortunate of men to have been delegated to come and fetch you?"

"You are *despicable!*" she raged. "Have you not insulted me enough?"

He put up his quizzing glass and scanned her flushed face with offended innocence. "Insulted you? How?"

"You know what you just did!"

"*I* do," he grinned. "But *you* should not, for you were swooning, I think."

"Well, I was, but— Oh! I thought you were Sir Peter!"

"You surprise me. I'd no idea he was such a naughty boy."

"He is not! You know—I mean—I would *not* have—"

"Not have objected had he—ah, caressed you as did I?" He swung the glass gently at the end of its red velvet riband, and murmured shrewdly, "Or did you perchance fancy you had entrapped him—at last?"

With a snort of impotent fury, Rebecca turned on her heel. And was seized, wrenched around by hands of iron, and crushed against his muscular body. "Foolish, most enchanting little creature," he breathed huskily. "Why will you persist in denying your heart?"

His mouth was very close; his eyes ineffably tender. And whether or not it was denied, her traitorous heart was trying its best to jump right through her poor abused ribs. "I—I do no such thing," she asserted, and demanded feebly, "Loose me . . . at once. . . ."

He did not loose her. Instead, his lips sought hers with a fierce insistence. She seemed to melt under them, and that same heady weakness was overpowering her faint decision to scratch him. A fundamental need to draw breath rescued her from this disgraceful delirium. She tore her head away and dragged a hand across her mouth.

Still holding her, de Villars murmured, "I love you, sweeting. More, I swear, than I have ever loved. Forget this sordid pursuit of fortune. It would not serve, for—"

"Sordid!" She pushed him away and, because she was very afraid, half sobbed, "Let me be! Oh—let me *be!* Can you not see that I do not *want* you? And you do not love me! You *desire* me, only, and try to force me. But—*love* cannot be forced! Have you never learnt that?"

He stiffened. With a curl of the lip, he said, "Were Peter Ward as—as penniless as I—would you choose him, I wonder?"

"Yes! And yes! Were he poor and had no title, I would still honour him, for he treats me always with respect. Not once has *he* grabbed me as though I were the merest trollop! Never has he forced so much as a hug upon me, much less crushed me like a demented bear and smothered me with odious unwanted kisses!"

His mouth became a thin, hard line. He gave a grunt of cynicism and with anger flaring in his eyes said curtly, "The more fool he!"

"How typical that *you* should think so! Oh, you may say 'tis only that I long for position and—and security. But the truth is that Peter Ward offers so much more!"

One brow lifted in surprise. "*Offers?* Have you then manoeuvred him into a proposal of marriage? My felicitations, ma'am."

The choice of words, the contemptuous sneer made her

shiver with rage. "I have manoeuvred him into nothing! But—
but if he should—"

"Come up to scratch?" he supplied.

"If he should offer," she said, fixing him with a look of
withering scorn, "I am perfectly sure it would be with honour!"

De Villars contemplated the small, angry face, the flashing
eyes, and his own gaze fell. "And—what if I were to make you
a—er, similarly 'honourable' offer?"

Was he truly offering her marriage? The Licentious Rake?
The Libertine of London? Astounded, and with a sudden
breathlessness quickening her bosom, she stared at him.

He glanced up from under his lashes. The expression he
had so hoped to see was not there. The incredulity in her
lovely face was instead a thing so wounding that his wrath
flared. "No title and small fortune present an insurmountable
barrier, I see," he said, and added with disgust, "How typical!
You women are all alike."

Rebecca gave a gasp. He was impossible! And how dare
such as *he* censure her? "How could you offer me a similarly
honourable proposal?" she countered, just as willing to hurt as
was he. "Sir Peter stands for all the things you do not!"

He whitened. "Does he, indeed? I must congratulate the
peerless gentleman. And amongst those things, you list—what?
A saintly morality? Nobility par excellence? In addition to looks
and money, of course."

Close to hysteria, Rebecca saw only his sneer and acid
eyes, while the little pulse that beat beside his jaw, the spas-
modic clenching of his hands escaped her. Gritting her teeth,
she ground out, "Yes! Honour above all things! Courage and
compassion and selflessness! Have *you* ever known such, Mr. de
Villars? Have *you* ever cared for anything but your own needs?
Have you ever imagined that love might be something other
than the brief passion of a night spent with some lightskirt?
That it might be a mutual caring and respect—a sharing of bur-
dens and happiness and sorrows, down through the years? A
growing together that becomes something more than love—
more of a oneness—a belonging. The lady so fortunate as to
wed Sir Peter Ward will know that, I am assured! She will

never face the unhappy probability that a—a bird of paradise lures him away, or that some lovely highflyer has been comfortably established nearby! For the ring *he* puts on her finger will stand for all that is beautiful and holy and lasting in a marriage!"

She paused, appalled by the forthright words temper had goaded her into uttering. She felt weak and shaken. What a speech she had made! And how still he was, how pale as he stood there, staring at her with that odd, blank look in his eyes! Lord knows, she'd not meant to scourge him so. But he had thoroughly upset and enraged her.

De Villars drew a deep breath. "Dear me," he murmured ironically. "I really have established myself as the complete blackguard, I see."

Tears blurred Rebecca's eyes, and a lump rose in her throat. She was overwrought, which was not to be wondered at after such a dreadful scene, but she did not want him to see her weep, and so stepped quickly to the door. He made no attempt to stay her, but she could not leave with such bitter words between them and, hurriedly drying her tears, she turned back.

He stood with head downbent, watching the quizzing glass swing slowly from one hand. He was very pale still, and on his lips that cynical mockery of a smile. Rebecca thought with a pang of remorse that, whatever else, he *had* spared Snow. He was not a blackguard, she thought repentantly, but before she could speak, he glanced up.

"You play fair, I see," he said. "Thank you for granting me time for a rebuttal." He wandered towards her.

Rebecca edged back uneasily.

He lifted one hand in a calming gesture. "Have no fears. I shall not again molest you. We have, perhaps, come to know one another better in our few stolen moments than many couples who stand before the altar together. For one thing at least, I must honour you, ma'am: your concept of the married state. The relationship you so graphically described is surely one that has been yearned for by countless maids and men." He gave a slight shrug and the sardonic lines beside his nostrils deepened. "It would surprise you to know that even I, in my—ah, dark depravity, have longed for such a blessed partnership."

Remorseful, she tried to speak, but again his slim hand made an imperative gesture, and he went on, "That type of paradise, however, has little to do with avarice and ambition. And I doubt will prove any easier to find by *your* methods, Mrs. Parrish, than by mine own."

ða

It was past two o'clock before the last card game was concluded and sleepy footmen began to snuff out the lights in the drawing room. Sir Peter handed a candle to the rather bosky commodore who still lingered in the hall, summoned a lackey to aid the befuddled gentleman to his bedchamber, and smothered a yawn. As was his habit before retiring, he went back into the drawing room to assure himself that the terrace doors were locked, and was mildly surprised to see the glow of a cheroot outside. He opened the door and, joining his guest, said, "What, you, Treve? Not quite in your style to gaze at the moon, is it, old fellow?"

Perched on the low wall that edged the terrace, de Villars surveyed him coolly. "Are you wearing your sword, Peter? No, I see you are not. Regrettable. I really think I might like to run you through." He blew a cloud of smoke into the air and, watching it spiral, grey against the night sky, added, "And through. And through."

"Good God!" Ward laughed uncertainly. "A fine way to treat your friends! What have I done?"

"I am informed on excellent authority that you are honourable, courageous, compassionate, and selfless."

Ward uttered a strangled exclamation, and de Villars amended, "Forgot one. That you will be a faithful and devoted husband."

Sir Peter's brows lifted. "Aha!" He sauntered to lean back against the wall beside his friend and, folding his arms, said, "The lady shows most excellent judgement. Are you acknowledging defeat, then?"

De Villars swore softly and savagely. "You shall have my draft in the morning. A thousand, I think?"

"Yes." Watching the lean profile outlined against the faint glow from the windows, Ward said slowly, "She properly sent you to the right-about, eh?"

"Oh, absolutely. She grassed me, stepped upon my loathsome carcass, and wiped her dainty shoes upon me. Had she not been such a gently bred chit, I do believe she would have spat upon me." He ground out his cheroot on the terrace wall, smiled without mirth, and said, "I am quite *hors de combat*, my Peter. The field is yours." He offered a flourishing bow, and started off.

Straightening, Ward caught his arm. "Wait."

De Villars looked over his shoulder. "Never say you do not want the lady?"

"Have I said it? She is a very choice little creature."

"Spare me."

They started to the doors together. Inside, Ward turned the key and said slowly, "What a gudgeon you are. You had two ace cards. Why not play them?"

"I played one." De Villars shrugged, his face unreadable in the dimness. "It did not serve. Even the glorious opportunity—so seldom given, you'll mind—to bear my name, did not move her."

"You—*offered* for her? *Marriage?*"

"Damn you, Peter! You sound as astonished as was she! Hell and the devil confound it, am I *so* base?" The lazy drawl had vanished, the words uneven and strained, as though torn from him.

Ward slipped a consoling hand onto one powerful shoulder. "No, Treve. Of course you are not. You only like to make everyone *believe* you are. 'Fraid it's caught up with you, dear old boy."

CHAPTER
❧ 12 ❧

"*Of* course I believe it!" Strolling through the dewy morning, one hand resting lightly on her escort's arm, Mrs. Boothe said indignantly, "It is *always* de Villars! I vow, Mr. Melton, he is Rebecca's Nemesis! Everything runs along nicely, and then up pops that wretched man and my poor niece's plans are scattered to the four winds! Oh, I beg you will not ask what it was he said last evening, for she refuses to tell me. I only know she was happy and hopeful of—er, enjoying a lovely time, and then *he* came! She was so enraged I dare swear she never slept a wink! Is a wretch, Mr. Melton! A libertine and a—a marplot! I wish he would be gone and allow my sweet Becky to be happy and carefree once again!"

"Well, he has, ma'am," soothed Mr. Melton, daring to pat the small hand upon his sleeve.

However lost in resentment, Mrs. Boothe was aware of this little caress, and she blushed becomingly. "He has?" she echoed. "De Villars is gone? Oh—are you perfectly sure, sir?"

"My man told me his bed was not slept in, and that his valet is properly in the boughs because there has been no word from him. He has a favourite mare he always rides here, and she also is gone. I have been unable to learn more, but—" He shrugged. "'Twould seem to indicate he has left."

"How famous!" exclaimed Mrs. Boothe. "Might we return to the cottage, Mr. Melton? I can scarce wait to tell Rebecca—'twill make her so exceeding glad!"

When the news was relayed to Rebecca, however, she did not seem at all glad. She said, "Oh," in a very small voice, and promptly burst into tears.

"My love!" wailed the dismayed Mrs. Boothe. "You had not wished that The Wicked Rake remain?"

"I hate him!" raged Rebecca.

"Of course you do, my sweet. Who would not?"

"He saved Snowden's life!" Rebecca gulped contrarily, glaring through her tears.

"Well, I know but, surely—"

"And he is *not* a wicked rake! He never forced— Well, he *did*, but I mean— He always let me go when—when I bade him. . . ."

Mrs. Boothe gave a gasp, and echoed weakly, "Let you . . . *go?* You—you mean he—"

"No, I do not," said Rebecca, sniffing crossly. "Not that he did not try!"

"Well, then, dearest, I do not understand why—"

"No. You could not, but—it is—it is only that he has . . . spoiled *everything!*"

"Yes, but—if he has gone away . . . ?"

"I hope he has!" Rebecca narrowed her rather reddened eyes. "I only pray I shall *never* see the revolting brute again!"

And she went off to join Sir Peter and rehearse the songs she would sing tonight, leaving her aunt staring after her, nonplussed.

Halfway across the park, Rebecca met Snowden. He came striding up the path towards her, head down. Astonished, she saw that he wore his sword and was booted and spurred and quite muddied. She was so taken aback by his sudden appearance at a party he had earlier stigmatized as being the greatest bore in creation that she halted and stood watching him approach.

He glanced up, saw her, and waved, and she ran to hug and be hugged.

"Rascal!" she cried, beaming into his face. "Had you meant all the time to surprise me by coming?"

He drew her hand through his arm and walked on with her. "Coming? Oh—to the ball, you mean. Well—er, that's it, of course. Only I was—ah, delayed. On business, y'know. And—"

"Forty's business?" She laughed. "But then you learnt The Monahan was to be here, so you raced back, am I right?"

"No, is she? Jove, that's splendid! Have you seen—er, anyone else?"

The tone was light, yet he scanned her face intently. Scrutinizing him in turn, she said, "Of course I have, silly. Who do you— Snow! You look downright exhausted. Is something wrong? Oh—is it your poor wrist?"

"Pho! Never! 'Tis only that—" He checked both words and stride.

Following his uncharacteristically stern stare, Rebecca saw that an old friend approached. "Why, it is Hilary Broadbent." She held out a welcoming hand. "Major! How very nice to see you here. Are you also come for the party?"

"Wish I was!" The dashing young officer bowed over her

hand and, straightening, said, "I'm on duty, I'm afraid, Rebecca. How do you do, Snow?"

Boothe said irascibly, "Dashed poorly, do you want the
truth of it. Forty and I went to look over some horses, and—"

"Went where?" asked the major with mild curiosity.

"Eh? Oh, Newcastle."

"Upon-Tyne?"

Boothe groaned an exasperated, "You too? My sister and I
had at that question before I left! It's all of a piece. Thing is,
I've lost Forty, and—"

"Dashed long way to go to look at a horse, was it not?"

Again, the tone was mild, but Boothe's eyes sparked. "No,
it was not! You going to arrest me for riding to Newcastle,
Broadbent?"

Shocked, Rebecca interpolated, "Snow! You are tired,
love. I'm sure Hilary did not mean—"

"Well, I'd like to know just what the devil the major *did*
mean! Ain't no law against riding north, south, east, or west, to
look at a *spider*, does a man take it into his head to do so! And
if there is, I'd like to know about it, so Uncle Quincy can raise
the question in the Upper House!"

It was one of the few times in his life that Rebecca had
ever heard him mention a distant, influential, and much disliked relation. Snowden, she thought, was unusually prickly today. She wondered uneasily if he had somehow learned of de
Villars' disgraceful behaviour towards her. The very thought of
de Villars brought dread of another duel, and she inserted a
nervous recommendation that both gentlemen come up to the
house and drink a glass of wine. The major declined, saying
that he must get back to his headquarters, but he would hope
to drop by for a short while this evening, if only to enjoy all the
costumes. He then smiled to Rebecca, nodded civilly to
Boothe, and went off stablewards.

Boothe scowled. "I'd no idea that blasted fellow was sta-
tioned hereabouts, had you?"

"'Blasted fellow'?" Bewildered, Rebecca protested, "But—
you've known Hilary for years and years. Whatever has come
between you?"

Boothe gave her a fulminating look. She smiled at him, hopefully, and his set jaw relaxed. "Sorry, m'dear. I must be just—tired, as you said. There were so blasted many military people on the road north. Dashed if I didn't get sick of the sight of 'em! Rushing and shouting about; searching every henhouse and dog kennel three or four times over like a blasted lot of treasure seekers, looking for those poor Jacobite gentlemen! I tell you, it was damned disgusting! Even had a sergeant and two troopers come bursting into my hotel room one night and roust me out of bed whilst they went through my clothes press. They had the unmitigated gall to pull off all the sheets and blankets! Confounded impertinence!"

Trying to banish the rage which had crept back into his eyes during this recital, she said, "Yes, indeed. And how fortunate you was alone, love."

Boothe glanced at her sharply.

"Well, only think," she said with a saucy smile. "Suppose it had been someone like de Villars. There's no telling who that sergeant might have rousted from *his* bed!"

Her brother laughed heartily. "Two or three ladybirds, at the very least—eh?" He squeezed her arm. "You little baggage! What a thing for a lady to say! Tell me now what has been going on—if anything. And who else is here?"

She told him about the mice, though without mentioning The Wicked Rake, and was satisfied from his amused reaction he knew nothing of it. "And as for who is here," she went on lightly, "everyone you might expect. The Streets, and Lady Ward, and de Villars. The Duchess of Chilton, The Monahan, the Reverend Boudreaux and his sister, Lord—"

"Letitia Boudreaux?" Having been apparently unimpressed by the fact that his recent antagonist and a duchess were present, Boothe brightened perceptibly. "I'd best go and change out of my dirt before she sees me."

As it transpired, however, he had no chance to observe this civility, for Miss Boudreaux and her brother came onto the front steps just as Boothe and Rebecca were mounting them. Letitia turned quite pink, and her eyes flew to Boothe's bandaged wrist. Boothe made his bow, shook her brother's hand in a left-handed grip, and exchanged cheery commonplaces with him, then turned back to ask Letitia if she would care to take a turn about the park with him. She said shyly that she would like very much to go for a walk on such a beautiful morning. Boothe offered his arm and led her down the steps.

Embarrassed, Rebecca said, "I do apologize, sir. That was rude beyond permission. My brother should have consulted you before taking your sister away. I beg you will excuse him. I fancy he is rather tired—he is only now returned from the north."

The reverend, who had been watching the departing couple with a faint smile, darted a glance at her. "Boothe is a perfect gentleman, I believe."

"Oh, indeed." Walking back into the house beside him, she said earnestly, "He is a very warm-hearted boy, and has usually the most sunny disposition."

"When he is not fighting duels, eh?"

A lackey had swung open the front door and, as they passed through, Rebecca looked up at Boudreaux anxiously. The grey eyes twinkled down at her, and with a sigh of relief she said, "That was not really Snowden's fault, for if—" She bit the words off hurriedly. Heavens, but she'd almost betrayed herself!

Boudreaux said in his shy way, "Ma'am, might I have a private word with you? I think most of the guests are not yet abroad. Could we go into the book room for a moment or two?"

Intrigued, she went with him. He left the door open and, having ushered her to a window seat, drew a wing chair closer, and occupied it. Rebecca felt a pleasant tingle of anticipation. He was undoubtedly going to speak of Letitia and Snow, for her brother's interest in the girl had been even more obvious this morning. How lovely it would be to have a wedding in the family! She could be matron of honour, and—

"I do not know how de Villars has alienated your brother, Mrs. Parrish," said the reverend, shattering her rosy dreams. "But I wish you will believe he is very far from the villain gossip has painted him."

Rebecca experienced a compelling urge to run from the

room. He had brought her in here to talk of de Villars? How unfair! Here was she, striving very hard to not so much as *think* of that Person, much less discuss him! Hoping to discourage this earnest young man, she said coldly, "Mr. de Villars' behaviour towards me, sir, cannot but lead me to believe that rumour has dealt exceeding kindly with him."

He looked distressed. Leaning forward in his chair, he clasped his long bony hands and said with sincerity, "I am indeed sorry to hear you say that. I know he is a trifle—er, reckless at times. But, truly, he has a great deal to recommend him. Had you but seen him as a youth, always full of energy and fun, and showing so much promise. He was easily the most popular man in his class. Kind, generous . . ." He sighed. "I never knew him to turn his back on a friend, or to give way to moods or distempered starts."

"Indeed? How much he is changed, sir."

"Yes." The untidy head was shaken regretfully. "By rights he should be setting up his nursery by now. Unhappily, the girl he chose did not—"

She did not want to know about it. She had not the smallest interest, but somehow she was saying a brittle, "Oh, come now, Mr. Boudreaux! You surely are not going to tell me about the lady who turned out to be his grandpapa's *chère amie?*"

The reverend's jaw dropped. "His . . . grandpapa?" he echoed, fascinated.

"Yes. And how de Villars eloped with her, but his grandpapa came up with them and nigh killed de Villars in a duel!"

The clergyman threw back his head and went into a shout of mirth. "He was hoaxing you, of course," he said, still chuckling. "Probably to draw you off the track."

"Of—what?"

"Why, the true story. I'll not paint him a saint, ma'am. I know him to be a fine man, but he has more than his share of human frailties, I own it. Among the worst is his pride." The laughter faded from Boudreaux's eyes. "He don't like his wounds touched. If he suspected you knew the truth, he would shrink from your sympathy."

"I see." Rebecca stood. "Then perhaps you should not tell me of it, sir. I certainly have no wish to—"

"So this is where you are hiding!" Sir Peter came into the room, elegant as ever, his eyes flickering over Boudreaux to come to rest with patent admiration on Rebecca.

Boudreaux, who had sprung to his feet, frowned. "If you could allow me another minute or two, Ward."

"Cannot be done, Fitz." Peter gave his arm to the willing Rebecca and said laughingly, "This charming lady and I have an urgent appointment—a musical tryst that must be kept before my other guests are up and stirring. You will excuse us, I know."

The reverend gentleman protested in vain; Rebecca was borne off to a music room now lacking mice, and the rehearsal began.

Sir Peter played well, as she had anticipated, and was the perfect accompanist for her not very strong voice. She had agreed to sing three songs, and it transpired that she was not to be the only contributor to the evening's entertainment. Lord Glendenning, said Ward, would play the harp for them, and Mrs. Monahan had also agreed to sing.

Unease stirring in her breast, Rebecca said, "I fancy you will wish to hasten then, sir, for you will want to practise Mrs. Monahan's music with her."

"Oh, no. I am accustomed to playing for Rosemary. We have plenty of time."

He had no sooner uttered these disquieting words than his butler put in an appearance. It seemed that my Lady Ward was having a spasm because an essential part of her costume was incorrectly sized; Major Broadbent required an immediate interview; and a courier from London was distraught because the urgent communiqué he had brought Mr. de Villars from my Lord Geoffrey Boudreaux could not be placed in the gentleman's hands.

"Egad, what a bumble broth!" Sir Peter stood and, reluctantly folding the music, said, "By your leave, Mrs. Parrish, I shall go to my grandmama at once. Greywood, you will please put Major Broadbent in my study, and tell him I shall be at his disposal in twenty minutes. As for Mr. de Villars, I take it he is not in his bedchamber?"

"Not since the wee hours, sir. I am told he rode out before dawn and has not as yet returned."

Briefly, Sir Peter looked worried. Then he turned his ready smile on Rebecca. "Mrs. Parrish, I am eternally grateful. Your pretty songs will greatly enhance my party. I shall look forward to seeing you at luncheon."

Rebecca returned to the cottage and went up to her bedchamber where she found Mrs. Boothe clad in a wrapper and settled in a comfortable chair at the window. She was sipping hot chocolate and looking mournful. In response to her niece's enquiries she answered sadly that Evans had taken the children to the village. And that although she was perfectly sure Mr. Melton's affections were engaged, it was the most shackle-shy gentleman ever created. "I am no more successful than you, my love," she sighed, twirling the remaining chocolate in her cup.

Rebecca sat down at her dressing table and inspected herself in the beautifully bevelled mirror. "This ball, dearest," she murmured, dusting some powder onto her pert nose, "may spell the *coup de grâce* for us both. I fancy The Monahan has her claws more firmly into Sir Peter than I had supposed."

"Oh, never say so! I was sure she is still fond of de Villars!"

"I rather think she is. . . . 'Twould seem she is a lady of— diverse interests. Whatever. Mr. de Villars has apparently vanished." Rebecca scowled at the inoffensive hare's foot and added a firm, "Fortunately."

"Fortunately, indeed!" Mrs. Boothe set aside her cup and saucer and hissed theatrically, "And just in time! You know that Snowden has come?"

"Oh, yes. And at once went for a walk with Miss Boudreaux."

"Did he so? Well, he is back and rushing about like any madman. He means to change his dress and ride into the village in search of a seamstress who can conjure him up something to wear this evening. Faith, one might think—"

"Hail, me proud beauties!" The object of their discussion came blithely into the room, looking very dashing in his leather riding coat. "And farewell." He grinned at Rebecca, and went on, "As saith the Immortal Bard."

Wrinkling her brow, she demurred, "Are you sure? I thought it was somebody else."

"Devil a bit of it. I only remember two quotations, and they both are his I feel sure. 'I come to bury Caesar, not to raise him,' and 'Hail and farewell, bother'—or is it 'brother'? Some such claptrap!"

Rebecca gave a trill of laughter, but her aunt said indignantly, "Claptrap! No, really, Snowden! You lack the proper respect!"

He shrugged unrepentantly. "For Shakespeare, perhaps. But not for certain other—celestial creatures. . . ."

Rebecca turned from surveying her brother's suddenly dreamy countenance in her mirror, and faced him fully. "You could not possibly refer to Miss Letitia Boudreaux?"

He flushed scarlet. "Eh? Oh . . ." He turned away, making quite a business of shooting the lace at his wrists. "Matter of fact, I was thinking of someone else. Not that Letitia ain't a jolly delightful chit. Pity she's so tall, though. When we were walking just now, I noticed her shadow was head to head with mine."

"What difference?" Vexed, Rebecca declared, "Miss Boudreaux is a girl in a thousand, and—"

"Yes, my love," Mrs. Boothe put in hurriedly. "But she is more than half promised to Jeremiah Kier-Byerby."

Rebecca stared at her aunt in amazement, met a faint flicker of one eyelid, and managed to assume a pleased air. "Why, I *had* heard a whisper of it! Is it truth then, dearest? What a famous match!"

"Famous?" Boothe exclaimed, his face dark with anger. "I call it *in*famous! Kier-Byerby ain't as tall as Letty. Deuce take it, he ain't as tall as *me!*"

"And what has that to say to anything?" Rebecca took up a buffer and began to polish her nails. "I fancy Mr. Kier-Byerby has known sufficient ladies to have a value for what is worthy and what is not."

"If by 'sufficient ladies' you mean half the women in Mayfair," Boothe fumed, "you have the right of't. Why, the man's a positive rakehell! I'll be dashed if it ain't downright indecent to pair that sweet chit with such an old *roué!*"

"Old?" said Mrs. Boothe mildly. "At three and forty? Is a fine-looking man aside from a few warts. And very flush in the pockets, besides."

"Thunderation!" Boothe ran an exasperated hand through the wig he had just tidied. "Does no one in this confounded Society of ours ever wed for anything save lettuce?" He stamped to the door, and left them, snorting, "Kier-Byerby, indeed! I've to go into the village, but so soon as I return I mean to put a few words into Fitz Boudreaux's ear, I can assure you!"

No sooner had the door closed behind him than Rebecca uttered a squeak and ran to hug Mrs. Boothe. "Oh, how very clever! Do you think it will serve?"

"We can hope." Albinia giggled. "Did you see how his eyes sparked? I never saw Snowden so provoked because a lady looked elsewhere! We shall have to warn dear Letitia!"

Miss Boudreaux was overjoyed to hear of the impending lecture. She prepared her brother for a protest from Mr. Boothe against her betrothal to a man she scarcely knew, and then ran upstairs to dress with especial care. She came down to luncheon looking very pretty indeed. Unfortunately, Snowden was not among those present, and to her disappointment and Rebecca's mortification, he did not put in an appearance for the balance of the afternoon. The only consolation to the three conspirators was that The Monahan was very much present, so at least Snowden could not be dallying with her. Rebecca's relief was, however, leavened with chagrin. The Monahan might not be exercising her wiles on Snow, but Sir Peter was receiving a large share of The Beauty's attention.

Luncheon was served al fresco, since the day was pleasantly warm, and the long tables set out on the front terrace, the colourfully attired guests, the flowers that blazed in the great urns constituted a charming picture. The company was happy and carefree, and the fare a triumph of gastronomic and organizational skill, especially when one considered that the great house was being readied for the ball, and the kitchens were swarming with extra servants from the catering company.

Afterwards, a walk was proposed by those having the energy to attempt it. There was some light-hearted rivalry for the escorting of the fair ladies, and when Sir Peter coolly offered his right arm to Rebecca and his left to The Monahan, outraged cries went up. Fat and jovial Colonel Shephard accused their host of taking advantage of his position; the Reverend Boudreaux said solemnly that such greed must bring a Dread Punishment; and Rebecca, in the midst of a trill of laughter, was suddenly seized from behind and whisked away.

Still laughing, she protested, "But, really, I—" Grave grey eyes transfixed her, and the words died in her throat.

De Villars said, "It seemed only fair—to prevent bloodshed, you know." He added softly, "Try not to appear too provoked with me, ma'am. We must not give cause for gossip."

"Th-there has been sufficient of that, indeed," stammered Rebecca, once more caught offstride. Fighting to appear at ease, she said the first thing that came to mind, which was an unfortunate, "Speaking of which, how is your hurt, sir?"

"De Villars—hurt?" Drawing level with them, The Monahan said an incredulous, "But not in your famous duel, surely, Treve?"

"The merest scratch, dear lady," he answered blandly.

Mrs. Monahan's white hand fluttered to her bosom, drawing with it the eyes of most of the gentlemen. "Can I believe this? The incomparable Trevelyan de Villars bested in a duel? And by Snowden Boothe? No, I think you quiz me."

A little flare of irritation lit de Villars' eyes as those within earshot crowded around.

"Every dog has his day," Walter Street observed with a grin.

A slight frown marring his smooth brow, Ward said, "Treve? How is it that I heard naught of this?"

De Villars shrugged carelessly. "Because there was nothing to tell. Boothe and I found an excuse to exercize our skills and did so with little of ill-will. I chanced to be clumsy, and—"

"*Clumsy?*" Colonel Shephard's tone was astonished. "In a duel? *You?*"

"It does sound incredible," agreed The Monahan dubiously. "Unless . . ." She glanced to Rebecca. "Aha. I think I have it."

Rebecca caught her breath as all eyes turned to her.

"Which reminds me," said de Villars lazily. "I should warn you, my Peter, that you play host to a cat."

The Monahan's malicious smile became frozen and her cheeks as pale as Rebecca's were red. Miss Street, aware of the implication, breathed, "Oh, Lud!"

Sir Peter asked innocently, "I do? Where is the creature?"

"Why—here," drawled de Villars, ignoring the savage glare from a pair of fine green eyes. "I saw her stalking a mouse when I returned from my ride this morning." There was an audible and collective breath of relief, and de Villars advised Ward to purge his estates of the predatory feline.

Rebecca recovered sufficiently to say, "Oh, no! You will not hurt her?"

"Of course he will not!" snapped The Monahan. "Not *all* men are monsters, dear Mrs. Parrish."

"Do you believe that, Miss Templeby?" De Villars turned his attention to Glendenning's shy and pretty sister.

Flattered by the attention of so notorious a gentleman, the girl glowed and stammered an inaudible response, and he offered his arm and led her away.

The little party reassembled, and the stroll across the park continued, tongues progressing faster than elegantly shod feet. With Sir Peter on one side of her and Horatio Glendenning on the other, Rebecca should have felt triumphant, whereas her spirits were somewhat depressed. Why she must be plagued by a sense of impending disaster was beyond reason, yet that premonition had been troubling her of late and would not be banished. She was surprised after a little while to find that Captain Holt had contrived to slip in between herself and the viscount. They talked in desultory fashion at first, and then he said mildly, "I understand your brother is to attend the ball this evening, ma'am. I saw him with you earlier, I think. You bear him quite a resemblance."

Rebecca thought, "I do?" and decided that he was attempting, not very skilfully, to be pleasant. "Thank you," she said. "Actually, I am held to be more like to my elder brother, Jonathan. He is in Europe at present. Have you made his acquaintance, Captain?"

"Unfortunately, no. But I hear Mr. Snowden Boothe has been off in search of horses. I envy him. Do you know if he found any likely ones?"

"Hail, my Fair!" De Villars neatly inserted himself between them. "And farewell, *mon capitaine*."

Diverted, Rebecca exclaimed, "Oh! Do you know who said that, sir?"

"I did. With my own ardent lips. Just now."

His ardent lips were smiling the smile she had seen only in their few private moments; the smile of such sweetness that it obliterated all memory of his cynicism and rudeness. With an effort she recalled that he was only playing a part for the benefit of the other guests, and said chidingly, "No, no. 'Tis a quotation, am I not correct, Captain?"

The captain said a terse, "I have no idea, ma'am."

Glancing at him, Rebecca surprised a set look to his jaw and a flash in his hard dark eyes, and wondered if he was annoyed because Treve—Mr. de Villars—had come up with them. The captain did not seem the flirtatious type, but one could never tell.

De Villars said, "You are quite correct, my erudite lady. The quotation is from—I had best say it softly!—Catullus."

She clapped her hands delightedly. "I was right! My brother *would* have it was Shakespeare!"

"Pray do not tell him 'twas I betrayed his want of knowledge. I go in dread lest he call me out once more."

Lord Glendenning scoffed, "Aye, but I can hear your knees knocking, Treve."

"Those are not de Villars' knees," the captain said. "I fancy you hear drums, sir."

All heads turned to him. The happy voices were stilled as they halted and stood listening. Sure enough, faint with distance a throbbing rose on the air.

Miss Street asked uneasily, "A military exercize, Captain?"

Holt shook his head. "My men are rousing the countryside, ma'am. There are escaped Jacobites hereabout. We've orders to take or kill them, before they reach the sea."

"Poor creatures!" said Rebecca, her eyes stormy. "Even as we are so carefree, others of our countrymen are being hounded to a cruel and shameful death."

"For which they have only themselves to blame." De Villars took the captain's arm in friendly fashion. "Come, sir, and tell me of these fugitives. Do you know how many there are?"

Frowning after them as they walked on ahead, Rebecca found Sir Peter at her side. "You must really be more careful, dear lady," he warned softly. "In the name of Christian charity, your sentiments do you honour, but the captain might easily have interpreted your remarks as treason."

"In which case," purred Mrs. Monahan, slipping her arm about Rebecca's small waist, "you would probably lose that pretty head. And even a jealous female such as myself should not wish to see that, my dear, so—pay heed to what Sir Peter tells you."

Rebecca laughed, but she was frightened. Such things did not really happen, surely? Not to people one knew. Yet she had the oddest feeling that The Monahan was sincere. She thought of the desperate fugitives, perhaps wounded and exhausted, fleeing before the relentless pursuit, and a shiver chased down her spine.

CHAPTER
❧ 13 ❧

Fearing that they would be easily identified were they seen leaving the cottage in costume, Sir Peter urged Mrs. Boothe and Rebecca to stay at the main house on the night of the ball. There was no formal dinner party that evening. Trays were carried to the bedchambers, and later, the butler was to call for the guests, one at a time, and escort them to the ballroom by way of a rear corridor so that they could enter unobtrusively and mingle with the guests who had already arrived. A most tempting meal was sent up, but Rebecca was too excited to do more than pick at the food. Mrs. Boothe had already donned her costume and was all enthusiasm as she watched Millie dress her niece. Rebecca fought against overconfidence, but when she was powdered, attired in the glorious gown, a paste necklace of rubies and diamonds flashing convincingly about her throat, and long earrings sparkling, she could not but be hopeful of success.

Overawed, but ever practical, Millie asked anxiously, "Can you balance them hoops, Mrs. Rebecca? Turn about—give us a twirl."

Rebecca did so, staggered, and caught her balance with a breathless laugh. "I shall have to take care," she admitted, "lest I make a quiz of myself."

Mrs. Boothe, her eyes misting, thought that never had she seen so beautiful a sight. If Sir Peter did not offer tonight, he must be all about in his head!

❧

By ten o'clock the grand ballroom was athrong with an incredible company. Shepherdesses and Grecian nymphs were ogled by several Julius Caesars and a rather embarrassingly authentic-looking Pan, who Rebecca later decided must be Trevelyan de Villars, partly because of his height and easy grace, and partly because of that naughty costume. There were Elizabethan ladies with high ruffs and standing collars and farthingales, gentlemen in doublet and hose with short cloaks and dress swords. The steeple headdresses and flowing veils of the sixteenth century vied with gold turbans from the mysterious East. A centurion danced with a gentle Juliet. Cleopatra arrived, escorted by a full-bodied Henry the Eighth, and an equally stout pirate. Brigands rubbed elbows with Chinese mandarins, ladies of the harem, and Puritanical gentlemen in wide white collars and vandyke beards. And everywhere laughter and jollity and the freedom of masked countenances.

Yet even this brilliant gathering was moved to stare and

exclaim when the next competitor appeared on the raised dais across which each new arrival had to pass so as to be seen by the judges and admired by the throng. Tall she was, a statuesque beauty clad in a flowing cream silk gown that left one dimpled shoulder bare, and was tied criss-cross about the breasts with ribands of green satin. Shining black locks were pulled back so as to descend loosely behind her shoulders—a wig, possibly. And her mask, edged with jewels, covered sufficient of her classic features as to leave most in doubt, but several wondering.

"Delilah!" announced the major-domo, ringingly.

To one side of the applauding crowd, a dashing buccaneer turned his scarfed head and nudged the lord justice at his side. "Choice, eh, Fitz?"

The gentleman of the cloth exclaimed, "Shocking! Why, I can see her *ankles!* And—Horatio, her toenails are gilded! Who is she, I wonder?"

"She is The Monahan, you great gudgeon," imparted Glendenning, disrespectfully. He turned back to the dais, watched the arrival of a milkmaid, and was contemplating the provocative smile of a thirteenth-century princess when his friend breathed an admiring, "Now . . . by Jove!" and his attention returned to the dais.

The major-domo proclaimed resonantly, "The Scarlet Signorina!"

With leisured grace came this Spanish lady from the perilous days that had closed the sixteenth century. The brilliant red velvet of her vast farthingale fell richly over an underdress of white brocade embroidered in silver. Bands of ermine edged the deep outer sleeves, front openings, and hem of her gown. The neckline was square and high, rising at the back to a very high-standing collar of white brocade trimmed in silver. Jet curls, piled on her head and threaded with strings of pearls, enhanced a skin almost transparent in its purity. A jewelled fan was clasped in one hand, and the other was gracefully extended as she swept into her curtsey. The roar of applause brought every head turning, and the applause swelled, luring a shy smile to the full-lipped mouth.

Sir Peter, his receiving done for the evening, had just wandered into the ballroom. He was the only person not masked, since his duties as host clearly established his identity, and he looked breathtakingly handsome in the flowing periwig, dashing green *justaucorps* jacket, and culottes of seventy years earlier. Catching sight of the dazzling vision on the dais, he gasped, "Now . . . by God!"

"Enchanting, is she not?" chuckled a buccaneer, and began to edge his way through the throng of gentlemen waiting to besiege The Scarlet Signorina.

Recovering his scattered wits, Sir Peter followed.

ও

The little abigail put down her tray of wine glasses and, sitting beside The Scarlet Signorina in a secluded corner of the refreshment room, said in a voice that quivered with emotion, "Oh, my love! Such a triumph for you! I vow you are the most sought after lady at the ball! *Everyone* is clamouring for your identity, and your company! You must be fairly exhausted."

"Aunt Alby," said Rebecca. "Whyever are you carrying that tray?"

"One of the guests asked that I remove it from his table," Mrs. Boothe giggled. "Is it not hilarious? I am *truly* incognito! What a relief to escape myself for an evening!"

Rebecca was rather indignant, however, and said that since only footmen and lackeys were at work in the big room, she would have thought the guest might have been more perceptive.

"Well, I expect he would, my dearest, only he was a little foxed. And I truly was flattered. How comes it about that you sit here alone? 'Tis the first time you've not been surrounded."

"A most persistent buccaneer brought me down to supper and has gone off to fetch me a plate." Beneath the table, Rebecca slid tired feet out of her high heeled slippers. "When other gentlemen came over, he flourished a great sword at them, so I have been granted a few moments of rest. I suspect he is Horatio Glendenning, and I think he has a suspicion of who I am, though I've adopted the most delicious Spanish accent so as to deceive him. Are you enjoying yourself, dear?"

"Immensely, but I have identified only a few people. Delilah is The Monahan, of course. Have you spotted Lady Ward
yet?"

"No. Have you? There is a Joan of Arc here, but she is too
plump."

"I thought the same. I'm not very clever at guessing people. I only identified Mrs. Monahan because she wears that
beautiful antique ring. Have you noticed it, love? A most cun-
ningly wrought golden dragon with red eyes."

"Yes, I admired it at the boat party. It is so unusual she
might have known it would betray her identity."

"With the gown she almost wears, I doubt any of the gentlemen would notice her *ring*," said Mrs. Boothe with a giggle.
"In fact—" She broke off, her chin sagging.

A female Viking had come into the room, escorted by Sir
Peter. The lady was not of great stature, but her enormous
helm boasted two very large, upcurving horns, which presented a distinct hazard to those in her vicinity. Thick flaxen
braids hung on both sides of her thin face. A beautifully embroidered blouse and full dark skirt completed her costume.
She carried herself with a prideful arrogance, and there could
be no mistaking her. Rebecca whispered an awed, "So she was
not Joan d'Arc . . . after all!"

Catching sight of The Scarlet Signorina, the Viking lady
glanced idly away, but as if comprehension was slow in dawning, her head fairly shot back, her eyes all but goggling. The
effect was, to say the least, alarming. The helm did not respond
with the proper degree of alacrity and settled midway on her
head, one large horn sticking out above her nose like some
demented unicorn.

Lord Glendenning, bearing two laden plates, strove vainly
to stifle an involuntary whoop. The golden Delilah, seated at a
nearby table, chuckled audibly. Highly diverted, Rebecca's
eyes swept the amused crowd, seeking de Villars, well knowing
how his appreciation of the ridiculous would be titillated by
this apparition.

Lady Ward uttered a squawk, clutched at the arm of her

grandson, and became so white that Rebecca sprang to her feet in alarm. "Ma'am? Are you ill?"

"That . . . that . . . gown!" gasped my lady.

Coming anxiously to join them, Delilah asked, "Is aught amiss, my lady Viking?"

"Do not *dare* to reveal my identity," snapped Lady Ward, recovering.

Behind her begemmed mask, the green eyes of The Monahan widened. "Lud! I'd not been aware of it—till now."

Sir Peter said uneasily, "Are you all right—"

At this point the lord justice, stooping to hear the remarks of a pretty milkmaid, passed by. He inadvertently collided with the horn of my lady's helm that, being now opposed to its fellow, swooped out behind her head. He gave a yelp as his wig was neatly speared and sailed away with my lady, who had stepped aside to allow him to pass. Another laugh went up. The reverend gentleman, good-naturedly accepting his premature unmasking, grinned, and reclaimed his property.

Lady Ward was less magnanimous. Whirling on him, she shrilled, "Pray *what* are you about, sir?"

"Allow me, ma'am," said Sir Peter and, with a deft tug, straightened helm and horns. Lady Ward was more irked than grateful and proceeded to deliver a withering indictment of dim-witted and unmannerly young men that petrified the unfortunate Boudreaux.

Lord Horatio handed one of his plates to Rebecca, seized her by the elbow, and guided her quickly away. "I knew I had seen that gown somewhere before," he murmured, as they left the debacle behind. "How ever did you acquire it? The old lady regards that collection as sacrosanct."

"Oh, dear! Does she? Mrs. Kellstrand was so kind as to allow me to borrow it," said Rebecca, abandoning the attempt to conceal her identity. "Will she be very angry, do you suppose?"

They found an unoccupied table and sat down, and the viscount said cheerily, "Never worry. Peter is the apple of her eye, he'll soon have her out of the boughs. And heaven knows, she shouldn't have flown into 'em—you look delicious. The colour is perfect for—Ma'am? You are not greatly distressed, I trust?"

Rebecca, who had been scanning the crowd as he spoke, apologized. "Forgive me. I was paying attention, only—if I appear upset, it is partly because of my brother. He went into the village this morning to attempt to find a suitable costume, and I've not seen him since. I cannot but be apprehensive."

"Oh, do not give it another thought, dear lady. In this crush it is impossible to find anyone. For instance, I have been attempting to spot de Villars, and quite without—"

"Is that you, Viscount?"

A Cossack, with huge moustachios, removed his mask to reveal the stern features of Captain Holt. "Cannot seem to get through the crush to Sir Peter," he said crisply. "I've to leave. Be so good as to convey my regrets?"

"Of course. Nothing wrong, I hope?"

"Only that we have cornered some of these blasted rebels. Broadbent already left, and I must not tarry. Your pardon, sir, ma'am." And he was gone, swallowed up in the chattering crowd.

A blaring fanfare from the orchestra very soon summoned everyone back to the ballroom. Six chairs had been placed at the rear of the dais, and five of these were occupied by the judges, consisting of the lord justice, a gypsy fortune teller, a very fat Chinese mandarin, a Dutch farmwife, and a tattered chimney sweep.

When everyone was assembled, Sir Peter held up his hand for quiet. Gradually, the noise died down, and he announced, "'Tis almost—the Witching Hour!" He clapped his hands sharply. Unearthly music struck up, haunting at first, then rising to a wild, tempestuous melody. From both sides of the great ballroom came witches, fairies, and warlocks, skipping and leaping to the dais, there to dance with skill and precision for the pleasure of the brilliant company. A lighter refrain brought elves and pixies who bounded and cartwheeled their way to join the dancers, mingling with them in a clever ballet that drew repeated bursts of applause. Then, with a clash of cymbals, the music stopped. The dancers all froze into attitudes of tense expectancy, everyone pointing to a black drapery that curtained off a corner of the room. The draperies were slowly drawn aside. Beyond, two silver-cloaked and hooded figures held flaming torches to illumine the face of a great clock. The small hand pointed to the hour, its fellow creeping toward it. The crowd watched breathlessly. The two hands met. A brief hush, then the first chime pealed, the guests joining in the count until "Twelve!" became a roar of triumph.

Four youths in blue and silver tunics and white hose now marched in and swung up glittering trumpets. A fanfare cut through the uproar.

Sir Peter stood once more. "It is time," he announced loudly, "for the judging. We have six finalists, and must choose one to reign as Ruler of the Midsummer's Eve Ball!" Again, he was interrupted by the excited crowd, and the trumpeters had to be employed to restore quiet. Sir Peter took up a sheet of parchment. "Will these ladies and gentlemen please come to the dais? The Great God Pan . . . Don Quixote . . . Queen Elizabeth . . ." Applause had greeted each name, but some confusion now ensued, since it seemed there were three Queen Elizabeths. It was settled at last, and a truly spectacular royal lady made her way to the dais. Sir Peter resumed his list. "Delilah!" More applause. "A Viking Princess." The shouts were laced with a few chuckles, but Lady Ward marched serenely to her triumph. "And—lastly," said Sir Peter, tantalizingly, "The—Scarlet Signorina!"

Rebecca's horrified gasp was lost in the roar of acclaim. Glendenning made his way through the enthusiastic crowd, leading her to the dais.

"I *cannot!*" she cried, trying to free her hand.

He grinned. "'Course you can. No call to be nervous," and, willy-nilly, she was drawn along.

She had no chance to protest further, and took her place among the other contestants, praying she would be rejected. Outrage gleamed in the eyes of the Viking Princess, but by not so much as a quiver did the smile change on Delilah's lovely face.

The judges were making notes and conferring gravely together; the onlookers watched eagerly; and Rebecca waited, probably the only person in that festive hall who was in utter misery. Why, oh *why*, had it never occurred to her that this might happen? She could take no credit for either the devising or creation of the magnificent gown she wore. If it became known that she had borrowed her finery, and from whom, it must look as though she stood on extremely close terms with the Wards. Even more deplorable, she now realized belatedly, in having loaned her a possession he was known to prize highly, Sir Peter might very well be judged as having publicly declared his interest. Tears of humiliation started to Rebecca's eyes. Her only hope was that The Monahan or the Viking Princess would win, although there was always the chance that de Villars would reign over the ball.

The judges had reached a decision! Sir Peter came to his feet and raised one hand. The room hushed. "Third place," he called, "goes to a very enchanting—Delilah!"

Cheers rang out. The Monahan curtseyed with superb grace and moved to stand to one side of Ward.

There was much cheering again when Ward said, "Second place to that authentic rogue—the Great God Pan!"

Pan bowed his thanks. Straightening, his eyes glinted at Rebecca from behind his mask.

Her knees shook. Surely—*surely* they would not name her?

"And the first place," Ward's voice rang with excitement, "goes to—*The Scarlet Signorina!*"

The storm of acclaim drowned Rebecca's moan. A sea of faces looked up at her with delighted approval. On the dais, the Viking Princess glared her frustrated fury. A faint smile touched the mouth of Delilah. Pan was grinning widely. Ward was at her side.

"Queen of the Midsummer's Eve Ball! Our two hundred and fiftieth Ruler! Lead us in unmasking. Who are you, lovely one?"

His hands were unfastening her mask. She said desperately, "Sir Peter! You must stop this. I *cannot* be—"

But the mask was drawn away. A roar went up. "The Little Parrish! It is The Little Parrish!"

De Villars' name for her. How widespread it had become. In desperation, Rebecca turned to him. Pan raised a fine-boned hand and removed his mask. Her heart thudded into her slippers. She was gazing at a lean, amused face she had never seen before. She heard Ward laugh and exclaim, "Kadenworthy! You rascal!" She thought, "*Kadenworthy?* The man Treve almost killed? Here?"

Everyone was unmasking. Amid the hubbub and laughter, Rebecca was not surprised, of course, that FitzWilliam Boudreaux was the lord justice, or that Delilah was indeed The Monahan. She managed a smile upon discovering that one of her judges, the Dutch farm wife, was Letitia Boudreaux, but she had not the acquaintance of the gypsy fortune teller, who was a Countess somebody or other; neither did she recognize the well-preserved elderly gentleman who was Don Quixote tonight. She'd had not the faintest suspicion that the rotund Chinese mandarin would turn out to be a well-pillowed George Melton, and she was thoroughly astounded when the tattered chimney sweep was revealed as her brother's immaculate bosom bow, Lord Graham Fortescue.

"Forty!" she gasped, as overjoyed as she was surprised. "I didn't know it was *you!*"

He blushed and said with simple pride, "Bet Snow a monkey I'd fool you!"

"Oh, is he here? Forty, I am in the most dreadful—" She broke off in consternation as Sir Peter dropped to one knee before her and took her hand between both his own in the ancient oath of fealty.

Her eyes sparking with wrath, Lady Ward cried, "One *moment*, if you please!"

There was no doubt of what she was going to say.

"Please!" said Rebecca firmly, overriding her ladyship and withdrawing her hand from Sir Peter's clasp. "I cannot accept such an honour!"

"Hah!" exclaimed my lady. "So I should hope!"

Dismayed, Sir Peter stood. "What? Whyever not?"

"Oh, Lud! What a gapeseed!" grated his grandmama, *sotto voce*. "Are you *totally* blind, Ward?"

The consternation among the watching crowd died down, and there was a tense silence as they all waited to know what was happening.

Rebecca said clearly, "I am more grateful than I can say. But I must decline the honour you do me. This gown, you see, is—"

She was interrupted by a cluster of sharp, staccato sounds. To her, they seemed like so many brittle tree branches snapping, but several gentlemen, obviously alarmed, sprinted to the terrace doors. Someone shouted, "Jacobites!" and another cry was heard, "Poor devils! Blasted close by!"

This set off a flurry of alarm and silenced Lady Ward, who had seized the opportunity to address a few pithy remarks to her grandson.

A footman came quickly to the dais and spoke to Ward in an urgent undertone. Sir Peter nodded, made an imperative gesture to the musicians, and shouted a cheerful, "On with the dance!"

The music struck up. Over it, Colonel Shephard demanded indignantly, "But who is to rule us, Ward?"

Sir Peter replied with smiling composure that the judges and the six finalists would adjourn to another room to thrash out the problem.

"I wager a monkey it will be Delilah!" offered a demon, and was at once surrounded by eager bettors.

The major-domo called a minuet. The ominous interruption was forgotten, and the guests prepared happily for the dance.

Lady Ward rasped, "I shall come, too!" and took her grandson's arm, leaving the dais after raking Rebecca with a contemptuous stare.

Following, her hand trembling on Fortescue's arm, Rebecca whispered, "Forty, my gown is borrowed from Sir Peter's Hall of Effigies upstairs. Is that very bad?"

"Not if you truly wish to wed old Peter," his lordship replied.

She thought, "Yes, but I did not mean to entrap him so blatantly as this!"

They had passed into the hall, and lackeys were swinging wide the door of a blue and gold ante-room. Judges, contestants, and a militant Viking Princess went inside.

No sooner had the doors closed upon the curious servants than Sir Peter turned to Rebecca. "Now, ma'am," he said kindly. "What is all this foolishness?"

"Gad!" his grandmother snarled at the ornately plastered ceiling.

"I quite understand that your gown is borrowed," he continued with a smile. "But it certainly has never been worn to greater advantage, and I fail to see—"

"Then you are a simpleton, sir!" his relation interpolated wrathfully. "You surely must realize what gossip would make of—"

A commotion on the terrace was followed by a fumbling at the outer doors which burst open suddenly, causing the heavy brocade draperies to billow inward. A small scream escaped my Lady Ward as a dishevelled figure staggered into the room and stood blinking around at the startled group.

All evening, Rebecca had been battling a ridiculous sense of ill-usage because Trevelyan de Villars had ignored her. Now she knew why, for he very obviously had not been at the ball. He stood swaying before them, clad in simple riding dress. His dark hair was wildly disordered, his pale cheeks were scratched, and mud streaked one side of his face. His right hand clutched a limply dangling left arm bound with a handkerchief that showed wet and crimson.

"Good God!" cried The Monahan, impulsively starting towards him. "What on earth has—"

From outside came shouts, the male voices harsh with excitement. "Did he go into the house?" . . . "Which room?" . . . "This way, men!"

One hand flying to her throat, my Lady Ward eyed her favourite and gasped, "De Villars! Never say *you* are a—a Jacobite traitor?"

"If he is, he'll not drag *me* down with him!" growled Kadenworthy.

At that, into every mind came the horror of the rope, axe, and block, and the nightmare of public dismemberment. The Monahan paled and shrank away from the wounded man.

De Villars gasped out, "My apologies . . . Ward. I—I'd not have come here but . . . they gave me little . . . choice."

Rebecca, who had stood in stunned silence, cried, "Never mind that! Quickly! We must hide him!"

"Where?" wailed Lady Ward, wringing her hands in anguish. "There is no cupboard in this room, gal!"

"Under the furniture! Anywhere!"

"And incriminate us all?" Kadenworthy snarled, "Are you gone insane, ma'am? This is *High Treason!* You may not value that pretty head of yours, but, by God! I've no wish for mine to adorn a spike on Tower Bridge!"

"You are no Jacobite, Treve," quavered Sir Peter, white to the lips. "You have only to tell them they mistake the matter, and—"

"Unhappily," said de Villars faintly, "I was—was seen, Peter."

"Doing what?" Fortescue demanded, with an unfamiliar air of authority.

"Aiding some . . . stupid damned fugitive onto . . . my mare."

"Good heavens!" moaned Lady Ward. "How *could* you, de Villars? Is *Peter's* mare! Now you have involved my grandson!"

"No." De Villars stumbled towards the door. "I'll go and throw myself on . . . their mercy."

"And get none!" Kadenworthy glared at him. "Curse you! How could you have been so stupid?"

Turning back, de Villars peered at them blindly. "Peter? I cannot . . . seem to . . . so—you . . . you must hand me over. Do not . . . risk . . ." And he sagged like a rag doll and lay in a crumpled heap before them.

They all stood as if frozen.

The hall door burst open. Rebecca all but fainted with terror. The butler hurried in and cried an agitated, "Soldiers are searching the house, sir, and—oh! My God!"

As though released from the paralysis which had gripped them, Boudreaux sprang to swing the door shut. "We must *do* something!" he said urgently.

"We cannot!" said Ward, his face twisted with grief. "I must think of—er, the rest of you! To aid a fleeing rebel is treason, even as Lord Kaden—"

"*No!*" Turning on him like a tigress, Rebecca cried, "Have you no loyalty to your own? Do you think he would turn his back on any one of us in such a tangle? De Villars is innocent of anything save kindness! We cannot condemn him to so hideous a death only to spare ourselves!" Ward stared at her in silence. She stretched out her hands pleadingly. "Oh—*hide* him! For the love of God! *Help* him!"

But it was too late. Military footsteps were marching along the hall. A brisk, cultured voice called, "The library, you two fellows! You three—this way!"

Rebecca thought in a numb, detached fashion, "It is Hilary Broadbent."

"Alas, dear lady," groaned Sir Peter. "I am sorrier than I can say, but Treve has brought it on himself. We cannot—"

With an incoherent snarl of impatience, Rebecca ran forward. While the rest of them watched, flabbergasted, she lifted her skirts, careless of the expanse of lace-trimmed bloomers that was revealed above her neat ankles. Turning carefully, she draped those wide, luxurious skirts over the insensible form of The Wicked Rake.

Lord Fortescue uttered an admiring exclamation and ran to lift one limp and bloody hand and shove it beneath the sheltering farthingale. The Monahan, leaping pantherlike to the candelabra, blew out as many flames as she might. My Lady Ward hurried to the credenza and extinguished the lamp there, so that only one branch of candles on the mantelpiece remained lighted.

"You are all run *mad!*" hissed Kadenworthy.

Letitia Boudreaux, who had neither moved nor spoken during all this, now recovered and moved to Rebecca's side.

"God bless you!" she gulped. "What can I do?"

"Pray he does not move, or cry out! And put on your mask—quickly!" Replacing her own mask, Rebecca called softly, "We are part of the collection from upstairs!" She barely had time to tie the mask and place one hand on Letitia's arm, before the door opened.

Major Broadbent strode in, three troopers following.

"Are they not realistic?" murmured Lord Fortescue, surveying the "effigies" with enviable aplomb. "I vow, Ward—"

"Sir Peter," the major interposed curtly, "I pray you will believe that I mislike what I must do. There is a Jacobite loose in the vicinity. We know he is winged, and suspect he sought shelter here. The house is being searched, and I must ask your co-operation, in the King's name."

Standing motionless, praying, Rebecca slanted a glance at Kadenworthy. He was watching the major, his face cold and calculating. He had good reason to hate de Villars. If he spoke . . . ! She fought back a sob of fear, and struggled not to tremble. Poor Letitia's arm was cold as ice under her fingers. Peter Ward was like a ghost. He had vowed he would aid any Jacobite friend who asked his protection. The man lying so limp and helpless beneath her gown was his *closest* friend. Surely, *surely*, he would not betray them?

His voice strained, Ward said, "Pray *do* search! Who is he, do you know, Broadbent?"

"We know only that two fugitives broke through our lines. One of them got away, but the other was shot. We followed him here."

"But—why here? He must know my home is full of people! He would be seen!"

"And hidden, belike," said Broadbent cynically. "There are Jacobites throughout Britain where one might least expect to find 'em, Ward!"

Behind the military men, a slow grin spread across Kadenworthy's lean visage.

"You men," Broadbent ordered, "search this room thoroughly."

The troopers hurried about, upending chairs and sofas, peering behind the curtains, and requiring guests to move so that they might look behind chests and under tables.

"Damned impertinence," drawled Kadenworthy, removing his hips from the credenza in response to a terse request that he do so. "D'you expect to find your fugitive in one of the drawers, you dolt?"

Lady Ward uttered a shrill titter.

Broadbent said thoughtfully, "You've brought down some of the effigies, I see, Ward." He marched forward.

Rebecca felt the blood drain from her face and thought she must faint as he halted before her.

There was an absolute, horrified silence.

Dropping to one knee, the major reached to grasp her skirt.

Choking with fear, her heart hammering, Rebecca leaned down and soundly boxed his ears.

Uttering a startled yelp, the major jumped back to sit sprawling on the floor before her.

"How *dare* you, sir!" she said, managing somehow to dimple roguishly at him, as she took off her mask.

"By . . . by Gad!" gasped the major, leaning back on his hands. "You like to scared the wits out of me, Rebecca!"

The guests laughed convincingly, though many of the knees in that perilous room were weak as water.

"For shame, Broadbent!" said the Reverend Boudreaux sternly. "You stand sadly in want of respect, sir!"

Unhappily aware of the wide grins on the faces of his troopers, the major clambered to his feet. "I thought—I thought the ladies were effigies, sir," he stammered, very red in the face.

"Disgusting!" snorted my lady.

"No, really, ma'am." Rebecca laughed. "'Twas what we strove for, after all. You see, Sir Peter? Hilary was convinced. Now own we fooled you, also!"

Ward shrugged and said wryly, "In this light, ma'am, I'll admit it was most effective."

The major drew out his handkerchief and mopped his face. "I beg you will believe that you fooled *me*, ladies."

"There!" Rebecca clapped her hands, but her eyes grew round as an unseen hand tugged at her bloomers. She had thought to have stepped on something when she boxed Hilary's ears. She must be crushing de Villars' fingers! She moved her foot, and the farthingale swayed heart-stoppingly. "I win my bet, Sir Peter!" she cried, a little too gaily. "You must pay me at once, sir!"

"I shall do more," he said, bowing. "You are undeniably the Queen of our Ball! Eh, Grandmama?"

With a tight little smile, Lady Ward inclined her head. "Hail to the Queen!"

The declaration was taken up and repeated lustily. Broadbent hesitated, watching as they all crowded around Rebecca. He could not know that for several of the ladies, tears were very close behind their rather shrill laughter. He was miserable in a task he loathed and thought that these people presented anything but the picture of a group of terrified conspirators.

"I would suggest, sir," sneered Lord Kadenworthy, sensing his indecision, "that you withdraw before word of your—"

Captain Holt intervened from the doorway, "Do you require assistance, sir?"

Rebecca's heart leapt with fright. Holt would know at once this entire scene was ridiculous, for he had seen her with Ward and would be aware there was no likelihood of Ward mistaking her for an effigy!

"Thank you—no," said Broadbent, his dislike apparent in his cold condescension. "Have you finished with the kitchen quarters?"

"We have." Advancing into the room, the captain said suspiciously, "If there is any difficulty with these people . . ."

"Perhaps," murmured Fortescue, "we should explain the nature of the difficulty. The captain might be able to tell us if it is customary to—"

The captain, Broadbent was bitterly aware, would be delighted to report an incident that, however innocent, might be interpreted as misconduct. He intervened sharply, "We waste time here! Holt, take your people upstairs!"

Holt frowned, but beckoned to his men and retreated.

"Peter," drawled Kadenworthy, "I saw your dear friend de Villars at the unmasking. He and I have an—ah, matter to discuss. I am becoming bored. If you will be done with the judging, I'd as soon return to the party."

Broadbent scowled at him resentfully, but he saw laughter brimming in the eyes of The Monahan and, beyond her, the stiff, disapproving countenance of the Viking Princess. "Dear God!" he thought, and led his troopers from the room.

Rebecca felt suddenly weak and giddy. As the door closed, she clapped both hands to her mouth and closed her eyes. Letitia began to weep softly. Boudreaux hastened to her and, sprinting forward, Kadenworthy slipped an arm about Rebecca. "You're not going to faint, m'dear," he said, a new warmth to his voice. "Jove, but if that was not the bravest thing I ever saw!"

"Indeed, it was!" admitted Lady Ward, her own voice shaking.

More practically, The Monahan said, "Do we not tend Trevelyan's wound, he's like to bleed to death."

At once, Rebecca lifted her skirts and stepped away. De Villars lay as before, giving no indication of having regained consciousness.

"Lud!" gasped Letitia, terror-stricken. "Is he dead?"

Fortescue had already dropped to one knee and was easing the wounded man onto his back. He felt for a pulse. "No, he ain't dead, yet," he said, and began to unwind the sodden handkerchief from de Villars' arm.

"Nor are we safe, yet," Kadenworthy warned as Letitia appropriated her brother's handkerchief and knelt beside de Villars. "He must be got upstairs."

"How?" said Ward helplessly. "We cannot carry him!"

"Could pretend he was foxed," Fortescue suggested. "But—he's all blood. Anyone sees him and we're properly dished."

De Villars sighed, and opened his eyes. For a moment he stared up at them blankly. Then, sitting up, he asked, "Am I not arrested yet? Or—do I dream this?"

"You are free for the moment," said Lady Ward. "Thanks only to Mrs. Parrish, without whose courage you would be on your way to the Tower!"

De Villars' tired eyes turned to search Rebecca's pale face, but he said nothing.

"If I might venture a remark, sir," said the butler, who had watched the dramatic interlude in silence. "The guests will be coming for the Ruler, at any second!"

Wringing her hands, Rebecca half sobbed, "Oh—I could not g-go out there just—just now. I *could* not!"

"Of course she could not!" said Ward. "She has risked enough!"

"Crown *me* Queen!" his grandmother suggested. "I'll go out there!"

"And right bravely," Fortescue agreed with rare tact. "But we shall need your nursing skills to help Treve, ma'am. If only we can smuggle him abovestairs."

The butler said, "Sir—were I to get another costume, could Mr. de Villars climb the stairs?"

"'Course I can climb the stairs," de Villars asserted. "D'ye think I'm foxed, Greywood?"

The butler smiled and, not waiting for his employer's consent, slipped into the hall.

Fortescue helped de Villars to his feet. Assuring them rather threadily that he was "much better now," the injured man took one tentative step and sagged weakly. "Confound it!" he groaned, clinging to his lordship's arm. "I—I imperil you all! Perhaps you *should*—render me up, Peter!"

His own voice strained with nervousness, Ward snapped, "To die? For doing no more than—than any one of us would have done?"

Kadenworthy said a contemptuous, "If you really believe that, Ward, you are a fool. I, for one, would not have taken such a risk. No more, I doubt, would you."

Rebecca scarcely heard them. Not until de Villars had

staggered into the room had she known how ghastly was the taste of pure terror. It was almost inconceivable that the vital arrogance of him could have been so swiftly reduced to this helplessness. And just as inconceivable the fact that he—the man who had sneered at the folly of aiding a fugitive—should have been the very one to commit such gallant folly. She heard again Anthony's childish voice: "I found out that his eyes say different to his words." Those eyes were fixed on her now. They were strained and tired and full of pain, but faint and familiar came that quirkish twist of the white lips. An undeniably suggestive wink was directed at her. She fought tears. The wretch was teasing her because he had recovered consciousness and given that outrageous tug at her undergarments! Blinking, she thought, "There is no propriety in him! He is the outside of enough!" But she also thought him exceeding brave, and his irrepressible grin gave her the strength she needed.

Her chin tossed upward. She took a deep breath and stood away from Lord Kadenworthy's supporting arm. "I am better now. I thank you, my lord." She summoned a quivering smile. "Shall we go, Sir Peter?"

He stared at her, pale and obviously panicked. His grandmother glared at him, and he recovered sufficiently to go and offer his arm. "Are you sure it will not be too much of a strain for you, Mrs. Parrish?"

She looked up into his handsome, concerned face. And she knew he would have stood by and allowed his best friend to be delivered up to a cruel and shameful execution, and lifted not a hand to help. He was trying now, because the rest of them had stood firm, but he was very frightened. The last scales fell from her eyes. Handsome Peter Ward had been her dream—her knight in shining armour. But the dream was false, and although someday she might wed him, the deep respect and admiration she had felt for him were gone forever. Sadly, she said, "Quite sure, I thank you."

As they walked past The Monahan, that lady bowed into a deep curtsey.

Rebecca glanced at her in surprise.

Delilah murmured, "Bravo!"

CHAPTER
🙟 14 🙞

*T*here was a good deal of noise and confusion when Rebecca and Ward returned to the ballroom. The guests were milling about angrily while soldiers searched behind draperies and furnishings, but also narrowly scanned the room's occupants.

"As though," protested one indignant dowager, less outlandishly than she could know, "we had Jacobites concealed about our persons!"

The major-domo conferred with Sir Peter, then announced from the dais that The Scarlet Signorina was definitely the Queen of the Midsummer's Eve Ball. A loud, defiant cheer went up. The orchestra began the introduction to a country dance, which Rebecca and Ward led. Gradually, the guests began to forget their pique, and soon the ball was in full sway once more.

Dancing, chatting, smiling, flirting, all were mechanical for Rebecca. Her mind was occupied with two things. Firstly, her dread that Trevelyan de Villars would be at any moment dragged forth by the soldiers and taken to meet a ghastly death. Secondly, Snowden. Again and again her eyes searched the crowd, but at length she was forced to the admission that her brother must not be here. And if he was not here, whatever had become of him?

She lost track of time and was able to maintain a happy manner only by virtue of the knowledge that she dare not deviate from her normal untiring ability to dance the night away. And it seemed that every gentleman present wished to dance with her. Kadenworthy claimed her for a quadrille and, when they came together during the movements of the dance, told her he was lost in admiration and begged leave to call upon her—a favour she gladly granted since she felt a kinship with

the peer, if only for the danger they shared. Mr. Melton won a
country dance and whispered that her aunt was abovestairs assisting with Mr. de Villars. "We dressed him as a footman,
ma'am, and I wish you might have seen how haughtily he
stalked up the stairs, and then collapsed in Lady Ward's bedchamber."

"Good heavens!" exclaimed Rebecca. "Whyever did they
take him there?"

"It had already been searched. Do you know, I believe we
may bring him off safely, yet. Is a fine gentleman, Mrs. Rebecca, but I've little need to tell *you* that, I am very sure!"

That last remark was somewhat puzzling, but she was too
weary to attempt to make sense of it. The events of the evening
had taken their toll, and she was deeply grateful when Graham
Fortescue begged that they pass his allotted time in sitting on
the terrace, rather than dancing. Once they were alone in the
cool evening air, she hissed, "Are they all gone, Forty? Are we
safe at last?" A trooper, looming up through the dimness, answered that question, and Rebecca gave a trill of laughter,
rapped his lordship's knuckles with her fan, and advised him he
was "such a naughty boy!" Fortescue was amused, but the sol-
dier loitered about so obviously that they were unable to speak
of anything but commonplaces. Leading her back inside, his
lordship breathed softly, "If de Villars is spared, Mrs. Rebecca,
it will be only because of your courage. Salute you, ma'am, and
all that sort of—er, bilge."

Rebecca's heart was warmed. It was truth, she reflected
with a stirring of pride. And de Villars was much too good a
man to end with his head on a pike! The thought of that cynical
grin so hideously impaled turned her bones to sand, and she
had to concentrate with determination on the gentlemen who
rushed to surround her.

At three o'clock a large rabbit was flirting persistently with
her in the refreshment room when Sir Peter came to claim her.
Instead of leading her into the ballroom, he took her by way of
a rear corridor to the stairs. He seemed quite restored and
announced jubilantly, "Well, we've done it, ma'am! De Villars

is undetected, and our bounty hunters are gone at last!"

Rebecca uttered a little cry of relief. "Thank God! Is Mr. de Villars' arm broken?"

"Fortunately not, but my grandmama says the musket ball may have scored the bone, for it came very close. He has lost a deal of blood and is in much pain, but Lady Ward says he will do. If you are not exhausted beyond bearing, poor girl, he begs that you will look in on him. I would not ask it, but he is becoming feverish and cannot seem to rest without he thanks you."

She nodded and went with him to his grandmother's chamber. Inside, Lady Ward was seated at a round table, engaged in rolling strips of linen for bandages. Lord Kadenworthy, who had been leaning against a chest of drawers, straightened respectfully when Rebecca entered. Most of her attention however, was fixed upon the astonishing sight of her brother, clad in rumpled riding dress, bending over the bed to grip de Villars' hand.

"Snow!" she gasped. "Where on earth have you been?"

He spun to face her, his comely face mirroring guilt. "Not as usefully employed as you, m'dear!" He strode to give her a buss on the forehead. "Jolly well done! Dashed if I ain't proud of you!"

He was *proud* of her? For protecting someone he despised and had sworn to fight again at the first opportunity? And why had he been shaking de Villars' hand as though they were the best of friends? Was there *any* understanding the erratic rules by which men lived? She wrenched her bewildered gaze from her brother. De Villars was white and haggard, yet looked oddly youthful lying in the great bed. He reached out eagerly, and she went to him at once and took that unsteady hand, only to be shocked by the dry heat of it.

De Villars saw alarm come into her face. "Do not be put about, ma'am," he said with a twinkle. "This time you are quite safe. I am genuinely indisposed."

She smiled, but said earnestly, "I honour you for that indisposition. 'Twas nobly done, sir."

A flush stained his pale cheeks. "Do not refine on it, I beg you. A stupid impulse of the moment, only—that should not have been heeded, since by it—I—I think I have contrived to ruin you."

Lady Ward agreed tartly, "You would have, save that word of your escapade must never leak out."

"Since all our lives are at stake, including your own, ma'am," said Kadenworthy in his dry manner, "I rather fancy 'twill be the best-kept secret in England. Speaking of which"— he turned to de Villars—"who is this confounded rebel for whom we all are at risk?"

For a moment he was not answered. De Villars, his hand still clasping Rebecca's, was gazing at her with an awed expression, and she, smiling compassionately down at him, was aware of no other.

Kadenworthy said, "Treve?"

Rebecca gave a gasp and hurriedly reclaimed her hand.

"Eh?" said de Villars blankly. "Oh—the Jacobite you mean, Kade? I am not—acquainted with the gentleman."

Rebecca looked at him sharply. His expression had not changed, but his good hand was clamped tightly on the coverlet.

Lady Ward had also noted that jerkily interrupted utterance. She poured a glass of barley water and walked up to scowl at her patient. "Paying a high price for your quixotic folly, are you?" she said sourly. "Well, I've no laudanum to give you and I'm sorry for it. I admire courage. Lord knows why, for 'tis a pretty mess you've plunged us all into."

"I know . . ." said de Villars, humbly. "And I am most deeply grateful."

Snowden said a defensive, "And a man's life is saved, perhaps."

"Perhaps, indeed!" snapped my lady, rounding on him. "From what Trevelyan said, the rebel was hurt and totally exhausted. He'll likely be taken again, and soon. And—then what? How if he tells who aided him?"

Rebecca cried, "Oh, but he would not! What gentleman would give so treacherous a return for chivalry?"

"A man may do anything is he put to the question," muttered Kadenworthy.

They looked at one another in new horror, even Lady Ward, having succeeded in frightening herself as well as everyone else, appalled by the prospect.

"Well, our poor fugitive will not do anything so craven," said Boothe defiantly. "He is safely bestowed and shall not venture forth again till he is well enough to be smuggled out of the country."

Astonished, Rebecca turned to him. He saw the question in her wide eyes and grumbled, "Fiend seize it, I'll say no more! Ward, should you not rejoin your guests?"

"Before he does," said my lady, "he can help raise de Villars. Boothe, pray slip the extra pillow behind him so he may sit up."

This painful operation being completed with as much gentleness as possible, de Villars drank gratefully, then leant back against the pillows, his right hand gripping his arm and his eyes closed, his "Thank you, my lady," very faint indeed.

Kadenworthy said, "He's properly knocked up. Let him rest," and walked to the door.

"What about you, Boothe?" asked Sir Peter. "Do you mean to stay?"

De Villars opened his eyes. "You'd better establish your presence, Snow."

Boothe nodded thoughtfully. "I will, if Ward has suitable raiment for me."

Albinia came in, carrying a pile of clean linens. "Hello, my love," she said, with a fond smile at Rebecca. "*What* an adventure we are having!" Ward having divested her of her burden, she began to extricate from it the various medical supplies she had concealed there, then produced some neatly folded garments of green satin. "Mr. Melton supposed you might need a costume, Snowden."

De Villars gave a croak of laughter. "*Boothe*—a footman? By God! You'll never carry it off!"

"Devil a bit of it!" Boothe held up the tunic with a grin.

"Try not to expire tonight, Treve, and I may serve you breakfast on the morrow!"

De Villars said, "Wouldn't miss that for the world!"

ⲥⲁ

It was almost dawn before Rebecca crawled between the sheets and she was asleep the instant her head touched the pillow. She awoke, refreshed, when the curtains of her bed were drawn back, and was surprised to see her brother dozing in a chair beside the windows and already fully dressed.

Millie plumped her pillows while she washed, and when she got back into bed put a breakfast tray across her lap, then went over to waft a cup of hot chocolate under Snowden's nodding head.

"What?" he exclaimed, leaping upright. "Millie—you saucy wench! Give me that."

She chuckled, gave him the chocolate, dodged the affectionate pat he aimed at her broad hips, and went out.

"So you're awake at last, are you?" Boothe yawned. "Thought you meant to snore all day."

"You know perfectly well I do not snore. And— Good lord! I'd forgot! What o'clock is it? Is Treve—I mean, is Mr. de Villars—"

"It is nigh eleven o'clock. And he is downstairs, having breakfast."

"Down . . . *stairs?* He must be mad! He was in no condition to—"

"With that confounded Holt," Boothe finished, his eyes grim.

"Dear God!" Rebecca put down her toast with a trembling hand. "Never say he suspects?"

He scowled. "He suspects something, but how much of the truth he has there's no guessing."

"Then . . . then all our lives are in de Villars' hands!"

"Never mind the dramatics, my girl! Treve will do his possible. It ain't him I tremble for, but your bird lover!" He came to his feet. "I'd best get down there before Ward faints dead away!"

"No—wait!" Rebecca put the tray aside and leaned forward, regarding her brother tensely. "I must know the truth of it. Snow, am I wrong, or are you involved in this?"

He stared at his cup, not replying at first. Then he said slowly, "Only to the extent that I was with de Villars, and—"

"*With* him? But—oh, if I could but comprehend all this! Snow, you mean to *fight* de Villars! Why on earth—"

His head lifted. He said with steady emphasis, "Trevelyan de Villars is a rake and a rascal. And he is also one of the finest gentlemen it has ever been my honour to know. I discovered it rather—late, is all." He raised his right hand to silence her astonished indignation, and the lace fell back to reveal the bandages about his wrist. Nodding to them, he continued, "This confounded sprain almost brought me to Point Non Plus last evening, I can tell you!"

Rebecca flung back the bedclothes, stepped into her slippers, and pulled a wrapper about her. Snowden put down his cup and returned to his seat resignedly and she drew up the nearest chair and sat close to him.

"We are not discussing boxing the watch, Snow. Or outrunning the constable. You and I, and many others, could yet stand accused of treason. I'll have the truth, if you please."

A twinkle came into his eyes. With a touch of admiration, he said, "You can be surprising regal at times, did you know it, Becky? Oh, very well. I will tell you as much as it is safe for you to know."

"Snow—*den!*"

"And that is *all!*" Boothe glanced to the door as though four troopers pressed their ears to the far side, and drew his chair even closer until he was almost knee to knee with his sister. "Firstly," he began, low-voiced, "I did not go up to Newcastle in Forty's behalf. An old and dear friend—I'll name him Jason—was, I knew, engaged in a desperate attempt to come south."

"A Jacobite gentleman?"

He nodded. "Poor fellow was badly wounded at Culloden, and it had taken weeks for him to recover to the point he dare venture from his place of concealment. He sent word to me that he dreaded lest the people who shielded him be discovered, and so he meant to strike out alone and would try for the home of a friend in Newcastle. I went up to help as best I might. Failed miserably. You will be thinking me a fine weakling to have involved Forty in it all. Truth of the matter is, he also knows our rebel and wanted to help."

"As would I, had you only taken me into your confidence!"

Boothe smiled, but said sternly, "The least you know of it, the better, at present! And you are to mention no word of this to my aunt—or anyone else!"

"Of course. How can you think me so henwitted? Do I know this poor fugitive?"

"You'll not get an answer to *that*, my girl. Next you'll be wheedling at me for his name—the which you shall not have, either!"

"All right, all right! Do go on. Did you find your friend in Newcastle?"

"No, blast it! I missed him by a day only. He had been all but caught and had to run for his life. I sought high and low, and came so near calling attention to myself that I finally had to buy a confounded slug of a hunter, only to try and fool the military. Egad! Wait till you see him! The most deceitful damned— Oh, well. Never mind about that. I had lost so much time pulling the wool over the eyes of a blasted persistent lieutenant, that I gave up, finally. My hope then was that—er, Jason might have headed for London and my rooms. He had not, of course, but I come back to Town and waited. Didn't know what else to do. It occurred to me that he might go to your house, so I stayed there, and Forty kept an eye on my flat. When Forty came to John Street after the duel, it was to tell me he'd received word that Jason had been hounded towards Bedfordshire. We decided that your being at Ward Marching would serve as a perfect explanation for our presence there."

"So *that* is why you urged me to return!"

"That is why. Forty and I come up, and rode hither and

yon, trying to keep as much in the open as possible, just as I'd done up north, hoping the poor fellow would spot us. Instead, de Villars found me."

Intent, she asked, "Accidentally?"

"No, as a matter of fact. He is already up to his neck in— Never mind. At all events, his great-uncle what's-his-name—"

"Geoffrey? Lord Boudreaux?"

"That's it. What a dashed fine old sportsman! He was also anxious for our rebel, and had sent word to de Villars to be on the lookout for him. Yesterday morning when I went into the village, Treve suddenly rid at me from a copse. Scared the wits out of me, I don't mind telling you! He warned me that Broadbent was in the vicinity and poor Jason heading this way and very likely to run right into a trap. We agreed to separate. Forty came here, I went north, and de Villars to the west. By purest luck, I found my man at sundown, but it was hell for leather then, and good old Jason so wrung out I could scarce keep him in the saddle."

"How awful! Poor soul. Had you planned to rendezvous with de Villars?"

"Well, of course I had. D'ye take me for a cloth head? I was almost there, too, when Jason tumbled head first from his horse. The troopers were close behind, and with this stupid blasted arm I could not lift him. Jupiter! I thought we were done for, I can tell you! Then Treve came up. He boosted Jason into his own saddle, for Jason's hack was nigh foundered, and told me to head for the hiding place we had decided upon earlier, and that he would lead the troopers off. I knew he had little chance. I was barely clear when they shot the poor hack, and then shot Treve. I started back, but I knew the horse would not carry all of us, and I damned well *had* to get Jason clear." He was silent for a moment, his lips tightly gripped together.

Rebecca waited breathlessly, her heart racing.

"I saw Treve trying to get away," muttered Boothe. "I could tell he would not last long." He swore under his breath. "I doubt I have ever felt quite so wretched in my life."

Rebecca leaned back in her chair. "And this—Jason?"

"Is safe. For the time, at least. No, really, Becky. He is tucked away where they could never find him, and with some of Boudreaux's loyal people caring for him."

She nodded. Then, smiling faintly, said, "De Villars once told me that any man so stupid as to embrace the cause of Bonnie Prince Charlie in effect *deserved* the retribution that must follow."

Snowden laughed. "Did he so? What a complete hand he is! Speaking of which—" He stood again. "I must go down and lend a hand. Treve is likely feeling as queer as Dick's hatband by this time."

When Boothe strolled into the breakfast parlour a few moments later, however, he found de Villars lounging in his chair, laughing at some remark of Ward's. Of the other guests, only Kadenworthy and Glendenning were present. Captain Holt sat next to de Villars. He was smiling, but very obviously on the alert.

"I wish I *might* have been your man," drawled de Villars. "For I vow 'twould break the monotony of life. I am like to die of boredom."

"Do you allow this impertinent clod to so criticize your hospitality, Ward?" enquired Boothe, sitting down, and very conscious of Ward's pallor and the two spots of colour high on de Villars' cheekbones.

"I am resigned," said Ward in a brittle voice. "Besides which, one must excuse a man who surely is still well over the oar."

"Indeed I am not," de Villars said aggrievedly. "Do I look bosky, Holt?"

The captain scanned the flushed features and shadowed eyes. "A touch, perhaps. Though I do not recall that you were in your cups at the ball. In fact . . ." He took up a fork and toyed with it idly. "I do not recall your appearing, at all." As he spoke his glance shot keenly to de Villars. He was disappointed. A look of elation came over the sardonic features.

"I win!" exclaimed de Villars, thumping one fist exultantly on the table. "He did not recognize me! Pay up, my Peter." And he reached out, snapping his fingers.

A pulse beating nervously under his eye, Sir Peter managed to grumble, "I shall write you a draft."

Holt scowled from one to the other, his hoped-for promotion seeming to fade with each passing second.

"Treve was a lackey," Boothe chortled.

"And tendered you a tray, *mon capitaine*," de Villars lied with an air of triumph.

"Indeed," said Holt silkily. "Of what?"

Ward's face became even whiter. Holt was not a drinking man, but de Villars could not know that. His heart pounded sickeningly.

De Villars shrugged. "Lord knows. I'll admit I do not recall last night very clearly."

"Well, I recall," said Rebecca teasingly, coming to join them at that moment. "And I saw the captain refuse your offering, de Villars."

The men stood as she entered. She saw de Villars flinch slightly, but his head was turned from the captain's relentless surveillance, and she kept her own smile intact as she begged that they be seated. Sir Peter pulled out a chair, and occupying it she said, "'Twas a glass of champagne, Captain. And I remember thinking how admirable it was that you would not take strong spirits whilst on duty."

"The captain never takes strong spirits," said Sir Peter, his tense gaze meeting de Villars' calm one.

"And I was not on duty at that time," said the captain. "But I am now and must be on my way."

Six anxious hearts were eased by this statement, but even as he seemed about to leave, Holt turned back. "By the by, de Villars. I understand you are related to Lord Boudreaux."

"The head of my house, Captain. Are you acquainted?"

His face cold and closed, Holt said, "Not well. But I suspect he is a Jacobite sympathizer."

Very aware of how narrowly he was watched, de Villars shrugged. "I wish you might prove it," he said dryly. "He disinherited me years agone, sad to tell."

"Did he so?" The captain's brows lifted. "You are to be congratulated, sir." And as if to make amends for his former coolness, he smiled and clapped de Villars heartily on the shoulder.

It was the left shoulder. De Villars' face convulsed.

Rebecca's heart seemed to leap into her throat and choke her.

"Now—curse you for a . . . clumsy clod," groaned de Villars, clutching his brow with a shaking hand. "Oh! My poor head!"

Kadenworthy laughed although he was suddenly deathly pale. "And you not bosky this morning, eh?"

Glendenning sighed. "To my sorrow, I know exactly how you feel, Treve."

The captain said an amused, "You had best give him the hair of the dog that bit him, Sir Peter. Good morrow, ma'am. Gentlemen . . ." And he walked out, Ward ushering him politely from the room.

De Villars leant back in his chair. "The devil!" he gasped. "That was a close run thing!"

&

The Midsummer's Eve Ball had provided Sir Peter's guests with a supply of *on-dits* that they would be able to recount for weeks to come. The fact of their host's obvious *tendre* for Mrs. Rebecca Parrish, and of my Lord Kadenworthy's sudden infatuation for the lady, were also well worth the sharing. The military involvement had, however, brought with it memories of the recent and tragic flare-up of the Rebellion and, disturbed, the guests did not linger. By early afternoon many of those who had overnighted at the mansion were preparing to depart. Lord Kadenworthy, the Boudreauxes, the Streets, Mrs. Monahan, Mr. Melton, and Lord Graham Fortescue were among those who remained. Neither Major Broadbent nor Captain Holt returned, but the presence of the several individuals who were unaware of what had actually transpired in the blue ante-room on Midsummer's Eve forbade that the matter be discussed. After a late luncheon, Rebecca and her aunt retired to the cottage and found Anthony and Patience awaiting them in a fever of excitement. They had seen the soldiers and, much to their delight, the cottage had been searched. Millie had been cross, but had thought the sergeant in charge of the search party was "quite a nice chap." "I think he must have liked her, too," said Anthony brightly, "for he has been here twice this morning."

Rebecca exchanged a swift, scared look with her aunt.

Not to be outdone, Patience chirped, "I helpt-ted the tholdierth look *everywhere*, ma'am. I wath a good helper. They telled me."

Again, the ladies looked at one another in horror. Chilled, Rebecca gulped, "Oh, Aunt! This *wretched* slaughter! Will it never end?"

She was shaking visibly. Mrs. Boothe thought, "Poor girl, she has been through too much these past few days." "You are tired, love," she said gently. "Go and lie down upon your bed and rest. 'Twill make you feel better."

Rebecca went to her room, but not to her bed. Sitting by the open window, gazing across the verdant grounds, she sought a peace of mind that eluded her. Peter Ward had looked at her with deeper admiration after the ball. He would offer now, she was sure of it. And his offer would mean security, a luxurious future, and no more worries over bills for either her or Anthony. But insidiously came the recollection of de Villars weaving into the ante-room. Of his gallantry, so opposed to Ward's— Desperate, she cut off that thought, but she could not banish the memory of de Villars, hurt and helpless; of that dauntless grin; of the awed worship in his eyes when he had looked up at her from his pillow. Tears blurred her own eyes. She bowed her head into her hands and wept. And when the storm was over, she was too exhausted to evade the truth any longer. She loved. For the first time in her life, she really loved. But she loved the wrong man. It would not *do!* If de Villars offered again, as he very well might, she could not accept. She *must* not accept!

Sighing, she glanced at the distant loom of the great house. That could be her future home. Anthony's future home. No, she would not think of Trevelyan de Villars anymore. She would concentrate on her future—a serene future with Sir Peter to stand ever between her and a sometimes cruel world. De

Villars' voice rang in memory. "I was hoping a vulture might captivate him." She laughed brokenly and then again burst into tears.

She did not see de Villars again that day, but Lady Ward whispered that he was uncomfortable and troubled of his wound. Rebecca's fears for him mounted. They would not dare to summon an apothecary, for Hilary or that miserable captain would learn of it. Treve must be suffering miserably. Suppose the wound became putrid? Suppose he was feverish? Suppose he *died*—before she could see him again? Frantic, she sought out her brother. Boothe scolded that she was fretting needlessly. "Old Treve" was made of steel and doing splendidly, by what Letitia had been able to tell him. He would be fine as fivepence by tomorrow. Later, a solemn and tired-looking Letitia told her that her cousin was at last asleep but had passed a miserable day and would probably be confined to his bed for at least a week.

The evening dragged past. The Monahan and Kadenworthy chattered brightly. The Streets, innocently unaware of the tense undercurrent to the easy conversation, contributed their joint observations in such a way as to amuse all and were never in the least offended by that amusement. Sir Peter looked at ease again, and his usual distinguished self. He carefully divided his attentions among Rebecca, Rosemary Monahan, and an unusually subdued Lady Ward. Snowden spent most of the evening hovering about Letitia Boudreaux and her brother. On the one occasion Ward dared to broach the subject of their ordeal, he was showing Rebecca a superb engraving of a pheasant, and being safely removed from the rest of the company, murmured softly, "You seem weary, dear ma'am. I trust you do not worry unnecessarily over de Villars. Have no fears on that score. I shall see to it that he gets safely away, I promise you. And very soon."

"Soon?" she asked anxiously. "Is he well enough?"

"Oh, assuredly. The sooner the better!" He met her rather shocked eyes and added a hasty, "For all our sakes! Indeed, he himself is desperate to be gone. The poor fellow is plagued with guilt and keeps telling me he bitterly repents his foolishness." He smiled. "As though I would blame him. I'll own that when I told you I would not fail any friend claiming sanctuary here, I never dreamed you would so bravely aid me."

Speechless, Rebecca stared at him, and was not a little relieved when Lady Ward called testily that they must come and make up another table for cards.

Sleep was long in coming that night, and Rebecca awoke feeling listless and worried. The final touches were being applied to her toilette when Evans came up to announce that ma'am was wanted in the parlour. Before Millie could discover who waited, the abigail's cheerful countenance was whisked away.

"Birdwit!" snorted Millie, threading a riband through Rebecca's curls.

Going downstairs, Rebecca decided that her early caller was probably Kadenworthy, his nose out of curl because Sir Peter had outmanoeuvered him last evening and led her back to the cottage whilst his lordship was lost in a game of chess with Fitz Boudreaux. She went smiling into the parlour and halted with a shocked gasp. Trevelyan de Villars, booted and spurred, stood by the mantel.

"Good gracious!" she exclaimed. "You should not be so soon up, sir!"

He spun to face her, his eyes brightening. He did not carry his arm in a sling, but of course he would not dare, and perhaps there was not the need, for he looked surprisingly well, and there was in fact a good colour in his face. Nonetheless, she crossed to him, saying anxiously, "You cannot be thinking of riding out?" Polite phrases, yet her heart was pounding madly, and her earlier resolution to give him no encouragement had vanished in the first instant of seeing him. She knew very well why he was here. He had come to thank her for saving his life. He had come to beg her to forgive his earlier naughtiness and plead with her to be his wife. And the anticipation of hearing those dear words was causing her pulse to flutter ever more wildly, her breathing to become erratic, and such a soaring joy to take possession of her that she dare not think what she would say when he asked her.

De Villars, noted Corinthian and whip and man about town, had not been at a loss for words any time these past ten years. He was at a loss for words now. Looking into this girl's bewitching face, he felt like an inexperienced youth again and said clumsily, "Oh, I am perfectly fit, never fear. But I must— must leave at once, for I've an—er, prior engagement, you see, that— I mean—there are certain claims upon me that I cannot—ah, neglect."

Rebecca stiffened. How nervous he was; how unlike the suave, self-assured man she knew. "A prior engagement?" A woman, no doubt! What a fool to have supposed that he meant to offer! She stepped back. "You should be laid down upon your bed for at least a sennight, Mr. de Villars."

He sensed that he had offended. The concern in her eyes had been replaced by storm clouds. His own fault, of course. In an effort to banish the vexation from her face, he said with his easy grin, "There was a time, ma'am, when I would have voiced a most improper response to such a remark."

She blushed and turned away. This was more in his usual style, to be sure. But it was scarcely the speech of a worshipful swain. It would seem that if the gentleman intended to offer her anything, it was a slip on the shoulder, not a marriage ring! She felt bruised and hurt, and said, "I am quite sure you must know many places where such remarks would be well received."

De Villars bit his lip. He was bungling this badly. If only his confounded head did not feel so completely detached from the rest of him. "I felt I must come and thank you," he said, absently taking up his whip from the sideboard.

That movement convinced Rebecca that he was in a passion to be gone. She glanced outside. His coach stood waiting on the drivepath, a groom holding the spirited horses. A woman's hand rested on the open window, and on that hand was a ring shaped in the form of a golden dragon. Rosemary Monahan's ring. Feeling as though she had been struck, Rebecca stared at that white hand. *She* had saved The Wicked Rake's life! And at considerable risk to her own. And he could scarce be bothered to thank her, so eager was he to be off with his bird of paradise! At any other time she might have openly taxed him with it, but the tensions of the past few days had wrought more havoc with her nerves than she knew. Tears of mortification stung her eyes as she recalled her earlier hopeful idiocy, and she could only pray he would not have the satisfaction of knowing what a fool she had been. She swung around and said airily, "Oh, pray do not refine on such a trivial thing, sir. I would have done the same for any hunted creature."

Shaken, de Villars tried again. "I have no doubt you would, ma'am. Still, there is—is a custom in some lands, you know, that—if you save a life, that life belongs henceforth to you."

How charming. His life belonged to her. Unless he chanced to have a "prior engagement" with the enchanting Mrs. Monahan! A lump rose in her throat. And it was silly, downright *stupid* to be so devastated! She had known what he was, for heaven's sake! Whatever else, however, she must not betray herself. "Indeed?" She crossed to a side table and straightened the fruit that had been set out in a large bowl. "In that event," she said with superb disdain, "it would behoove one to take care lest all kinds of undesirables might hang upon one's sleeve."

De Villars whitened. "I came here to thank you," he began grimly.

"So you said."

He stepped forward to grip her wrist with his right hand, and although she averted her head, he grated, "You saved my life. . . ." The memory of that intrepid action, combined with the sweet scent of her, the nearness of her warm loveliness, conspired to overpower him. With a folly his friends would have found astounding, he burst out, "How can I ever repay you? Marry me!"

Rebecca's mouth fell open. *This*—from an accomplished lover? A renowned rake? This crude excuse for a proposal, lacking all tenderness and polish? This vulgar reward for services rendered? Why, he must feel the most utter contempt for her not even to have tried to pretend affection! Infuriated, she wrenched away. "You are much too generous, sir! So *grand* a payment is not necessary!"

"I know! I know!" He ran a hand through his hair in distracted fashion. "God! I did not mean it!"

How well she knew! The villain! The savage! "One would hope you did not, indeed. I had fancied to have made my future plans sufficiently clear. There was no call for you to come here and insult me, Mr. de Villars!"

So an offer from him was an insult. Scarcely to be wondered at, after all. He should apologize, but his head was so muddled—he could not even think. . . . Words failing him, he reached out to her imploringly. Had Rebecca seen that tremblingly outstretched hand, so much might have been changed. But in an attempt to hide the tears that welled over, she stood with her back turned. "Perhaps," she said icily, "it would be best if you went upon your way, sir."

It would have been best had he not come. By heaven, what a frightful mull he had made of it! Well, there was no undoing it now. He said quietly, "Yes. Forgive me. I had no thought to insult you. But I owe you— I must make amends— somehow. And I will—I swear it. If—if you still want—Peter, I—I will help. In any way I can."

He would help her into marriage with another man! Oh, but here was a lover *par excellence!* One who could scarce wait to be rid of her! The tears cold upon her cheeks, she said, "You are too kind. But pray do not trouble yourself. It is neither asked—nor necessary."

De Villars walked blindly to the door and closed it gently behind him.

CHAPTER
❧ 15 ❧

"*P*eaceful?" Snowden Boothe reined back his rambunctious steed so as to stay more or less beside his sister's polite gelding. "A *cemetery* is peaceful, yet I'd as soon not dwell there as yet! I wonder all this peace has not sent you riding *ventre à terre* back to Town!"

"Oh, no," said Rebecca, stifling a sigh.

Slanting an oblique glance at her, he thought that no matter what she said she was not happy. He knew her too well not to suspect that she had thrown her heart over the hedge, and, knowing also for whom she nourished a *tendre*, reached over to pat her gloved hand. "Cheer up, lass. Your dashing beau will return on Friday. I take it you mean to wait for him?"

Alight with eagerness, her eyes flew to his face. "Are you sure?"

"'Tis what he told me when he rid out to take his grandmama back to Cornwall."

"Oh." The glow faded from Rebecca's eyes. "Well, yes, I shall wait, of course. I—we promised Sir Peter we would stay a month, and that will be up next week."

"Just as well. It will— Blast and damn this glue pot! Becky, I cannot talk while he persists in standing on his tail. Can we walk?" And when he had swung from the saddle and handed down his amused sister, they walked on together while he went on more evenly, "It will give me time to get our rebel to London and gone before you come back. He's much restored already, and well able to travel can we only elude that damned Hilary Broadbent. Lord! Who'd have thought a boy we've known since childhood could turn so curst treacherous?"

"Oh, never say so! Hilary is but doing his duty. Indeed, I have often thought that if Captain Holt had been in the anteroom that night . . ." She shuddered. "Hilary means us no harm. It is this—this loathsome Rebellion!"

"If he means us no harm, why does he continually lurk about with that revolting sycophant of his?"

"You *know* why! And you should not even attempt to—" She bit the words back. He must attempt it, of course. In his shoes she would do the same, if she had as much courage. And so she finished lamely, "Snow—do *pray* be careful!"

"I shall, never doubt it." He glanced at her fondly. She was a good chit. Not once had she suggested he let the fugitive take his chances, yet how many women would have flown into the deuce of a pucker over this nasty business? He thought, "And how many women would have had the courage to conceal a hunted man beneath their skirts?"

"Perhaps," Rebecca worried, "I should come back with you. It might look less—"

"Devil it would! No, madam! If aught *should* go wrong— which it won't—I'll have a better chance to get clear am I not hampered by the need to get *you* clear as well."

Startled by a new thought, she said, "Dear heaven! You never have him in your flat? Or at John Street?"

They were alone out here, and yet he instinctively glanced around and lowered his voice. "Never you mind where I have him, my girl. Least said, soonest mended!" She looked frightened, and he went on in a more breezy fashion, "At all events, he will be gone by the middle of next week at the very latest. After that, I've—ah, certain plans of my own to bring to fruition." He added rather wryly, "Do I summon up the gall."

"A lady? Snow, you villain! Is it The Monahan you pursue?" Guilelessly, Rebecca murmured, "I saw how you ogled her."

"Ogle indeed! What a widgeon you are, Becky! Rosemary Monahan is a true Fair, but scarce the type for whom I would form a lasting attachment."

Rebecca clapped her hands, her face more animated than he had seen it for days. "*Have* you done so? Oh, how exciting! Is it someone I know well? Is it—I *do* hope it is a certain very lovely girl who is just a little taller than I, perhaps."

"She ain't so very tall since she's taken to wearing slippers with lower heels," he said defensively. "Just about perfect, in fact."

"Yes, she is indeed the very dearest girl."

"Well, I am, er, very glad you—ah." Boothe flushed. He seldom flushed and, feeling his face grow heated, averted it, coughed, then stammered, "If—er that is, *should* Letty—er, Miss Boudreaux . . . would—er, *might* you—oh, dashitall, Becky! You know what I mean."

She leaned to hug him impulsively. "I do. And she is the *very* girl for you. I have so prayed you would choose her, for she has been in love with you this age!"

He scanned her face with betraying eagerness. "Do you really think so? I scarce can tell whether I'm on my head or my heels. When first we met, I thought her a nice chit, y'know. But the more I saw of her, the more I saw what a truly delightful lady she is. So kind, Becky, and gracious. And gentle. And you must admit she's beautiful."

"And brave," Rebecca contributed. "Only think how she stood by me at the ball. Snow, you will *never* know how frightened I was, thinking that at any minute someone would give de Villars away, and we both would be dragged off to the Tower! When Letitia came up so staunchly, I could have kissed her!"

"Yes." He frowned darkly. "I cannot like her to have run such a risk."

"Oh, can you not? And what of the risks *you* are running, sir?"

"Fustian! I'm a man."

She laughed. "Are you, so? I have always fancied you a great, silly boy!"

"Wretch," he said with a grin, tugging the nearest ringlet. "Poor Letty, to have such a madcap for a sister."

"Have you offered already, then? Good gracious! You waste no time."

"I've wasted too damned much already!" But he added rather shyly, "I ain't offered formally, of course. Cannot, you know, until I've approached the old gentleman. Ecod! He's like to judge me a very poor prospect, eh?"

She looked at the fair young face, the clear eyes, the proud tilt to the head, the broad shoulders and athletic build of this loved brother, and said a fond, "He could only be delighted."

"Silly cabbage!" But he took up her hand and dropped a rare kiss on it. "Never mind about my manly beauty. What about my reputation?"

"What fustian! You've never been much in the petticoat line, nor—"

"Deuce take it, girl! You *must* not use such vulgarities! Whatever would Ward say? Or—my Lady Ward?"

"I know." But peeping at him mischievously, she said, "I have to overcome the habits picked up from my wicked brothers! Oh, how thrilled Johnny will be by your news! I shall write— No, *you* must, of course. He will come home, and we shall have the most beautiful wedding, and I shall help Letitia choose her bride clothes, and—"

"And—heigh-ho, off we go!" he intervened, shaking his head at her. "Becky, Becky! Do you never mean to stop romancing and start growing up?"

He helped her back into the saddle, swung astride his own mount, and led the way down into the lane.

Rebecca protested his remark indignantly. "And this from a man who only last April walked backwards to Clapham and then lost his wager because he fell into a horse trough!"

He chuckled. "No, but you see I am in love now, and everything in the world so changed! But—you know the feeling, eh?"

Rebecca's smiling gaze fell away. She said rather unevenly, "What did you mean about your reputation? A few escapades, merely, unless— Snow! You were not *deeply* involved with the Uprising?"

"No. I meant only that I'm known to be pockets to let. Trust his lordship to know that. The old boy's keen as a cross-eyed walrus, and I ain't at all sure I'll blame him does he deal me a leveller."

She frowned. It was very true that they were far from comfortably circumstanced. And Letitia was a considerable heiress. If her great-uncle judged Snow a fortune hunter . . . Uneasily, she said, "Lord Boudreaux is likely happy as a minnow. He must be does he love Letitia, for I am very sure she is *aux anges*, dear girl."

"I pray you have the right of it." They rode on in silence for a short while. Then Snowden said, "One thing, when the old boy learns how you saved de Villars' life, that may turn the trick!"

Rebecca was properly reassuring, but she could not place much dependence upon that fact. After all, my Lord Boudreaux *had* disinherited his notorious grandnephew.

❧

"Why so dismal, my dearest?" Tripping across the back garden to where Rebecca sat alone under the apple tree, Mrs. Boothe held up the paniers of her charming gown of primrose muslin, all decked about with tiny bows of yellow satin, and was herself as light-hearted and bright-eyed as a girl, from dainty beruffled cap to tiny slippers. "I have been looking for you this age," said the little lady blithely. "Anthony and Patience went blackberrying, and he teased her, so she pushed him into a bush and is now overset with remorse. Can you not feature it? That tiny mite of a child!"

Amused, Rebecca said, "I do not blame her a bit. Anthony treats her as though she were a loved but rather wooden-headed pet dog. Is he badly damaged?"

"Physically, no. But mentally—" Albinia threw up her hands and sat beside her niece. "He writhes, poor boy. As all males do when a girl outwits 'em. Speaking of which, has Snow heard aught of poor de Villars? He was much too ill to go riding off like that, and I am convinced did so purely to remove his dangerous presence from— Good gracious, dearest! Are you feeling feverish? Your cheeks are so flushed and your eyes look—"

Attack, thought Rebecca desperately, was ever the best means of defence, or so Papa used to hold. And so she intervened, "Never mind about my cheeks, you sly creature! Only look at your own! I vow you look no older than cousin Evaline, and twice as lovely. Whence cometh these pretty blushes and the stars in your eyes? Eh? What have you been up to that you keep from me?"

Albinia lowered her lashes at once, but could not extinguish the betraying glow from her cheeks. "It must be this pure country air. Now *why* must you stare so, horrid child? I declare one cannot put on a new gown without—"

"He has *offered!* Why, you shameless little jade! Mr. Melton offered and you said naught of it!"

Blushful and fluttering and quite beside herself with agitation, Mrs. Boothe responded, "Why, Becky, I would not— I mean, I did not— I had no thought to say anything until you yourself were— Oh, *wretched* girl! *Yes!* Is it not superb? Your silly aunt is to be *wed* again! Oh, I feel—"

But her feelings were smothered as she was swept into a hug, kissed, exclaimed over, and congratulated, and all with such a depth of love and joy that her eyes became bright with more than happiness and she had to grope blindly for the scrap of cambric and lace she designated a handkerchief.

"Naughtiest of aunts," Rebecca chided, her own cheeks aglow with excitement. "I demand to know the how and why and where of it! Did he go down upon his knees? Was he too bashful to make a proper offer? Where shall you live? Can he support you in the fashion to which you are accustomed? Is he richer than Croesus? Come—speak up now!"

Between laughter and tears, Mrs. Boothe cried, "Mercy! What a plethora of questions! He proposed last evening whilst we walked back to the cottage. And it was on this very bench, bless the dear object! As for *how*—we were speaking of somebody else, as a matter of fact, and I said that I was sure this particular gentleman was head over ears in love with a certain lady, only it was hard to guess whether or not he might propose. And George—Mr. Melton, I mean—said he had always believed ladies knew long before gentlemen when they had won hearts, and then he—he sort of rushed with great speed into saying, 'For instance, dear Mrs. Albinia, you must know the depth of *my* esteem for *you*.' And—" She clasped one hand to her rapidly rising and falling bosom, and said happily, "Oh, Becky! I was so *astonished*, and before I could utter a word he had indeed fallen to his knee—well, you may look incredulous, though to be sure it was not very far to fall, since we were sitting down at the time—and begged I grant him my hand in marriage."

"How splendid!" Rebecca's hug was so boisterous that her aunt wailed she must be quite jellied did she not desist. "And when shall you be wed? The gentleman has a home in the country, I believe?"

"Near Richmond. He is to take me down there tomorrow, if you would not object to stay here alone, dearest. His mama is quite lonely there, so George thinks she must be pleased to know we shall live in the house for much of the year." She clung to Rebecca's hand and went on earnestly, "I shall expect you to come to us very soon, my pet. You cannot stay in Town alone, though if Sir Peter should make an offer, things would be quite different, of course. And I do believe he will, for he can scarce tear his eyes from you when—"

"When he is not gazing at Mrs. Monahan," Rebecca put in dryly.

"Oh, but every gentleman looks at The Monahan. Even George. And one can scarce blame them—she's a striking woman. Besides," continued Mrs. Boothe carelessly, "everyone knows she was de Villars' fancy piece, and even *he* did not offer for her."

Her eyes flashing, Rebecca flared, "Why do you say '*even* he'? Trevelyan de Villars is as well-born as any man!"

Her aunt blinked, but persisted, "I do not dispute that. But—his reputation . . . ! Horrors!"

"Reputations are all too often created by unconscionable gabble-mongers."

"Very true. But not in this case. All London knows he ruined a lady when he was no more than a boy, and—"

"And has been paying a cruel price ever since for that piece of folly!" Her brows drawn into a fierce scowl, Rebecca said hotly, "And if it comes to that, Aunt Alby, I would give a deal to know how this sadly disgraced lady contrived to make an excellent match not a year later. It appears to me there is more to that tale than has ever been revealed!"

"Why, there always is, my love. And do not mistake, I think de Villars charming. Despite the fact he so recklessly endangered us all—and you in—"

"*Endangered* us! He risked his life for a poor wounded fugitive! I would not call that reckless. Gallant, unselfish, courageous, rather!"

It became necessary that Mrs. Boothe purse her lips so as to hide a smile. "Hmmnnn," she mused. "Nonetheless, I cannot believe Sir Peter to be seriously enamoured of The Monahan. So soon as he returns he will make *you* an offer, dear one. I *know* it!"

Rebecca sighed. "I hope so," she said, forlornly.

Mr. Melton called for his betrothed at a very early hour the next morning, and they drove off in his light carriage,

bound for Surrey and his country estate, with Albinia's handkerchief fluttering from the open window, and her promise to
be back next day before sunset echoing in Rebecca's ears.

They had been gone scarcely two hours when a sleek black
travelling coach bowled up the drivepath and Lord Kadenworthy and Viscount Glendenning alighted. Rebecca had walked
out onto the porch to greet them and, chancing to glance at the
handsome vehicle, was struck by the absurd notion that one of
the footmen was Lord Graham Fortescue. The coach was in
motion before she noted the resemblance, and Kadenworthy
was planting an ardent salute upon her hand.

"My lord," she said urgently, "I know it is foolish in me,
but I am sure that footman was—"

"Well, well, more company," drawled Horatio Glendenning, and sure enough another carriage made its way along the
drive, this time bearing Martha and Walter Street. Delighted,
Rebecca welcomed her callers, sent Millie scurrying to warn
Evans they would sit down five to luncheon, and forgot all
about the footman. He did not, in fact, come back into her
thoughts until she and her guests went inside after a merry
game of croquet and found the dining table readied for lunch
and my Lord Fortescue dozing in an elbow chair in the parlour.

"Forty!" exclaimed Rebecca. "So it *was* you!" She went
over to give him her hand. "And why the business of wearing
Kadenworthy's gold livery?"

Fortescue looked down in apparent bewilderment at the
elegant maroon coat and pearl grey satin small clothes he wore.

Glendenning asked with sublime innocence, "Business,
Mrs. Rebecca? I assure you old Kade ain't a Cit."

"You are too good, dear boy," murmured Kadenworthy.
He looked levelly at Rebecca. His eyes held a warning. She felt
suffocated. How could she have been so dense? She had
thought her part was played, but once again she was involved
in desperate deeds. "Oh, I suppose there must have been a
faint resemblance," she said lightly. "I thought Forty was playing one of his pranks."

Fortescue protested, "Now that ain't fair, ma'am! Fact is, I rode my new hunter. Snow found him in Newcastle. Care to see, gentlemen?"

To these men born and bred in homes where horses were a ruling passion, such a question was superfluous, and they all trooped out to the stable to congregate about a stall containing a very large but unlovely grey hunter.

There was a moment of silence, Fortescue smilingly expectant, his prize grey munching with closed eyes and sublime indifference, and the assembled viewers solemnly restraining their reactions.

Lord Kadenworthy, less inhibited than his companions, murmured, "You did say Boothe—er, found *him*, Fortescue?"

Surveying the equine through his quizzing glass, Glendenning uttered a muffled snort, but said kindly, "Good shade of grey, that."

"He is very . . ." said Walter Street,

"—er, large," his sister finished.

Anthony, galloping into the stable with his satellite trundling along behind, halted, staring.

"Oh," said Patience, and added with the devastating candour of childhood, "What a funny-looking horthy!"

"He may *look* a trifle odd," Fortescue defended, his unfailing good humour unruffled by the resultant burst of laughter, "but he can go like the very deuce. Old Snow thought he had bought a proper slug, so I took him. There was a look about the eyes, y'know. Had a sort of premonition. Jolly glad."

Mr. Street asked, "Why would Boothe buy a horse—"

"—if he thought it was a slug?" appended Martha.

Fortescue looked stunned, floundered, and threw a frantic glance at Rebecca.

"It—it was a wager," she declared brightly.

"A sort of—who can buy the biggest hay-burner wager," murmured Kadenworthy.

Awed, Glendenning said, "Only look at him eat! Your other cattle may well starve, Forty."

Rebecca's attention had wandered during this exchange.

From the moment they had entered the stable she had experienced the oddest sensation that she was being watched. She directed a quick look up at the hay loft and caught a glimpse of a powdered wig hurriedly ducking from view.

Miss Street asked, "Is something amiss, Mrs. Parrish? You are quite pale."

"I—I thought," stammered Rebecca, "I saw a rat!"

Miss Street uttered a piercing shriek. She had, it developed, a terror of rodents. They left the stable at once, Anthony and Patience running ahead, lured by the prospect of luncheon, and the gentlemen still teasing poor Fortescue because of his gluttonous hunter.

Striving to appear at ease, Rebecca's heart was hammering. Her brief sight of the man in the loft had also revealed the sheen of gold satin. Forty had worn the footman's livery, sure enough. But he had changed clothes, probably in the loft, with the man now clad in those garments.

For the balance of the afternoon, her nerves were strained, and she dreaded that Hilary or that horrid Captain Holt appear. Not until Kadenworthy's carriage went bowling down the drivepath was she able at last to breathe easily. Watching it out of sight, she prayed silently for the footman sitting up behind—the one who was a desperate Jacobite fugitive.

❧

Friday was warm and sultry. Millie took the children to the pond after luncheon, and Rebecca sat at the parlour window, her work box beside her, repairing a torn flounce on her pink muslin while pondering gloomily upon how many more years she might be doomed to exist. It was so quiet in the cottage that she jumped when a knock sounded at the front door. She waited for Evans to answer it, but that expert in the art of occasional deafness did not put in an appearance. Rebecca laid aside her work and went to the door.

Sir Peter stood there, a lackey behind him holding a great bouquet of golden roses. Sir Peter's coat was also golden.

"Oh, how lovely," said Rebecca. "Welcome home!"

He beamed and, bowing over her hand, kissed her fingers gallantly. "And what a delight to come home and find so lovely a lady—waiting."

A few weeks ago that remark would have sent Rebecca into raptures of anticipation. She thought in an interested way, "So he is going to offer at last," and said calmly, "Thank you. Will you not come in?"

Evans appeared belatedly and took lackey and flowers into the nether regions, and Rebecca led Sir Peter to the parlour, poured him a glass of wine, and enquired after the welfare of his grandmama.

"Oh, she is very well," he said, waiting courteously for her to seat herself before he occupied the wing chair. "I took her down to Cornwall, you know. It is a long journey for the poor soul, but she endured it uncomplainingly."

"I am sure of it. And how fortunate that she has so devoted a grandson."

He made a deprecatory gesture, and said with a wry smile, "Sometimes I fear I become a trifle impatient. She is not always easy to please, but I do hope you have not taken her in dislike, ma'am?"

"Good gracious! As though I should! I thought her splendid—especially when she played her part so bravely."

He nodded. "She did not let us down, did she?" He set his glass aside, stood, and paced slowly to the window, to stand in silence with hands clasped behind him.

Rebecca smiled. He was nerving himself. And if he did offer . . . ? She gave herself a mental shake. What nonsense! This was what she had prayed for, was it not? She considered him speculatively. A rich, handsome, charming gentleman. She would be extreme fortunate to secure such a husband. A tiny voice, as disturbing as it was unwanted, whispered, "He will never say, or do, anything outrageous. There will be polite smiles, but no spontaneous laughter. His wealth will protect you against poverty, but when you face a family crisis, he will assure you of his support and then leave you to handle matters as best you may. . . ." She bit her lip, and, shutting out the painful memory of a cynical grin and twinkling grey eyes full of mischief, told herself firmly that she would not only say a most grateful "Yes," but that she would try with all her heart to be a good wife.

"She thinks very highly of you," murmured Sir Peter, watching the flight of a swallow across the sunny park. "In fact—" He turned about and asked gravely, "But perhaps the memories you associate with Ward Marching are not happy ones? You have known great peril here. Indeed, I wonder your nerves are not completely overset, poor creature."

"But I have been very happy here," said Rebecca with a degree of truth. "It is so beautiful."

Obviously pleased, he walked closer, that grave regard still fixed upon her face. "De Villars feels very badly because he spoiled it for you."

Her heart giving a tremendous leap, she stammered, "Y-you have spoken with him? He is recovered?"

"Oh, one does not worry about Treve, he is indestructible. We had a good chat, and he is in fullest agreement with my grandmama. You will be thinking me a silly fellow to mention that, I daresay, but the opinions of those I cherish weigh heavily with me. And in this case, reinforce my own."

Rebecca lowered her lashes demurely and was silent. So Trevelyan had given her a good reference. She wondered what Sir Peter would say if he knew that The Wicked Rake had recovered consciousness while shielded beneath her gown and had tugged on her—

"Wherefore," said Sir Peter, coming to stand directly before her, "I have decided they both are perfectly right, dear Mrs. Parrish." He reached out his hands. She put hers in them, and he drew her tenderly to her feet. "You are the perfect lady to become my wife. Will you allow me the very great honour to ask your brother for the right to pay my addresses to you?"

It was done. She had triumphed at last. Smiling into his kind hazel eyes, Rebecca murmured, "It is I who will be honoured, sir."

Sir Peter pulled her into his embrace and kissed her passionately.

On the forehead.

❦

"By Jove!" Boothe ushered his aunt and sister into the warm parlour. "I thought the royal coach was rumbling up John Street! *Four* outriders?"

"Sir Peter is extreme devoted," said Albinia with a twinkle.

"Oh, what a fine blaze!" Rebecca crossed to the fire and sat in the chair the beaming housekeeper pulled up for her. "I am so glad you have a fire, Falk. I vow one would think it November rather than July!"

Boothe ushered his aunt to another chair, then seized his sister's hand. "Hey! Falk—see here! Be dashed if this ruby ain't the size of a pigeon's egg!"

The betrothal ring having been properly exclaimed over, he opened the door for Mrs. Falk, then returned to take Rebecca's hand again and look searchingly into her eyes. "Happy now, m'dear?"

"Of course I am. Where is Anthony? Had he a comfortable journey with Millie yesterday?"

"Very. They are gone to the park, but will be home soon, I fancy. How improved the boy is. The country air was good for him."

"Yes. Thank heaven, he is quite his old self again." She tugged at his coat skirt and said fondly, "Do sit down and tell us your news, Snow. How does your suit prosper?"

Boothe disposed himself on the arm of her chair, watching her with a slight frown in his blue eyes. He glanced at his aunt. Her smile was bland. He thought, "There's a roach in the rum . . ." but said cheerfully, "Oh, I gave it up. I've decided to remain a carefree bachelor. For the time, at least."

"*What?*" Rebecca seized his arm with a dismayed exclamation. "Oh, dearest! I am so sorry! I *knew* something had you in the hips. Whatever has happened?"

"Nothing more than a change of mind," he said nonchalantly, removing her clutch. "Always better to be safe than—"

"Stuff!" his aunt interposed with a stamp of her little foot. "Snowden, have you not yet learned you can hoax neither one of us? The truth, dear boy. At once, if you please! 'Twas my Lord Boudreaux! High in the instep, is he? I had half expected it, I own."

Rebecca said indignantly, "Why should the man hold us in contempt? Our lineage needs no apology!"

"It is not our lineage the old boy objects to," Snowden said ruefully. He paused and moved a bowl of roses so that Falk might put a laden tray on the table. When the housekeeper had left again, he went on, "Your irresponsible here-and-there-ian of a brother just don't come up to his lordship's notion of a husband for Letitia." He sighed. "I ain't at all sure but what he's in the right of it, at that."

Mrs. Boothe went over and began to pour the tea. "What *does* he expect? A Prince of the Blood for the girl?"

"She deserves it, Lord knows. But—" He took the cup his aunt offered, added four teaspoons of sugar, and began to stir absently. "I must own the old boy was decent about it. But he gave me to understand, in his gentle way, that I have no aim in life. I just—skitter about. But then, if you come right down to it, we *all* do—pretty much."

Rebecca sank her teeth viciously into a steaming crumpet, then wiped butter from her chin. "I collect," she said rather indistinctly, "that were you a coal-heaver, he would approve. Is there no reasoning with the man?"

"I tried. Don't mean to give up, you know, but—" Briefly, despair came into his face. "He's rather—daunting. And it's—well, Letitia is the worst part of it. She's heart-broken, dear soul."

He looked older, suddenly, and Rebecca saw the same shock in her aunt's face that she herself had experienced. She said slowly, "There must be *something* you can do to win him over?"

"Buy a pair of colours, perhaps. Or get on to an Ambassador's staff. But there's nothing I do *well* that could offset my lack of property and tenants."

"Of course there is! We shall have to study it—all three of us. Oh, if only Jonathan were here! He'd know what to do!"

"*Someone's* here!" Boothe put down his cup hurriedly. "Gad, but I clean forgot! There's a gentleman waiting to see you." He clapped a hand to his brow. "I'd best go and get the old fellow, or would you care to come? Falk put him in the book room."

"A gentleman?" Standing, Rebecca straightened her gown. "Lud! And I've not taken time to change my dress! I must look a fright."

He grinned. "Well, you do, of course."

Mrs. Boothe laughed. "Wicked boy! Who is it?"

"Dashed if I can recall. Frail-looking old duck. Said his name was Andrews, or Anderson, or—Apperson! That's it! Mr. Gervaise Apperson."

Rebecca excused herself and, en route to their small book room, racked her brains, but the name was completely new to her. When she opened the door she found that a small fire had been lighted on the hearth, which was as well for the room was chill and the elderly gentleman warming his hands before it looked frail indeed.

"I must apologize, sir, for having kept you waiting," she said. "I hope you have . . . not . . ." The words trailed into silence.

He had stood at her coming and turned to greet her. His wig was moderate, his clothing neat but certainly not of the first stare of elegance, his manner almost humble. It was difficult to determine his age, for although the face was thin and lined, the eyes beneath the heavy white brows were bright and youthful.

Rebecca experienced the same breathless sense of excitement that had seized her in the stable at Ward Marching when she had glimpsed the rebel fugitive hiding in the hayloft. This man was old, with a scar down one cheek to disfigure what might otherwise have been a pleasant face. And yet . . .

"Have we met . . . before, sir?" she said hesitantly.

"Not for—quite some time." His voice shook. He took her hand, and her heart all but stopped when she saw the glint of tears in those very blue eyes. It was not . . . it *could* not be . . . but—"*Johnny!*" she screamed. And throwing herself into her brother's ready arms, she sobbed between kisses, "Johnny! You rogue! How *could* you so . . . tease me? Look at those eyebrows! And you are so *changed!* I scarce recognized . . . Have you been ill, love? And—this scar on your face! Oh, my dear! My dear!" And hugging him, laughing, crying, and hugging him again, she gradually passed from shock and joy to puzzlement and a presentiment of trouble, while Jonathan Boothe, overcome, could do no more than try to smile at her, even as he blinked away unmanly but very human tears.

Snowden came in and leaned beside the door, arms folded, and an unwontedly sober expression on his face.

"Snow," called Rebecca, "how wicked of you to pretend so! And here is our Johnny, after all this time, and . . . and . . . Oh, my heaven! What *is* it? Why does he look so changed and ill? Johnny? Snow? Tell me!"

Snowden looked at his brother, but Jonathan shook his head and walked to stand with one hand on the mantel and his back to them.

Snowden crossed to Rebecca's side, asking, "How long, Johnny?"

"A moment only," Jonathan replied unsteadily. "When I spoke—touched her hand, she knew."

"But of course I knew! You are my dear brother, could you doubt? Why? Because of the scar on your face? I am very sorry for that, John, but—"

Jonathan turned, smiling wryly, and Rebecca gave a gasp. The scar and the bushy white brows were gone. He held out his hand and they lay on his palm.

"The scar is wax only, dear girl. An actor friend made it for me, and taught me how to apply both it and these brows that age me so well."

"But . . . why? Oh, John! You are never thinking of treading the boards?"

He laughed shortly. "'Twould be an honourable career

compared to the disgrace I must bring down upon you am I discovered." He came over swiftly to grip her hands again. "Oh, Becky, with your lurid imagination, can you not guess why I am here and so—changed?"

Terror rested its clammy touch upon her. Refusing to credit her intuition she said numbly, "No. You have been on the Grand Tour . . . you *could* not have been—"

"A Jacobite? A captain for Bonnie Charlie? Ah, but I was, love. I am! Did he call again, I'd to him in a flash!" His eyes sparked. He declared ringingly, "*He* is England! Not this German usurper!"

Snowden said a warning, "Have a care!"

Rebecca's knees had turned to water. She swayed dizzily, and both young men leapt to support her. "It is not . . . truth . . ." she gasped out. "It cannot be!" But she knew it *was* truth. It was why Snowden had rushed to Newcastle-upon-Tyne; it was why he had behaved in so strange a fashion that day after the duel. Snowden urged her to sit down. Jonathan offered a glass of wine. Briefly, she clasped her hands to her mouth, her eyes closed, but in a moment she looked up into her elder brother's face and, dashing tears away, drew him down beside her. "What a frightful time you have had, poor darling! Snowden, why do you not smuggle Johnny out of the country with the other fugitive gentleman? The one who—" Shock silenced her. Snowden looked so grim. With a shaking hand she reached for the glass Jonathan still held, and swallowed a healthy gulp. Choking, her eyes watering, she strove to comprehend. "Then—it was *you*? All the time? Oh—*never* say you were the fugitive whom de Villars helped to escape at Ward Marching?"

Jonathan said quietly, "Is a very brave gentleman. Save for him, I would lie in the Tower this day—if I lived at all."

Rebecca sat motionless, scarcely able to control her emotions. When de Villars had staggered into that ante-room and been so desperately in need of help, he certainly must have known he would only have had to mention Jonathan's name to have won her aid. But even in that ghastly moment he had taken the entire risk to himself. And later, when he had tried

to thank her—to thank *her* for helping him, what had she said?
That she would have done the same for any hunted creature.
She felt sick with shame, and thought an aching, "What have I
done?" But she knew what she had done—and why. She had
been jealous; mad with jealousy and hurt pride because The
Monahan had been in his carriage. And so she had sent him off
with bitter cruelty to remember her by, never knowing how
deeply she was indebted. A fine reward for "a very brave gentleman"!

Jonathan said wretchedly, "You see how I have upset her?
I should not have come!"

Rebecca pulled herself together. "I am—all right now,
dearest. Come, sit by me, and tell me of it all. How did you
join the Jacobites?"

He sat beside her and told her something of this past year.
He had been deeply interested in the Jacobite Cause for a long
time, and when he had completed the Grand Tour with
Durstin McCloud, had gone to France, joined The Pretender
under an assumed name, and returned to Scotland to fight with
him.

"And you were badly wounded at Culloden! Oh, dearest
boy! To think I never knew—never so much as suspected.
Snow, *whyever* did you not tell me? Did you think I was not to
be trusted?"

Jonathan said gently, "I charged him to say nothing. It was
a deadly secret, love. Better you should not know."

"Gad, but it was," Snowden confirmed. "Each time I
looked at Hilary Broadbent I yearned to strangle him! You
would likely have jabbed him with your hatpin or some such
thing, Becky."

She laughed shakily. "Perhaps I would. At all events, the
important thing is that you are safe, Johnny." She saw the swift
look that passed between the brothers and said in deeper anxiety, "He *is* safe, isn't he, Snow? You *will* be able to get him
away?"

"Yes. Can I but get him to the coast. Forty and— Forty's
at work on that now, just in case I am watched."

"My God! Do they suspect *you*?"

Jonathan gripped her hand tightly. "Never shake so, little bird."

"Do not! Oh, do *not* call me that!" she flared.

Snowden burst into a laugh. Jonathan looked from one to the other uncertainly. Snowden explained, "Rebecca's affianced is a bird watcher. Jolly good chap, for all that."

Inspecting the great ruby on his sister's hand, Jonathan said, "How grateful I am to know you will be well provided for. Now—you are not to worry, I shall be away tonight."

"By posing as a footman atop Kadenworthy's coach again?" He smiled. "I thought you had seen me."

"And should have known my own flesh and blood was close to me, for I had such a sense of danger threatening—I must have sensed what you were suffering. For days I had been troubled, and—oh! What about Anthony? Does he know you are here?"

Snowden said, "No. And must not. I wouldn't put it past that Holt fella to question the boy. I gave Millie strict instructions not to come back until five o'clock."

"And Aunt Alby? Oh, she would so love to see him, Snow."

"Yes," said Jonathan. "I would love to see the dear soul. But the fewer who know of my perilous presence, the better."

Snowden glanced at the clock on the mantelpiece. "Johnny, man, we must be off. Put your years back on."

Rebecca watched as he replaced his disguise. Her eyes dimming, she thought, "Shall I ever see him again?" He looked at her, his own eyes sad. She summoned a smile somehow. "I must not send you off with tears. But . . . oh, my dearest! Be safe! You will—" She broke off with a gasp of fear as the door burst open.

A dirty, smelly, disreputable street pedlar entered, cap pulled low over stringy hair, and insolence in every line of him.

"Arternoon, ma'am," said my Lord Graham Fortescue, his accent as atrocious as his grin was broad. "All aboard wot's goin' aboard, guvnor. Got a lovely bargeload of winkles ready to 'ead north, sir. All aboard!"

"Going—*north?*" Rebecca echoed. "But—"

"Last place they'll look, love," said Snowden, assisting her to her feet. "They are on the alert for those trying to head south; not someone going right back to the trouble. Come, Johnny. It's a smelly road for you, old fellow, but with safety at the end, I'll warrant. Forty, you'd best go out by the tradesmen's entrance."

Rebecca threw herself into Jonathan's arms and kissed him lovingly. My lord, watching in mild amusement, gave a gasp of fright as Rebecca turned to him. Dirt, smell, and all, he was embraced and kissed just as soundly. Red to the roots of his hair, he gabbled something wholly incoherent, and fled.

They were gone then, and she was alone. Before she had time to gather her thoughts, Mrs. Boothe hurried in. "Whoever was that poor old gentleman, love? The most awful street hawker came with a message for him."

Rebecca's heavy heart lifted a little. If Albinia had not recognized Jonathan, there was hope indeed. "What did he say?" she asked.

"Some nonsense about the carriage being in the way of his barrow. The impertinence! I vow, Becky, the commoners are becoming—" She wrinkled her dainty nose. "Lud, but it smells downright fishy n here!"

The door creaked a little wider. Whisky waddled in and began to sniff interestedly about.

Rebecca laughed. "Your opinion is shared, dear Aunt!"

CHAPTER
❧ 16 ❧

Mrs. Albinia Boothe drew the lacy shawl closer about her dainty shoulders and, affecting an altogether spurious air of bewilderment, echoed, "Boudreaux House? But whyever should you go there, love? I understood Sir Peter to say he was coming today to take you to meet an aunt of his."

"Yes, but he finds he must postpone the call." Rebecca rose from her dressing table, easing the long kid glove over her wrist. "So I shall beard the lion in his den."

She looked, thought Mrs. Boothe with satisfaction, utterly

delectable in the pale orange *robe battante* with its richly embroidered train and the neckline that plunged into a froth of lace. Her hair was piled in high, powdered curls, and a small black patch in the shape of a half moon set high on her right cheekbone drew attention to her big dark eyes. "So you mean to intercede for Snowden and Letitia," said Albinia. "How brave you are! Poor lion—he is doomed to go down to defeat."

Those words bolstered Rebecca's courage all the way to Boudreaux House. It would be so wonderful to have good news to carry back to dear Snow. There had been no word of him for three days now, but she was sure she would have heard if her brothers had been taken. The hardest part was to carry her terrible secret alone. There was no one to confide in, no one to help her through the long, anxious hours that were made even more trying by her personal misery. She had tried to keep very busy and had accomplished several long-neglected tasks. And one, more recent, but of such import that she had still not been able to bring the details to her aunt. How odd that, expecting that particular task to be so distressing, it had turned out to be not only easy, but resulting in such a tremendous sense of relief. . . .

The carriage reached Grosvenor Square, and the home of Lord Boudreaux loomed so large and menacing behind its noble trees that her knees began to weaken. But she must not weaken. Her own mistakes were irrevocable, and she had no one to blame but herself. Heaven knew what the future might hold for Jonathan. But Snow, bless his warm brave heart, *must* have his chance at happiness.

The butler received her graciously and showed her into a charming saloon. She had no sooner sat down and removed her gloves than Letitia Boudreaux slipped into the room and ran to kiss her. "Becky, dearest! I saw your carriage, but no word was brought me. Is Snowden all right? I have heard nothing for days and days!"

Rebecca touched the wan cheek tenderly. "No more have I. But if aught had gone amiss we would have heard, I feel sure. I am here to see your great-uncle."

"Because of—us?" Letitia's clasp was very tight. "Bless

you! I am so grateful! I thought perhaps you had come because you heard about Treve, but—"

A low-pitched, singularly attractive male voice could be heard from the hall.

Letitia gave a gasp. "Uncle Geoffrey! I must go!"

"Wait!" begged Rebecca. "What did you mean about Treve? Is he—"

But with a flash of petticoats and a swirl of faintly perfumed air, Letitia had run to a door leading to the garden and was gone.

"Mrs. . . . Parrish . . . ?"

Rebecca turned, her anxiety so plainly written in her eyes that the slight gentleman who had entered the room halted, surveying her in some surprise. "Good gracious!" he exclaimed, as she rose from her curtsey. "How distressed you are. Dear lady, how may I—" He had come swiftly to take her hand, but now stood motionless, gazing into her face.

His fine-boned, delicate features were not at all what Rebecca had expected. He seemed more the frail scholar than the inflexible tyrant. And just now the clear eyes—so reminiscent of another pair of eyes—reflected stark astonishment. There was something vaguely familiar about him. Her brow wrinkled. Where on earth had she met this man before?

"My angel!" he breathed. "After all these months, I have found you!"

"Good God!" thought Rebecca. "He is indeed like his grandnephew!"

The silver head was bowed over her hand with exquisite grace. Straightening, he saw consternation in her eyes, and his own began to twinkle. "Sink me, but you must take me for a clod! And probably imagine— No, I pray you, do *not* imagine. Recollect, rather." He led her back to a chair and, when she was seated, occupied the sofa beside it. "A year ago, almost . . . on Bond Street. I was—"

"Oh, la! Yes, yes!" She clapped her hands, quite forgetting to be regal and distinguished, the unaffected gesture brightening the glow in Boudreaux's eyes. "You are my poor man who was taken ill and those stupid people would not help!"

"And you are my avenging angel who swooped down to rescue me before I was trampled to death! I had been struck with the pneumonia, but recovered, as you see. My dear child! How ever may I express my gratitude? If it is within my power . . ." He gestured expansively.

The delight in Rebecca's eyes faded. "You—ah, you *do* know who I am?" she asked cautiously.

"Your card proclaimed you to be Mrs. Parrish, I believe."

She sighed. "Ah. I see you do not know who I am, sir. My maiden name was Boothe. And my brother is—"

"Oh, dear," said his lordship. "Well now, we have rather a pretty predicament, do we not?"

A faint flush of embarrassment lit his fine features.

Ever impulsive, Rebecca reached out to place a consoling hand on his wrist. "No. I shall not take advantage of your gratitude. If I am to win you over, it must be because of my dear brother's sterling qualities. Not because you quite mistakenly consider yourself beholden to me."

The corners of the well-shaped mouth twitched. He leant back, his elbow on the arm of the sofa, his chin against the palm of his hand, while regarding her with faintly amused anticipation. "May I ask, dear ma'am, why you feel my indebtedness to be 'mistaken'?"

She hesitated, searching his face, but if there was a smile in his eyes, it was a friendly smile, and not the kind that would lead to mockery. "Because, my lord," she said earnestly, "you gave me a very rare chance to make amends. Only think of how many times one sees a poor soul who is crippled perhaps, or maimed, or blind. Or one meets a bright young person so full of brilliant promise, yet doomed from some dread affliction, and one's heart is wrung. If *only*, you think, you could give them a magic potion, or tell them some cure, or know of a physician who could help. But there is *nothing* you can do! How lucky was I! You were there—needing help, and I *was* able to help you! Do you see?"

His eyes, initially puzzled, had become very soft. He said gently, "Yes. But you said, 'make amends.' For what, child?"

"Oh." She flushed and looked down. "So many things. Kind words I have left unsaid; gossip I have repeated; my dreadful daydreaming which quite drives my poor aunt into the boughs; my improvidences! My"—she smiled at him, awakening a roguish dimple in her cheek—"my hoydenish behaviour and often dreadful temper!" She sighed. "Perhaps, when we *are* able to be of help to someone, it may be noted down on our—our celestial records, do you not think, sir?"

He chuckled. "And be a golden mark to wipe out some black ones? A lovely notion, my dear, though it would seem to me that your sins are small indeed—compared to most."

"Perhaps," she said dubiously. "But they are an exceeding heavy burden at times."

"Then you must be faint under such a weight." He stood and crossed to tug at an embroidered bell-pull. "Allow us to refresh you—a dish of Bohea, a glass of ratafia, and some cakes perhaps. And then you shall tell me why you think your brother would make my very beloved grandniece a good husband."

His eyes twinkled merrily at her. How gracefully he moved, and with what sweet courtesy he spoke. "A true gentleman," thought Rebecca, and blessed the lucky chance that had enabled her to be of service to him. She felt as though she had known him for years. Surely, it would be easy to convince him of Snow's worth. . . .

Half an hour later, she was far less confident of success. She had spoken of her brother's warm-heartedness and loyalty, of his unfailing care and kindness to her and Anthony after her husband's untimely death. Of his excellence at all things athletic, and of his high courage, but although Lord Boudreaux's questions had been few and gentle, they had also been dismayingly shrewd, and had proven difficult to answer in such a way as to refute the obvious impression that, having no fortune of any size, Snowden had done little to better himself, and did, in fact, continue to dress and conduct his life as though he were a very wealthy young man, existing as did so many others on the expectation of a lucky win at the track or at play, and managing somehow to stay always one jump ahead of the constable. Biting her lip after one such daunting admission, she looked up to find a grave and level gaze fixed upon her.

Disheartened, she said, "Oh, I know what you must think, sir. But, truly he is *not* a wastrel. He showed a marked bent for engineering and cartography at university. As a young boy he was most desperately eager to be a naval ensign, only Mama made him promise he would not go, and Snow never breaks his word, you see."

"He certainly has a most eloquent defender," said his lordship with his kindly smile. He put aside his teacup and asked mildly, "Tell me but one thing. You are a mother; had you borne a daughter instead of a son, would you wish her, when the time comes, to marry such a one as Snowden Boothe?"

It was a home question. Hesitating, Rebecca stammered, "W-well, I—yes! Snow may not have a comfortable independence, but—but we do have a small income from the funds that we share each Quarter Day." (She did not add that it was invariably spent before they got it!) "And he is loving and kind. The lady who weds him will know what it means to be cherished."

He smoothed a wrinkle from his peerless sleeve and said gently, "And—do you think that will weigh with her when she cannot close her desk drawer for the bills that clutter it? When her daughters cannot have pretty clothes, or her sons be enabled to attend Eton or Harrow, or go to university? When she has to weep in secret, each time the reckoning arrives from the milliner or the mantua maker, or the grocery shop?"

Rebecca whitened and stood suddenly, so that he at once followed suit.

"Ah, sir!" she said accusingly. "You *do* know of me, then. And use my own weaknesses against me!" She reached for her reticule, but he was before her, to sweep it up and hold it behind his back.

"I did not know you when you first arrived. When I learnt who was your brother, I knew also that you were the lady of whom my grandnephew has spoken so often."

"And—and so," she said unsteadily, "you teased me and

made mock of my pleas. That was cruel, sir. I will go now, if you please."

"I do not please. And there are many kinds of cruelty, my dear. . . . In truth, I had not meant to hurt you. Even though . . ."

"Even though—what, sir?"

"I have no right to speak for another. Yet—" He frowned. "You have accused me of judging your brother harshly. I wonder if you, too, perhaps, have judged—not being aware of all the facts of the matter."

Rebecca caught her breath.

His lordship sighed, and held out her reticule. "But—I have no right. I will think on what you—"

"What—what facts, sir?" she interposed tremulously, taking her reticule but sitting down again with it clasped very tightly to her bosom.

Lord Boudreaux bowed his head to hide a sudden smile, and seated himself also.

"You meant Tre—I mean, Mr. de Villars," she said in a rush of anxious words. "You cannot know how *grateful* I am for all he has done. I should never have answered him in such haste and—and anger. If you but *knew* how I have reproached myself! No wonder you hold us in contempt, for if he told you what I said . . . ! Unforgivable!"

He leant forward to remove the reticule from her nervously twisting fingers. "My nephew has told me very little. I know only that when he recovered, he—"

"*Recovered?*" Her eyes huge and dark with fright, she faltered, "But—he was almost well when he left Ward Marching."

"No, ma'am. He had come to such a state when he arrived here that he was, for a week, very ill indeed. But surely you must know that a musket ball seldom inflicts a trivial wound?"

"He said he was perfectly fit! And—he seemed well!" She realized she was babbling, and bit her lip to steady herself. "I—I had no notion— Oh, my lord, tell me, I beg you. Is he very ill now? Is he here?"

Boudreaux regarded her thoughtfully. "He is much better,

praise God. And out at the moment, which would enrage our estimable physician. The ball nicked the bone, you see, and aside from the fact it was excessive painful, we were afraid— well, the fever was extreme high, and Treve apparently with no will to fight it, so— Good God!" Aghast, he stood, looking down at the lovely face that was suddenly drenched with tears. It was most improper, but my lord's heart was as warm as that of the lady he hosted and, unable to resist that crumpled little face, he sat beside her, put an arm about her shoulders, and drew her into a fatherly embrace. "There, there," he said, in time-honoured fashion. "My poor girl, how very unhappy you are."

"Oh, yes," sobbed Rebecca, clinging disastrously to his Mechlin lace cravat. "I have made . . . such a dreadful mull of . . . it all. Tr—Treve was so—so sneery at first, and such a *wicked* flirt! And then, when I knew him better . . . he seemed more kind. And so full of—of laughter and fun. And the children *loved* him, which I should have paid more . . . heed to. Only, I did not, and when he was shot, I felt so . . . oh, so *awful!*"

"And saved his life, right nobly," he soothed, managing to detach her death-grip from his laces and contriving to extricate his handkerchief so as to offer it.

Rebecca wiped her eyes and blew her nose lustily, but did not relinquish either the handkerchief or her position, resting her head comfortably on his lordship's long-suffering and very damp cravat and not appearing in the slightest offended by the arm that again cherished her. "Yes," she sniffed, "I did help save his life. At least, I did *that* right. But then—when he offered, I was—oh, horrid! I kept thinking, just as you said, about the bills and Anthony and—Lud!" She sat up suddenly, and fixed him with a watery but militant eye. Wiping tears from her chin, she exclaimed, "Oh, how naughty you are! Tr—Treve is no better than Snowden, for he asked me to wed him, well knowing he has not a sou! And you refuse Snow for the self-same reason!" She gave a shuddering little gulp, but continued to fix him with that shocked frown.

His lordship sighed. "I am devious," he admitted. "Was

that why you refused him?" He added with a rather apologetic smile, "I'd no idea he had offered. He told me only that his case was quite hopeless."

"Oh." Her shoulders slumped. "Well—no. It was not that, entirely. It was mostly my . . ." She gulped again, and said threadily, "My wicked jealousy. And—and . . . well, he really has such a *dreadful* reputation, and Snow had insisted I have nothing to do with him, and—"

"Yes, and fought for your honour," interpolated Boudreaux, approvingly. "I begin to think better of your brother, my dear."

She stared at him. "You—you do? But—if you love your grandnephew, which I had thought you do not . . ."

"But I do. Very deeply."

"Yes, but—you said . . . and you cut him off because he ran off with that poor lady. So I thought . . . oh, dear!" She put one hand to her brow. "I do not know *what* to think!"

"Of course you do not, poor child. And if you keep on trying to understand it all, you are sure to get the headache. May I ask you just one thing, however? I flatter myself that I am a broad-minded man, but—I'll own it does seem just a shade odd to me that a lady so newly betrothed should be cast into despair in behalf of a—er, another admirer."

He saw at once that his question, however gently voiced, had been unwise, for those great dark eyes began to glisten ominously, and that tender mouth to tremble in the way that really was heart-rending.

"Yes," said Rebecca on a sob. "I know what you mean—exactly. It is purely dreadful, and has been since—since first I met your nephew, and I might, I might have done differently had he not been so *very* naughty. Well, there was his deathbed in the London house, you know, to say nothing of manoeuvring Peter and the children with the bat and ball—as though we were all the merest *puppets!*—only so as to . . . and then that *awful* thing with—with the mice! And then, when I saw him lying there—and stood over him, but he pulled at my— Oh, *wicked!* But—worst of all—The Monahan was in his *coach* . . . even while he—he offered for *me* . . . !"

Lost in all this, but vastly titillated, his lordship seized upon the one item he could comprehend. "No—was she? How very stupid of him."

"Yes, wasn't it? And then he—he threw an offer at me—like—like a dog to a bone. Oh—I mean a bone to a dog, of course. A *prize*, I mean, sir. Or in payment for—for services rendered. And then—" The tears were flowing in earnest again. "And—then," she wailed, "he said he hadn't *meant* it!"

"Good God! What a gapeseed! I wonder you did not strike him!"

She sniffed, and essayed a watery smile. "I—felt like it. But I did not dream how ill he was, poor— But—but even if he *was*, oh, you *see* how hopeless it is. He is just . . . just a natural born lecher, I suppose."

His lordship's brows shot up. Hurriedly, he put a hand across his mouth. Rebecca disappeared into his handkerchief once more. She looked very small, and grieved, and forlorn. Touched, he recovered his aplomb. "My poor girl. I can see I must divulge some secrets. Not that I have the right. But under the circumstances . . ."

He was briefly silent, and when Rebecca emerged from the handkerchief his expression had become so grim that she was dismayed.

"Trevelyan," Boudreaux began slowly, "was not quite eighteen years of age when he fell in love with Constance Rogers. She was the child of neighbours at his parents' country estate. Not a great beauty, exactly, but she had a fascinating way with her, and Treve worshipped her. He used to call her his Madonna, so his mama wrote me. I was in Holland at that time, and I was not 'my lord,' but plain Major de Villars, for a cousin and a brother were before me in the line of succession. However, I did know the families, and gained a fair picture of what happened. Constance had been always much courted and indulged. Her house was not a wealthy one, nor was his, but Treve had an adequate competence, and Constance would have a dowry of five thousand pounds, so that they were not like to have starved. All went well for a time, but then it began to be apparent to Treve that Constance was distressed. It developed that a very wealthy lad named Dutton had fallen head over heels into love with her. He was, I suppose, a pleasant enough boy, but his father was a Cit. The girl was horrified by Dutton's advances. Her family, however, was impressed by his riches, and her father heartily approved of him as a suitor. Trevelyan was frantic and begged his own parents to intervene, but he was so young, and they knew Constance . . . Well, at all events, they represented to him that he was under age, and that it would be several years before he should even be thinking of taking a wife. Time passed, and Constance grew ever more harassed until at last, driven to desperation, Treve took her away, and they made a dash for the Border."

"Gretna *Green?*" breathed Rebecca.

"He fancied it their only chance. But Mr. Rogers and his son and young Dutton came up with them." His lordship's hand clenched. He said after a brief pause, "There was a duel, of course."

"My heavens! But—he was just a boy!"

"True. But Dutton thought to use his horse whip. Treve was a high-couraged lad . . . but he was only eighteen. Dutton was not only five and twenty, but a most skilled swordsman. It was a—desperate affair. Some passing travellers chanced by, just at the finish of it. Otherwise—I shudder to think what might have occurred. As it was, the girl was packed off home in deep disgrace, and Treve was flat on his back for six months."

"Dear God! How awful."

"So we thought. We discovered that was not the worst of it, alas." He took a breath, then went on harshly, "The truth came out at length—as always it must. It was all a ruse, ma'am. At the start I believe Constance truly had a fondness for Trevelyan, insofar as she was capable of that emotion. But when young Dutton came along she found him handsome and was flattered by the interest of an older man. More compellingly, she discovered him to be immensely rich. She determined to have him, but—contrary to what she had told Treve—her parents were most violently *opposed* to the match. Dutton's father was in the City, as I said. He had no name, no background. Nothing would move Mr. Rogers, whose house goes back into antiquity, and who was, besides, a man obsessed with pride. Constance decided there was but one way to achieve her ends. She would allow herself to be compromised by Treve, and in the process be so disgraced that her parents must only be grateful to marry her to any man who would have her. Need I add that she was very careful to arrange that her father would catch them before the knot was tied; and also to engineer wide circulation of the horrible scandal her family were desperately attempting to suppress. A scandal that quite ruined my nephew."

Appalled, Rebecca stammered, "I—cannot *credit* it! What lady would ruin a man's life? See him almost slain just—just so as to marry wealth? And he cared deeply, you said? Poor boy! How frightful! I wonder he did not die."

"He is made of stronger stuff than that, praise be! But his father's health was broken by it all. He had never been strong, and his pride in his son was such that it was a terrible blow to him. The more so because the Rogerses had put it about that there had never been an elopement; and that Constance had in fact been abducted. Philip suffered a heart seizure, and my poor sister had two invalids to care for. When I learnt the facts of the case, I advised her to tell Trevelyan. She was distracted, poor soul, convinced it would send him into a decline. But I was right, thank God! At first he would not believe. When he knew it for truth, he just lay there, day after day, saying not a word. But it saved him. He was so enraged that he was soon on the road to recovery." Boudreaux paused, then went on soberly, "Before the tragedy—for I can only call it such—Treve was a happy, warm-hearted boy. He recovered as a cynical, embittered man. He had many loves after that, but he swore that never again would he be so foolish as to give his heart. And so far as I am aware, has not done so. Until—recently." His gaze flickered to the silent girl. "I hope I have not offended you by so savage a tale, my dear."

Rebecca turned a pale, horrified face. "I never dreamed people could be so cruel—so heartless! I hope—oh, I *hope* that evil girl was repaid! I hope she is miserably unhappy!"

"I wish I could say that she is. However, I believe her to

be an extreme satisfied woman. Her husband died a year or two ago, so the entire fortune is hers now. Retribution does not always follow wickedness, does it?"

"No." Her brow puckered. "But—I still do not understand. If it was as you say, whyever did you—"

She checked as the door opened and the man they had been discussing came into the room. His rapid steps halted. He all but staggered with shock as he saw Rebecca.

"Treve!" Boudreaux sprang to his feet. "Is it done, then? Did all go well?"

His unblinking gaze fixed on the blushing girl, de Villars offered a stiff bow. "Good afternoon, Mrs. Parrish."

Speechless, Rebecca inclined her head.

Boudreaux glanced from one nervous face to the other, and smiled faintly. "Trevelyan?" he prompted.

"Oh!" De Villars started. "Your pardon, sir. Yes—it went along very nicely, I'm glad to say."

"And—you are feeling . . ."

"Satisfied?" de Villars said hurriedly. "Perfectly, sir."

"Are you—alone?"

"Yes. We—ah, separated. It seemed—expedient."

My lord frowned uneasily. "Still, there must be financial arrangements. I will go and—"

De Villars' chin tilted in the way Rebecca had come to know was associated with an affront to his pride. "No. I thank you, but there is not the need."

"Fustian, m'boy! Why should you stand the huff—which must have been considerable?"

Beneath their long lashes, de Villars' grey eyes slanted quickly to Rebecca. "A most imperative need. A—right, in this particular instance."

"I see. Well, I must have a word with your wilful cousin, so—" Boudreaux started to the door.

"Sir!" cried Rebecca in alarm.

"I—w-wish you will stay, Uncle," stammered de Villars.

"Trevelyan, pray try to be not *quite* so foolish," quoth his lordship, and took his leave.

De Villars stared helplessly at the closing door, then gathered his wits and swung around. "Mrs. Parrish." He lifted his quizzing glass and scanned her with slow impertinence. "How very fetching you look in that gown. I am sure my uncle must have enjoyed your visit. I was not aware you are acquainted."

"Well, we are." Managing not to reveal that her heart was lodged somewhere in her throat, Rebecca stood, and once again retrieved her reticule. She took a step towards the door, and stopped, peering at him. "You are excessive pale, Mr. de Villars."

He shrugged. "My life of debauchery, alas."

"Your life of stuff and nonsense," she countered, frowning.

He blinked at her. "You have been here long, ma'am?"

"Yes. And if you are wondering what your uncle has told me about you, be at ease. He told me everything!"

The faint flush in his thin face faded to a dead whiteness. "Did he so?" His mouth twisted into the cynical sneer she hated. "Then, how very logical that you should be here."

She tilted her head, confused. "Oh. Yes. Indeed it is. Treve, oh, *Treve*, why did you not tell me you were ill that day? Your idiotic high in the instep pride! If only I had guessed your colour was the result of fever, I would—that is, I might—"

At the start he had listened, his lips tightly compressed. Now, sauntering to the mantel, he stared at the large Chinese urn full of hollyhocks that occupied the empty grate, and interposed a sardonic, "Might have done what? Accepted a penniless rake? Taken an odious, womanizing lecher to husband?"

Rebecca winked away a renewed onslaught of tears. This was no time to be a watering pot. If he truly loved her and was trying not to reveal how deeply she had hurt him, she must somehow bring him up to scratch again—she *must!*

"Perhaps not," she said sadly. "For my mind was quite made up, you see."

He laughed shortly. "Oh, I *do* see. Well, you made an excellent choice, ma'am. Now, if you will excuse me, I've an engagement, so—"

Frightened, she summoned her courage and marched to stand in front of him. The top of her head came to his lips. She glared up at him ferociously. "Enough of this nonsense! Tre-velyan de Villars, I demand—" She broke off, sniffing. "Where have you been?"

"In a most—delicious bower," he leered. "A place of silken sheets, warm, soft arms, and a heady alluring perfume—"

"Of winkles!" she cried, triumphant. "Oh, you wicked liar! You wretched, wretched man! Tell me—do pray *tell* me! My brothers? Oh, for God's sake, Treve, do not dissemble! I *know* you were with them, risking your life again, even though you are not nearly as well as you claim. Are they safe?"

A reluctant smile dawned. "And well," he acknowledged. "And Johnny en route to La Belle France."

She closed her eyes, bowed her forehead against his cra-vat, and breathed a small prayer of gratitude. And thus did not see the agony of longing in the grey eyes, the strong white teeth that clamped down on his lower lip, or the fists that clenched at his sides to keep from seizing her and sweeping her into a crushing embrace.

"Madam," he drawled, as soon as he could trust himself to speak, "you must remember you are promised to my best friend. This is not seemly."

She looked up into stern eyes that held all the warmth of an icicle. "You think to stop me from thanking you." She stood on tiptoe. "I will!" She put her hands on his shoulders.

De Villars uttered a stifled exclamation and wrenched away. "'Fore God! Have done, woman! Is not one conquest enough for you? I am as much a rogue, as unprincipled a lecher as ever. Go to your model of perfection! Go!"

Rebecca touched one loving finger between the broad shoulders thus presented to her, her mind busy. "I am here," she sighed, wandering back to the sofa, "to yet again ask your help."

De Villars glanced up. His haggard eyes found her reflec-tion in the great convex mirror that hung above the mantel. How little she looked, huddled at the end of the sofa. How utterly dejected. Intrigued, he half turned and murmured idly, "You require the services of a—lecher, ma'am?"

Her voice almost inaudible, she said, "You once told me . . . that if ever I needed you . . ." The great eyes came up, so desolate that hurt and pride were banished on the instant.

"My Lord! What is it?" He strode to her, then jumped back so hurriedly that he all but fell into the chair behind him.

Rebecca bit her lip. Fortunately, de Villars mistook its quivering for distress. He sprang up. "You are distraught— why? If Ward has made you unhappy—! No, by God! It's that hound Broadbent has been terrorizing you! I'll have his liver out!"

Her eyes opened wide. Lud, but the man was a flame! "Oh, pray do not! It is not Hilary, it is . . . Peter."

He stared his astonishment.

She added, blinking pathetically, "He is—a harsh man . . ."

There was no doubt but that she had been weeping. Her eyes were red and slightly swollen. A blinding rage possessed him. "That damned milquetoast? Lord, I'd not have thought him capable of— What did he do? Tell me, ma'am, did he dare— Did he lay hands on you?"

Rebecca bowed her head into her hands, convulsed, but gasped as she was seized and dragged to her feet.

"That stinking swine!" he uttered through shut teeth. "I might have known he'd be all gentleness in public and something quite different—!" He all but flung her from him and, his face livid, marched for the door.

Rebecca was appalled. She'd not dreamed in her playacting that he would react with such Puritanism. Especially when he himself had dared far more than she had implied, and with far less justification! She ran to throw herself against the door. Looking up into his grim face, she said, "Treve! Wait! I—"

"Stand aside!"

"What do you mean to do?"

"Get my sword! He'll answer to me, damn his eyes!"

"Good God! You cannot!"

His hands closed over her wrists. She tore free and

gripped his arms desperately. "No—do but listen—" He pulled away, and her grip instinctively tightened so that he gave a sudden gasp, his face twisting.

She drew back her hands as though he had burned her. "Ah! I have hurt you! Forgive me!"

De Villars stared, grasped her wrist, and gasped, "Your—your ring . . . ? I heard you wear the Ward ruby?"

"He—took it back," she said, yearning to cherish the pained bewilderment from his eyes.

"Took it—back?" He peered at her. "Why?"

The pained bewilderment was vanishing of its own accord. Blushing, Rebecca slipped away and went back to stand beside the sofa, her heart beating a thunderous tattoo.

"Little Parrish." His voice was so close behind her. So husky, and tremblingly uncertain, and dear. "Answer me. Why? Why did Peter take back that ridiculous monstrosity?"

"I—I told you he is—a harsh man. He has the oddest notions. He did not seem to . . . to want a wife who . . ."

He stepped closer. So close that she could smell the winkles very strongly. "A wife who—what?"

"Whose heart was given to . . . another gentleman."

She heard him gasp. From the corner of her eye she saw him reach for her, but that outstretched hand stopped, clenched, and fell away. There was a long silence. Waiting, praying, certainty became doubt, and doubt—fear. She glanced around. He had left her and was sitting on a chair beside the door, head down, and hands clasped between his knees.

"Treve!" She was at his side with a flutter of petticoats, bending to touch his shoulder, her anxious eyes scanning him frantically. "Is it your arm? Oh, my dear one, I—"

"Do not! For the love of God! Do not call me that!" He bowed his face between gripping hands for an instant, then, his head still lowered, asked in a stifled voice, "When did you return Peter's ring?"

"Yesterday. I had to, before he sent the notice to the newspapers."

"And you had not met my uncle before today?"

"No. Well—yes, long ago, as it chances, but I never *spoke* to him until today. Is that what you mean?"

He nodded. "And—you said he told you . . . all about . . ."

"About you and that perfectly wretched girl. Oh, my love—never grieve so. She was not worth one minute of—"

He stood, and faced her with a look of such anguished desperation that Rebecca was aghast. "Is that *all* Uncle Geoff told you? Nothing about my inheritance?"

"No." Confused, she said, "I knew he had cut you off, of course, but—Treve, is that what so distresses you? It is worrying, I know. But I have thought and thought. I have existed for so long on the edge of insolvency. And I am sure we could manage, if—"

He groaned. And she was seized and crushed to him while he gazed down at her with such yearning, such a depth of love that she waited in trembling eagerness for his kiss.

"Dear God, how I love you! Oh, Little Parrish, if only . . ." He flinched, his head lowered and he spun away, one hand pressed to his temple. "But—you do not know! You do not *know!*"

"Do not frighten me so. Treve—I love you, too. Whatever it is cannot be so base that I could *stop* loving you!"

"Oh, can it not!" He laughed, a wild bitter laugh that heightened her fear. Then he turned, but he could not force his eyes to meet her anxious ones and concentrated instead on a small tapestry on the far wall, just beyond her head. "When Constance betrayed me," he said stiffly, "I was utterly disillusioned. I had brought the whole ghastly imbroglio on myself, for any man with half an eye could have seen what—what manner of lady she was, except—"

"Lady!" Rebecca intervened hotly. "She was a scheming witch! Not worthy to clean your shoes. And you—a gentle, trusting, honourable boy! How could you have known?"

De Villars closed his eyes. When he opened them, Rebecca was aghast to see them bright with tears. "Please," he managed huskily. "Please, do not defend me. You must—understand. . . . I have lied to you. From the first."

Thoroughly frightened, she stared at his averted face.

"In my colossal arrogance," he went on grimly, "I decided that women were all alike: predatory, scheming, fortune hunters."

At this, Rebecca shrank away, still gazing at him.

"Wallowing in my misery," he said, "I decreed that until I found one who could . . ." He bit his lip and turned his head farther away. "Who could pass my test, I would not marry."

She whispered, "Your test . . . ?"

"Yes. You see, the final irony was that my grandfather died suddenly of heart failure. He was a miserly old recluse who had always claimed he could scarce afford to buy candles. Everything he had came to my father, and when my father followed him to the grave a year later, I inherited. It turned out to be a considerable fortune. Suddenly, I was a very rich man. I thought of how Constance had schemed to get her hands on Dutton's wealth, and I vowed no girl would do that to me. So I set it about that my great-uncle, the dearest, kindest, most generous of men, had control of the funds, and had cut me off, leaving me to manage on a small competence. By then, my reputation would have more than justified such an action, but I was too selfish to think of his feelings, or that it must necessarily restrict our meetings. Nor had I the right so arrogantly to condemn all womankind. I know that!" He risked a quick glance over his shoulder. Rebecca was moving away. His heart twisted. To lose her now—just when he had been given a chance for love and happiness, did not bear thinking of. "Becky," he pleaded. "Oh, dearest Little Parrish—can you not understand . . . ?"

"I—do understand," said Rebecca faintly. "When you asked me just now for how long I had been here . . . when you said it was—*logical* for me to be here now . . . you thought I had learnt that you were rich. Is that it?"

His head bowed. Racked with shame, he could not answer.

"I see." She felt dazed, and went and took up her reticule. "Of course," said she, pausing. "It is true, really. You were quite right. I *was* a fortune hunter." And she moved away.

He ran after her. And not touching her, pleaded, "Do not leave me! Oh, Becky—most brave and lovely and adored girl—please, *please* do not go out of my life. I am not worthy—God! How well I know it! I have been all—and worse than you know! But I swear I will do everything in my power to make you happy! I will try to—to be better, if only—"

"I do not think that possible, Mr. de Villars," she said, still turned from him. "You see . . . in my entire life I have known only one gentleman who could have so instantly won the hearts of a lonely little boy and girl; only one gentleman who would so valiantly risk his life to save an unknown fugitive and ask nothing in return. Only one, sir—and he is the finest gentleman I have ever met. The man who stands here beside—" She turned then, her eyes soft with love, but de Villars was not standing beside her.

On his knees, he gazed up at her, a look of such humble adoration on his pale face that she cried, "No, my dearest! Pray get up!"

He raised one hand. With a twitching attempt at a grin, he said, "You had best not cut this short, love. I—I doubt I shall ever manage it again." The levity disappeared. In a very shaken voice, he went on, "My beloved girl. If you can stoop to lift this . . . truly wretched rake to the—the glory of your arms . . . as God be my judge, I will never, *never* give you cause to regret it. Little Parrish . . . you cannot know how . . . I worship you."

"Treve. My darling . . ." She reached down, took his hands, and drew him to her arms. "Oh, Treve, I do wish . . ."

"What, my treasure?"

"That you would stop talking so much, and just—kiss me. . . ."

It was several dizzying moments before Rebecca put back her head and, looking up into his adoring eyes, said softly, "Treve . . . you really *do* love me?"

For answer, he bent to her again, but she put a finger

across his lips. Kissing it tenderly, he murmured, "With all my heart . . . and soul . . . and for ever."

"No matter how naughty I am?"

He laughed rather unsteadily. "How could you be naughty, my heart?"

"Well, I think I must be, dearest. Because—do you know, I simply cannot help thinking how much nicer it is that—that you are very rich. . . ."

CHAPTER
❧ 17 ❧

"Mr. de Villars, ma'am," beamed Mrs. Falk, opening the door to the cosy parlour of the little house on John Street.

Rebecca stood and reached forth both hands, and Trevelyan de Villars came eagerly to take them, press each to his lips and then drop a kiss on her dewy cheek. "Are we to be alone for a space?" he breathed hopefully into her ear.

"Mr. de Villars!" cried Anthony, bounding into the room and seizing the skirts of an impeccable coat. "Come and see how I have mended the boat you gave me!"

"Cease hauling at me, vile brat," said de Villars. "Can you not see I am occupied?"

"Come along, sir! You can kiss Mama any time. Though why you want to is beyond me."

"Is it indeed? If you do not desist, I shall return her hand to Sir Peter!"

Anthony stared his dismay. "That knock-in-the-cradle? Oh—no, sir!"

"Anthony!" exclaimed Rebecca, horrified.

"Repulsive whelp," de Villars said with a broad grin.

Anthony laughed joyously, and dragged his protesting captive towards the steps.

The door opened. "Treve!" said Mr. Melton. "I hear our mutual friend is clear? That was well done, my dear fellow!"

Shaking hands with him, de Villars said, "Thank you, George. I hope you shall be dining with us?"

"I shall be, as a matter of fact. You look prodigious well. Be dashed if Cupid don't agree with you!"

De Villars laughed, but Rebecca thought lovingly that it was truth. The cynicism was gone from Treve's eyes. He looked younger, and completely happy. "And I shall keep him looking so," she vowed silently.

Mrs. Boothe hurried in. "So there you all are! Patience, hurry up, dear. They're in the parlour."

Anthony, who had begun to look glum, brightened joyfully, but he said with proper male boredom, "The shrimp is here? Well, that will make mice feet of everything!"

Patience ran happily down the steps, stumbled, and sprawled at his feet. "Cawker," he said, bending to help her up.

She hugged him briefly, then squealed, "Mither De-Vil! Mither De-Vil!"

De Villars swung her into his arms and was the recipient of a smacking kiss.

Half strangled, he looked at Melton. "She means you, of course. Must."

Melton laughed. "An apt name, I'll admit. But I disclaim the honour."

"No," cried Patience, pulling de Villars' ear. "I meaned *you!*"

Anthony asked condescendingly, "Want to come and see my boat, shrimp?"

"Oooo! Yeth, pleath, Anthy!"

"Fickle wench," mourned de Villars, setting her down.

"We told Ward we would keep her for the week." Mrs. Boothe threw an apologetic glance at her radiant niece. "I hope you will not object, love. The dear mite was so lonely, and poor Sir Peter really has no faintest notion of what to do with her. Besides which he is—ah, so busy just now."

Rebecca sat beside her and said anxiously, "Is he? I am so glad. He was so despondent when I—er—"

"Jilted him?" put in de Villars, with a condemning shake of the head.

Rebecca blushed. "Wicked creature! There is no shame in you!"

"None, thank God! But I am sure our Peter is up to his ears in feathers, eh, Aunt Albinia?"

Mrs. Boothe looked startled by this form of address, then gave a ripple of laughter. "Not feathers—*nephew*—exactly. Though his—ah, new friend does affect exotic . . . plumage."

Rebecca, her eyes very round, breathed, "The Monahan?"

De Villars said exuberantly, "Excellent! They will deal very well."

"How can you say such a thing?" Rebecca protested. "They are worlds apart. I shall always have an affection for Rosemary Monahan—how could I do otherwise when she helped protect you, love? But—" She was interrupted, de Villars slipping an arm about her. Their eyes met and held through a hushed pause.

Her eyes alight, Mrs. Boothe gave a small cough.

Rebecca started, and went on hurriedly, "But what can they possibly have in common? She so—so clever and sophisticated. And Peter—"

"Such a bumbling ornithologist." De Villars grinned. "No, do not eat me! I am quite aware how much I owe the good fellow. But you mistake it, my dear. Rosemary is both kind and a sensible lady. She knows exactly what she can expect from Peter, and will ask no more of him. For her part, she will be devoted and patient. She will set up her court and her cicisbeos, Peter will have his birds, they will lead totally different lives with much amiability, and likely develop a deep affection one for the other."

"I hope so," said Rebecca dubiously. "But whatever is to become of dear little Patience?"

"I have already asked Ward if he will allow us to adopt her," said Melton rather shyly.

"How splendid!" exclaimed Rebecca.

"Yes," said de Villars. "But she must spend part of the year with us, if you please. She and Anthony quarrel so happily together. Besides which, she will keep that repulsive brat out of my hair!"

"It is far more likely you'll have 'em *both* in your curly locks, old chap," said Snowden Boothe, coming in and handing his lady down the steps.

Letitia ran to kiss Rebecca. "Dearest! Only guess! Uncle Geoffrey has given us his blessing! How may I ever thank you?"

Rebecca looked narrowly at her right hand. "By telling me where you got that dragon ring!" She looked at her future sister-in-law wonderingly. "I thought it belonged to—"

"Rosemary Monahan? It did. I admired it after the Midsummer's Eve Ball, and she gave it me."

"You mean—*you* were the lady in Treve's carriage when— . . ."

"When he went in to say goodbye to you. Yes, dear. I was worried, because I know how he will never admit it when he is feeling poorly. Why?"

"I share your mystification," said de Villars. "Why, Rebecca?"

"Because, I saw . . . and I thought . . ." Rebecca stopped, gave a tiny sigh, and, her eyes like stars, said, "It doesn't matter. Oh, it does not matter at all! How lovely this is. All of us together. What a jolly evening we shall have!"

The room was becoming quite crowded, but a new voice was heard. "Do you fancy one more person could squeeze in?"

"Uncle Geoff!"

"Welcome, sir!"

Lord Boudreaux trod down the steps, as elegant and distinguished as ever, to be hugged, his hand shaken, and his shoulder pounded. Eyes twinkling, he said to Rebecca, "Do you know, my dear, that this brother of yours has some of the most interesting notions? We mean to build a canal together."

De Villars said an interested, "The devil you do!"

"Whatever for?" asked Rebecca, curiously.

"Why, to carry off some of the rainwater, I suppose," said her aunt, with considerable logic.

The men laughed.

"For shipping, my love," explained Mr. Melton. "Capital idea, Boothe. I just may want to be in on this."

Falk returned, Millie following, with glasses and decanters.

Rebecca looked around that crowded, merry room and felt drenched with happiness.

Later, when smells of dinner were drifting fragrantly through the house, de Villars took her by the hand, and they slipped quietly away. He stopped in the entrance hall and kissed her. "My apologies, Little Parrish. I could not wait another second," he said, opening the front door.

"Where are we going?"

"Not very far." He took a ring case from his pocket and opened it. "Do you know, I cannot think who this is for. Unless I have been so reckless as to offer for someone."

"Rogue!" Rebecca peered at the small cluster of diamonds, winking in the light of the setting sun. "Oh . . . Treve!"

He slipped the ring onto her finger and kissed it reverently. "Be warned. You cannot give it back to me with some tale of loving another. For," he gazed into her eyes, "I shall not believe you, my fishwife. . . ."

He drew her hand through his arm and led her around the side of the house and into the alley. A groom waited there, walking a fine Arabian stallion up and down. Rebecca stood very still, her heart leaping. The horse turned its head and whickered a greeting. She said on a sob, "*Saracen!*" And ran to throw her arms about the silken neck, while the Arabian snorted and blew gustily down her back.

Her eyes full of happy tears, Rebecca asked, "Treve, my dearest dear! How did you *know?* How ever did you find him?"

De Villars nodded dismissal to the groom and, as man and animal moved off, took his lady into his arms. "My betrothal gift to you, beloved. And—it is my business to know everything about you—now and for ever."

He bent to her. Rebecca darted a nervous glance to the street. "What if someone should see? Treve—*no!* I—"

And after a blissful moment, she sighed, "Trevelyan de Villars, unhand me! Oh! Now *that*, sir, was *very* naughty!"

"My love," the miscreant breathed, "you have not yet begun to know how naughty I am!"

"Have I not?" she asked, with more eagerness than scolding. "And—and shall I like your naughty ways, sir?"

He smiled down at her, his heart in his eyes, and murmured, "I venture to believe, Little Parrish, that you shall like them very well."

In this particular instance, time proved the beliefs of Mr. Trevelyan de Villars to be perfectly justified.